TARGETED

A DEADLY OPS NOVEL

KATIE REUS

A SIGNET ECLIPSE BOOK

SIGNET ECLIPSE
Published by the Penguin Group
Penguin Group (USA) LLC, 375 Hudson Street,
New York, New York 10014

USA | Canada | UK | Ireland | Australia | New Zealand | India | South Africa | China
penguin.com
A Penguin Random House Company

First published by Signet Eclipse, an imprint of New American Library,
a division of Penguin Group (USA) LLC

First Printing, October 2013

ISBN 978-0-451-41921-7

Printed in the United States of America
10 9 8 7 6 5 4 3 2 1

For my husband, who puts his life on the line every day. Your sacrifices are appreciated more than words can ever express. Thank you for your love and support of your family and the way you selflessly give to strangers.

Prologue

Marine Corps Scout Sniper motto: one shot, one kill.

S am Kelly could see his GP tent fifty yards away. He was practically salivating at the thought of a shower and a clean bed. But he'd settle for the fucking bed at this point. He didn't even care that he was sharing that tent with twenty other men. Showers were almost pointless at this dusty military base in hellish sub-Saharan Africa anyway. By the time he got back to his tent from the showers, he'd be covered in a film of grime again.

Four weeks behind enemy lines with limited supplies and he was also starving. Even an MRE sounded good about now. As he trekked across the dry, cracked ground, he crossed his fingers that the beef jerky he'd stashed in his locker was still there, but he doubted it. His bunkmate had likely gotten to it weeks ago. Greedy fucker.

"There a reason you haven't shaved, Marine?"

Sam paused and turned at the sound of the condescending, unfamiliar voice. An officer—a lieutenant—he didn't recognize stood a few feet away, his pale face flushed and his skin already burning under the hot sun. With one look Sam knew he was new in-country. Why the hell wasn't the idiot wearing a boonie hat to protect his face? Hell, it had to be a hundred and thirty degrees right now. Yeah, this dick was definitely new. Otherwise, he wouldn't be hassling Sam.

Sam gave him a blank stare and kept his stance relaxed. "Yes, sir, there is. Relaxed grooming standards." *Dumbass.*

The blond man's head tilted to the side just a fraction, as if he didn't understand the concept. God, could this guy be any greener? The man opened his mouth again and Sam could practically hear the stupid shit he was about to spout off by the arrogant look on his face.

"Lieutenant! There a reason you're bothering my boy?" Colonel Seamus Myers was barreling toward them, dust kicking up under his feet with each step.

The man reminded Sam of an angry bull, and when he got pissed, everyone suffered. He was a good battalion commander, though. Right now Sam was just happy the colonel wasn't directing that rage at him. Guy could be a scary fucker when he wanted.

"No, sir. I was just inquiring about his lack of grooming." The officer's face flushed even darker under his spreading sunburn. Yeah, that was going to itch something fierce when it started peeling. Sam smiled inwardly at the thought.

"You're here one week and you think you know more than me?"

"N-no, sir! Of course not, sir."

The colonel leaned closer and spoke so low that Sam couldn't hear him. But he could guess what he was saying because he'd heard it before. *Stay the fuck away from Sam Kelly and the rest of my snipers or I'll send you home.* Rank definitely mattered, but to the colonel, his few snipers were his boys, and the man had been in more wars than Sam ever wanted to think about. Sam had seen and caused enough death himself to want to get out when his enlistment was up. That wasn't too far off either. He'd been to Iraq, Afghanistan, a few places in South America that weren't even on his official record, and now he was stationed in Djibouti, Africa. Or hell, as he liked to think of it. He loved his job and he loved his country, but enough was enough. Sam just wished he could figure out what the hell he wanted to do if he got out of the military.

He watched as the colonel started talking—loudly—to the new guy. Getting right in his face as only a pissed-off Marine could. Sam almost felt sorry for the guy, but what kind of stupid fucker didn't know that since the environment here was so dirty that staph infections were rampant, grooming standards were *different*? That was one of the reasons he and a thousand other guys his age had relaxed grooming standards in the bowels of this hellish place. But they also cut him slack because he was a sniper. Sometimes he had to blend in with the populace, among other things. He might be stationed in Africa, but he'd just gotten back from—where else?—Afghanistan. He'd stayed holed up for days in that dank cave just waiting—

"Sergeant, in my tent. Now."

Sam blinked and realized Colonel Myers was talking to him. He nodded. "Yes, sir."

The colonel was still reaming out whoever the newbie was, but Sam always followed orders. Looked as though that shower was going to wait. The walk to the big tent in the middle of the base was short.

As he drew the flap back and stepped into the colonel's tent, he stilled when he spotted a dark-haired man leaning against a table with maps on it. He looked as if he thought he had every right to be there too. Interesting. A fly landed on Sam's face, but he didn't move. Just watched the man, ready to go for one of his weapons if need be. He didn't recognize him and he wasn't wearing a uniform.

Just simple fatigues and a T-shirt that stretched across a clearly fit body even though the guy had to be pushing fifty. There was something about the man that put Sam on edge. He was like a tiger, coiled and waiting to rip your head off. The man's eyes weren't cold, exactly, but they were calculating.

Carefully the man reached for a manila folder next to him and flipped it open. He glanced down at it. "Sam Kelly. Originally from Miami, Florida. Grew up in foster care. No known family. One of the best damn snipers Myers has ever seen. Sniper school honor grad, aptitude for languages, takes orders well, possibly a lifer." He glanced up then, his green eyes focusing on Sam like a laser. "But I don't think you're a lifer. You want a change, don't you?" The man's gaze was shrewd, assessing. Sam didn't like being analyzed, especially by a stranger. And the guy didn't even have an accent, so he couldn't place where he might be from. Nothing in his speech stood out.

Who the hell was this guy? And how the fuck did he know Sam wanted a change? It wasn't as if he'd told anyone. Sam ran through the list of possibilities. He'd been on different operations before, sometimes working for the CIA for solo things, and he'd been attached to various SEAL teams for larger-scale missions, but he'd never worked with this guy before. He did have Sam's file, though—or Sam guessed that was his file in the man's hand. He could just be bluffing. But what would the point of that be? He dropped all semblance of protocol since this guy clearly wasn't a Marine. "Who are you and what do you want?"

"You did some good work in Cartagena a few years ago." He snapped the file shut and set it back on the table.

Sam just stared at him. His statement said a lot all by itself. That mission wasn't in his official jacket, so this guy knew classified shit and was letting Sam know it. But since he hadn't asked a question or introduced himself, Sam wasn't inclined to respond.

The man's lips quirked up a fraction. As they did, the tent flap opened and the colonel strode in. He glared at the man, cursed, then looked at Sam, his expression almost speculative. He jerked a thumb at the stranger. "Whatever this guy tells you is the truth and he's got top secret clearance." He snorted, as if something was funny about that, then sobered. "And whatever you decide . . . Hell, I know what you'll decide. Good luck, son. I'll miss you." He shook Sam's hand, then strode out of the tent.

Miss him? What the hell was he talking about? Sam glared at the man in front of him. "I asked you once who you were. Answer or I'm out of here."

The stranger crossed the short distance and held out his hand.

Sam ignored it.

The man cleared his throat and looked as if he was fighting a smile, which just pissed Sam off. "I'm Lieutenant General Wesley Burkhart, head of—"

"The NSA. I know the name." Sam didn't react outwardly, but the gears in his head were turning. "What do you want with me? I thought you guys were into cryptography and cyber stuff."

"We are, but I'm putting together a team of men and women with a different skill set. Black ops stuff, similar to the CIA, but with less . . . rules. I want to offer you a job, but before I go any further, you need to know that if you come to work for me, Sam Kelly will cease to exist. You will leave your past and everything in it behind."

Sam stared at the man, overwhelmed by too many feelings. Relief being one of them. Leaving his identity behind didn't seem like such a bad thing at all. Finishing the rest of his enlistment in shitholes like this wasn't something he looked forward to. He'd seen and caused so much death that sometimes he wondered if God would ever forgive him. The idea of wiping his record clean was so damn appealing. Maybe this was the fresh start he'd been looking for. Except . . . he touched the hog's tooth hanging from his neck. He'd bled, sweated, and starved for this thing. For what it represented. It was part of him now. "I'm not taking this off. Ever."

The other man's eyes flicked to the bullet around his neck, and the corners of his mouth pulled up slightly. "Unless the op calls for it, I wouldn't expect you to."

Okay, then. Heart thudding, Sam dropped his rucksack to the ground. "Tell me everything I need to know."

Chapter 1

Black Death 9 Agent: member of an elite group of men and women employed by the NSA for covert, off-the-books operations. A member's purpose is to gain the trust of targeted individuals in order to gather information or evidence by any means necessary.

Five years later

Jack Stone opened and quietly shut the door behind him as he slipped into the conference room. A few analysts and field agents were already seated around the long rectangular table. One empty chair remained.

A few of the new guys looked up as he entered, but the NSA's security was tighter than Langley's. Since he was the only one missing from this meeting, the senior members pored over the briefs in front of them without even giving him a cursory glance.

Wesley Burkhart, his boss, handler, and recruiter all rolled into one, stuck his head in the room just as Jack started to sit. "Jack, my office. Now."

He inwardly cringed because he knew that tone well. At least his bags were still packed. Once he was out in the hall, heading toward Wesley's office, his boss briefly clapped him on the back. "Sorry to drag you out of there, but I've got something bigger for you. Have you had a chance to relax since you've been back?"

Jack shrugged, knowing his boss didn't expect an answer. After working two years undercover to bring down a human trafficking ring that had also been linked to a terrorist group in Southern California, he was still decompressing. He'd been back only a week and the majority of his time had been spent debriefing. It would take longer than a few days to wash the grime and memories off him. If he ever did. "You've got another mission for me already?"

Wesley nodded as he opened the door to his office. "I hate sending you back into the field so soon, but once you read the report, you'll understand why I don't want anyone else."

As the door closed behind them, Jack took a seat in front of his boss's oversized solid oak desk. "Lay it on me."

"Two of our senior analysts have been hearing a lot chatter lately linking the Vargas cartel and Abu al-Ramaan's terrorist faction. At this point, the only solid connection we have is South Beach Medical Supply."

"SBMS is involved?" The medical company delivered supplies and much-needed drugs to third-world countries across the globe. Ronald Weller, the owner, was such a straight arrow it didn't seem possible.

"Looks that way." His boss handed him an inch-thick manila folder.

Jack picked up the packet and looked over the first document. As he skimmed the report, his chest tightened painfully as long-buried memories clawed at him with razor-sharp talons. After reading the key sections, he looked up. "Is there a chance Sophie is involved?" Her name rolled off his tongue so naturally, as if he'd spoken to her yesterday and not thirteen years ago. As if saying it was no big deal. As if he didn't dream about her all the damn time.

Wesley shook his head. "We don't know. Personally, I don't think so, but it looks like her boss is."

"Ronald Weller? Where are you getting this information?" Jack had been on the West Coast for the last two years, dealing with his own bullshit. A lot could have changed in that time, but SBMS involved with terrorists—he didn't buy it.

"Multiple sources have confirmed his involvement, including Paul Keane, the owner of Keane Flight. We've got Mr. Keane on charges of treason, among other things. He rolled over on SBMS without too much persuasion, but we still need actual proof that SBMS is involved, not just a traitor's word."

"How is Keane Flight involved?"

"Instead of just flying medical supplies, they've been picking up extra cargo."

Jack's mind immediately went to the human trafficking he'd recently dealt with, and he gritted his teeth. "Cargo?"

"Drugs, guns . . . possibly biological weapons."

The first two were typical cargo of most smugglers, but biological shit put Keane right on the NSA's hit list. "What do you want from me?"

His boss rubbed a hand over his face. "I've already built a cover for you. You're a silent partner with Keane Flight. Now that Paul Keane is incapacitated, you'll be taking over the reins for a while, giving you full access to all his dealings."

"Incapacitated, huh?"

The corners of Wesley's mouth pulled up slightly. "He was in a car accident. Bad one."

"Right." Jack flipped through the pages of information. "Where's Keane really at right now?"

"In federal protection until we can bring this whole operation down, but publicly he's in a coma after a serious accident—one that left him scarred beyond recognition and the top half of his body in bandages."

Jack didn't even want to know where they'd gotten the body. Probably a John Doe no one would miss. "So what's the deal with my role?"

"Paul Keane has already made contact with Weller about you—days before his accident. Told him he was taking a vacation and you'd be helping out until he got back. Weller was cautious on the phone, careful not to give up anything. Now that Keane is 'injured,' no one can ask him any questions. Keane's assistant is completely in the dark about everything and thinks you're really a silent partner. You've been e-mailing with her the past week to strengthen your cover, but you won't need to meet her in person. You're supposed to meet with Weller in two days. We want you to completely infiltrate the day-to-day workings of SBMS. We need to know if Weller is working with anyone else, if he has more contacts we're not privy to. Everything."

"Why can't you tap his phone?" That should be child's play for the NSA.

His boss's expression darkened. "So far we've been unable to hack his line. I've got two of my top analysts, Thomas Chadwick and Steven Williams—I don't think you've met either of them." When Jack shook his head, Wesley continued. "The fact that's he's got a filter that *we* can't bust through on his phone means he's probably into some dirty stuff."

Maybe. Or maybe the guy was just paranoid. Jack glanced at the report again, but didn't get that same rush he'd always gotten from his work. The last two years he'd seen mothers and fathers sell their children into slavery for less than a hundred dollars. And that wasn't even the worst of it. In the past he hadn't been on a job for more than six months at a time and he'd never been tasked with anything so brutal before, but in addition to human trafficking, they'd been selling people to scientists—under the direction of Albanian terrorists—who had loved having an endless supply of illegals to experiment on. He rolled his shoulders and shoved those thoughts out of his head. "What am I meeting him about?" *And how the hell will I handle seeing Sophie?* he thought.

"You supposedly want to go over flight schedules and the

books and you want to talk about the possibility of investing in his company."

Jack was silent for a long beat. Then he asked the only question that mattered. The question that would burn him alive from the inside out until he actually voiced it. The question that made him feel as if he'd swallowed glass shards as he asked, "Will I be working with Sophie?"

Wesley's jaw clenched. "She *is* Weller's assistant."

"So yes."

Those knowing green eyes narrowed. "Is that going to be a problem?"

Yes. "No."

"She won't recognize you. What're you worried about?" Wesley folded his hands on top of the desk.

Jack wasn't worried about *her*. He was worried he couldn't stay objective around her. Sophie thought he was dead. And thanks to expensive facial reconstruction—all part of the deal in killing off his former identity when he'd joined Wesley's team with the NSA—she'd never know his true identity. Still, the thought of being in the same zip code as her sent flashes of heat racing down his spine. With a petite, curvy body made for string bikinis and wet T-shirt contests, Sophie was the kind of woman to make a man do a double take. He'd spent too many hours dreaming about running his hands through that thick dark hair again as she rode him. When they were seventeen, she'd been his ultimate fantasy and once they'd finally crossed that line from friends to lovers, there had been no keeping their hands off each other. They'd had sex three or four times a day whenever they'd been able to sneak away and get a little privacy. And it had never been enough with Sophie. She'd consumed him then. Now his boss wanted him to voluntarily work with her. "Why not send another agent?"

"I don't *want* anyone else. In fact, no one else here knows you're going in as Keane's partner except me."

Jack frowned. It wasn't the first time he'd gone undercover with only Wesley as his sole contact, but if his boss had people already working on the connection between Vargas and SBMS, it would be protocol for the direct team to know he was going in undercover. "Why?"

"I don't want to risk a leak. If I'm the only one who knows you're not who you say you are, there's no chance of that."

There was more to it than that, but Jack didn't question him. He had that blank expression Jack recognized all too well that meant he wouldn't be getting any more, not even under torture.

Wesley continued. "You know more about Sophie than most people. I want you to use that knowledge to get close to her. I don't think I need to remind you that this is a matter of national security."

"I haven't seen her since I was eighteen." And not a day went by that he didn't think of the ways he'd failed her. What the hell was Wesley thinking?

"It's time for you to face your past, Jack." His boss suddenly straightened and took on that professorial/fatherly look Jack was accustomed to.

"Is that what this is about? Me, facing my past?" he ground out. Fuck that. If he wanted to keep his memories buried, he damn well would.

Wesley shrugged noncommittally. "You *will* complete this mission."

As Jack stood, he clenched his jaw so he wouldn't say something he'd regret. Part of him wanted to tell Wesley to take his order and shove it, but another part—his most primal side—hummed with anticipation at the thought of seeing Sophie. She'd always brought out his protective side. Probably because she'd been his entire fucking world at one time and looking out for her had been his number-one priority.

He'd noticed Sophie long before she'd been aware of his existence, but once he was placed in the same foster house as her, they'd quickly become best friends. Probably because he hadn't given her a choice in being his friend. He'd just pushed right past her shy exterior until she came to him about anything and everything. Then one day she'd kissed him. He shoved *that* thought right out of his mind.

"There's a car waiting to take you to the flight strip. Once you land in Miami, there will be another car waiting for you. There's a full wardrobe, and anything else you'll need at the condo we've arranged."

"What about my laptop?"

"It's in the car."

When he was halfway to the door, his boss stopped him again. "You need to face your demons, Jack. Seeing Sophie is the only way you'll ever exorcise them. Maybe you can settle down and start a family once you do. I want to see you happy, son."

Son. If only he'd had a father like Wesley growing up. But if he had, he wouldn't have ended up where he was today. And he'd probably never have met Sophie. That alone made his shitty childhood worth every punch and bruise he'd endured. Jack swallowed hard, but didn't turn around before exiting. His chest loosened a little when he was out from under Wesley's scrutiny. The older man might be in his early fifties, but with his skill set, Jack had no doubt his boss could take out any one of the men within their covert organization. That's why he was the deputy director of the NSA and the unidentified head of the covert group Jack worked for.

Officially, Black Death 9 didn't exist. Unofficially, the name was whispered in back rooms and among other similar black ops outfits within the government. Their faction was just another classified group of men and women working to keep their country safe. At times like this Jack wished the NSA didn't have a thick file detailing every minute detail of his past. If they didn't, another agent would be heading for

Miami right now and he'd be on his way to a four-star hotel or on another mission.

Jack mentally shook himself as he placed his hand on the elevator scanner. Why was Wesley trying to get under his skin? Now, of all times? The man was too damn intuitive for his own good. He'd been after him for years to see Sophie in person, "to find closure" as he put it, but Jack couldn't bring himself to do it. He had no problem facing down the barrel of a loaded gun, but seeing the woman with the big brown eyes and the soft curves he so often dreamed about—*no, thank you.*

As the elevator opened into the aboveground parking garage, he shoved those thoughts away. He'd be seeing Sophie in two days. Didn't matter what he wanted.

Sophie Moreno took a deep, steadying breath and eased open the side door to one of Keane Flight's hangars. She had a key, so it wasn't as though she was technically breaking in. She was just coming by on a Sunday night when no one was here. And the place was empty. And she just happened to be wearing a black cap to hide her hair.

Oh yeah, she was completely acting like a normal, law-abiding citizen. Cringing at her stupid rationalization, she pushed any fears of getting caught she had to the side. What she was doing wasn't about her.

She loved her job at South Beach Medical Supply, but lately her boss had been acting weird and the flight logs from Keane Flight for SBMS's recent deliveries didn't make sense. They hadn't for the past few months.

And no one—meaning her boss, Ronald Weller—would answer her questions when she brought up anything about Keane Flight.

Considering Ronald hadn't asked her over to dinner in the past few months either as he normally did, she had a feeling he and his wife must be having problems. They'd treated her like a daughter for almost as long as she'd been with SBMS, so if he was too distracted to look into things because of personal issues, she was going to take care of this herself. SBMS provided much-needed medical supplies to third-world countries, and she wasn't going to let anything jeopardize that. People needed them. And if she could help out Ronald, she wanted to.

She didn't even know what she was looking for, but she'd decided to trust her gut and come here. Wearing all black, she felt a little stupid, like a cat burglar or something, but she wanted to be careful. Hell, she'd even parked outside the hangar and sneaked in through an opening in the giant fence surrounding the private airport. The security here should have been tighter—something she would address later. After she'd done her little B&E. God, she was so going to get in trouble if she was caught. She could tell herself that she wasn't "technically" doing anything wrong, but her palms were sweaty as she stole down the short hallway to where it opened up into a large hangar.

Two twin-engine planes sat there, and the overhead lights from the warehouselike building were dim. But they were bright enough for her to make out a lot of cargo boxes and crates at the foot of one of the planes. The back hatch was open and it looked as if someone had started loading the stuff, then stopped.

Sophie glanced around the hangar as she stepped fully into it just to make sure she was alone. Normally Paul Keane had standard security here. She'd actually been here a couple of weeks ago under the guise of needing paperwork and there had been two Hispanic guys hovering near the planes as if they belonged there. She'd never seen them before and they'd given her the creeps. They'd also killed her chance of trying to sneak in and see what kind of cargo was on the planes.

When she'd asked Paul about them, he'd just waved off her question by telling her he'd hired new security.

One thing she knew for sure. He'd lied straight to her face. Those guys were sure as hell *not* security. One of them had had a MAC-10 tucked into the front of his pants. She might not know everything about weapons, but she'd grown up in shitty neighborhoods all over Miami, so she knew enough. And no respectable security guy carried a MAC-10 with a freaking *suppressor*. That alone was incredibly shady. The only people she'd known to carry that type of gun were gang-bangers and other thugs.

So even if she felt a little crazy for sneaking down here, she couldn't go to her boss about any illegal activities—if there even were any—without proof. SBMS was Ronald's heart. He loved the company and she did too. No one was going to mess with it if she had anything to say about it.

Since the place was empty, she hurried across the wide expanse, her black ballet-slipper-type shoes virtually silent. When she neared the back of the plane, she braced herself for someone to be waiting inside.

It was empty except for some crates. Bypassing the crates on the outside, she ran up inside the plane and took half a dozen pictures of the crates with the SBMS logo on the outside. Then she started opening them.

By the time she opened the fifth crate, she was starting to feel completely insane, but as she popped the next lid, ice chilled her veins. She blinked once and struggled to draw in a breath, sure she was seeing things.

A black grenade peeked through the yellow-colored stuffing at the top. Carefully she lifted a bundle of it. There were more grenades lining the smaller crate, packed tight with the fluffy material. Her heart hammered wildly as it registered that Keane was likely running arms and weapons using SBMS supplies as cover, but she forced herself to stay calm. Pulling out her cell phone, she started snapping pictures of the inside of the crate, then pictures that showed the logo on the outside. In the next crate she found actual guns. AK-47s, she was pretty sure. She'd never actually seen one in real life before, but it looked like what she'd seen in movies. After taking pictures of those, she hurried out of the back of the plane toward the crates sitting behind it.

Before she could decide which one to open first, a loud rolling sound rent the air—the hangar door!

Ducking down, she peered under the plane and saw the main door the planes entered and exited through starting to open. Panic detonated inside her. She had no time to do anything but run. Without pause, she raced back toward the darkened hallway. She'd go out the back, the same way she'd come in. All she had to do was get to that hallway before whoever—

"Hey!" a male voice shouted.

Crap, someone had seen her. She shoved her phone in her back pocket and sprinted even faster as she cleared the hallway. Fear ripped through her, threatening to pull her apart at the seams. She wouldn't risk turning around and letting anyone see her face.

The exit door clanged against the wall as she slammed it open. Male voices shouted behind her, ordering her to stop in Spanish.

Her lungs burned and her legs strained with each pounding step against the pavement. She really wished she'd worn sneakers. As she reached the edge of the fence that thankfully had no lighting and was lined with bushes and foliage behind it, she dove for the opening. If she hadn't known where it was, it would be almost impossible to find without the aid of light.

Crawling on her hands and knees, she risked a quick glance behind her. Two men were running across the pavement toward the fence, weapons silhouetted in their hands. She couldn't see their faces because the light from the back of the hangar was behind them, but they were far enough away that she should be able to escape. They slowed as they reached the fence, both looking around in confusion.

"Adonde se fue?" one of them snarled.

Sophie snorted inwardly as she shoved up from the ground and disappeared behind the bushes. They'd never catch her now. Not unless they could jump fences in single bounds. Twenty yards down, her car was still parked on the side of the back road where she'd left it.

The dome light came on when she opened the door, so she shut it as quickly as possible. She started her car but immediately turned off the automatic lights and kicked the vehicle into drive. Her tires made a squealing sound and she cringed. She needed to get out of there before those men figured out how to get through the fence. She couldn't risk them seeing her license plate. Only law enforcement should be able to track plates, but people who were clearly running weapons wouldn't care about breaking laws to find out who she was.

She glanced in the rearview mirror as her car disappeared down the dark road, and didn't see anyone in the road or by the side of it. Didn't mean they weren't there, though. Pure adrenaline pumped through her as she sped away, tearing through her like jagged glass, but her hands remained steady on the wheel.

What the hell was she supposed to do now? If she called the cops, this could incriminate SBMS and that could ruin all the good work their company had done over the past decade. And what if by the time the cops got there all the weapons were gone? Then she'd look crazy and would have admitted to breaking into a private airport hangar, which was against the law. Okay, the cops were out. For now. First she needed to talk to her boss. He'd know what to do and they could figure out this mess together.

Chapter 2

Legend: an agent's alleged background and personal history, usually supported by documents and memorized details.

Printing out flight logs from Keane Flight's most recent deliveries, Sophie frowned at the computer screen in front of her when her intercom beeped. She'd been too terrified to get more than a couple of hours of sleep last night, and her calls to Ronald had gone unanswered. Since she hadn't wanted to leave a message on his phone about what she'd found, she'd decided to talk to him this morning. Right now he was in a meeting, but as soon as he was free, she was telling him everything. She'd e-mailed herself the pictures, but she'd also printed some to give him. He needed to see everything in color. Then they could figure out how to move forward. If that meant involving the police, then so be it.

"Sophie, I've got Hannah Young on line three. She says it's urgent," Mandy, her assistant, said.

"Got it. Thanks." She wanted to ignore the call, but Hannah was her best friend and she needed to act normal at work right now. "What are you doing up at seven thirty on a Monday?"

Her best friend groaned. "I can't sleep. I'm still reliving the horror of last night's date."

Despite the rampant adrenaline still pumping through her, a small smile touched her lips. Talking about Hannah's dating life would be a welcome momentary distraction. "I thought you were going out with the 'hot Italian.' What happened?"

"After dinner we went back to his place. We're on his couch, making out, when someone knocks on his door."

"How late was this?"

"Ten. He looks through the peephole, freaks out like a little girl, and makes me hide in his closet."

"Uh, what?"

"Thank you! Ridiculous. He told me it was his ex-girlfriend and that she's crazy, so I asked him why he didn't just ignore her. He says that if he does, she'll keep knocking all night."

"What did you do?"

Hannah sighed. "What else? I hid in the closet until they started going at it. On. His. Bed."

Sophie choked out a sound.

"They actually started having sex on his bed with me in the closet. Freak," she muttered.

"I can't believe you stayed that long!"

Hannah chuckled, the sound wicked. "Just as he was about to, you know, I walked out and told him never to call me again. His expression was priceless and I could still hear her shrieks by the time I was outside."

"If I didn't know you, I'd swear you made this stuff up." Sophie had been listening to these stories since college. If there was a crazy in a ten-mile radius, Hannah would find him. It was as if she had a homing beacon attached to her.

"Now that you've heard my horror story, you have to take pity on me and meet me for happy hour after work. If that doesn't convince you, two-fifty martinis better."

Under normal circumstances Sophie would have loved to have met her friend. But she couldn't say yes to anything until she'd talked to her boss. "I can't tonight. Work is insane right now." Okay, not exactly a lie.

"Come on, one night off won't kill you."

Sophie shut her eyes and massaged her temple. She was desperate to tell someone what she'd seen. It was like a need growing inside her to just get the information off her chest, but she bit it back. There was no way she'd ever put anyone she loved in danger. "I can't, but I swear I'll make it up to you."

"You suck, but okay." There was laughter in Hannah's voice, so Sophie knew her friend wasn't actually mad. "By the way, my mom wants to know why you haven't been over in the past couple of weeks. She thinks you've found some-one else to cook for you."

She snorted. "Right. Will you tell her I've been busy?" Sophie had met Hannah's mom during her first spring break in college, and the woman had taken her in as her own. After Sophie's growing up in foster care, having a real mother fig-ure was a new experience but one she'd embraced.

"*You* tell her. I talked to her last night and she wanted to know why I haven't married a rich doctor yet. I'm taking a couple days off from torture."

Sophie shook her head. "Fine. I've got to go but I'll see you tonight."

As soon as they disconnected, she pulled the logs she'd been reviewing back onto her screen. Gas charges and mile-age weren't matching up, and after last night she knew why. They were carrying way too much cargo. She clicked her pen up and down as she stared at the screen. Damn it, why wouldn't Ronald call her back? She wanted to scream. When an e-mail marked *urgent* from one of their biggest suppliers popped up on the bottom of her screen, she sighed and closed the other file. She could stare at her computer all day or keep herself distracted with work.

After taking care of her client, she made a serious dent in

the quarterlies, though images of grenades and guns hovered at the back of her mind. She'd tried buzzing Ronald three more times, but he hadn't been in his office and no one had been able to find him. Just as she stood, ready to hunt him down, her assistant buzzed her office. "Sophie, Mr. Weller wants to see you in his office. There's a man from Keane Flight here. He's yummy." Mandy whispered the last part before clicking off.

Sophie's knees weakened for a moment. Someone from Keane Flight? Oh God, what if it was one of those scary men from last night? Maybe they'd figured out she'd been the one to break in. There hadn't been any video cameras—she'd noticed that Paul had taken them down when she'd been there for her last surprise visit—but maybe they'd seen her car. Sophie swallowed hard and shoved the folder containing the pictures she'd taken into her desk. She'd wanted to bring them to Ronald, but she wouldn't risk it with someone from Keane Flight in there.

She swallowed hard but found her voice. "Thank you, Mandy." Mandy had been her intern last year and, when she graduated, had applied for a job. She definitely didn't have the experience Sophie had been looking for, but the woman was a fast learner.

After straightening her pencil skirt and smoothing on lip gloss, Sophie grabbed a notepad and pen. She had to appear normal when going to Ronald's office. Plus, holding something felt a bit like having armor. She shut her office door behind her and stopped at Mandy's desk. "I sent some stuff to the printer. Would you organize everything and put it in a binder for me?"

"No problem."

"One more thing." Sophie glanced behind her. Two other administrative assistants shared the open space with Mandy, and she didn't want them overhearing. "Don't let *anyone* into my office while I'm gone. I've locked it and you have the only other key."

A slight frown marred her pretty face. "Is there a problem? Did I do something wrong?"

"No. I'm just working on some stuff right now that Mr. Weller wants to keep private."

Immediately Mandy's mouth relaxed into a smile. "Oh, okay."

Sophie clutched her notebook to her side as she headed down the long hallway toward her boss's office. In addition to what she'd discovered last night, lately she suspected that things in her own office had been out of place. A paperweight and paper clip holder had been moved on more than one occasion. It was small stuff and maybe she was being paranoid, but she'd learned long ago to trust her gut. Considering what she'd found last night, she was never ignoring her instinct again.

She half knocked as she entered Ronald's office. She was officially his assistant, but not in the sense that Mandy was her assistant. He didn't like to deal with anyone but her, which was why Sophie was surprised he'd told Mandy he needed to see her instead of coming to her directly. Maybe he really was ignoring her calls.

"Good morning, Sophie." Ronald gave her a tired smile as he looked up from his desk. Deep lines etched the grooves around his mouth.

There was no one in his office, so whoever they were meeting with must have stepped out. Which gave her the perfect opportunity to talk to her boss in private. "Ronald, we need to talk. Didn't you get my calls last night?"

He shook his head, but the guilty flush spreading up his cheeks gave him away. Sophie reeled back as if slapped. He *had* been ignoring her. What the hell? She gritted her teeth, quickly moving past the hurt. "I discovered something . . . important." She nearly snorted at that understatement.

His face paled. "Can it wait?"

"No, it *can't*." As she stared at the man in front of her, she tried to find the right words to just come out and say what she'd found. Something about his expression was just off. He looked almost haggard, so unlike the man she'd come to love and trust. She'd been twenty-two and right out of college when he'd given her a job. Not to mention that the company had paid for her master's degree. She didn't have any family and he'd always been a father figure to her. Anyone would have been better than the asshole foster fathers she'd endured over the years, but Ronald was truly kind. Even with the panic humming through her, seeing him this way pulled at her heartstrings.

Ronald sighed and his eyes flashed with something she couldn't define. Pain? "We'll talk, but not here. Just wait—"

He abruptly stopped talking and his gaze trailed over her shoulder at the sound of the door opening. Sophie shifted in her seat and glanced behind her.

She blinked once as she made eye contact with the stranger entering the room. Staring into those eyes made her feel as if she'd been punched in the stomach. A raw sort of awareness stirred inside her, making her throat tighten and somewhere a lot lower heat up completely against her will. Mandy's description of "yummy" was so very incorrect. A *cupcake* was yummy. This man was like a decadent triple-chocolate truffle cake with chocolate shavings sprinkled on top. Considering the crap she needed to deal with, noticing someone in such a sexual way—someone she clearly couldn't trust—was beyond stupid. And definitely not like her. Only one man had ever had this raw effect on her. Though he hadn't been quite a man. He'd been growing into a very handsome one and—damn it. She shook herself, trying to quash this strange sexual awareness that had erupted inside her.

Almost against her will, Sophie's eyes trailed over him. The man seemed to make the room shrink just by stepping inside. It wasn't that he was overly tall. He was maybe six feet, but he had a strong, domineering . . . presence. His shoulders almost appeared to strain against his suit, as if he'd be more comfortable chopping lumber or something else equally and ridiculously masculine. When the sudden—unexpected and definitely absurd—thought of what it might feel like to have those strong arms around her popped into her head, she felt herself blushing furiously. This visceral reaction was too weird and brought up too many unwanted memories. When she focused on his face once again, her heart skipped a beat. "Holy shit."

The man jerked to a halt and she realized she'd said the words out loud. She cringed and ordered herself to get it together.

"Ah . . . sorry." What else could she say, that she'd suddenly developed a mild case of Tourette's?

"Sophie, this is Jack Baldwin. He's been a silent partner with Keane Flight until recently." Ronald's words blew right past her as she continued to watch the stranger.

He had pale bluish gray eyes she'd never seen on anyone before except . . . *Sam*. Eyes with the seemingly endless depth of the unforgiving ocean. So deep she could drown in them. She wanted to look away, but couldn't even pretend not to stare. And he was definitely looking back. Watching her with a mix of curiosity and something she couldn't begin to define.

The harsh lines and angles of his face gave him a unique, almost statuesque quality. As if he'd been carved out of stone. He wasn't handsome in the typical Hollywood sense, but any woman with a pulse would certainly do a double take. Maybe even a triple take. He even had the same dark hair as Sam. For a brief moment she could feel herself drowning as memories attacked her.

Sam carrying her books home from school. Protecting her from neighborhood bullies. Staying up late with her when she needed help studying. Sam kissing her, making love to her, going with her to the beach even though he hated it, holding her when she'd had a bad day.

Sam is dead. The jarring thought was the only thing that gave her the power to tear away from this stranger's far-too-intimate gaze. Feeling an ache deep inside, she absently rubbed the middle of her chest until she realized what she was doing. She nervously cleared her throat and hoped her blush had started to recede as she found her voice. Right now Keane was at the top of her shit list. She wasn't going to let a handsome face distract her. "Recently?"

"Yes . . . Please, have a seat." Ronald half stood and motioned to the other man to sit. Sophie noticed his voice shook a little. Maybe he was intimidated by this man.

Not that she blamed him.

In a few long strides, Jack Baldwin was sitting on a burgundy high-backed chair identical to the one she sat on a mere foot away. The briefest whisper of a familiar scent tickled her nose. Something spicy, masculine, and earthy that made her toes curl in her sling-backs. Clearly it had been too long since she'd had sex if even the intoxicating scent of a possible arms dealer was affecting her. It was the only thing that explained her raw reaction.

The corners of his lips pulled up slightly as he nodded at her—as if he *knew* what she was thinking. The very thought was horrifying. "Pleased to meet you."

Against her will, she found herself staring at his mouth. Instinctively she moistened her own dry lips. When she did, his jaw muscle flicked, drawing her attention back to those intoxicating eyes. *Oh, crap.* The blush was back. She could feel heat creeping up her neck and cheeks, and for a brief moment she thanked God for her Cuban heritage. She vainly hoped her darker skin would cover her embarrassment, but knew it was unlikely.

"Likewise, Mr. Baldwin." She shifted in her seat, turning

slightly away from him. God, she needed to get whatever this feeling was under control. Maybe if she didn't look at him she could tune out all that raw, unwanted sexuality.

"Call me Jack." His voice was low and sensual. It rolled over her with the subtlety of a tidal wave, sending unexpected shivers to all her nerve endings. Why was it so familiar? It reminded her slightly of Sam, but it was deeper, more masculine. Like what Sam would have sounded like if he'd been allowed to grow up fully. She shook herself at the depressing, and insane, thought.

Why did she have the urge to say Jack's name out loud? Just to feel it on her tongue. Her nipples tightened at the thought of saying that name under very different circumstances. Right then and there, Sophie felt like a crazy person. This was so unlike her, this . . . sexual hunger. And there was no other word for what she was feeling.

Ronald's voice grounded her, forcing her to look away again. "Like I was saying, Jack here will be filling in for Paul."

She frowned at her boss, wishing she could tell him everything she'd found last night. "Why?"

The other man answered before Ronald could speak. "He was in a terrible car accident and is unable to handle the day-to-day dealings, so you're stuck with me." His lips pulled up again, this time self-deprecatingly.

Or she was under the impression that was what he was going for. The action was a little too practiced. Sophie chewed on her bottom lip as she tried to gauge his expression. There was something else underneath that charming and sexy veneer that didn't sit right. This was the first she'd heard about a car accident. It was also the first she'd heard of a silent partner and they'd been working with Keane for about eight years. Since the year she'd started at SBMS, in fact.

"Paul was in an accident? Is he going to be okay?"

"The doctors aren't sure yet. He's in a coma and it's touch-and-go right now," the newcomer said quietly.

She glanced back at her boss for confirmation. Ronald just nodded. Even if Paul was hurt she was still unsure why Jack Baldwin was even here. It wasn't as though they worked for Keane. No, it was the other way around. So why was his partner here now? And why was this the *first* she'd heard of him? And why the hell were there freaking weapons in the plane she'd broken into last night?

As if the other man read her mind, he said, "I'm sure you're wondering why I'm here. Ronald has agreed to let me borrow you for the day as my personal tour guide of the company."

"Why?" she asked bluntly, not caring how rude she sounded.

His eyebrows lifted as if she'd taken him off guard. The movement was slight, but she couldn't help feeling as if she were under a microscope.

Oh, crap, did he know she was the one who'd broken into Keane Flight last night? She fought the urge to squirm in her chair. The way this man was studying her was unnerving. "Uh, why do you need a tour guide?" she asked, this time more politely.

"Mr. Baldwin is thinking of investing in SBMS and wants to see the day-to-day operations," Ronald said smoothly.

"I see." Though she didn't. Not at all. "When would you like to start? I can schedule something tomorrow—"

"How about I take you to lunch and then we get started?" Somehow the man's question sounded more like an order.

"Uh, sure." Now she definitely sounded rude.

"Is La Marea okay?" There was a slight touch of amusement in his voice.

"That sounds wonderful." Okay, that was a much politer response. Good for her. La Marea was an expensive restaurant for a work lunch, but it was also her favorite place. For some reason, it annoyed her that he'd picked it. As if he knew more about her than he should.

Jack followed suit as she stood. She looked at her boss. "You coming?" *Please say yes.* She tried to will him to respond. All she needed was a few minutes of his time.

Ronald shook his head and grabbed his briefcase. "You two go ahead. I've got a meeting to head to."

A strange panic settled in her gut at the thought of being alone with Jack Baldwin before she'd spoken to Ronald. Ignoring the newcomer, she looked pointedly at her boss. "I need to talk to you in private before I leave."

"It'll have to wait, Sophie." His voice was tired, strained.

"But—"

"I have a meeting," he snapped, taking her completely off guard.

She recoiled at the abrupt tone. Ronald had never spoken to her like that, and even though it was childish, she felt stung. Fighting the sudden onslaught of emotions, she turned and found Jack staring at her as if he could see straight through to her innermost thoughts. How the hell did he do that? It was so damn jarring, but she couldn't tear her gaze from those pale eyes.

He was definitely good-looking in that rugged, muscular Marlboro man sort of way. And something told her he didn't get those muscles from a gym. Which made her wonder exactly what kind of exercise he did to warrant that clearly fit body.

There was something about him that triggered her feminine awareness. He wasn't doing anything outwardly offensive. It was something *primal* he exuded. Something akin to death clung to him, and it put all of her senses on red alert. Yeah, she definitely needed to get away from him. Maybe she could call Ronald on the walk to her office and make him listen. Short of tackling him and forcing her boss to sit and listen to a few words, she had no other choice but to play it cool and act normal. At least until she knew what was going on and especially in front of this particular stranger. "I need to grab my purse if you don't mind wait—"

"I'll walk you to your office." There he went with that deep voice again, sending tingles straight to her toes.

It rankled her that when he spoke it sounded like a command. He was quiet the entire walk to her office. Sure, it was only at the other end of the hall, but it dragged on for an eternity. Unable to help herself, she snuck a quick glance at him. Even his profile was intimidating.

Well, except for his mouth. It looked absolutely kissable. Which was plain wrong. A man with such a hard exterior shouldn't have inviting lips.

His square jaw clenched as if he was aware of her scrutiny. Swallowing, she glanced away, horrified that she was having these thoughts about a possibly dangerous stranger. She blamed her response on his eyes. They looked so much like her first love's it was beyond startling.

As soon as they stepped into the receptionist's area, Mandy smiled and handed her a white binder. "This is the information you requested on K—"

"Thank you, Mandy. I'll go over it later." Sophie quickly grabbed the binder and tucked it under her arm, hoping the man next to her didn't notice the Keane cover Mandy had thoughtfully put on it. He definitely didn't need to know she'd been looking into his company before he arrived. Not until she knew what his deal was or why he was really here.

Thankfully Jack didn't follow Sophie into her office. She unlocked her drawer and pulled out her purse. She started to put the binder in her drawer, but slipped it into her purse instead. She also shoved the pictures she'd planned to show Ronald into her purse, then tucked the flash drive she'd saved them on into her bra. She might have e-mailed herself the pictures and have them saved in her online mobile album, but she wanted another backup and she was taking it with her.

Ronald might be acting like a jackass right now, but after this stupid lunch she was hunting him down and *making* him listen to her. If she had to spend a little time with the sexy, intimidating, and probably criminal Jack, so be it.

Chapter 3

Contract killer: a person hired to kill a selected target or targets for money.

From the doorway of Sophie's office, Jack watched her walk around her desk. Her slim-fitting skirt hugged her in all the right places. Even though she had on a jacket, her small breasts were outlined perfectly. Nothing about her outfit was overtly sexual, but simply watching her move around her office got him hotter than anything any other woman had ever done. She didn't just move. The woman flowed with a grace that made staring at her an addiction. Something about the sleek tailored outfit made him wonder what she had on underneath. Plain cotton, or silk and lace? Or maybe nothing at all. When they were seventeen she'd usually worn Brazilian-style bottoms that showed the bottom half of her butt. Those things had driven him crazy, so of course she'd loved to walk around wearing only that when they'd been alone.

At *that* thought, his entire body tensed. When they were teenagers he'd wanted her so badly he couldn't think straight most of the time, but this reaction was different. It was . . . more. *Intense.* Like thirteen years of pent-up need clawing its way to the surface and just begging to be set free. He'd known coming on this mission so soon after that last op was a mistake, but hadn't been able to force himself to tell his boss no. Not when he'd been dying to see Sophie.

When she leaned over her desk to grab something, her dark hair cascaded over her shoulder and he couldn't help remembering what it had been like to run his hands through that thick mass as she rode him. Or as he'd taken her from behind. Or as they'd simply held each other and watched the ocean waves. Memories of their short time together had kept him sane during some of his nastier missions. Her smart-ass attitude and sense of humor had kept him entertained back when there wasn't much bright in his life. She'd been one of the few bright beacons in his world. He'd even categorized his life into "before Sophie" and "after Sophie." Because after he'd met her, he'd known on a fundamental level that she was meant for him.

Watching her now felt too surreal. The outline of her jaw, the gentle curve of her neck, her dark, intoxicating eyes. Despite the sharp angles of her exotic cheekbones, everything else about her compact body was soft and inviting. Especially her hips. She had just enough curves for a man to hold on to. Well, not any man. Only him. He wanted to bury his face against her neck, between her breasts, and definitely between her legs. God, if she knew what he was thinking now, she'd run. Or maybe not. He'd seen a hint of awareness in her eyes back in Ronald's office. It had been tempered with almost outright anger at his presence—which made him curious—but he was pretty sure she was attracted to him.

She paused before slipping the binder her assistant had given her into her purse, and then it looked as if she tucked something into her shirt. Since she had her back to him, it was difficult to see, but he found it interesting.

"Hey, Mandy. Is Sophie in her office?" A man's voice caused Jack to turn.

Jack quickly sized up the man standing at the receptionist's desk. He recognized him from one of the dossiers he'd studied. Benson Pollard. Been with the company six months. No red flags.

But Jack didn't like the familiar way he said Sophie's name.

Sophie walked out and smiled warmly when she saw the other man. A punch of need slammed into Jack, along with a healthy dose of jealousy. He hadn't seen that smile in too many years, and he didn't want her sharing it with anyone else. Crazy? Definitely. He just didn't care.

She hoisted her purse higher on her shoulder. "Hi, Benson. I'm just heading to lunch."

"I was actually coming by to see if you wanted to join me for lunch. Where are you headed?"

"It's a private lunch." Jack surprised himself and everyone else around him with his heated tone. Mandy's mouth dropped and the other man's eyes narrowed at him with barely concealed annoyance . . . and disgust?

Sophie's dark eyes widened, but she quickly recovered before turning back to her coworker. "Sorry, Benson, it's a working lunch. Maybe later this week."

"Sure, or maybe we can do drinks after work?"

Jack watched Sophie finger a strand of dark hair. Something she'd always done when she was uncomfortable. Not that he blamed her. What kind of jerk asked a woman out in front of people?

"I'll buzz you when we get back." She looked at Jack, but her eyes were shuttered. "You ready?"

He was silent until they reached the elevators. The short walk didn't bother him, but it was obvious Sophie was uncomfortable around him. The tiny pulse point on her neck was visible and it was working overtime. He was still unsure if it was because of him or if it was because he worked for Keane Flight and she had something to hide. Once they stepped into the elevator, he broke the silence. "I'm sorry if I was rude to your boyfriend." If this had anything to do with work, he would have been subtle, but something primal inside him wanted to know exactly who that guy was to Sophie.

She glanced at him as he hit one of the buttons. "What . . . Oh, Benson's not my boyfriend."

"He wants to be." He inwardly cringed. Today he was definitely not a superspy. More like a randy teenager who couldn't keep his mouth shut. He was supposed to be getting close to her, getting information from her, not grilling her about her social life. And certainly not alienating her. Jack couldn't seem to stop his apparent repressed Neanderthal behavior, though. Being around her put him on edge, and the close confines of the elevator didn't help. His skin felt too tight for his body, and the urge to reach out and touch her just for a moment was so real it scared him. For a former, highly trained Marine Corps Scout Sniper and an even better-trained government agent, he was fucking pathetic.

A delicate blush rose on her tan neck and swept across her cheeks. "That's slightly inappropriate and none of your business."

"Just making conversation," he murmured as the elevator dinged that they'd reached their destination.

When the elevator doors opened he stepped forward to intentionally crowd her. In her boss's office he thought he'd detected some physical awareness from her, but he wanted to be sure. Her shoulder brushed his as she exited into the parking garage. She tensed at the contact. Looking away, Sophie started to dig into her purse, but he hit the unlock button on his key chain. "I'll drive."

Her eyes slightly narrowed at him, but she didn't argue. She also had something grasped in her fingers as she withdrew her hand from her purse. He couldn't see it clearly, but he was guessing pepper spray when she subtly tucked that hand into her jacket pocket and left it there. Damn. Okay, she might feel a little attraction for him, but she definitely did not trust him. The fact that she thought she could actually need a weapon against him pissed him off even if his reaction was irrational. She was just watching out for herself, as any woman should. Still, he'd never hurt Sophie.

Guest parking was right up front, so they didn't have far to go. He held the passenger door open to the SUV, earning him a wary but curious look from Sophie as she slid into the front seat. Her exotic familiar scent assaulted his senses, bringing back unwanted memories.

"How long have you worked with SBMS?" He started the engine and tried to ignore the way her skirt kept sliding up against the leather seat.

There was a pause, and then she answered almost grudgingly, "A little over eight years. Since I graduated from college, actually." She crossed her legs away from him, her body language crystal clear. She wasn't comfortable sharing personal details with him.

He glanced in the rearview mirror before reversing. "That's rare, to stay with a company so long, especially your first one after graduating. At least nowadays it is." He was fishing for information, but she didn't seem to notice.

Sophie shrugged and shifted against the seat, pushing her pencil skirt up an inch higher. The three-inch heels she wore gave her calf muscles even more definition. Taking this job had been monumentally stupid when even her calves had the ability to distract him. Of course when he could clearly remember having her legs wrapped around him as she climaxed, it was damn hard not to be distracted.

"Ronald gave me a chance when I had no experience, and the company offers tuition assistance. And . . . he and his wife have been really good to me."

She said Ronald, not SBMS. That could mean that she was loyal to him, not the company. Jack made a mental note and tried to ignore another flash of her smooth, toned skin. She was still petite and fit, but she'd definitely acquired some more curves. She'd been a knockout at seventeen, but she was all woman now. And she could never be his again.

He rolled his shoulders, trying to ease the foreign tension humming through his body. Missions never affected him like this. He'd always been able to compartmentalize and detach from things.

Always.

Except with her. Seemed now was no different. He'd only lived under the same roof with Sophie for six months, and once they'd crossed that line into more than friends he hadn't been able to keep his hands off her. But he'd been seventeen. He shouldn't still be reacting the same way to her. His attraction should be dulled and he should damn well be able to control his thoughts. But Sophie had always been his one soft spot and he hated that his boss was using that against him.

Jack was only a month older than her, so he'd signed up to go to boot camp until she could move out on her own—at her insistence. They'd graduated from high school, but she'd still had a month left in the system because of her age. So he'd been gone when she was attacked, brutalized. He hadn't been there to protect her. Her last words to him, shouted in anger, haunted him to this day. *"I hate you and I never want to see you again."* She'd been a hurting, terrorized girl and on one level he knew she'd said them in the heat of the moment, but those words had buried themselves deep in his psyche and latched on with eagle talons. And she'd never tried to get in contact with him after that. Had never returned any of his letters. Eventually he'd lost track of her—until he'd been recruited by the NSA. Then he'd found out everything there was to know about her current life. Like a masochist.

"So, what about you? I didn't realize Paul Keane had a partner." Sophie's soft voice brought him back to the present.

Game face on, he ordered himself. Jack wasn't some rookie, and if he didn't get his shit together, this entire op could fail. That was unacceptable. Biological weapons were the wave of the future, and the fallout was terrifying. Hospitals, religious centers, schools—terrorists had no problem hitting innocent civilians. In fact, they thrived on those targets. And Vargas had no conscience; the man would strike where he could hurt the most. Translation: the most innocent victims, which would likely be children. The monster had done just that in his own region to instill fear and to keep locals in line.

Thankful for the mental reminder of what was on the line, Jack recited the cover story he'd gone over half a dozen times in the past couple of days. "I gave him the start-up for Keane Flight. Until now I've never had any interest in his company, but when he got in that accident, I stepped in to take over things for a while."

"So, what did you do before this? Or what *do* you do?" There was a definite note of anxiety in her voice.

He risked a quick glance at her. Sophie's face was impassive, but she was twirling a strand of dark hair. Why was she nervous? The information he had didn't suggest she was involved, but until now he hadn't realized how loyal she was to her boss. Maybe she wasn't nervous because of that. If it was because she was attracted to him—no, he shut that thought down. It didn't matter. "I own a few restaurants, and I've been fortunate enough to make wise investments over the years." This was all part of his cover, but he didn't divulge too much information.

She nodded and glanced away. As he pulled up to La Marea at the Tides Hotel, she tugged at her skirt almost self-consciously, and when one of the valet guys opened the door for her, she jumped. It was subtle, but enough for him to notice.

Jack's hands clenched around the steering wheel, but he forced himself to get out. He rarely used a valet—didn't ever like giving up control of his keys—but for the role he was playing, it only made sense.

"Is the terrace okay?" he asked as he held open the front door to the restaurant for her.

"That sounds great." The smile she gave him was tight and brittle, but it didn't detract from her full lips and he couldn't help staring at them.

All he wanted to do was nibble, tease, and stroke them. The urge to lean forward and do just that was startlingly real. He sighed. Being so close to Sophie again was going to put him in an early grave.

From the file Wesley had given him, he knew this was her favorite place, so he hoped to soften her up while he subtly grilled her. Once they were seated and the hostess had taken their drink orders, he jumped right in to professional mode. "Ronald tells me you're like his right hand."

She blushed and damn if his cock didn't jump to attention. Again. It gave her a deliciously innocent quality that made him ache. She was quick to brush away his compliment. "I don't know about that."

A light breeze blew up, ruffling the open table umbrella sheltering them. He instinctively glanced around. The terrace was blocked by thick hedges, giving them a decent amount of privacy, but his senses had been on high alert since they'd left SBMS. At first he thought it was because he was around Sophie, but his gut told him otherwise. A familiar tingle spread across the back of his neck, as if someone was watching him. He'd been in the crosshairs of a sniper scope before, and the sensation he had now was damn familiar. Jack started to respond when a reflection from the hedges caught his eye. It danced and flickered for a second and raw adrenaline kicked in.

There wasn't time to make any other decision. Even though there was a slim chance he was making a mistake, it would be worth the embarrassment. He shoved the iron and glass table on its side and tackled Sophie. The last thing he saw as he flew at her was her wide brown eyes. He attempted to soften the blow as he fell over her by rolling the chair, but a few cuts and bruises or even a broken arm would be nothing compared to a bullet in her chest.

"What the hell are you doing?" Sophie yelled, and struggled underneath.

A huge potted plant exploded behind them, followed by screams and shouts from the other patrons. She immediately stilled, her mouth falling open.

"There's a shooter. We have to get out of here." He shifted and grabbed one of the iron table legs, pulling it around so they had more cover.

Face pale and eyes wide, she nodded likely because the word "shooter" sank in.

The glass tabletop exploded, showering them with shards. Which told him the shooter had suitable visibility. At least he had lousy aim. Jack kept his body over Sophie.

"Get ready to run. Stay low," he ordered.

Still shielding her, he grabbed her arm and they sprinted for the open glass doors to the interior of the restaurant. Luckily there were other patrons doing the very same thing, inadvertently giving them cover. Once inside, he scanned the area for a backup shooter. Patrons, servers, and other staff of the hotel were all running around in a blind panic, so if there was a backup shooter, he would be the only calm person. Jack didn't spot anyone like that and at least now they were inside. Short of being hit with a missile, they had cover for the moment.

Keep moving, keep moving. Moving targets were a hell of a lot harder to hit. As a veteran sniper, he had firsthand experience.

He glanced at Sophie as they continued running through the restaurant. "You okay?"

She nodded shakily, her face pale. "Yeah."

Jack still held on to her arm. And he didn't plan to let go anytime soon. "I promise we'll get out of here."

Jack had been in far worse situations, but always during missions and usually in foreign countries. Everyone he worked with knew the risks associated with their chosen profession. Not Sophie. She was just a civilian and hadn't asked for this.

He continued through the restaurant, dodging shouting men and women and jerking Sophie along with him. Once they neared the sliding glass doors on the other side of the hotel, he tugged her to the side of the entrance. "Stay here."

When the doors whooshed open he ducked outside and behind the valet desk. Crouching down, he scanned the wooden board until he saw his keys. In all the chaos, no one was paying attention to him. And if they were, they didn't care what he was doing.

Seconds later he was back inside. Fear punched through him when he didn't spot Sophie.

"I'm here." She jumped up from behind one of the huge potted palm trees against the wall, still clutching her purse like a lifeline.

"Come on." He kept his hand at the small of her back as they ran toward one of the side exits.

"Where are we going?"

"To get my vehicle."

"How do you even know where it is?" she asked as he pushed open the exit door into an empty tiled hallway.

"I know where they valet the cars." Before he went anywhere, he made it a point to memorize the schematics of the building. It always amazed him that people would give up their car keys to strangers without knowing anything about where their property was being taken.

Sophie's heels clacked along the floor, and even in her restrictive skirt, she almost matched his stride.

"This way." He motioned to turn left at the next open hallway.

She tripped on the slick floor as they made the sharp turn,

but he caught her before she fell. A burst of raw adrenaline and lust surged through him in equal doses when his hand snaked around her waist. Sophie tensed, shoved away from him, and kept running on her own.

"We're almost there." When they made it to the last door, he held up a finger to her and pulled out the SIG, which had been nicely tucked into his shoulder holster and hidden by his jacket.

"What the hell?" She stared at the gun with wide eyes, real fear in her gaze.

"Stay close to me, please." Jack wasn't sure whether it was the unexpected weapon or the "please," but Sophie jerkily nodded.

He eased the door open. No one was in this section of the parking garage. He pressed the unlock button. Two rows over, the SUV beeped and the lights flashed.

After one more visual sweep, he reached behind him without turning around. "Come on."

When he felt Sophie's delicate hand in his, an invisible vise tightened around his chest. She was trusting him with her life and he'd be damned if he screwed this up.

Crouching low, they slipped out the exit door and ducked behind a four-door sedan. With their backs against the passenger door, Jack motioned with one hand. "My SUV is about two rows over. We're going to make a run for it."

"Is there someone in this parking garage after us?" she whispered.

"I don't know, but I'm not taking a chance." There were too many variables right now, and Sophie's possible involvement was a very big one.

He'd considered the fact that someone from one of his previous jobs might have tracked him down—almost an impossibility considering that most people he'd worked with were dead or in prison—but something told him that shooter hadn't been aiming for him. The potted plant had been a lot closer to Sophie. No, someone had been after her. Which might mean his cover had been compromised, but more likely someone didn't want her talking. About what? He had no idea. The only thing he knew for sure was that he was getting her out of here and getting some answers.

Fast.

"On the count of two, we go." Using his fingers, he counted. On two, they sprinted across the concrete, using the other cars as cover. Her shoes smacked loudly, ruining any chance of covertness they had.

Before getting inside the SUV, he lay on the ground to make sure someone hadn't planted a bomb. Definitely paranoid, but he'd rather be that than dead. Once they were inside his vehicle, he started the ignition, kicked it into drive, and pulled out of the spot before she had a chance to strap in.

He barreled through the first level, keeping his eyes open for anyone suspicious, but the level was clean. Jack paused at the exit, then took a left. His tires squealed loudly as he zoomed away.

"What the hell is going on? And why are you carrying a gun? Who are you?" Sophie's questions came at him like machine gun fire as she gripped the armrest with a white-knuckled hand.

"Why don't you tell *me* what's going on?" he asked.

"Excuse me?" Her voice rose a few octaves.

"Whoever was shooting at us wasn't aiming at me." He quickly scanned her. She was rumpled, but he couldn't see any blood.

"What . . . You think someone was shooting at *me*? You're insane." She shook her head and tucked a few strands of hair behind her ear before glancing down at herself. Her crisp white button-down blouse was missing a couple of buttons and her jacket was ripped at one of the seams. "Why aren't we calling the police?"

He glanced in the rearview mirror. No one was behind

them, so he took a right onto Ocean Drive. It was Miami's most famous and most crowded street. They'd be able to blend in and get lost if they needed to. At least until he could secure another vehicle.

"You never told me why you're carrying a gun."

He ignored her and switched lanes while keeping his eyes on the rearview mirror. If someone was tailing them, they were good because Jack didn't see anyone.

"Okay, are you just ignoring everything I'm saying?" Her voice rose again, that temper he remembered so well flaring brightly.

It shouldn't turn him on, but damn if he didn't love and miss that fire in her. "I'm trying to get us away from here in one piece. I'll answer your questions once we're safe."

Out of the corner of his eye, he saw her dig into her purse. Before he realized what she was doing, she was on the phone.

"What the hell are you doing?" He risked a glance at her as they came to a red light.

"Calling Ronald."

"Damn it, woman—" He lunged for the phone, but she jerked away from him lightning fast at the same time a horn blasted from behind.

He accelerated and gritted his teeth. Technically, he could forcibly take the phone from her, but he wasn't sure if that was necessary yet. The thought of hurting her, even inadvertently, sliced up his insides.

"Hi, Mandy. It's Sophie. I need to talk to Ronald. . . . *Homeland Security* . . . They want to talk to *me*. . . . Are you sure? . . . I don't understand—"

Screw it. Jack grabbed her phone and pulled the battery out in a few short moves. She squawked and reached for it, but he shoved both pieces into the side of the door.

He was surprised by her silence, but considering he had a gun, he knew he shouldn't be. She had to be scared out of her mind. But after a few long beats she started cursing at him in rapid-fire Spanish—and he inwardly smiled. Back when they were teenagers and she got pissed, she'd always had the same reaction. It was probably messed up, but he liked the sound of her cursing at him like this. It meant she was angry, and that was an emotion he could always deal with.

When she finally caught her breath and seemed to calm down a fraction, she said, "Where are you taking me, *cabron*?"

Okay, she wasn't that calm if she was cursing at him. "I have a backup car stashed not far from here. We're going to retrieve it; then I'm going to get you somewhere safe."

"Safe? You think I'm going to trust you?" She snorted, the sound irreverent, but he didn't miss the way she nervously wrapped her arms around herself.

Winding his way through Miami, he was watchful of anyone that might be following them. Sophie was fidgety as he drove but didn't ask any more questions, probably because she was now terrified of him. Or *more* terrified than she had been already.

When they finally neared their destination, he didn't let his guard down but allowed a sliver of relief to slide through him. The expansive parking lot was nearly empty as he drove across it toward a bundle of empty warehouses perched on Biscayne Bay. He'd parked another vehicle roughly a mile away in a grocery store parking lot, but just in case they were being tracked, he didn't want to lead anyone directly to his backup.

"What is this place?" Sophie finally said as she slowly pulled out the pepper spray from her pocket.

He'd parked in between two unused warehouses he'd scouted out earlier. Bayside Marketplace wasn't that far from where they were—hell, he could actually see Port Boulevard Bridge jutting over Biscayne Bay—but for how quiet and desolate the area seemed, they might as well be a thousand miles away. He glanced at her hand and shook his head.

"You can keep that if it makes you feel better, but you don't need it against me. In fact . . ." Jack reached down and lifted up his pant leg. He handed her a simple revolver. "Take this. There's no safety and you don't have to pull back the hammer. It'll make for a smoother shot if you do, but it's not necessary. All you have to do is pull the trigger."

Swallowing hard, she eyed him with surprise. But she didn't hesitate to take the weapon. "Why are you giving this to me?"

"Because I don't like that fucking fear I see in your eyes when I'd *never* hurt you," he snapped, losing his tight control for a moment.

Her eyes widened, but she still held the weapon in her lap. At least it was turned away from him. "You still haven't told me where we are."

"Just somewhere to ditch this vehicle." He pulled out another weapon from under his seat. Jack was all about backups. He needed to call Wesley to have someone pick up the SUV and sanitize it, but now his only priority was getting Sophie to safety.

After popping the locks he gave a cursory glance over his shoulder, then froze. There was a black Humvee gunning right for them. With a warehouse on either side, they had nowhere to go. Making a split-second decision, he pressed the button to open the sunroof. He'd been in worse circumstances, but having Sophie with him now made his heart beat just a little faster.

Sophie looked back at him. Her mouth dropped open, but before she could ask any questions, he pointed up. "These guys are going to ram us and there's nothing we can do. As soon as we hit the water, you're going to clear the sunroof."

"What? What about you?" Panic laced her voice as she tucked the revolver into the waist of her skirt.

"Sophie!" he shouted, needing her to listen, needing to get through her adrenaline-jagged brain. They only had seconds now. In his periphery vision he could see the black vehicle closing in on them. Instinctively he tensed, bracing for the impact. This was gonna hurt like hell. He prayed Sophie wouldn't be injured too badly to escape. He'd disabled the airbags—as he always did—in the SUV so at least they wouldn't suffer under that impact. "Promise you'll climb out the sunroof. I'll be behind you, but I can't worry about you while trying to save myself."

Eyes wide, she nodded and slipped her heels off the moment before the impact. She still had her purse slung across her body like a satchel. He wanted to tell her to lose it, but there was no time.

A jarring crunch wrenched through the vehicle. Sophie let out a little scream as her body slammed forward, but she held on tight as they were propelled toward the water.

"Why aren't you shooting at them?" she shouted as the Humvee driver gunned the engine once more, shoving them inexorably toward the small pillars that wouldn't stand a chance under the force of the two vehicles. She quickly jerked the purse off, but snagged her wallet from it as she tossed it to the floorboards. Shoving the thin wallet down her shirt, she looked over her shoulder again, fear clouding her eyes.

He ignored her question. "We're going to go over in a second. Through the sunroof, then swim east. Swim as hard as you can until you find cover! Don't surface until you're safe!" There was a lip that curved over where the string of warehouses sat. They had to reach it.

The SUV jerked forward again and the scent of burning rubber filled the air as they teetered and plunged over the edge.

Grabbing her waist, he unceremoniously shoved her upward as they hit the water. She'd have seconds before the water rushed through the opening. Then they'd be trapped until the water pressure had equalized enough for them to swim out. Jack wasn't waiting.

Sophie let out a yelp as he kept pushing at her, but eventually her feet cleared the opening. Frigid water gushed over him in a powerful torrent, so he clutched the armrest and held his breath as the vehicle filled and the coolness submerged his body. He could hold his breath for five minutes, and he knew it wouldn't take that long.

In the back of his mind, fear clawed at him at the thought of whoever had rammed them into the water hurting Sophie while he was trapped here, but he could only focus on one problem at a time. He'd gotten her clear of the immediate danger. The SUV rapidly filled up and he hit the bottom of the bay floor—he guessed it was maybe nine or ten feet down. Finally the interior water pressure stabilized. Weapon in hand, he blinked a few times as he swam through the sunroof. The salty water stung his eyes, but the visibility was decent. At least it was murky enough that he couldn't see the surface clearly, which meant whoever had rammed them couldn't see him either.

As his head cleared the opening, he nearly jerked back at the sight of Sophie swimming toward him. She grabbed his hand and pointed frantically in the direction of the warehouse. The knowledge that she'd come back for him slammed into his chest, but he didn't have time to dwell on it. Maybe he never would.

He pushed free of the SUV and began swimming toward the warehouse. She let his hand drop and swam in short, surprisingly powerful strokes away from him. Her sleek legs kicked furiously as she kept pace with him. When she started ascending, he followed. It was dark above them, with very little sunlight pouring through the water. Weapon raised, he was ready to defend them, but they were under the protective lip.

Adrenaline punched through him as muted male voices above them talked in rapid-fire Spanish. He spoke many languages. Spanish wasn't one of them. He might not know what they were saying, but he did know that he and Sophie needed to get the hell out of there.

Sophie's face was pale and her teeth were chattering as she quietly treaded the icy water. A shot sounded above them as someone fired into the water where the SUV had plunged in. Her entire body jerked at the sound, but she didn't let out a peep. Reaching for her, Jack wrapped an arm around Sophie's waist and tugged her close. To his surprise, she curved into him, wrapping her arms and legs around him. He tried to ignore the way his entire body reacted to the familiar feel of her slim body molded to him like a second skin, but a certain part of his anatomy wouldn't listen. Later he'd blame it on adrenaline.

"Hold on to me. I'm going to swim us until this cover ends. They won't be able to follow," he whispered against her ear so quietly he wasn't sure she'd heard.

Until she nodded and tightened her grip on him. Her breasts pressed up against his chest, torturing him. After tucking his gun in his shoulder holster with his free hand, he slowly and quietly made his way along the length of the wall. Water lapped at them, splashing their faces and covering their movements. Sophie was quiet, if shaky, as he moved through the water. Once they passed under one of the warehouses, he felt a modicum of relief.

A rapid-fire round of shots sounded behind them, and Sophie let out a distressed mewling sound as she buried her face in his neck. He stroked a hand over her head, hoping to soothe her.

The farther they moved away, the more distant the voices got until he couldn't hear them at all. Sophie still clung to him. He worried she'd gone into mild shock, which might be a small blessing. If he could just get her on dry land and retrieve his vehicle, they had a fighting chance of getting out of this alive.

About five hundred yards down, a rusty ladder hung over

the walk above them. It seemed to take forever, but finally they made it. Grabbing it, he took Sophie's face in his other hand, gently stroking her cheek with his thumb. Her eyes were wide but alert. "I need you to let go of me so I can climb up."

"O . . . kay," she said through clenched teeth as a chill snaked through her.

He peeked his head over the top and let out a shaky breath. A lone warehouse with boarded-up windows was to his right. An older-model Grady White with no engines on a trailer sat next to it. To his left was the back of the grocery store where he'd left his backup. Jack looked down at Sophie clinging to the metal ladder. Her hair was plastered to her face, those dark eyes of hers hauntingly wide, making her look young and vulnerable. It reminded him of the last time he'd seen her. He swallowed hard, fighting the urge to pull her into his arms. "Do you have enough energy to run about a hundred yards?"

"Will there be . . . d-dry clothes?"

Grinning at her attitude, he nodded.

"Then hell yeah," she said through clenched teeth.

Chapter 4

Going dark: when an operative cuts all communication for a certain period of time.

Sophie kept stealing glances at Jack as they drove down the highway, but so far she hadn't said anything. Her hair was slicked back and her arms were wrapped around her still-shivering body. Jack had turned on the heat in his backup car, and she'd stripped out of her wet clothes into a pair of sweatpants and a T-shirt he had in his duffel bag. The clothes were too big for her, but they were dry.

"I'm not going to hurt you," he told her as he pulled out one of his backup cell phones from the duffel. After the way he'd just carried her to safety, she should know that, but maybe she needed reassurance.

"Why should I believe you?"

"First, I gave you a loaded weapon. Second, if I wanted you dead, I'd have let that shooter blow your head off—or I could have drowned you myself back there."

She winced at his words and her already pale face turned almost gray. Instantly he wanted to kick his own ass. Yeah, he really needed to learn some subtlety.

"Where are we going?" Her voice was even quieter now.

"Somewhere safe."

"Where?" she persisted.

"You're just going to have to trust me."

"I barely know you." She mumbled a few Spanish words under her breath, and though his knowledge of the language was limited, he was pretty sure she called him a lying criminal.

Despite the situation, he had to bite back a smile at her attitude. She impressed him with how well she was handling everything. Ignoring her annoyance, he called his boss.

"Yeah?" Wesley answered immediately.

"Are you on a secure line?"

"Of course. What's going on?"

"Someone just tried to kill Sophie Moreno."

"Who?"

"Don't know yet, but they were highly trained. Got a brief look at one of the guys right before we crashed into Biscayne Bay. He was Caucasian, dark hair, couldn't tell how tall he was."

"Russian?"

"No way to tell, but I heard them speaking Spanish, so I'm guessing no." He briefly filled in his boss on what had happened.

Wesley was silent for a long beat. "You can't take her back to SBMS or the condo."

"I know. Do you know anything about Homeland Security wanting to talk to her?"

"What?"

"I didn't think so. Looks like we might have a leak or they've been watching SBMS too. Homeland Security was at SBMS waiting to question her before we were attacked. I'm en route to a safe house, but as soon as we disconnect, I'm going dark until tomorrow."

"Damn it, Jack, I need a way to contact you."

"Too bad." He pressed the END button, then took out the battery. Jack couldn't chance that someone was tracking them with a satellite. The NSA had better security than all their government agencies combined, but if there was a mole, all the security in the world wouldn't matter.

"Who was that?" Sophie scooted back in her seat, as if she could hide from him.

He sighed but kept his eyes on the road. "That was my boss."

"How does he know who I am? And what do you mean there might be a leak? Who are you? After what just happened I think I deserve to know." The pitch of her voice rose steadily with each word.

Jack couldn't afford to have her freak out now. Especially not when he was pretty sure she was in mild shock. "Listen, I know you're scared, but I need to get you to a safe place and we really need to clean up your wound." He didn't know when she'd been hit, but he was assuming a piece of glass or something else had hit her at the restaurant. The outside of her left jacket sleeve had been soaked with blood, and a tiny portion covered the back of her new T-shirt.

"Wound?" She glanced down at herself and ran a hand over the front of her shirt and sweatpants.

"Blood's seeping through the back of your shirt, so I'm assuming you were hit." If they'd had time, he'd have cleaned it up when they first reached the backup car. But time was not on their side.

She reached around with her right hand and felt the left side of her ribs and upper back. She winced in pain when she touched her shoulder blade. "Why didn't I feel anything before?" she asked through gritted teeth.

"Adrenaline."

When she pulled her hand back, there were a few specks of blood on her fingers. She took in a few deep, ragged breaths.

Shit. The sight of blood used to make her sick. He'd just assumed that she'd gotten over it. Up until now she'd been handling everything relatively well. Even though he hated wasting time and stopping, he glanced in the rearview mirror and steered into a gas station parking lot.

"Lean forward and put your head between your legs," he said quietly.

She shook her head, her breathing ragged. "I'm fine."

"Humor me, then."

Muttering another curse, she did as he said. He reached out and rubbed her back in small, soothing circles, careful to stay far away from the wound. The action was instinctive for him. She might not realize it, but her body needed comforting. It was pure biology. Instead of calming down, however, she tensed and her erratic heartbeat increased. He could feel the thumping against his fingers.

"Sophie? Talk to me." He kept his words low and even.

Still leaning forward, she shook her head. "Can't breathe . . . Today is insane. . . . We were shot at and . . . you could have drowned. . . ." She sucked in another uneven breath.

"Sophie."

When she still didn't respond, Jack made a decision. He knew he'd regret this later, but for now, it was the only thing he knew that would get her under control. "Look at me." His words were a sharp order.

Immediately she sat up, her dark eyes wide. Against his better judgment, he reached out to comfort her. He just wanted to wrap his arm around her so she'd calm down. Well, he wanted more than that. After she'd been plastered against him in the frigid water, he ached to feel her lean body around him once again. Because she wanted to be, not out of necessity. His fingers threaded through the curtain of her damp hair as he pulled her close. Her breathing was still erratic, and she practically fell across the console as she buried her face in his chest and dug her hands into his shoulders. Jack continued rubbing her back in soothing, rhythmic patterns until her heart rate slowed to normal. Comforting her like this was better than anything he could say with words.

"I'm sorry," she mumbled as she pulled her head back.

"You have nothing to be sorry for." Immediately he missed the warmth of her body against his. Instead of removing his hand as he knew he should, he remained immobile.

When her eyes locked on his, Sophie stared at him without blinking. Her dark eyes seemed to swallow him whole and when her soft lips parted invitingly, his entire body reacted with primal awareness.

Before he could change his mind, he brushed his mouth over hers. A bare grazing of his lips over her soft ones. She let out a tiny gasp of surprise and her hands pressed against his chest as if she meant to push him away. But just for a moment. Then she clutched his shirt, grabbing onto him as if he were a lifeline.

He pressed his tongue deep into her mouth, tasting her sweet essence. For years he'd fantasized about kissing her again. It was like fucking heaven. Pure Sophie. He was consumed with greediness, already wanting more from her. Wanting to strip her bare and take everything she had to offer. As their tongues meshed and collided, a deep moan released from her. The erotic sound drove straight to his core and wrapped around the part of him he kept locked away from everything and everyone.

The part that dared to want someone for more than a night. The part that wanted to feel and experience more than meaningless sex. The part that wanted Sophie Moreno in his bed and in his life permanently. Just as they'd planned when they were younger.

Jack hadn't been prepared for his primal reaction to her. It was even more intense than when they'd been seventeen. His stomach clenched as she wrapped her hands around the back of his neck and returned his fervent kisses with a heated intensity he hadn't expected given the situation. With his free hand he grasped one of her thighs and bunched a section of the sweatpants she wore. It was the only way he could remind himself of restraint. He wanted to rip them off her and plunge deep inside her. To feel her tight sheath clenching around his cock until they were both sated and tired. The fact that they were in a car and on the run didn't matter.

She made a soft moaning sound into his mouth and he was afraid he might combust on the spot. Moving higher because he needed actual contact, he slid his hand underneath her cotton shirt. His fingers burned as he caressed her silky stomach. Actually touching her brought all his memories back like a raging fire. Memories and fantasies would never compare to the real thing.

When the blast of a car horn ripped through the air, he jumped back. The horn wasn't meant for them, but it had shattered the moment just the same. Breathing hard, he forced himself to move away from her and turned the ignition back on. What was he doing? He was a government agent on a critical mission, trying to get this woman to safety and to save the country from a potential catastrophic threat. Not a randy teenager on his first date who couldn't control his dick.

Sophie's soft pink lips were swollen and by the dazed look in her eyes, she was surprised, but also turned on. Her damp hair was messy and framed her face in a way that made him think of raw sex. *Great.*

"I'm sorry . . . I shouldn't have done that. It won't happen again." His hoarse, shaky voice sounded foreign to his own ears.

In response she touched a trembling finger to her lips, then leaned back against her seat. He glanced out his window to give her a moment of privacy.

"Jack?" The sound of her voice pulled him back around.

When he faced her, her eyebrows were pulled down, as if she might ask him something. Instead she leaned forward and twisted in her seat so that her back was turned toward him. "Can you see where I'm cut?"

There was some blood covering her shirt, but it wasn't spreading and appeared almost dry. "It looks like you got hit with some glass. Probably from the table at the restaurant. I don't want to risk taking it out right now and making things worse."

"Okay." She leaned back in the seat but twisted so she wasn't pressing against the wound.

He rubbed a hand over his face and tried to banish the memory of that kiss. It was a mistake and he'd just leave it at that. This hadn't even been in the realm of possibilities of how he'd expected things to go today. Normally he got a rush of adrenaline during firefights, but the only thing he felt at the moment was relief for Sophie's safety. Well, that and he was still turned on. Unfortunately there wasn't a damn thing he could do about that.

Following the signs and keeping to the speed limit, he made his way to 95 South. Technically he wasn't going to a safe house, but Wesley didn't need to know that. He'd purchased a place in Marathon, Florida, years back. It was listed under a bogus corporation, and it wasn't connected to him. It was his contingency plan in case things ever went south. Only one other person knew about it, and there was no way in hell his friend would tell anyone about it.

Right now this was the best and closest option for Sophie and him to escape to. There were too many unknown variables and he wasn't trusting her safety to anyone but himself.

Chapter 5

Safe house: a house in a secret location, used by spies or criminals in hiding.

Ronald Weller somehow managed to keep his stride even as he walked toward the elevators. He couldn't call Miguel Vargas from his office. Now that Homeland Security was in the building, he couldn't risk being overheard. So far they were just asking routine questions about SBMS's business practices, but he wasn't fooled for a second. The government wouldn't have shown up unless they suspected SBMS of *something*.

And after Sophie's insistent calls last night and then again this morning, he knew she was on to something. She was a damn good worker and she could be relentless when she wanted to know something. For the past few months he'd been able to brush off her questions about Keane, but with this new guy suddenly showing up and now Homeland Security—Ronald couldn't stop sweating. His entire world was crumbling and he couldn't help the one person in his life who needed him most. He felt as if he was between that proverbial rock and a hard place. Except that rock was a terrorist with a gun.

Once he reached the parking garage, he scanned the rows of cars and trucks. No one was following him and no one was in the garage. He pulled out one of the throwaway phones he'd been instructed to purchase and dialed a familiar number.

Someone he didn't recognize picked up. A woman. "Yes?"

"I need to talk to Miguel. Now."

"Who is this?"

"None of your damn business." He sounded a hell of a lot braver than he felt. Fear was the only thing spurring him on, though.

There was a shuffling, then Miguel came on the line. "Who is this?"

"It's Ronald. What the hell is going on?"

"What do you mean?"

He heard the ding of the elevator, so he headed in the direction of his car and lowered his voice. There weren't any video cameras in this garage, so he didn't have to worry about anyone seeing him either. "Homeland Security is here. They want to talk to Sophie Moreno."

"She won't be a problem. I don't know why you're always worrying. I've taken care of her." Vargas's condescending voice grated on him.

Ronald's throat tightened as the possible meaning of Vargas's words sank in. "What the hell does that mean? Of course she's not a problem. She's not involved in any of this."

"She's been sticking her pretty nose where it doesn't belong. One of my men saw her car fleeing a certain hangar last night."

Iciness engulfed Ronald, chilling his entire body. "What are you talking about?" That was probably why she'd wanted to talk to him. He had assumed it was to discuss the books. He'd just wanted to blow her off, to buy some damn time. She'd been at Keane's hangar?

"You should have kept a tighter leash on your employee."

Ronald swayed for a moment. Sophie hadn't returned from lunch yet. In the eight years she'd worked for Ronald, she'd *never* been late without calling first. He'd told her time and again she didn't need to check in when she was going to be late, but she always did. Truthfully he'd thought she was just pissed at him for being so rude earlier. "What have you done to her?"

"She will be eliminated shortly." His clipped tone left no room for doubt.

"You son of a—"

"Remember who you're talking to."

How could he forget? Ronald rubbed a hand over his two-day-old stubble as his stomach pitched. Sophie was like family to him, but he didn't have a choice. "I haven't forgotten."

"Good. I'll be contacting you shortly regarding the next shipment."

"And this is the last one?"

"If things go according to plan, yes."

Ronald would believe it when he saw it. Before going back in, he tossed the phone into a trash can. With Homeland Security snooping around, he couldn't give them any excuse to take him into custody.

Not now. Not when he was so close to having his life back.

Sophie clutched her chemistry books tighter against her chest as she came up on Second Street. The smell of freshly cut grass tickled her nose. All the lawns in the neighborhood were perfectly mowed. Except her home, of course. Her foster mother was older and didn't care about stuff like that. As Sophie rounded the corner, her stomach tightened when she saw Inez Reyes standing in her front yard talking to two of the neighborhood kids.

Hoping to avoid another confrontation, she crossed the street. It was useless. Out of the corner of her eye, she watched Inez say something to them, then run across the street.

"Sophie! Where're you going so fast?"

The knot in her stomach tightened. She didn't stop walking. "I've got to get home."

"I'm having a party Friday night. Ricardo was asking about you," the tall, curvy girl cooed.

Somehow Sophie doubted that. With her flat chest and nonexistent curves, boys never looked at her. Not that she cared. They were a waste of time and she wasn't going to end up pregnant before she'd graduated from high school because of some loser. For some reason unbeknownst to her, Inez just liked to pick on her. And she'd never done anything to the other girl. "Whatever," she mumbled.

"I don't know what your problem is, perra flaca. You think you're so much better than all of us. At least I have parents."

Sophie didn't respond. If she did, she'd start crying. And she refused to let this stupid girl see her tears. Three more houses to go. Only three more and she'd be home. It might not be much, but at least it was safe.

"I'm talking to you, stupid!" Inez grabbed her arm, but before Sophie had a chance to react, a heated male voice interrupted them.

"Get away from her, you fucking cow." It wasn't exactly a shout, but there was a deadly edge to that voice.

Sophie and Inez both jerked to a halt and turned. Sophie wasn't sure who he was talking to, but her stomach did a little flip-flop as the cute dark-haired boy closed the distance between them. Casting a withering look at Inez, he positioned himself in between them. "If you talk to her again, I'll tell everyone in school that you've fucked the entire basketball team and now you're making your way through the baseball team. You know they'll believe me too."

Sophie watched as the other girl's face paled a deathly white beneath her normally caramel skin.

"Fuck you." Inez flipped her dark ponytail over her shoulder before running back across the street.

The tall—really cute—boy glanced down at her. "You okay?"

"Yeah. Uh, thank you." The afternoon sun beat down on her face, but the heat rushing to her cheeks had nothing to do with that. Boys rarely looked at her, and the careful way he was watching her made her nervous.

He shrugged and took her books from her hands. "I'll carry these for you."

She was too stunned to argue, so she fell in step with him. "Do you even know where I live?"

"Yep, you're Sophie Moreno and you live with Ms. Bigsby."

An alarm bell went off in her head. She stopped on the sidewalk and refused to take another step. There weren't many white boys who lived in her neighborhood, and he wasn't one of the few who did. Cute or not, she wasn't going anywhere with him. "Who are you?"

"My name's Sam. I just moved into Ms. Bigsby's house today. She told me about the problems you've been having with that stupid girl." He jerked his head in the direction of Inez's house.

"Oh . . . I didn't know we had anyone moving in." For a foster mother, Renee Bigsby was one of the nicer ones, so Sophie was surprised she hadn't said anything.

"It was last minute. My last house was . . . It doesn't matter. Since I already attend Miami Beach High, my social worker wanted to keep me in the same district since I graduate soon."

"You go to Miami Beach High too?" Sophie frowned at him. He had unmistakable pale blue eyes. Kind of like a wolf. She'd definitely have remembered him.

"Yeah. I play baseball. I've seen you around." The corners of his eyes crinkled as he looked at her.

"Oh." She bit her bottom lip, unsure what to say. Now she wished he hadn't taken her books. They provided a nice bar-

rier and she felt exposed as this strange boy stared at her with barely concealed interest. It didn't make her feel uncomfortable exactly, but she didn't know what to do about the tingly sensation in her stomach.

He averted his gaze and a light shade of red crept up his neck. "She's just jealous, you know."

"Who is?"

"Inez."

"Somehow I doubt that." She turned and started walking toward her house.

Sam kept pace with her. "She is. Trust me. You're pretty without trying and she hates you for it."

Another strange flutter settled in her stomach. He thought she was pretty? Sophie didn't say anything. She wasn't sure what to say anyway. Talking to the same sex was hard enough. Talking to boys—cute ones at that—no, thank you.

Sophie opened her eyes and groaned, banishing the long-buried dream she'd been having. What the hell was that about anyway? She hadn't dreamt about Sam in a while, and she didn't like that she was doing so now. It made her feel vulnerable and edgy.

Blinking a couple of times, she tried to orient herself. She felt as if her body had been through a blender. It took a moment to realize she was on her side and lying on a couch. She remembered being drowsy in the car. Must have dozed off, but . . . where was she?

"You awake?" a deep voice from behind her said.

She jerked up at the sound but immediately regretted the abrupt action. Piercing pain fractured through her body. Her arms and legs were stiff and achy. As if she'd just run a marathon in her heels. Probably from being tackled by Jack at that restaurant and then from the impact of that vehicle slamming into them. She shifted around so that she was sitting upright on the blue couch.

It took a few seconds to adjust to her surroundings, but she was in a sparsely decorated living room. Two large prints of underwater ocean life hung on the wall above the flat-screen television in front of her. She focused on them as she steadied herself.

The large room was attached to a kitchen where Jack stood behind a counter. It was the only thing separating them. She eyed him warily. After that hot—and unexpected—kiss, feelings of long-dormant lust battled the soreness shooting through her arms and legs. It was one thing to fantasize about kissing the sexy stranger, but quite another to actually do it. Especially since he was probably a criminal. "Where are we?"

"Marathon."

"In the Keys?"

"Yes."

She reached around and gingerly touched her shoulder blade. What if it was already infected? Why hadn't he woken her up?

As if he read her mind, Jack said, "We *just* got here. You haven't been asleep long and I was letting you rest a couple minutes."

Using the couch arm as a crutch, she pushed up and tugged her oversized T-shirt down. She had about a hundred different questions—like who the hell he really was—but first she wanted to make sure she wasn't going to bleed to death.

Jack was completely immobile while she walked into the kitchen. The tile cooled her bare feet as she stepped toward him. She figured he was trying to keep her calm, and that was fine with her. He'd already laid out towels, bandages, tweezers, peroxide, and alcohol.

She stared at his large, callous hands as he opened one of the butterfly bandages, and suddenly she felt very small. And terrified. She was in a strange place with a strange man. A man she'd recently shared an intimate moment with. Yes, he'd saved her life, but kissing strangers wasn't something she did. She'd never even had a one-night stand, yet she'd let a man with a scary gun and sexy muscles kiss her senseless.

Worse, she'd enjoyed it. A lot. The timing had been insanely inappropriate, and even so, she wouldn't mind a replay. Not to mention she'd fantasized about doing a whole lot more than kissing Jack. But what if he expected more from her? Her throat seized as violent scenarios played in her head. For all she knew, his name probably wasn't even Jack. From what little she'd gathered, she knew he didn't work for Keane Flight.

"I need you to take off your shirt." His words sliced through the quiet room like a machete.

A momentary burst of panic skittered across her skin. She'd been at the mercy of a man before. Defenseless and hurt so badly it made a shiver snake through her even thinking about it. She clutched the counter, fighting to take a full breath.

Jack didn't move. Just watched her with a preternatural stillness. As if he was trying to reassure her without words, but actions. The man might be a criminal, but he'd also given her a gun—which she'd lost during her swim to freedom. He hadn't had to do that. The rational voice in her head overrode her fears. If this man wanted to hurt her, he would have by now. He'd had plenty of chances. And she seriously doubted he'd have laid out bandages for her if he didn't care about her injuries.

She pushed out a long breath and turned so that her back faced him. "Can you help?" Her left arm was too stiff, so he helped her lift it over her head. Aware of how exposed she was, she froze, unsure what to do when the shirt was off.

He cleared his throat nervously, which actually made her feel better. "Uh . . . you might want to use this," Jack said as he handed her a hand towel.

Sophie was thankful she wasn't looking at him and hoped he couldn't sense her embarrassment. With her back still to him, she covered her breasts with the towel, using one hand to keep it anchored in place. She'd had to lose her bra earlier because it had been soaked through just like the rest of her clothes, and getting warm and dry had been a priority.

She glanced over her shoulder to look at him and saw he was averting his eyes. The apprehension she'd been feeling almost dissipated completely. Almost. He might not be who he said he was, but he wasn't going to attack her like a rabid animal.

"I'm going to pull out a few shards of glass, then cleanse the area with alcohol. It'll sting, but these are all surface wounds. You probably won't even be able to see the scratches in a few days. Do you need to sit down?"

"No. Sorry about earlier. It doesn't happen every time I see blood. I don't know why it did this time." She was beyond embarrassed by the way she'd handled herself. Hyperventilating like that made her cringe.

"A lot happened today. Some people have higher levels of tolerance for stress. You were pretty impressive, so cut yourself some slack." His deep voice was like a gentle salve against her worries.

Her shoulders bunched when his fingers grazed her skin. As he pulled a piece of glass from her shoulder, her back automatically arched. "What about you? Does this sort of thing happen to you all the time?" Maybe if she talked, it would take her mind off the pain. And the fact that she was standing half naked and alone with a very dangerous man. Hurting her might not be part of his agenda, but this man was an absolute predator. It was clear in his every move.

He chuckled as he pulled out another piece. "More than you'd think."

She stiffened again and gritted her teeth as he withdrew yet another. The pieces he placed on the counter were so small, she couldn't believe she'd bled so much.

"That's it. Now I'm going to cleanse it."

"Okay." She liked that he was walking her through each step. It gave her a tiny sense of control, something so important to her. She also appreciated that he wasn't touching her more than necessary. It was a small thing, but it spoke volumes about the kind of man he was.

The cool wet cloth against her skin soothed her. Even the alcohol felt good. It burned, but it was a relief knowing she was okay.

He cleared his throat again. "You might want to shower before I put on the bandage. If not, I'll have to rebandage it later."

Clutching the towel to her chest, she turned to face him. "Then you'll answer all my questions?"

He stared at her with those somehow familiar pale bluish eyes that reminded her so much of the boy she'd once loved, and an explosion of butterflies launched in her stomach. Maybe it was the dream she'd just had, but watching him— unwanted memories played in her head with a vengeance.

"As much as I can." His voice was slightly strangled, mirroring how she felt.

But there was no way he could be feeling or thinking the same thing as she. Sophie decided to take a chance. "Can you answer one now?"

"Maybe."

"Is your name really Jack Baldwin?"

He paused for a long beat and she wasn't sure he would even answer. That alone pretty much gave her an answer. Finally he spoke. "It's Jack Stone."

At least he was being honest. Or maybe that was simply *another* alias. She inwardly sighed when she realized it didn't matter how truthful she thought he was being. She had no way of knowing truth from lies or how to check out who he was. "Where's the shower?"

He turned around and led her down a short hallway. "This is your room." He motioned to the room on the right. "That's mine." He indicated to the one on the left. "They both have private bathrooms. I managed to dig up some clothes for you, but we'll get you something more suitable tomorrow."

"Tomorrow?" They *still* hadn't called the cops, Homeland Security was apparently at her work, someone definitely wanted her dead, and he expected her to stick around?

"Shower first. Answers later." That pale gaze of his was so damn intoxicating.

Maybe he thought he could hypnotize her into staying. She blinked and forced herself to glance away. After the way he'd tackled her at the restaurant, then their running for their lives, only to be followed by a car crash and an unexpected swim in the freezing ocean . . . Yeah, she could do with a hot shower. "Okay."

He stopped her with a gentle hand on her upper arm as she stepped through the bedroom door. "I noticed earlier that you've got a few scratches on your leg. Will, uh . . ." He scrubbed a hand over his face, and something told her he rarely stumbled over his words.

It was all she could do to ignore what the feel of his callous hand against her skin was doing to her senses. There was something so frustratingly familiar about it, and it was driving her crazy. This man was likely a criminal! She'd never been one to get turned on by the bad-boy image, but apparently her body was making decisions for her now. Her nipples hardened involuntarily under the thick towel. "What?"

"There's probably a little blood on your legs too. Do you want me to wait outside the bathroom or anything?" He rubbed his hand over his face in a manner so similar to the way her Sam had done, it made her breath catch.

"I'll be fine. I promise." Despite the sudden heavy sensation in her chest at the thought of a man who had died way too young, the ghost of a smile teased her lips as she shut the bedroom door behind her. Jack's tripping over his words gave her a strange comfort.

The bedroom was furnished but sparse. There was a bed with a white-and-yellow paisley comforter, a dresser, a nightstand, and two inexpensive pictures of palm trees hanging on the wall. A man had definitely "decorated" this place.

He'd laid out a green halter-style summer dress on the bed for her. It looked a little too big, but at least she had something to put on. A small part of her wondered where he'd gotten it from, but she really didn't care. Clean clothes sounded pretty damn good at the moment. No underwear, though, so she'd be going commando for a day. Thankfully the dress had a built-in bra.

After stripping off the sweatpants he'd given her, she opened the bathroom door and some of the tension ebbed from her shoulders. There was a toothbrush, a washcloth, shampoo, a razor, and bath soap. She pulled back the nautical-themed shower curtain and twisted the shower knob. As soon as steam rose, she stepped under the pulsing jets, but quickly turned the pressure down.

Bruises were starting to show up on her right hip, and she could only guess where she'd gotten them. She also had a few dark splotches dotting all down her arms and legs. And they were only going to get bigger. She'd probably look as if she'd been in a bar brawl.

Her movements were sluggish, but she managed to wash her hair and scrub the dried patches of blood off her legs.

When she was younger, she used to pass out at the sight of blood all the time. But she hadn't passed out since after . . . *that* night. Bile rose in her throat as a sudden image of her last foster father flashed in her mind. To this day the smell of whiskey made her ill. Despite the hot water, a chill skittered over her skin, giving her visible goose bumps. When another unwanted shudder snaked through her, she grabbed the bar of soap and began vigorously scrubbing her arms. She had more important things to worry about. Like why was someone trying to kill her and who was the man supposedly helping her?

Jack Stone. The name lingered in her mind and on the tip of her tongue.

Sophie wished she was dealing with anyone but him. Every time she looked at Jack, she was reminded of Sam. He'd been her best friend. The boy she'd lost her virginity to. He'd been her everything. Her whole damn world at one time. The one person she could count on for anything and the one person she'd been able to completely be herself around.

Inevitably, she was also reminded of the last hateful words she'd said to him. She tried to pacify her guilt by telling herself she'd been young and hurting, but there was no excuse for the way she'd blamed Sam. Nothing that had happened had been his fault. And she'd never get the chance to tell him how sorry she was for shutting him out of her life. They'd been so close and she'd just ended things. She'd been in pain and as awful as it was to admit, she'd wanted him to suffer too. God, she'd been a wreck back then.

A few errant tears escaped. For Sam's memory, or for herself, she wasn't sure. She brushed them away as the last soapy suds rushed down the drain; then she turned the water off. Despite her burning questions, Sophie took her time. She found lotion under the sink and smoothed it over her arms and legs. After running a towel over her hair and combing it with her fingers, she slipped the dress on. The thin material was soothing against her skin. She spared herself one last glance in the mirror before opening the bedroom door.

Jack wasn't going to hurt her. Nothing he'd done so far indicated that was his intention. She found him in the living room on a laptop and hated that little tingling sensation she got when she saw him. He was working on a laptop, his long fingers flying across the keyboard. His forearms slightly flexed, drawing her eyes up the length of his arms to those wickedly broad shoulders. She wanted to smooth her hands over them, dig her fingers into his bare flesh while he kissed her again. *Okay, not the time to indulge in that fantasy,* she chided herself. "Where'd you get the computer?"

He closed the computer and looked up. "It was here."

For a brief moment, his eyes darkened as they raked over her body. The look was quick, but he did a complete sweep from her head to feet and there was no denying the way his gaze lingered on her breasts. *Men.* Not that she could judge since she'd been checking him out too. She curled her toes into the plush carpet as she stood in between the entrance of the hallway and the living room, every inch of her aware of his raw masculinity.

He saved her by standing. "Come on. I want to bandage your shoulder before we do anything else."

Sophie nodded and followed him to the kitchen. At least with this dress she didn't have to take off her clothes again. His hands were gentle as he pressed the butterfly bandage to her exposed shoulder. A flutter settled in her stomach as his fingers glided across her skin, but she ignored the strange sensation. He still hadn't mentioned that kiss and it was doubtful he ever would. She'd been freaking out and it had obviously been the only way for him to calm her down. He had enjoyed himself, though. Of that much, she was sure.

When he was finished she took a couple of steps forward and turned to face him. Using the counter as a support, she found her voice. "Ready to answer my questions?"

"Do you want to sit?"

"No. I want to know who you are and who you work for and why you wanted to meet me today. I know you don't work for Keane Flight, so don't even go there. And I want to know who the hell was shooting at me."

His dark eyebrows rose slightly. "That's a lot of questions."

She crossed her arms over her chest. "Why don't you start with who you are?"

He leaned against the other counter, eyeing her with an

expression she didn't understand. "That's a complicated question."

Her temper ignited. "Well, how about you try to answer anyway?"

He was silent for a long beat and she was under the impression he was sizing her up. What, did he think *she* knew what was going on? The thought was so stupid she almost rolled her eyes.

"I work for the government . . . in a clandestine capacity."

Okay, that wasn't what she'd been expecting. "Like a spy?"

His lips twitched. "Something like that."

If someone hadn't tried to kill them multiple times today, she'd probably laugh in his face. "What agency?"

"I can't tell you that."

"Why not?"

He ignored her question and asked another. "What's your next question?"

For a split second she contemplated grilling him, but something told her that he was the kind of man who would only crack under torture. And probably not even then. He stood there watching her, his face completely impassive, like a granite statue.

She tried to bite back her frustration. "Okay, who was trying to kill us?"

"*You.* Not us. And I should be asking you that question." One of his eyebrows lifted almost mockingly.

She gritted her teeth at his confident tone. "Me? How could you possibly think someone was shooting at me? You're the hotshot spy. Maybe it was you they're after."

"They were after you, and that means you have something they want. Or you're working with them." His deep voice might be an aphrodisiac, but right now his calm attitude was simply annoying her.

Her hands automatically clenched into fists. "Working with *who*?"

His shoulders lifted casually, as if the answer should be obvious. "Terrorists."

"Terrorists? You *are* insane." She shoved away from the counter and tried to move past him through the kitchen entryway.

Jack shifted so that he stood in front of her, completely blocking her exit. In her bare feet, she was barely five foot two and he had to be at least six feet tall. She bit her bottom lip. If he wanted to keep her there, there wasn't a lot she could do about it. No matter that she didn't fear him physically hurting her, that didn't mean he couldn't restrain her.

"Move," she ground out, hoping her voice sounded stronger than the trembling one inside her head.

Her order fell on deaf ears. "Sophie, you have something they want or you've seen something you shouldn't have. If you're not involved, then think about the last few months at work. Have you noticed anything different about anyone you work with?"

She didn't have to think about the last few months because she knew that if someone wanted her dead it was because of what she'd seen last night. "You don't actually think I'm a terrorist, do you?" She needed to get that out of the way first because if he did, she wasn't going to bother talking with him.

Something passed over his features as he shook his head. It was brief, but she knew what it was. Sincerity. "No, I don't. But my superiors aren't as convinced. So why don't you tell me what you know?"

"My purse . . ." She'd left it in the SUV, which was now at the bottom of the bay. And it had that file with Keane Flight's records.

"Left behind, though your wallet sort of survived. Your credit cards and ID are still inside."

"Where?" There was nothing tied to SBMS in it, but she was glad he'd saved it. After she'd changed out of those wet clothes, she hadn't even been aware of what he'd done with them or the wallet.

"Your room."

Wordlessly she made a move to leave the kitchen mainly because she wanted to get out of the enclosed area. Jack made her feel almost claustrophobic.

"I'll come with you." He shifted to the side so she could pass, but not enough that she could avoid touching him. Her shoulder brushed against his muscular chest, sending a rush of heat to her lower abdomen. She hated her purely physical reaction to him. It made her feel out of control, and right now that was the last thing she needed.

He wasn't more than a foot behind her as she made her way to the bedroom. Something about his scent was familiar. It was spicy and just plain masculine, but there was something else. Something that triggered familiar memories. Memories she wanted no part of. He might have the same dark hair and same pale eyes as Sam, but she had to be imagining any other similarities. Her mind was seeing what it wanted to see. Nothing more.

Her damp black wallet was on the small nightstand next to the bed. She hadn't even noticed it earlier. It was wet and still zipped up. The few receipts inside were ruined, but her credit cards were fine. She didn't see her flash drive anywhere, which meant either he'd found it or it was still in the lining of her bra. Wherever that was.

"What was in your purse?" Jack asked quietly.

She raked a shaky hand through her hair, hating that she'd had to leave it behind.

"I had my assistant compile a list of flight logs, flight patterns, and a few other accounting mysteries connected to Keane Flight that I've been looking into." She left out the part about the incriminating pictures.

He nodded as if he already believed her. "We know about most of this."

Okay, then. "We?"

Of course he ignored her question. She was starting to get used to that. "Was that file the only information you have on Keane and SBMS?"

She wasn't going to answer just yet. "Where's my bra and panties?" Jack hadn't proven that he worked for the government and he hadn't even told her which branch. Her boss might have been acting strange lately, but before she told this stranger anything, she was going to call Ronald and get more answers. She owed him that much. Jack might have saved her life, but doing that could still be for his own purposes, and Ronald was more than just her boss. He was her friend. Hell, he was like a father to her.

The question took Jack off guard. He rubbed the back of his neck, clearly uncomfortable. "I, uh, hung them up in the closet to dry. Didn't know if you'd want them later."

She tried not to let her elation show. Instead she held a hand to her forehead and swayed on her feet, hoping he bought her act. "Thank you . . . I'm feeling a little weak. Do you mind if I lie down for a bit?" She stumbled to the bed before sitting on the edge of the mattress. His eyes narrowed and she wondered if she'd overdone it.

When he shook his head she relaxed a fraction. "There's not much here in the way of food, but I'll be cooking rice and beans. Want me to wake you up in an hour?"

She gave him what she hoped was a reassuring smile. "Perfect."

Once he shut the door behind him, she rushed to depress the simple button lock. The satin nickel lock was flimsy, but if he tried to open it, she'd hear the door jangle. Or if he really was a spy, maybe she wouldn't. Either way, it made her feel better. She hurried to the window and pulled back the yellow curtain. They were on the first floor. Perfect.

Jack might not want to hurt her, but that didn't mean she trusted him.

Blood rushed in her ears as she slid open the closet door. Even the rustling of her dress seemed overly pronounced as she dug the flash drive from the lining of her damp bra. It was so lightweight she wasn't surprised he'd missed it. Of course, he probably hadn't thought to search her undergarments because, well, why would he? She snagged the lone pair of tennis shoes on the floor and slipped them on. They were too big and looked ridiculous with the dress, but she wasn't running around in bare feet. She grabbed her wet wallet and eased open the window. After a quick glance around she hoisted herself through and dropped onto a grassy incline. No alarm had gone off when she opened the window, so she figured she was safe.

Unless he had a silent one. The thought sent a jolt of adrenaline snaking down her spine.

As she surveyed her surroundings, Sophie realized she was in an end condominium near a body of water. Taking her chances, she headed toward the dock. Maybe she'd find someone to help her. She slowed and peeked around the corner of the building. There was a screened porch, but she didn't see Jack anywhere.

She picked up her pace and jogged toward the dock. Jack's place was one of four condominiums facing the water. There was a small marina and restaurant at the end of the row of buildings. She didn't want to draw attention to herself, so she kept her walk steady as she headed down the wooden planks and toward the faint reggae music.

The entire bar was built out over the water and completely open. There was a thatched roof covering the place, but there were no walls and no air-conditioning, just a long, rectangular wooden bar, ten high-top tables, and random nautical pieces hung up everywhere. There was even a fake parrot perched next to the cash register and a ship's wheel dangling above it. She didn't see a bartender, so she took a chance and sat next to one of the six older men drinking at the bar. He was the only one sitting by himself.

"Do you know if there are any pay phones around here?"

The man with the gray beard glanced up from his beer and frowned as he took in her appearance, no doubt noticing her faint bruises. "You don't have a cell phone?"

"My car got a flat tire about half a mile back. When I went to use my phone, I realized the battery had died. I'm vacationing with friends and need to tell them where I am."

"Here. Use this." He fished a phone out of his pocket and handed it to her.

Damn. People weren't this nice in Miami. "Thanks. I'll be quick."

She took a seat at an empty table a couple of feet from the bar and dialed Ronald's number. He picked up on the second ring. There was a cautious note in his voice. "Hello?"

"Ronald? It's me."

"Thank God you're all right. Where have you been? It's been all over the news that there was a shooting at La Marea. Were you there when that happened?"

Until she knew more she decided to be evasive. "It's a long story. Why was Homeland Security at work today?"

He sighed. "They weren't very clear, but they want to talk to everyone in the office. Including you."

"Why?"

"I have no idea. They said it's just a routine thing." Something in his voice told her he knew exactly what was going on.

A bead of sweat trickled down her spine. Why would Ronald lie to her? "Listen, I'm in a little trouble and I don't know where else to turn."

"Where are you?"

"I'm not exactly sure." A tiny voice told her not to say the city even though she desperately wanted to trust him.

"Wherever you are, you need to stay there. Get out of town for a few days at least. I'll tell everyone you're sick."

"You don't think I should come back to Miami?" More alarm bells went off in her head. This wasn't the behavior of a man in the dark. Maybe she couldn't trust him either. Did he know about the weapons Keane Flight were apparently delivering or selling or whatever?

"I can wire you some money if you need, but you *have* to stay hidden." His tone bordered on frantic.

"I don't need money, I need *answers*. What the hell is going on?"

"I can't explain everything without risking . . . Damn it, Sophie, I can't tell you. You'll just have to trust me. In a few days I'll be able to tell you everything. Promise me you'll stay hidden and don't trust anyone."

No problem there. She didn't even trust Ronald at this point. "What about Jack?" She glanced over her shoulder.

"Are you still with him?"

"Not anymore."

"Good. I don't know much about him, but I don't think he works for Keane Flight. Since Paul is in a coma, there's no way to ask. You need to disappear. Just for a few days. Can I contact you on this phone?"

"No, I borrowed it and I need to give it back soon."

"Try to get your hands on another phone and call as soon as you can."

"Okay." Feeling numb and confused, she disconnected and walked over to the older man. "Thanks."

She'd turned to leave when a hand clamped around her waist in an iron grip. She whipped around and found herself staring up into Jack's pale blue, hard eyes. Before she had a chance to react, Jack had her back pressed up against the bar. "Where've you been, *sweetheart*?"

His tone might be endearing, but his eyes glinted with a deadly edge. Out of the corner of her eye, she could see the man who'd let her use his phone watching them. When she tried to move, Jack pressed harder, his muscular stomach and chest an immovable force. The wooden edge of the bar dug into her spine.

An icy chill crept up the back of her neck as she tried to shift again and failed. The man was like stone. "I got a flat tire and, uh, my cell phone died."

Jack leaned down close to her ear so that only she could hear. "Don't make a scene."

His hot breath on her skin sent a wave of clamminess over her entire body. She hadn't been too afraid of him before, but now she was rethinking her escape attempt. Maybe she should just have run and hidden somewhere. She nodded, hating that his close proximity rattled her physically. Taking his extended hand, she let him lead her from the bar. "What are you going to do?"

"*You* are going to eat dinner and then we're going to talk."

He wanted to feed her? That didn't seem like the actions of a man bent on hurting her. He still hadn't let go of her hand. She tugged once, but he simply tightened his grip. It was almost deceptively gentle even if he was immovable. Her palm was sweaty, but it didn't seem to matter to him. He was holding tight.

"Are you going to hurt me?" She hated the fear she heard in her voice but couldn't hide it. He was a lot bigger and stronger than her and he was clearly deadly.

His lips pulled into a thin line. "I don't hurt women, Sophie, and I would *never* hurt *you*. But I will get my answers."

She bit her bottom lip. The way he said her name was too familiar. It rolled off his tongue as if they were friends. Maybe more than friends. Lovers even. She swallowed at the abrupt, ridiculous thought and forced herself to look away from his granite profile. She also tried to ignore the sudden heaviness in her breasts.

Something else was happening here between them, but

she couldn't wrap her mind around the implications. Every time she looked into his eyes, she saw Sam. It actually explained her insane erotic draw to the man who could be her enemy. Her body was at war with itself. Desire and fear battled each other for dominance. Unfortunately desire was kicking fear's ass.

Chapter 6

Operative: an intelligence officer or agent operating in the field.

Wesley tried Jack's cell again, but it went straight to voice mail. He didn't need to bother one of his analysts to figure out Jack had taken out the battery. If he'd turned off his phone, he'd definitely taken out the battery. And he would have been sure to avoid civilian CCTVs or traffic cameras if at all possible. All easy ways to track him, and if Wesley had been keeping physical tabs on him before he'd gone dark, he likely *could* have tracked the man. Then again, maybe not. Jack was trained well and he was familiar with Miami in a way he wasn't anywhere else. He could disappear if he wanted to bad enough.

Wesley's best agent had gone dark without explaining why, and now he wondered if he'd sent Jack into the field too soon. Even though the final purpose of Jack's last op had been to bring down those Albanian terrorists, any undercover operation dealing with the exploitation of kids was brutal. But Jack had never had a problem acclimating to another situation in the past. The man was like a machine sometimes.

Sophie Moreno was the only soft spot he had. Wesley could have sent someone else in for this job, but he wanted Jack to get over her and find some kind of normal life with someone. Anyone. Wesley had recruited Jack when he was only twenty-six. After eight years in the Marines, Jack had been physically tough and the best sniper he'd ever seen, but he'd also been his youngest recruit for the new black ops team he'd been putting together at the time.

Five years later, Wesley had never regretted his decision. He simply wanted Jack to find a life *outside* his job. The rate for substance addictions and broken relationships in this line of work was high, but Jack didn't have a problem with either. Hell, the man would have to have a damn relationship in the first place for the latter to be an issue.

Wesley tapped his finger against his mouse and pulled up Sophie's file. He'd read her dossier half a dozen times and had everything he could possibly want to know about her boss. Still, he wanted more. Especially if the woman was fucking with Jack's ability to do his job.

Wesley hit one of the intercom buttons on his phone, connecting him to Thomas Chadwick, one of his best analysts. "Thomas?"

"Yes, sir?"

"I need you to run another detailed check on Mandy Abarca, Benson Pollard, and Hannah Young. Go as deep as you can." He'd had another analyst run their information before, but he wanted this check to see if they'd missed anything.

"What's their connection?"

"Sophie Moreno."

"Got it. I'll send it to your screen as soon as I have the information."

"Thank you. If you need help, ask Williams to help you. He's familiar with Ms. Moreno's file." As soon as he disconnected, he dialed a friend of his at the Drug Enforcement Administration.

"Deputy Director Southers's office," a perky female voice answered.

"Connect me to Max, please." They hadn't spoken in a few months, but he'd served with Max decades ago when they were both in the Navy.

"I'm sorry, sir, he's gone for the day."

Wesley glanced at his watch. It was only six. "Tell him Wesley Burkhart is on the line."

"One moment, sir."

A few seconds later his longtime friend picked up. "Wesley, how are you?"

"Hey, Max. How are the wife and kids?"

"Mary's good and the boys are still in college, but I know that's not why you're calling. What's going on?"

"Do you have any contacts at Homeland Security?"

"I work with a couple of those guys every now and then. Why?"

The DEA and Homeland Security were bound to overlap, especially in a place like Miami. Thanks to the drug and slave trade, it was a cluster of acronyms in south Florida. "Have you heard any chatter lately about South Beach Medical Supply?"

"SBMS? Yeah, Homeland's been watching them and so have we because of suspected unusual activity. Why?"

"What about a woman named Sophie Moreno? Any red flags on her?"

"Not that I know of, but I'll ask around," Max said.

"Thanks. I'll be at the office for the next hour." In reality, probably longer than that.

"Why is the NSA interested in them?"

"It involves a separate mission. Don't worry, we're not invading your territory."

"So you don't know anything about a possible sniper shooting at a restaurant downtown this afternoon?"

He didn't even pause. "Not a thing."

Max was silent for a moment. "All right. I'll call as soon as I know anything."

"I owe you one."

As they disconnected, Wesley pulled up one of the files Thomas sent him. It was on Mandy Abarca, Sophie's assistant. His gut told him Sophie wasn't involved, but without having any way to contact Jack, he couldn't take a chance that Jack would let his guard down.

A sharp knock on his door interrupted his reading. "Come in."

Steven Williams, one of his better analysts, opened the door. "Got a second, boss?"

"What is it?"

"I found some interesting information on Benson Pollard, one of the men working with Ms. Moreno."

"And?"

"He's recently acquired a lot of gambling debts. He's into his bookie for about fifty thousand dollars."

Very interesting. "Have you e-mailed me the information?"

"Yep. I just wanted to let you know." He stood by the door expectantly.

"Is that all?"

"Uh, yeah." Without another word, he shut the door behind him.

Wesley scrubbed a hand over his face. Steven was a bit of an ass-kisser, but he was good at what he did, no doubt about it. He'd graduated from MIT with a degree in political science and he was a genius with computers. Sometimes Wesley wondered why he was working for the NSA instead of a private firm.

Jack sat across the kitchen table from Sophie, watching her push her food around her plate. She hadn't said much since they'd been back, but every time they made eye contact, she averted her gaze. As if she was afraid of him.

His grip on his fork tightened. He understood she was

scared, but so far he'd done nothing but protect her. Hell, he'd even given her a weapon. Sure, he could have taken it from her if she attempted to use it against him, but it had been a peace offering. The only way he knew how to make her feel more at ease. Maybe that was his damn problem. He should be more focused on the op than with Sophie. Unfortunately the need to keep her happy won out over everything. Always had. And that kiss had just reminded him how much he still wanted her.

"Did you use your credit card at the bar?" His voice held more heat than he'd intended.

She shook her head. Her dark hair fell forward over her shoulders, making him itch to thread his fingers through it again. To pull her body close to his and feel her soft breasts pressing against his chest. Not because she was in shock or needed to get warm, but because she wanted him as much as he wanted her.

"Did you call anyone?"

She started to shake her head, then shrugged. "Yes. My boss."

Damn it. "What did he say?"

She squirmed in her seat. "He told me not to come back to Miami for a few days."

Interesting. "Did he say why?"

"No, but . . . I don't think he was being completely honest with me."

He started to ask her another question when she cut him off. "How do I know you really work for the government?"

Knowing he had no other choice, he pulled his phone and battery out of his jeans pocket and put the battery back in. He hated breaking silence, but she'd tried to escape. Honesty was the only thing that would work with Sophie. She wasn't involved with any sort of terrorist activity. Gut instinct had gotten him far and he simply knew she wasn't dirty. That didn't mean he couldn't use her relationship with Ronald Weller to his advantage.

Wesley picked up on the first ring. "Where the hell are you?"

Jack didn't know why he bothered asking. Now that he'd broken silence, all his boss would have to do was trace his phone. It would take less than forty seconds. "I'm with Sophie right now and she wants proof of who I work for."

"You told her who you are?"

He cleared his throat. "Not exactly."

"Put him on speaker." Sophie's demanding voice cut through his conversation.

He bit back a smile at that flare of temper he loved. "Hold on, Wesley. I'm putting you on speaker." Jack changed the setting and placed the phone in the middle of the glass table.

"Ms. Moreno?" Wesley asked.

"Yes, who is this?"

"Lieutenant General Wesley Burkhart."

Sophie looked at Jack with raised eyebrows. "So you're in the Army or something?"

Jack suppressed a smile.

Wesley cleared his throat. "No, ma'am. I was in the *Navy*, but I'm now the deputy director of the NSA."

Sophie's eyes widened as she looked at Jack and he could practically see the wheels turning in her head. "How do I know you're telling the truth?"

"You don't, ma'am. You can look me up online, but I have no way to prove anything to you until we meet in person."

"What about Jack? Can I look him up online?"

Wesley chuckled softly. "No, ma'am. If you can, we're not doing our job."

"What exactly does Jack do?"

"I'm sorry, ma'am, but that's classified. However, I can assure you that you're in good hands."

She snorted derisively. "You can make all the assurances in the world and it still proves nothing. What do you people want from me?"

Wesley paused and Jack knew it was time to take over the conversation. He hadn't run anything by his boss yet, but this was Jack's call. "Your boss, Ronald Weller, is being watched under suspicion of dealing with terrorists. We've found a link between terrorist cells with ties in North Africa and a drug cartel in South America. SBMS is that link."

Jack carefully gauged Sophie's reaction. Her lips pulled into a slight grimace and all color had fled her pretty face, but she didn't seem surprised exactly. As if she knew *something*. "So why did you come into SBMS under the guise of working for Keane? And why did you want to work with me?"

"We weren't sure of your involvement and figured the easiest way to get to Ronald would be through you."

Her dark eyes narrowed. "What about now? Do you still think I'm involved?"

"No, I don't."

Some of the color returned to her cheeks.

Jack glanced at the phone, just to force his gaze away from her piercing one. Staring at her too long was bad for his sanity. "Wesley, send me a complete file on Vargas, including pictures of some of his handiwork." He was going to show Sophie exactly what kind of man they were trying to stop from unleashing terror on U.S. soil. The file would be encrypted and normally he'd have had the information with him, but he didn't have much on his current laptop since it was his backup.

"Will do. . . . Jack, I've got to take this call." Wesley disconnected before either of them could respond.

Jack took out the battery as Sophie stood and picked up her plate. She reached out to take his empty one, though her hand slightly shook. "Are you through?"

He nodded and let her take it. He cleared off their glasses and the serving dish and followed her into the kitchen. When she started washing the dishes, he stopped her. "Leave it, Sophie. Please."

At the word "please," she dropped the dishrag in the sink and turned to face him. Her expression was wary and he got the feeling that she was still holding something back from him. It was another reason he wanted to show her that file on Vargas. She needed to see that he was being honest with her—as honest as he could be. "What exactly do you want from me?"

Jack hadn't gone over anything with his boss, but he had no doubt Wesley would be on board with whatever he chose to do. "I know you're not telling me everything. I want to go over your past few months at SBMS, see if you remember anything out of the ordinary. The fact that you printed out all those logs from Keane tells me you're suspicious of something. I'd also like to show you a file on the man your boss is in bed with."

Leaning against the sink, Sophie clasped her hands in front of her stomach and tried to force herself to stop trembling. It was too hard to believe that Ronald was dirty, but his response to her call earlier had left her rattled. Why the hell would he want her to stay out of town? She might as well glean as much information from Jack as she could. He might not be telling the truth, but she was willing to listen. Mainly because she didn't have any other option at this point. "What man?"

"Miguel Vargas."

The name was vaguely familiar, sending off a small warning bell in her head. She frowned, unsure if she was supposed to know it.

Jack continued. "He's head of a violent South American drug cartel."

"Vargas . . . I *do* know the name, if it's the same man. About a year ago one of the planes we hired was hit before they could deliver supplies. Now there are a few places in Brazil and Chile we can't hire anyone to fly to for us. I think

I heard someone, maybe Ronald, say something about Vargas being involved."

"I thought Keane flew everything for SBMS." Jack watched her carefully.

She figured he probably already knew this but was just testing her. Besides, there was no reason to lie. It wasn't a secret. "Keane Flight flies supplies to different countries, but we often outsource to locals once he's in-country because they'd rather deal with their own people for the final deliveries. It's not personal to Keane and we care about getting those supplies to where they're needed most."

He nodded once, clearly accepting her answer. Then he nodded toward the living room. "I'd like to show you some files."

"Okay." She pushed up from the counter and let him leave the small kitchen first. Sophie needed some space from the man, but there was nowhere to go.

He sat on one end of the longer couch and she sat on the other, trying to put a little space between them. The room seemed to grow smaller in the silence as he turned on his laptop. It was a newer computer, sleek and thin. She watched his hard profile as he typed. His expression was grim as he stared at the screen, his fingers flying over the keyboard.

Suddenly he looked up, those pale eyes pinning her, and she flushed as if she'd been doing something wrong. She couldn't help staring at him, though. Watching him was like watching a tiger only feet from her. The man just screamed *danger*, but everything about him begged her to reach out and touch. To see if she'd get bitten. Her mouth and lips were dry, but she forced herself not to lick her lips even if the action was instinctual.

She could almost swear the man read her thoughts, though, because his gaze strayed to her lips for a fraction of a second before he turned back to the screen. He shifted the computer screen toward her.

Scooting closer, she couldn't ignore that spicy scent or what his mere presence did to her. She moved until their knees almost touched, but she kept a little space between them.

Jack eyed the small distance, frowned as if it annoyed him, then moved until they were touching. The action took her so off guard she didn't know how to respond. She wondered if he was even aware of what he'd done.

Before she could contemplate it, he handed her the laptop. "Scan the files if you like, but the pictures start on page five."

When she went to look at what he'd given her, he stopped her with a light touch on her arm.

"Fair warning, the pictures aren't easy to look at. Everyone in them is dead and . . ." He trailed off, shrugging. "This is what happens when someone crosses Vargas and why he must be stopped. These are his own countrymen and women, and he did what he did because someone went to the authorities because he was using their town as part of his supply route."

He stopped talking, but the dark look in his eyes was predatory. It was almost as if she could sense the rage in him even though he wasn't outwardly reacting. He was so still it was unnerving, as if he was reining in his anger. Sam had been just like that. Whenever he got angry, everything burned deep beneath his surface. And the quieter he'd gotten, the angrier he'd been. The sudden comparison between the two men jarred her enough to tear her gaze away.

Sophie started scrolling through the pages of text. On the third one, she glared at him accusingly. "I can barely read any of this." There were big paragraphs completely blacked out.

He looked almost apologetic as his broad shoulders lifted in a half shrug. "The classified stuff is redacted."

Gritting her teeth, she looked back and read what she could. The details were scant and she gleaned bits and pieces basically telling her what Jack had just told her. But when she got to the section of pictures, what little food she had in her stomach roiled. Men, women, and children had been massacred.

There were so many of them wearing threadbare clothes, some with no shoes, and their bodies had been ravaged with bullets. In some, the bodies of the women were missing skirts or they were completely naked, telling another story of the carnage. Some bodies were piled on each other, just dumped in ditches. Some had been left in the street and ripped apart by hungry scavengers. Swallowing hard, she closed her eyes, but the images remained.

Having seen more than enough, she snapped his computer shut and shoved it at him.

"I told you," he murmured.

"Vargas did that and he's supposedly involved with my boss? And Keane?"

"I don't know for sure about your boss, but it's more than probable." Jack's eyes were unreadable. He just stared at her, as if waiting for something.

Screw it. She reached into the built-in bra of the too-big dress and pulled out the flash drive. She had backups and someone wanted her dead. If Jack wanted to kill her, he could have done so. Multiple times. She handed it to the intimidating man next to her, then wiped her damp palm on her dress. She had no idea what his reaction would be.

His eyes slightly narrowed. "What is this?"

"I stopped by Keane's hangar—well, I guess I technically broke in—Sunday night and took pictures of some very illegal stuff. Grenades and guns were all I managed to get before some scary-looking thugs showed up and chased me. Luckily I'm a fast runner." She said the last part semijokingly, but even remembering the fear from the other night sent a shiver rippling through her. The thought of what could have happened to her seemed even more real after looking at those pictures.

Jack went impossibly still. "You broke into Keane's hangar. Alone. With no backup." His voice vibrated with anger.

She blinked, surprised by the tone. "How is this not a good thing? Well, the weapons aren't good, but I have proof that Keane is involved in bad stuff. Maybe this will tie him to Vargas. Isn't that important?"

His jaw clenched and he all but ignored what she'd said. "Anything could have happened to you! Do you realize how dangerous that was?" He cursed, the sound surprisingly savage.

Sophie slowly inched down the couch as a burst of fear detonated inside her. He was seriously angry at her and she couldn't figure out why.

When he saw her move, his expression really darkened. Shoving up from the couch, he stalked to the love seat, putting distance between them. "I hate that you think I'd ever hurt you."

The words elicited so much confusion she wasn't sure how to respond. "Why are you so angry at me?"

He completely ignored her question and picked up his laptop. As he plugged in the flash drive, he said, "So what prompted your break-in?" He wouldn't even look at her, something she found really annoying.

But she answered, "Ronald has been acting strange the past few months. Agitated, forgetting to do simple things, he's been blowing off my concerns about the anomalies I found in the Keane flight logs, and this is really small, but he hasn't asked me over for dinner in months."

"Why is that strange?"

"I assumed he and his wife were having problems—it would have explained his distraction at work—but after what I found and what you showed me, I don't know what to think anymore. Then when I just called him, he told me to stay hidden for a few days and that I had to trust him. About what, though, he didn't explain. He also offered to send me *money*.

That's not normal behavior for someone with nothing to hide."

Jack was silent for a moment, his expression thoughtful. "Who knew you were going to lunch with me today?"

"Well . . . Mandy, Benson, and Ronald, though I'm sure they could have mentioned it to practically anyone. Why?"

"Just trying to get a feel for the people you work with. Is there anyone you don't trust?"

"No. Other than Ronald—" She frowned as another thought hit her.

"What is it?"

"Lately I've noticed things in my office moved around. It's not something I'd swear to in court, just a feeling I've had."

"How would you feel about returning to Miami to question Ronald?"

"What about the people who want to kill me?"

"I'm talking about a private meeting. We would name the time and place. You'll wear a listening device—"

"Wait, what?" Was he crazy? A sniper had tried to kill her and now she was pretty sure that whoever she'd run from at the hangar was probably behind it. Someone knew where she worked and probably where she lived. And he wanted her to go back there? Even Ronald had told her to stay away.

Jack continued as if she hadn't spoken. "—convince your boss you're in trouble and need to meet with him. If you can get him to give up his partner or partners and, more important, bring Vargas to Miami for a meeting, we can bring him in immediately."

Her head swam as she tried to digest his words. "You're saying all this stuff as if it's normal. I'm not wearing a freaking wire anywhere. What if those people come after me again? Who's going to protect me? Where will I be staying? Because it sure as hell won't be my house." She instantly regretted the last question because it implied that she'd be going back soon. But if those pictures Jack had shown her were real, they said so much about what Vargas was capable of—and that terrified her.

Jack was silent for a moment; then he shook his head slightly. "I'm sorry—sometimes I forget. . . . Why don't you turn on the news and see if there's anything about what happened earlier today?"

"What about you?"

He stood, ready to head back to the kitchen. "I'm going to finish the dishes, then work some stuff up on my computer. I'm also sending those pictures you gave me to my boss."

She wondered what that would mean for her, but didn't ask because she didn't want the answer. Not yet. "I suppose it's out of the question to ask if I can use your phone?"

"Why?"

"To check on a friend." Even though she'd told Hannah that she couldn't have drinks tonight, she still wanted to check on her—especially with everything going on.

Something dark flashed in his eyes, but then it was gone so quickly she wasn't sure what to make of it. "No, sorry."

"What about e-mail? Can I use your computer?"

He shook his head. "Someone wants you dead and I'm not going to let that happen."

Maybe it was stupid, but she felt oddly warmed by the conviction in his voice. As though this was personal for him. Deep down she knew that was wishful thinking, but it evoked a long-buried sensation inside her anyway. "And you think someone can kill me through e-mail?"

"No, but they found us too soon today, which tells me that whoever is after you has government contacts. If they were able to use satellites to track us earlier, they might be monitoring your e-mail, and if you check it, they'll be able to track your IP address. I have an encrypted router on my computer, which would make it difficult, but nothing's impossible."

Sophie rubbed her temple. "Okay, no phone and no

e-mail. I guess I'm going to watch the news. Could you ask your boss to have someone check in on Hannah Young? She's my best friend."

"No problem." He turned then and strode toward the kitchen.

She tamped down the annoyance that stirred inside her. "Don't you need to know who she is?"

He glanced over his shoulder. "She grew up in Miami, her family owns two of the best Korean restaurants in the city, she graduated from the University of Miami with honors, she's the head nurse at Miami Children's Hospital—the youngest they've ever appointed—and she has terrible taste in men."

Sophie's jaw went slack, but she recovered quickly. "If you ever meet her, her parents own *the* best restaurants. Not two of the best."

"Noted." He shot her a lopsided grin that sent the butter-flies in her stomach into a tailspin.

If he looked at her like that more often, she was so screwed. She already knew how inviting his lips were, but when he smiled it softened his entire face. Which was the last thing she should be thinking about.

Another thought settled inside her. If he knew so much about her friend, he must know a lot about her too. "Do . . . you have a file like that on me?"

He nodded, his expression remote.

She swallowed hard. "How far back does that file date?"

"It covers your whole life." His quiet words pierced her deep.

That meant he knew things about her he had no right to. What had happened to her growing up should be sealed, but somehow she didn't think the NSA would have a problem getting those records.

Not wanting to talk anymore, she sat back on the couch. Tucking her feet underneath her, she flipped on the television. Maybe it would take her mind off the past twenty-four hours—though she knew that was impossible. She caught the tail end of the news and sure enough, there was something about the shooting at La Marea. There weren't any details, though. Just speculation that it was somehow gang-related.

"Do you want a glass of wine or a beer? Or water?" Jack asked through the kitchen archway.

"Wine works for me." She didn't care if it was red or white, just so long as it was wet and dulled her senses.

A few moments later he joined her on the couch. After he handed her the glass, he flipped open his laptop. "I'm sorry about earlier. I didn't mean to lay so much on you. I do this stuff every day and forgot that not everyone else thinks the same way."

She set her wineglass on the coffee table and shifted to face him. "It's okay. You did scare me talking about wearing a wire. . . . So what exactly would that entail? Me, wearing a wire?" Oh God, was that actually her talking? Those pictures flashed in her mind and deep down she knew she'd do whatever she could to stop a man like Vargas.

Jack turned away from his computer, pinning that laser-like focus completely on her. It was a little unnerving. Even more so when she briefly wondered what it would be like to have all that focus in a naked setting. Something told her he'd be a very dedicated and giving lover. Thankfully he had no idea what she was thinking or she would have been mortified. She was kind of freaking herself out with the thoughts.

His voice was all business as he said, "*If* you do this, and that's a big if, I'll be listening the entire time and I won't be far away. If anything happens or if you feel uncomfortable for any reason, we'll have a code word."

"What do you mean, *if*?" If he wasn't confident in this, how could he expect her to be?

"If you're too nervous, your boss will know something's wrong. I'm not sending you in anywhere if you're uncomfortable. He might not be a pro, but you're a terrible liar and he'll be able to see right through you."

"These people you think Ronald is dealing with? I know what you said earlier, but exactly what kind of terrorist activity do you suspect them of?" It couldn't just be weapons dealing. Yeah, that was bad but it didn't seem like the kind of thing to warrant this sort of attention from the NSA.

Something dark lurked in the depths of his pale eyes, and before he spoke, she knew the answer would be horrific. "We think he's helping a terrorist faction in North Africa get biological weapons into our country through his drug cartel in South America. Vargas has a long history with his hatred of the U.S., so it's not a stretch that he'd want to target us."

"Why does he hate our country?"

"His youngest son was killed by an ICE agent."

ICE? Sophie frowned, but didn't ask what he meant. He must have read her expression, because he continued. "They're part of Immigrations and Customs Enforcement. Vargas's other two sons were killed almost a decade ago by warring drug factions and it was no secret his youngest was his favorite. I'm sure there are other reasons he hates the U.S. A man like that doesn't need an excuse for violence and terror." Jack shrugged.

Sophie shook her head, trying to get back on track of their original conversation. "Okay, so biological weapons? Like nerve gas?" She'd only heard those words on the news, usually uttered by the president or in conjunction with something happening thousands of miles away. The devastation of that kind of attack could be catastrophic.

He nodded, his face grim. "Yes."

"And you know this for sure?"

"No. Paul Keane has been some help, but he doesn't know much. He's just a mule. He handles deliveries and pickups, but he doesn't have the details we need."

"Paul Keane who's in a coma?"

"He's not in a coma."

Okay, then. Something told her that would be all she got out of Jack on the subject of Keane. "You really think Ronald is involved in helping terrorists?"

"Someone tried to kill you *and* your boss told you to stay away from Miami. What do you think?"

"I don't know what to think." Or say for that matter. What the hell did one say after almost being killed twice in one day? Now it seemed pretty clear that her boss might be in league with terrorists. Freaking awesome.

When she didn't say more, Jack returned to his laptop. Sophie stared at his profile and tried to digest everything he'd told her. Tried to piece that knowledge together with the way Ronald had been acting lately and then her very recent phone conversation with him.

Focusing on Jack's profile proved incredibly distracting, though. Which was what she needed right now. A giant distraction. At least that's what she told herself as she covertly watched him.

He was in good shape. Okay, *great* shape. Something she'd known from the moment they met. He wasn't overly muscular, but trim and sleek. Definitely the body of a runner. Actually seeing him in action, however, had proven just how trained he was. When they were running from that shooter, he'd moved with the grace of a jungle cat. Then he'd moved through that water like a damn fish all while she'd been clutched on to him. She'd been too cold to even think about swimming any farther, but he hadn't seemed winded even with her as an anchor. Everything that was happening was so surreal, but for some reason, her instinct told her to trust this man. Even after she'd tried to run, there had been no hint of violence from him. He'd been angry, yes, but he didn't scare her.

Hell, he was almost . . . protective.

Jack glanced over from the computer, and her lower abdomen tightened in a *very* feminine way. He held her gaze for a long moment before turning away. Unless she was mistaken, she detected more than a hint of lust in those haunting eyes. When she was younger Sam had looked at her the same way. Her foster brother had been one of the few people in her life who had looked out for her and hadn't expected anything in return. He'd been her one constant for a little while.

Sometimes she wondered what would have happened if things hadn't ended so horribly between them. Maybe he'd still be alive. And maybe they'd have started a family and . . . maybe, maybe, maybe. *Fuck maybe.* Thinking about Sam was messing with her head at a time when she needed to keep alert and ready for anything.

She turned back to the news but wasn't actually seeing anything. Too many thoughts tumbled through her brain. Could she wear a wire? What if Ronald was innocent and she helped the government trap him? And what was she going to do about her attraction to Jack? It seemed insane to even contemplate doing anything, but she didn't want that kiss to be the only time she got a taste of him. That thought was depressing. Sophie pulled the soft afghan blanket from behind the couch and wrapped it around herself as an unwanted shiver racked her body. She clearly needed her head examined.

Chapter 7

Treason: violation of allegiance toward one's country
or sovereign, especially the betrayal of one's country
by waging war against it or by consciously and pur-
posely acting to aid its enemies.

He glanced around as he opened a new file on his computer
screen. The computer stations were completely open, so
he had to be extremely cautious. Most of the analysts had
gone home for the evening, but security was always tight
regardless of the time of day. Technically he shouldn't be on
these computer workstations, but no one would question him
if he was. He was one of Wesley's favorites. A fact he used
to his fullest advantage.

Covering his tracks had been tricky, especially lately, but
his growing offshore bank account was the only incentive he
needed. His boss wasn't stupid. Neither were his coworkers.
They'd catch on soon. Probably sooner than he wanted, but
he wasn't worried. He only needed a couple more days; then
he'd get the rest of his money and he could disappear forever.
He'd already paid off his gambling debts and gotten those
loan sharks off his back. Now he was actually in the black
and swimming in cash.

A few strokes on the keyboard and images from the private satellite he'd been using popped up on his computer. He

made a note of the woman's probable location, deleted his tracks, then made his way to one of the restrooms. He fished his cell phone—which had a nearly impenetrable filter—out of his pocket and locked himself in a stall once he was sure he was alone. Now was not the time to get sloppy.

Miguel Vargas picked up on the first ring. "Tell me you have her location."

"I have it narrowed down."

"That is not good enough!"

"It's going to have to be for right now. I can give you the area only. It'll take some time to pinpoint it. This will give your men enough time to get into position." He'd been able to track the woman when she called Weller at SBMS. Luckily she'd stayed on the phone long enough.

"What am I paying you for?"

He gritted his teeth. To say Vargas grated on his nerves would be a serious understatement. The drug lord expected to snap his fingers and have things happen. Ironic coming from a man who could barely check his e-mail. What he lacked in brains he made up for in firepower. "Do you understand where I work? I only have so much access. If you can find someone else to do my work for a better price, feel free to let me go."

A long moment of silence followed. "Call me when you have the exact location."

"Why do you even want this woman?"

"She poses a possible threat."

"Possible?" He rubbed the bridge of his nose. It didn't seem as if the woman knew anything. At least not according to the notes from her file. Going after her was a waste of resources and a waste of his time. Worse, it put him in danger of being discovered.

"She's been sticking her nose in places she does not belong," Vargas snapped.

"Unbelievable," he muttered at the man's vague response.

Vargas was making him jump through hoops for something that might not even be a problem? He was risking his life for this shit? *Idiot.*

"You've got your money. The rest will be wired to you when this job is over. I don't expect anyone to question me, so if you have a problem, explain yourself now." There was a razor-sharp edge to Vargas's order.

It reminded him that even though he was smarter than Vargas, the other man was a hell of a lot more ruthless. "There's no problem."

"Good," Vargas snapped.

As soon as they disconnected, he slipped his phone back into his pocket. He wasn't supposed to have a personal phone at work, but so far security hadn't noticed it. He just hoped his luck would hold out a couple more days. That was all he asked for. Then he'd be sipping margaritas on a beach and free of this pathetic job.

Levi Lazaro bit back his disgust as Vargas snapped his phone shut. Working with this piece of shit went against every fiber of his being, but it was the way things had to be. He needed the man to solidify his new cover, and he was willing to do *whatever* it took. If that meant selling a small part of his soul, so be it.

"That your contact at the NSA?" Levi kept his expression a mask, his voice monotone. As if he were simply asking for the time. If Vargas thought he actually cared, he'd wonder why.

Someone in the NSA had sold Levi out, and it might be the individual Vargas was currently working with to hunt the Moreno woman. If it was the last thing Levi did, he was going to find out the mole's name, kill him, and destroy the men who had murdered his wife. He would rip their lives apart the same way they'd done to him.

"Yes. He's closing in on the woman and the man she's with."

Levi glanced out over the veranda and watched the palm trees sway in the wind. He contemplated how much he could—or should—tell Vargas. One of Vargas's men had managed to snap a brief picture of the man the Moreno woman was with. Levi had nearly choked when he saw Jack Stone's face. At least Vargas hadn't noticed his reaction. Whoever had taken the picture had gotten damn lucky. Stone was like a fucking ghost. Whatever Vargas was getting into, Levi wanted to tell him to walk away and cut his losses. If he crossed a man like Jack, he'd make a very resourceful and brutal enemy.

Unfortunately Levi was about to make an enemy of Jack too. It burned a crater-sized hole in his gut that he would have to work against a man he considered a friend—one of the few he had—but Levi had little choice in the matter. He *needed* Vargas for the time being. Hated it, but there was no way around it.

While Levi knew the identity of the man the Moreno woman was with, he couldn't reveal *that* information to Vargas. He owed Jack that much. And it was clear Vargas's contact with the NSA didn't know who Jack was either. That usually happened when Burkhart sent one of his guys into the field on a solo mission. Levi knew because at one time he'd been on his fair share of those exact missions.

That didn't mean he couldn't tell Vargas their location. He knew Jack, and if he was a betting man, he knew *exactly* where he was going if the mole had tracked the Moreno woman to the Keys. Unfortunately Jack would realize Levi had given up the location since he was the only person Jack had taken there. "What city does your guy think they're in?"

Vargas's shoulders lifted casually. "Somewhere in Marathon."

Oh yeah, he knew where they were going. "I might know how to locate them." Wordlessly, Levi strode across the perfectly manicured lawn, toward the small gazebo, and pretended to dial a number on his cell. Ignoring Vargas's penetrating gaze, he had a conversation with himself. This would go a long way in establishing his credentials. Once he'd stayed on the phone long enough, he returned to the covered veranda. "I know where they are. Give me some of your men. If we leave soon, we'll be able to avoid the Coast Guard and make it by midnight." They were in Cuba, barely a stone's throw from the Keys. By boat, it would take a few hours depending on how fast they drove, but it would be easy enough to avoid detection.

Vargas's dark eyes narrowed. "You're sure your information is good?"

Levi scoffed. "I wouldn't waste your time or my time if it wasn't."

He paused for a moment. "Very well. Take who you need."

If at all possible, Levi planned to signal to Jack that he was coming and hope he got out alive with the Moreno woman. If not, that was life. No one had given a shit when his wife was tortured and killed. If his boss had, he'd have let him track her murderers down. Instead Wesley had told him to "take some time off." He'd taken time off all right. And he wasn't ever going back. If the U.S. government didn't think it was important enough to hunt down the fuckers who'd stolen his wife and unborn child, he'd do it himself.

This time, he didn't have to play by the rules.

Chapter 8

Traitor: one who betrays one's country, a cause, or a trust.

*S*am sat against the tree in his backyard, embracing the feel of the rough bark scratching him through his shirt. Anything to erase that image of Sophie coming out her bedroom earlier. She'd been wearing long pink pajama pants and a tank top. He'd seen the outline of her nipples through it and hadn't been able to stop staring. He scrubbed a hand over his face, then froze at the sound of soft footfalls moving over the grass behind him.

Swiveling, he glanced around the tree. Sophie gave him a tentative smile when she saw him and wrapped her arms around herself in that defensive way she often did. He didn't want her to be like that with him.

"What are you doing out here?" she whispered as she sat directly next to him.

Holy shit, she was so close and smelled so good. Everything about her got him hard and he felt like a jerk because she looked at him with such innocent trust and gratitude. As if no one had ever been nice to her before except him. Swallowing hard, he lifted his arm and motioned for her to lean in.

Smiling, she scooted closer and laid her head on his shoulder as she tucked her body against his. He fought a *groan. She was so compact, but with the right amount of curves. And she was soft and warm. God, what he wouldn't give to—nope, not going there. He shifted uncomfortably, cursing his hard-on, and was thankful for the relative darkness of Ms. Bigsby's backyard.*

"I couldn't sleep," *he finally whispered back. He wasn't really sure why they were whispering in the first place, but decided to go with it.*

"Me neither. It's so quiet."

He nodded, his chin brushing the top of her head. Her shampoo had a tropical scent to it, and it reminded him of the beach and coconuts. It was very quiet, especially for a Friday night. Normally someone in the neighborhood was having a party, so he savored the stillness. He didn't have school or baseball practice tomorrow, which meant he could sleep in if Ms. Bigsby let them.

"Do you want to go to the beach tomorrow?" *she finally asked after a few minutes of silence.*

His entire body tightened. The beach. With Sophie. In a bathing suit. Being tortured by seeing her and not being able to touch, or stop other guys from staring at her. He tried to find his voice but failed.

She pushed up and looked at him, her dark eyes guarded as she inched away from him. "You don't have to if you don't want to. It's not like we have to be friends just because we live in the same house."

He'd been living under the same roof as her for a week, and he sure as hell didn't want just friendship. Clearly she'd misunderstood his silence. "I want to!" *he blurted, then felt stupid.* "I was just thinking I don't have a bathing suit." *Okay, that sounded lame, but she seemed to believe him.*

Her shoulders relaxed a fraction as she leaned back against him. "You're lucky because you're a guy. You can just wear shorts. Or I've got some money saved up. I can buy you a suit at the boardwalk on the way."

She was offering to buy him something? He tightened his grip around her shoulders as something foreign settled in his chest. He wasn't sure what it was, but it made him feel warm. "Nah, I've got some cash saved too." He was always socking it away. Never knew when he'd get stuck in a shitty house and have to split. There was no way he'd let her pay for anything, but it amazed him that she'd offered in the first place.

"So . . . did I hear Inez stop by earlier?" There was more than a little hesitation in Sophie's voice.

Sam snorted. "Yeah. Stupid cow." He didn't understand girls at all. He'd told Inez to leave Sophie alone and had been pretty mean to the neighbor girl. It wasn't like he wanted to be mean, especially to a girl, but she tortured Sophie and that shit was gonna stop. So what did the crazy girl do? Inez came over wearing practically nothing and asked him if he wanted to "hang out" with her tonight. As in hook up. Fucking gross. The thought of touching Inez like that was enough to turn his stomach.

"You can hang out with her if you want. Just because she's—"

"No." He couldn't even let Sophie finish that thought when he could hear the pain in her voice. He shifted their bodies so she had to look up at him. She stared at him with big eyes and he forgot to breathe. What he wouldn't give to kiss her. Just once. He swallowed hard. "You think I'm that shallow?" He didn't expand because he didn't need to.

Smiling shyly, she shook her head and tucked it back against his shoulder. "I'm glad you don't want to hang out with her," she said after a few minutes of silence.

Jack hated the memory that played through his head, but he couldn't slow it down or stop it as he tried to lift Sophie's head without waking her. He slipped a pillow under her head, but she opened her eyes immediately. Instead of the fear he expected, her espresso-colored eyes were confused.

"What are you doing?" she mumbled.

"You fell asleep out here and I don't want you to get a crick in your neck." His hand hovered under her head. For a moment he stared at her parted lips. She wasn't quite awake, still in between that dream state and awareness. What he wouldn't give to taste her again. The soft sighs she'd been making in her sleep made him wonder what she'd been dreaming about.

"What time is it?" Her voice was quiet.

Slowly he withdrew his hand and sat on the floor even though moving away from her was the last thing he wanted to do. "A few minutes before midnight."

She rolled over on the couch and faced him. Jack had pushed the coffee table out of the way and laid out a blanket and pillow on the floor next to the couch. In the quiet living room, slivers of moonlight peeking through the long blinds covering the sliding glass door were their only illumination. It was still light enough for her to see that he'd fashioned a makeshift bed next to her.

"Why are you out here?" There was a slight trace of panic in her whispered question.

"I'm sleeping next to you." Occasionally he opted for boxers, but he normally slept naked. He knew that even boxers would freak her out, so he'd stayed in his jeans and T-shirt. Not exactly comfortable, but he'd dealt with a lot worse.

"Why?"

"If something happens, we need to be able to move together and quickly."

"Oh." She pulled the blanket up higher on her chest.

"Try to get some sleep. In the morning we have some decisions to make." He closed his eyes and tucked one hand under his head. Sleeping next to Sophie again like this wasn't exactly the way he'd imagined it. Once he joined the NSA he'd kept tabs on her. From afar he'd watched her develop into a beautiful woman. But beautiful women were a dime a dozen. There was something else about Sophie that called to him.

Always had.

From before they'd even spoken to each other. Jack didn't know what it was about her that got under his skin. Maybe it was the fact that she understood where he came from. They'd both had similar upbringings. Both had grown up in foster care because of shitty drug-addicted mothers who'd abandoned them to the system. Neither knew who their fathers were. They'd both been unwanted. They were both survivors.

Of course she'd survived a lot worse than him. He'd dealt with the occasional beating from asshole foster parents, but she'd been terrorized by a sick bastard when she was seventeen. And Jack hadn't protected her.

"Jack?" Her quiet voice cut through the even quieter night air.

"Yeah?"

"Please talk to me." The pleading note in her voice surprised him.

It was dark, but he could make out the delicate lines of her face. "What do you want to talk about?"

"Anything."

"Can't sleep?"

Her hair rustled softly against the pillow as she shook her head.

"For what it's worth, you're handling this better than most civilians would."

She chuckled and in the dark he couldn't tell, but he thought she smiled. At least it sounded like it when she spoke. "*Civilian.* I guess you've been doing . . . whatever it is you do for a while?"

Wesley would probably be pissed if he found out, but it wasn't as if Jack was spilling state secrets. "I've been working for Wesley for five years."

"Sorry if it's rude, but how old are you?"

"Almost thirty-one."

"Oh."

"What?"

She shifted again, this time onto her back. "Nothing. You just remind me of someone and he would have been the same age."

Jack knew that he should keep his mouth shut. He should try to get some much-needed sleep. Unfortunately he didn't give a damn about what he *should* do. Thoughts of Sophie had been torturing him for years. *Shut your fucking mouth,* he tried to tell himself again but lost the battle. "Do I remind you in a bad way or a good way?"

"Both." Her answer was soft and immediate.

"Who was he?"

She was silent for a moment, but finally spoke. "You've obviously read my file, so you know I was in the foster system."

He remained completely still against the pillow. "Yes."

"You remind me of one of my foster brothers. His name was Sam."

"You two were close?"

"Very . . . He meant everything to me." The last part was almost a whisper. The honesty and grief in her words hit him square in the chest with the intensity of a fifty-cal sniper rifle. Why the hell did she have to admit *that* to him?

He rolled back over and stared at the ceiling. It wasn't the best distraction, especially since her exotic, earthy scent was teasing him, but it was better than staring at her profile. When he did that it was hard to concentrate on even speaking. "What happened to him?" Jack felt like an asshole even asking since he knew the answer, but a long-buried part of him wanted to hear what she truly thought about Sam. About him.

"Life." The word came out bitter, strangled. She cleared

her throat and continued, quickly changing topics. "Do you like what you do?"

Talk about a loaded question. "Sometimes yes. Other times I wonder how different my life would have turned out if I'd made another choice."

She snorted. "I actually understand that. The boy, well, man, I was in love with died. We weren't even talking or friends at the time, but I'm pretty sure he'd planned to propose to me before my life turned to hell."

Jack struggled to draw in a breath. There were some things he'd known as a young man, like the fact that she'd loved him. Sophie had never said the words, but he'd known how she felt. But she'd known he planned to propose? *Don't ask the question,* he ordered himself. But there was no force on earth that could stop him. "Would you have said yes if he proposed?"

"Yes."

Fuck, fuck, *fuck.* He did *not* need to know that. He shifted against the floor, his attempt at getting comfortable pointless. Raw energy hummed through him and he fought his growing agitation. Why the hell had she admitted that?

"You probably can't even tell me, but do you have family?"

He scrubbed a hand over his face and shut his eyes tight. She wasn't holding anything back. No one who got into his line of work had family. "No."

"I guess we have that in common. We're both alone." Her whispered words wrapped themselves around his chest and squeezed with startling intensity.

You have me. You've always had me. The words were on the tip of his tongue, but of course he didn't voice them. They wouldn't make sense and they'd probably scare the hell out of her. He might not have been in her life, and with the exception of the last two years when he'd been deep undercover, he'd always watched out for her, wishing things could be different. It was the only way he'd been able to keep a link to her. Something that had always pissed off his boss, but it had been one of his contingencies when he was recruited.

"Jack . . . why did you kiss me in Miami?"

"You were in shock. It was the only way to get you to calm down." *Liar.*

Silence descended on the room.

He stared at the ceiling for a long moment, telling himself to stay quiet, but his mouth wouldn't listen to his brain. Being around Sophie had completely upended all his training. She wouldn't even have to torture him to get information out of him. "I didn't say I didn't enjoy it, Sophie."

She sucked in a quiet breath. "Oh—"

He didn't know what she was going to say, but he didn't want to hear whatever it was, so he cut her off. "It can't happen again." Because it would only torture him, remind him of what he could never have.

She didn't speak after that. Instead she curled up on the couch so that her back faced him.

Why the hell couldn't it happen again? he kept asking himself even though he knew damn well why it couldn't. The closer he got to her, the more he let her into his life, the harder it would be when he walked away. Even the *thought* of walking away from her was excruciating. Actually doing it after having had another taste—he wasn't a masochist. If he took things further, it wouldn't just be torture, it would be impossible.

The floor beneath him dug into his back. He rolled onto his side, but that didn't help either. Years ago while still a sniper in the Marine Corps, he'd slept sitting straight up in cramped caves in Afghanistan with no problem. Tonight, visions of Sophie's perfect mouth swam in front of him, rendering sleep impossible. And his fantasies didn't stop at her mouth. He kept envisioning what the rest of her looked like. It might have been years, but he knew *exactly* what she was hiding under those clothes. And he desperately wanted to see, touch, and stroke all of her with his mouth and hands.

Sighing, he got up, folded the blanket, and threw the pillow back onto his bed. Out of habit he rechecked the windows and doors and headed back to the living room. Sophie hadn't stirred once since he'd gotten up. Good, maybe she'd get some rest. At least one of them should, and he'd rather it be her.

He walked to the sliding glass door and shifted one of the floor-length blinds to the side. Most of the people who stayed in the building were snowbirds, so the place was empty half the year. One of the main reasons he'd purchased it. The building was unassuming and the tenants were quiet. More often than not, hiding out wasn't necessarily about the best security. It was about being untraceable.

Hiding in plain sight.

The intracoastal water glistened under the pale moonlight and stars. It was unlikely anyone would be out this late, but he wanted privacy if he decided to work on his laptop on the porch.

Jack started to let go of the blind when two large, dark shadows moved from behind a palm tree. The movement had been slight, but he wasn't taking any chances. Not with Sophie's safety.

Without making his movements overt, he let the blind slip back into place, then went to wake Sophie. Using one hand he covered her mouth. Immediately her dark eyes opened in a wide-eyed panic, but when she saw that he had one finger over his mouth, she simply nodded.

Jack removed his hand and motioned that she should follow him. It was too late to get out. If someone was outside, they'd have the entire place surrounded. He grabbed his laptop and phone and headed to his room. He also picked up her pillow and shoved it into the hallway closet. The place needed to look as if they'd left a while ago.

He opened the sliding closet door in his room and shut it behind them. It was damn near pitch–black, but he was thankful Sophie wasn't outwardly reacting. Her breathing was slightly erratic, but that was it. Reaching up, he felt along the top shelf until his hand landed on a flashlight. Jack flipped it on and handed the computer to her. This place was off the radar, but experience had taught him to always have a contingency plan. *Always.*

He'd brought only one trusted friend here years ago during a long weekend of fishing: Levi Lazaro. They'd rarely gotten downtime and it was right before his buddy had tied the knot. Sort of an impromptu bachelor getaway. Even then, he still hadn't told his friend about this. There'd been no reason to. Jack put the small flashlight in his mouth, then felt along the wall until his hand ran over the almost invisible seam. Seconds could mean their survival, so he tried to block out Sophie's presence. Normally he wouldn't break a sweat, but knowing that her life depended on him had changed everything. Perspiration trickled down his face and neck.

Jack pulled the wall covering away and turned his flashlight toward Sophie. He motioned for her to get inside. Without pausing she ducked down and crawled in. A muted thud sounded somewhere in the condo. He hurried in after her and pulled the false wall back into place behind him. He'd originally built this crawl space for one person. Hunched over, Sophie wordlessly stared at him, but he could see the questions in her eyes. He sat first and guided her so that she was sitting in his lap before he flipped the light off.

There wasn't much insulation through the plaster, so it wasn't too difficult to hear what was going on. The bedroom door creaked as it opened. Sophie tensed in his arms, so he placed what he hoped was a calming hand on her back.

The sound of the closet door sliding open caused his stomach to roil. This was it. He heard the sound of hangers sliding across the pole, a quiet curse, then the door sliding shut. Sophie's back relaxed slightly against his chest, but he could feel the pounding of her heart.

"They're not here," a familiar voice said.

Jack's entire world shifted when he heard Levi talking. He'd wondered how anyone had found this place, had briefly wondered if there was a leak in the agency—one he'd gladly ferret out—but for a friend to betray him seemed impossible. What the hell was going on?

When his friend—or former friend—continued, Jack assumed he was on the phone since there was no audible response. "No, we've swept the place. There are recently washed dishes and food in the kitchen trash can, so they were here earlier, but they're gone now. . . . Yes, I'm sure. I'm not leaving a man behind. You're being paranoid. . . . Damn it. Miguel, they're *not* here. It's not my fault you got bad intel. Find a new contact, then. . . . Fine, we'll head back to Miami. . . . Hannah Young? . . . You're bringing too much heat on yourself. . . . No, I'm not involving myself with her. . . . She has serious ties to the community. . . . Kidnapping her will serve you no purpose." He argued for another few moments, then hung up the phone.

Sophie gripped Jack's arm tightly. Her short fingernails dug into his skin, but he ignored the pricking sensation. He couldn't tell her now, but he wouldn't let anything happen to her friend.

Silence descended around them, so he slowly moved his arm up and pressed the backlight on his watch. It was almost one thirty. He brushed back Sophie's hair and leaned close to her ear. "We'll leave in one hour. Want to make sure they didn't leave someone in the condo."

Her hair tickled his nose as she nodded.

From Levi's conversation, Jack couldn't figure out if they'd decided to leave someone behind. If they had, he doubted the person would stick around long. And just what was Levi doing working with Miguel Vargas? It was possible he was undercover, but Jack's boss hadn't mentioned anything. Considering that they were trying to bring Vargas down, that was something Wesley would have told him. Hell, if he had an inside man it was unlikely he'd even have needed Jack. Or if he had, they would have been working in conjunction.

The way Levi had spoken to Vargas had been insubordinate, and that surprised Jack, especially if this was an undercover op. He couldn't dwell on that now. He'd get his answers soon enough.

Sophie shifted slightly in his lap, and his body instantly reacted. Years of training had ensured that he knew how to react under any circumstances. His body was his to control. Having a sexy woman work her charm against him had never been a problem. Unfortunately Sophie wasn't working anything. She was simply trying to get comfortable. He tried to focus on anything to take his mind off the way her petite body fit perfectly against his, but it was impossible. Jack couldn't believe he was reacting like the randy teenager he'd once been around her, but there it was. Her backside shifted against his erection, intensifying his pain. It was as if every single memory he had of their time together erupted inside his head at once. All he could think about was how they'd been in this very same position before—with no clothes on. When they were younger, he'd loved getting creative in bed and she'd been up for anything. He bit the inside of his lip, hating his lack of control. It reminded him too much of how he'd felt when he was helpless in certain shitty foster homes. When he first became friends with Sophie, she'd evoked that same feeling, but he hadn't cared then. Now it was like a warped, out-of-control sensation.

She moved again, jerking him out of those thoughts, and this time she must have realized his reaction because her back went ramrod straight. He wanted to apologize, but there wasn't anything he could do, so he laid his head against the wall, closed his eyes, and drew on his shittiest memories from the past decade.

Human beings sold for mere hundreds of dollars, women shot in the street for showing their ankles, images of children being forced to work in brothels . . . yep, that did it. As vicious memories assaulted him, his body obeyed. The last thing he needed was for her to think he got his rocks off like some kind of pervert. Not when nothing could happen between them anyway. Her mere presence was shredding all his hard-won control.

When he whispered in her ear that it was time to move, she jerked unsteadily. They were taking a risk exposing themselves, and as much as he enjoyed holding her, they couldn't hide out forever. Sophie still clutched the laptop, but managed to help him remove the paneling. When they both stepped out, he motioned with his finger to stay quiet. The room was dark, but there was enough light coming in through the blinds that they could see what they were doing.

Jack bent down and withdrew a gun from his ankle holster. "Stay here," he whispered in her ear.

After a quick sweep of the condo, the prickly sensation on the back of his neck was gone. A few things had been moved around, but they were alone. He found Sophie sitting on the edge of his bed, clasping the computer to her chest.

"Grab whatever you need. We're leaving."

"Where are we going?" she whispered.

"A motel for now."

She opened her mouth as if she might say more, but she ended up nodding and grabbing her wallet she'd hidden in one of the dresser drawers while he packed up his computer, his cell phone, and a few extra changes of clothes.

He hoisted a backpack on his shoulder as she entered the room. She wore those ridiculous sneakers from earlier. It bothered him that Sophie didn't have anything else to wear, but he'd fix that soon enough.

"I took the toothbrush and toothpaste if that's okay," Sophie whispered.

"It's fine." Despite the situation, he felt a smile tug at his lips as he watched her. She looked a little vulnerable, but the woman had a spine made of steel. "Stay behind me until I tell you otherwise."

"Okay."

Weapon in hand, he led them to the front door and opened it an inch. If a sniper was waiting, there was realistically little they could do, but one of the reasons he'd picked this place was that it was across the street from a golf course. Not many places to hide.

When he was as sure as he'd ever be they were alone, he stepped outside.

"Where's the car?" she whispered.

There was a single line of parking spaces in front of the building, but on the off chance they'd been tracked, he hadn't wanted their vehicle too close. "I parked at another building."

Using the darkness to their advantage, they jogged down the street until they reached the packed parking lot.

"We're three rows down." He motioned for her to stay close.

As they maneuvered through a row of cars, he slowed when they reached the back of a dark van. He hadn't heard or seen anything, but the adrenaline rush he'd gotten earlier was still pumping overtime. Being out in the open with Sophie for an extended period of time wasn't good for his sanity. Normally he was able to gauge any surrounding danger, but with her around, his internal meter was off balance.

As he paused and listened, a dark blur came out from behind the van.

"Take cover," he ordered Sophie, going into battle mode.

A man dressed in all black lifted a gun at Jack, but he was only two feet away. If he'd wanted to kill them, he should have waited until he had a little distance between them.

Close-quarter combat was Jack's specialty. Hell, anyone with decent training should know to take down an opponent without having to get too close.

In a quick move, Jack struck out with his arm, knocking the man's weapon out of his hand. It clattered to the pavement noisily in the otherwise silent parking lot. The man attacked, trying to punch Jack. He grunted as he moved and left his face unprotected.

Jack slammed him in the nose, fast and hard, with his fist. A crunching sound rent the air as the stranger howled in pain. At the same time, Jack kicked the guy's inner thigh. It was a move he'd used many times before. The body reacted instinctively and this guy didn't know what to protect right now. When the man stumbled, blood rolling down his face, Jack gave him a swift punch to the throat and another shot to one of his shins. The guy was big, but a tiny bundle of nerves ran along the shinbone. And pain was pain, no matter a person's size.

As their would-be attacker wheezed for air, Jack grabbed one of his arms and twisted it behind his back before slamming him face-first against the van.

"Sophie? You okay?"

"I'm fine!" She sounded as though she was a few cars over.

"Stay where you are!" He couldn't do his job if he was worried about her, so he was glad she'd listened and hidden.

The man started to struggle, so Jack lifted his arm higher, threatening to break it. "Who sent you?" Jack knew the answer, but his first response would tell him a lot about how informative this guy would be.

"Can't breathe . . ."

"Who?" Jack pressed harder.

"Miguel Vargas."

Interesting. "Why do they want Sophie Moreno?"

"I don't know."

Jack lifted his arm a fraction of an inch higher and gave him a rapid kidney punch. The man howled in pain but couldn't move unless he wanted to break his arm.

"Okay! She knows something or saw something, but I don't know what. I swear! Our instructions were to take out the girl. That's all I know."

If Jack had been working against the Russian mob or even against men directly inside Vargas's cartel, it would take months to garner information. If he ever did. From the easy responses, Jack guessed this guy was just hired muscle with nothing to lose. "What about the girl in Miami? Why are they going after her?"

This time the man didn't pause. "She's the backup plan. She's friends with the Moreno woman and the only person they could find as leverage against her. Vargas thinks if they threaten her friend she'll come out of hiding. I don't know any more! They don't pay me enough for this shit!"

"Jack?" Sophie's scared voice jerked his head around. She was too close.

In the instant he turned, he wanted to kick his own ass for giving in to his stupid instinct and not following his training. Everything around him slowed down. The man he held turned with his entire body, using the momentum of his free elbow, and swung back at Jack's head.

Leaning back, Jack nearly missed what could have been a crippling blow. The man came at him full force this time. Jack slammed into another car as the guy tackled him. Sophie shouted, but he tuned her out. He had to bring this man down and keep Sophie safe. That was all that mattered.

Jack deflected two blows and managed to get in a few kicks, but the other man was pumped up now. After Jack struck him in the jaw, the guy already had his fist drawn back. Jack realized he'd have to kill him. Dragging out a fight wasn't something he had time for. He hated the thought of killing someone in front of Sophie, but it had to be done.

A loud shot reverberated through the quiet night air, causing them both to freeze.

"Stop!" Jack turned at the sound of Sophie's voice.

In trembling hands she held the gun he'd knocked away from the man earlier. Next to him the dark-haired thug lifted both his hands in the air.

Keeping his eyes trained on the man, Jack walked backward to Sophie. "Give me the gun," he murmured when he stood directly next to her.

Wordlessly she handed it over, a slight tremor in her hands.

"On the ground. Now," he ordered the man.

"What are you going to do to him?" Sophie's voice shook.

Jack pulled his cell phone out of his pocket with his free hand. "Turn him over to the police."

"What about us?"

"Don't worry, we'll be long gone." The Keys were the worst place for criminals to hang out. The FBI, DEA, and U.S. Marshals were all stationed in Key West. Not to mention the locals. For small-town cops, they were all well trained. They worked with so many different federal agencies, they had to be.

After he made a quick call, he fastened the man's wrists behind his back with flex cuffs from his backpack and locked him in the trunk of one of the older-model cars. The man didn't struggle much, probably because he knew that unless the locals or feds had something on him, he'd simply be deported. And Jack wasn't worried about him being a problem. The man would probably disappear for a while considering he'd given out information on Vargas. Either that or Vargas would kill him for failing.

Once he and Sophie were on the road, she asked, "Did I hear that guy right? Those guys are definitely going after my friend?"

"Sounds like it." He glanced in the rearview mirror. This

late, there shouldn't be many people on the road. There was only one road in and out of the Keys, so if anyone was following them, he'd know.

"We need to call her."

He agreed, but there were other things to consider. "We can contact her now, but if she's being watched, our call might simply alert them."

"Then why don't you tell your boss?"

"Remember the man we heard on the phone at the condo?"

"Yeah."

"His name is Levi Lazaro. We're friends—or we used to be. And he works for the NSA."

She gasped, fear rolling off her. "He *works* with you?"

"Yes." Jack gritted his teeth. Or at least Jack thought he did. He couldn't believe Levi would betray his country, but Jack had been gone for two years. A lot could change in that amount of time. Money was a powerful motivator, and while he would like to think Levi was above that, things looked bad.

"So, what, your boss knew about this?"

"No." There was no way in hell Wesley was involved in any of this. The man had sacrificed so much for his country that nothing could sway him.

"Jack, you're going to have to give me a little more than one-word answers. I'm not a mind reader and I'm terrified for Hannah. We've got to help her. *Now.*" Panic punctuated every word.

"Sorry. I'm running through scenarios in my head."

"Well, please involve me. We're in this together."

He felt a small cracking around his chest at the way she said "we." "Wesley is my handler. We're all part of the same organization, and everyone who works for him knows each other. I don't know what missions any of the team goes on unless we're on the same mission. And if Levi was working with Vargas, I would have been informed. It would have been a joint op. As it stands . . ." He shook his head, not wanting to say the words aloud.

She frowned. "Okay, so how did they track us down? Your friend sold you out?"

"I don't know, but it's possible." He didn't tell her that Levi was the only other person who knew about Jack's personal safe house. It would make her even less likely to trust him, and right now he needed her.

"So why can't we call your boss?"

"If someone's hacked the NSA or if there's a mole in the agency, it's possible they're watching him too."

"We can't sit by and do *nothing*."

"I know. I just wanted you to know our options."

"We need to call Hannah now. Those guys left over an hour ago. They'll be in Miami soon."

Sophie was right. It didn't matter what option they chose. Her friend was in danger. Jack handed his phone to her. "Call your friend. Make sure she understands the urgency of the situation, but don't waste time explaining. She needs to leave and go somewhere no one would think to look, not even you. Tell her not to use her credit cards and to take the battery out of her phone. She should get money out of an ATM and use cash for now. She can buy a throwaway with cash tomorrow and leave a message on my phone that she's safe."

Sophie swallowed and took the phone from his hand. He didn't miss the way her hands trembled as she slipped the battery into place.

Jack listened as Sophie convinced her friend to leave. To give her credit, she didn't take no for an answer and she didn't waste any time.

"You sure she's going to listen?" he asked as she hung up.

"She's my best friend and she's not stupid." It was hard to miss the defensive note in Sophie's voice.

"You met her in college, right?" He needed to keep her distracted right now, and talking was the best way to do it.

Plus, he wanted to know the things about her life that a file simply couldn't tell him. He'd missed Sophie so fucking much. More than he'd realized until he'd found himself face-to-face with her, her tantalizing scent messing with his head and making him remember how great things had been between them.

She nodded, the action jerky. "Yeah."

"And? Come on, give me more than a one-word answer." He gave her a lopsided smile, hoping she'd let her guard down.

She gave him a small smile as the tension in her shoulders loosened a fraction. "Freshman year I got stuck with this horrible roommate who talked to her boyfriend for hours every night, but after a week she got homesick and moved out. That's when Hannah got placed with me. I was really shy and she *really* wasn't, but somehow we clicked instantly. We've been best friends ever since. Her mom—" Sophie bit her lip and stared at her clasped hands as if she was afraid she'd said too much.

To him, it wasn't enough. "What is it?"

"Nothing. Sorry if I'm rambling. I do that when I'm nervous."

"You're not rambling. What about her mom?" He could listen to Sophie talk for hours.

She shrugged. "I love her mom, but lately she's been hounding Hannah to get married and have kids even though she has four older brothers, all of whom are single."

"Isn't she a nurse?"

"The *head* nurse of the pediatrics ward. She's young and ambitious, but it's not what her family wants for her. Don't get me wrong, her mom is really great. If it wasn't for her, I'd have probably starved in college. She bugs me about settling down too, but she's not as hard on me." A small smile tugged at Sophie's lips, and it nearly undid him.

From Sophie's file he knew she was close to Hannah

Young, but it was obvious she was close to the whole family. Hell, it sounded as though she considered them her family. It had been a long time since he'd prayed, but he decided to take a chance and throw up a silent one for her friend's safety. If her friend died, it would shred Sophie. And anything that caused her pain was unacceptable.

Sophie barely concealed a yawn as they pulled into a cheap motel on the next island closer to the mainland. "Where are we?"

"Islamorada, and this place accepts cash. Stay here while I get us a room."

She didn't audibly respond, but nodded instead. Her red-rimmed eyes were glassy and tired. The one-story baby blue building looked the same as it had six years ago.

Once he'd secured a room and two keys, he found Sophie dozing against the headrest of the car. When he knocked on her window, her eyes flew open in a panic until she realized it was him.

She grabbed her purse and stumbled out. Luckily they were parked two spots down from their room, so he didn't have to move the vehicle.

After opening the door, he gave her one of the keys. "Don't open for anyone. I've got my own key."

"Where are you going?"

"I'll be back in five minutes." He shut the door behind him without further explanation. Jack might not be able to do much for her, but he was going to make sure he took care of whatever needs he could.

Chapter 9

Kidnapping: the crime of unlawfully seizing and carrying away a person by force or fraud.

Sophie was too tired to argue or question him, so she simply locked the door and surveyed her surroundings. On
the outside, the blue paint was chipping and a green-looking
fungus covered the bottom half of the walls, but the room
itself wasn't too bad. There were two double beds, both with
pink and blue floral comforters, and a table with a rotary
telephone. She dropped her purse on the bed farthest from
the door and stepped into the bathroom. At least they had
soap and two toothbrushes. She quickly washed her face,
then stripped out of her dress and wrapped one of the white
towels around herself.

There was no telling when she'd have a decent change of
clothes, and she wasn't sleeping in this dress if she was going
to have to wear it all day tomorrow. She left the bathroom
light on, but turned off the lights in the main room.

As she slid under the crisp cotton sheet, the thin material
had a cooling effect. She could practically feel the knot in the
back of her neck loosen. So much had happened since that
morning, it was hard to grasp that her world had turned up-
side down in the span of twenty-four hours. The only reason
she was remotely able to relax now was that she'd talked to

Hannah. Knowing her friend was getting out of town made dealing with everything else bearable.

She tensed at the sound of the doorknob rattling until Jack stepped in carrying a bundle of clothes. Like a laser, his gaze immediately narrowed as he fixated on the dress she'd draped over one of the chairs. Then he looked at her. Pure sex was in his eyes. It was so brief, but the look he gave her made her toes curl. He might not want to want her, but he definitely did. She didn't know how it was possible, but his pale eyes seemed to darken as they raked over her face, all hot and hungry. For her. She actually got wet as he watched her. Her cheeks flushed and she was thankful there was no way he could tell her reaction. That hadn't happened to her since she was seventeen going on eighteen. Only one person had ever gotten that reaction out of her. Being around Jack and those annoyingly familiar eyes brought back too many memories of Sam. Not to mention she couldn't deny her growing attraction to the actual man in front of her. Not a memory.

Jack had such a dangerous yet sexy edge to him that it got her impossibly hot when it was the last thing she should be feeling. After that one escape attempt back at his condo, she'd been full-on prepared to try to run again. But after her boss's shady behavior and then those men who'd stormed Jack's place, she realized that she was a hell of lot safer with him than on her own. If she tried to leave she had no clue where she'd go. Not to mention that Hannah was supposed to be calling him and leaving a message when she got to safety. And strange as it sounded even to herself, Jack was the ultimate protector. He'd seemed so pissed that she'd been afraid of him. As if he could ever hurt her.

The gaze on his face right now was so raw she wasn't sure what to do. Instinctively she pulled the sheet up higher, hoping he didn't think she was trying to get him into bed. Although the thought was pretty damn appealing. So much so that the thought of dropping her cover and asking him to join her was sounding better and better. She couldn't remember exactly how long it had been since she'd had sex—which said a lot about the state of her love life—but after the insanity of the last day she had no problem admitting she could find comfort in Jack's arms. There was no doubt it would be a mistake, but it was one she'd make with open eyes.

She nodded at his hands and found her voice. "What is that?"

"A couple changes of clothes for you. And two pairs of shoes. These should fit." Was it just her or was his voice unsteady?

"Where did you get those this late at night?"

He shrugged, but his heated stare never wavered from hers.

Warmth spread across her lower belly as her nipples hardened. The way Jack stared at her was different. He looked at her as if she was special. Not just another pretty woman. And she wanted . . . *him*. Damn it, she wanted him so bad her body ached for the feel of his hands and mouth stroking over her entire body. Maybe if she imagined or willed it hard enough, he'd do something about it. She was tempted to make a move on him or at least let him know she was willing, but if he rejected her after the day she'd had, she'd probably die of embarrassment. And there was nowhere to go if he did. She'd be stuck with him and her own humiliation.

When he cleared his throat she realized she'd been staring at his mouth. "Did you steal those from someone's room?"

Jack lifted a dark eyebrow, a hint of amusement in his expression. "I can return them if you'd like."

"No way." She smiled and fell back against the pillow. She was tossing those stupid sneakers tomorrow.

They stared at each other for a long moment. Cotton filled her mouth when his gaze fell to her lips. She wondered if he was remembering that kiss. Unable to take his scrutiny any longer when it was obvious he didn't plan to do anything about it, she rolled onto her side and punched her pillow. Behind her, the creaking of his bedsprings cut through the otherwise silent room. Sophie bit back a frustrated groan. She'd been ready to pass out minutes ago, but now she was wide awake and wondering what was going on in Jack's head. She shouldn't care, but the man was a mystery. A very sexy mystery. She should just keep her mouth shut and stay as detached from him as she could until this whole mess was over. Too bad that wasn't going to happen.

"Jack?"

"Hmm?"

"Can I ask you something?" Oh boy, she was so going to regret asking this, but there was no way to stop herself.

"Sure."

"Earlier, in the closet . . . Did I misread, uh . . ." Her face heated as she struggled to voice what she meant.

"No, you didn't. . . . I'm attracted to you. *Very* attracted. We have to keep this professional, Sophie. There's too much at stake." His deep voice was exceptionally low in the quiet room.

So he wanted her and she wanted him. She'd known it, but hearing him say it sent tingles racing along her nerve endings. Unwanted heat pooled between her legs as she imagined all the things he could do with those big hands. At that moment she was very thankful he couldn't see her expression.

With her back still facing him, she spoke again. "Where are you from?"

"What?"

"You have a file on me, right?"

"You know I do."

"So you know things about me you have no right to know. I just want to know where you're from." It was a fair request.

He was silent for so long she wasn't sure he'd answer. "I'm from Miami too."

His pause made her think he was actually telling the truth. Or maybe that was just some spy trick to make her believe him. "Really?" It wasn't actually that surprising, considering the way he'd maneuvered around the city, as though he was extremely familiar with the area in a way only locals were.

"Yes, really. Will you please try to get some sleep?" He yawned and she knew it wasn't real.

"That fake yawn is pathetic and just so you know, the attraction isn't one-sided. If you change your mind I'm right here." Sophie's chest tightened as she said the words she'd never have been able to say if she'd been facing him. It was out of character for her to be this bold, but with people trying to kill her, she was going to do exactly what she wanted.

From the moment they'd been introduced, she'd been more than aware that Jack was a good-looking man. Even when she hadn't trusted him and had thought he was a potential criminal, her body had flared to life with something raw and unexplainable. Something that had only happened to her in Sam's presence. In her experience, outward appearance didn't mean anything. Looks would fade and good-looking, charming people could be angry and cruel underneath the surface.

Truth be told, despite her original primal draw to him, it was seeing him in action and a strange familiar quality about him that triggered real awareness on her part. When he'd kissed her back in Miami, she'd felt it all the way to her pinky toes. It was as if she'd been hit with a live wire and it had woken up some long-dormant part of her. None of the men she'd ever dated after Sam had been able to affect her with just a kiss. Until Jack. Mr. Tall, Sexy, and Inappropriate Timing.

The sound of Jack moving against the sheets interrupted the quiet of the dark room and silenced her thoughts. For the first time in as long as she could remember, she actually felt safe in a bone-deep sort of way. Ironic, considering the circumstances. Tomorrow she'd have a billion things to worry about. For now, her body and mind needed time to recover. Or at least rest. Closing her eyes, she let the blackness of sleep overtake her.

Sophie flopped down on the towel next to Sam, stretching out on her stomach. "It's getting so hot," she complained. "Come in the water with me."

He hated the fucking beach with all the sand and nothing to do, but with Sophie, he had plenty to do. Namely, watch her. Well, and watch out *for her. It pissed him off how many guys checked her out. It was so blatant. She didn't seem to notice, though. That was the only thing that made the constant tension humming through him ease.*

They'd been coming to the beach the past two months every weekend. She loved it and it was free entertainment. And it kept them out of Ms. Bigsby's hair, which was a big plus. He'd learned long ago not to piss off decent foster parents. Ms. Bigsby wouldn't win any parenting awards, but she didn't beat them and she kept them fed and clothed. Both he and Sophie tried to be as trouble free as possible, and the lady liked them well enough. Being away from the house gave the old woman her space and she got a paycheck for letting them live there. They were all happy. And safe.

He started to roll over onto his stomach to talk to her, but stood when he saw Marco, a guy from his baseball team, walking toward them. "Hey, man." He nodded at the guy. They weren't tight, but they were close enough.

"Hey, Sam. Some of the guys are grilling and playing volleyball. Bring your girl and join us if you want." He nodded politely at Sophie, who had turned over and smiled at him.

Sam forced himself not to stare at her. When she was wearing a bikini that covered practically nothing, it was

*damn hard not to. She was so tan and lean, and all he wanted
to do was feel her body against his. He kept his gaze off her,
though. He'd just gotten his body back under control and he
refused to embarrass himself in front of her and his team-
mate.*

*"We were just about to hit the water, but we'll come over
later?" he asked.*

*Marco nodded, then gave Sophie's body a lingering look
that Sam recognized all too well before heading back to the
group of six guys and three girls about twenty yards from
them.*

*"We can go over now if you want." Sophie stood, brushing
sand off her slender legs.*

*His gaze strayed down the length of her lean body and he
abruptly turned away from her, facing the direction of the
water. "We'll go later," he said curtly.*

*"Jeez, what's wrong with you? I thought you liked
Marco." She nudged him with her hip as they headed to the
glistening Atlantic.*

*She'd left her dark brown hair down so that it fell in soft
waves down her back, and the plain black bikini she wore
barely covered her breasts. Probably because it was a couple
of years old. The little triangles should be illegal; they barely
covered her nipples. So what was wrong with him? He was
starting to get a hard-on at the beach and they were surrounded by hundreds of people—some of them his friends.*

*As soon as they reached the water, relief coursed through
him. When he was waist deep, he breathed out a sigh—until
Sophie jumped on his back and wrapped her legs around
him. She was so much shorter than him and she always did
this so he could carry her out deeper. He loved the feel of her
almost naked body on his, but today he was edgy. It was getting harder and harder not to make a move on her.*

*"You want to see a movie later tonight?" she asked, her
mouth right next to his ear.*

The feel of her warm breath made goose bumps break out across his skin. "Sure, what do you want to see?" *He couldn't tell if his voice sounded strangled or not.*

She didn't seem to notice. "I don't care. Anything that keeps us out of the house is fine."

When they reached a short sandbar, she jumped off his back and dove underwater. As she came back up, she slicked her hair back and grinned at him before splashing him. She was the combination of every fantasy and wet dream he'd ever had. Water rolled down her tan body and he could see the outline of her nipples—which had been taunting him for months. He was dying to see what they looked like, to taste them. To know what color they were. He couldn't even smile at her when she splashed him again. He felt like such an asshole, but he couldn't force the muscles to work. Sitting on the sandbar, he rubbed a wet, salt-tinged hand over his face.

"What's wrong? Are you mad at me?" *She sidled up next to him, hesitation in her voice.*

He hated that he'd put it there. She was so damn sensitive and sweet. She'd been dealt a shitty hand in life and she always kept up walls. It was why she never even noticed when the guys at school checked her out. Either she didn't want to notice or she didn't care. But with him she was different and he knew he had to be careful with her. He could never hurt her. It would kill him inside if he did.

"I could never be mad at you, Soph. I just . . ." *He trailed off, not wanting to say something stupid that would hurt their friendship. He felt so much for her. So much that it scared him, but he wouldn't risk accidentally pushing her away if she didn't feel the same. Some days he really thought she might want him, especially when she looked at him as if she wanted to kiss him. But she was so guarded it was too hard to tell.*

"What? Tell me now," *she demanded in that haughty voice she only used with him. The girl had such a temper some-*

times. It was buried deep, but when she let it out, it stunned him—and turned him on.

"Or what?" he teased, needing to lighten the mood. If he could get her mind off the way he'd been acting and what he'd almost admitted, things could go back to normal. And he could act normal. He just needed to get on even footing again.

"Or . . . or . . ." She sputtered for a moment before lunging at him, tackling him in the shallow water. "I'll make you tell me." She took him off guard, rolling over him and pushing him back in the water with a splash as her body covered his. Soph started to tickle him, but froze as her legs splayed over him.

It was the worst possible position for them to be in. Usually he could hide his erection or get it to go away by thinking of things not-Sophie, but she was practically straddling his lap. Lifting herself up on her legs, she tried to back away, but her knees sank into the sand and she rubbed her groin right over his hardness. He let out a groan and she sucked in a deep breath, but neither looked away from each other.

Her dark eyes widened and she sat back down, completely straddling him now. The water was calm, the waves small and barely rippling around them. He could hear people on the beach and there were a few in the ocean a good distance from them, but all his focus was on Sophie and her reaction to this. To him.

She swallowed hard. "Are you . . ." Her cheeks flushed bright red.

He was pretty sure his face matched hers. "Yeah."

"Is it because of . . . me?" She bit her bottom lip nervously.

He wanted to lie. He ordered himself to. But he couldn't. Lying to Soph was damn near impossible. How could she not know how he felt about her? "Yeah."

At that, her cheeks flushed a dark crimson, but she didn't

pull away. She leaned closer and, taking him completely by surprise, brushed her lips softly against his. "Good."

Jack opened his eyes and realized his hand was wrapped around his cock. Which was rock hard.

Fuck me.

He'd always been in control of his body. Until twenty-four hours ago. He shifted against the sheets, which had suddenly turned to sandpaper against his skin. After the last thing she'd said before she went to sleep, it was as if Sophie had waved a bright red flag in front of him and he felt like the raging bull she was teasing. Only she wasn't teasing. He glanced over at her bed. She was still turned on her side, her back facing him and her breathing steady. Sound asleep. Thank God she hadn't seen him.

He closed his eyes and tried to block out her face, but it was impossible. Not after that damn dream. It was the second one he'd had of her recently—and in such a short time period. Before that it had been years.

He'd never forget the day he found out he was being placed in the same foster home as Sophie. He'd known who she was from school, but she'd never looked twice at him. She'd never looked twice at *any* guy. She'd walked around with her head down everywhere she went. Half the baseball team had wanted a shot at her, but she'd been oblivious of her own attractiveness. Before he'd actually talked to her, he'd been so sure she was a snob.

When he'd realized she was just quiet, things had drastically changed and his attraction had grown overnight. In his world, survival of the fittest was the rule and he'd never been particularly protective of anyone. *Until her.* He'd definitely never had the urge to hit a girl until he'd seen some stupid neighborhood girl bullying his Sophie.

His.

The word echoed in his head. Some days he cursed ever meeting her. She made him want things he couldn't have.

Made him feel protective and proprietary when his world didn't allow those kinds of emotions. He didn't give a shit what Wesley said about him getting rid of his demons. It didn't matter if he did. He'd never be able to settle down. There was no way he could subject a woman to the kind of life he led. Never knowing where he was or how long he'd be gone.

So why even fantasize about taking just a night with Sophie? Or even a few hours? Even when they were younger he'd known they belonged together, and that feeling was still so damn overwhelming. Being around her brought back all those feelings of insecurity. He had the best training in the world, but put him in the same room as Sophie Moreno and he felt like that tongue-tied seventeen-year-old kid again who would do anything for the girl he'd loved.

Groaning, he grabbed the extra pillow on the bed and held it over his face. What the hell was wrong with him?

Hannah's hands shook as she pulled her duffel bag out from underneath her bed. She'd never heard Sophie—or anyone for that matter—sound so scared before. Hannah wasn't sure what was going on, but she trusted her best friend.

Sophie was sometimes a control freak, but the woman always kept her head on straight. Even in college, she'd been responsible and dependable as hell. Always the designated driver. Always studied before a big exam. Never late to a class. If Sophie said something was wrong, Hannah believed her.

After tossing a few pairs of jeans, sweaters, and undergarments into her bag, she cleaned off her bathroom counter with one swipe of her arm and just dumped everything in at once. Her mind raced as she tried to think of where she'd go. Sophie had told her to choose somewhere that not even Sophie would know about. That didn't leave many options.

Her parents had a house in Fort Lauderdale and they also had a cabin in North Carolina. She didn't think anyone knew about the cabin, but it was still connected to her family. Sophie had been pretty clear about avoiding any place like that. As Hannah shrugged into her coat, she shoved those thoughts away. Hell, she'd grab some cash and keep driving until an idea came to her if that's what it took to stay alive. Because Sophie had sounded *terrified*.

As Hannah entered the hallway from her bedroom, she started to turn on the lights out of habit, but jerked her hand back as if burned. If someone was watching her house, she didn't want them to know she was awake. Her feet were silent along the carpeted hallway. Right about now she wished she owned a gun or some kind of weapon other than pepper spray.

For a brief moment, she thought she heard a creak come from her living room. Numbness settled in her bones at that sound, making her feet lead. Waiting, she listened but didn't hear it again. Trying to steady her nerves, she reminded herself that her house had been built in the fifties. If she wasn't scared out of her freaking mind, she probably wouldn't have noticed it. With shaking hands, she clasped the handle of the door that led to her garage and quickly ducked inside.

It was empty except for her car.

Without pause she dumped everything in the backseat and slid into the driver's side. She cringed at the sound of the garage door opening, but she had no choice unless she wanted to drive through it.

Her slick palms slid against the steering wheel, but when she saw that there was no one visible in the rearview mirror she let out a harsh, high-pitched laugh that sounded a little maniacal in the enclosed space of her vehicle. Nothing about the situation was remotely funny, but her nerves were fried. As she pulled out of the garage, she screamed as glass shattered around her. Instinctively she ducked and covered her face as shards flew at her.

A dark shadow reached through the broken window.

She screamed again and tried to press on the gas but jerked back when a fist connected with her jaw. Her entire body jolted back against the seat. She was vaguely aware of pain slamming through her face, but her adrenaline spiked hard. Using her hands as a weapon, she tried to fend off her attacker. Punching at the man, she connected briefly with someone's arm, but the contact was pitiful.

Someone grunted and then very fast fists and something shiny—a knife maybe—flashed around her. She tried to hit the gas again, but hands were everywhere and her attacker yanked the keys from the ignition. Her car shuddered as it turned off. It all happened so fast she couldn't stop it. Before she could contemplate an escape, rough hands grabbed her shoulders.

As she tried to pull away, the door opened and she toppled through. Then she was shoved facedown on her hard driveway. Her face rubbed against the gravel, and a sharp burst of panic punched through her like a live blow.

"Quit struggling, little *puta*," the man on top of her growled in a Spanish accent. His knee dug into her back. She tried to struggle, but his weight proved too much.

"Hey!" another male voice sounded somewhere nearby.

Hope jumped inside her for a brief moment. Maybe someone was coming to help her. She tried to shout, but the man was pressing her into the concrete and it hurt to even breathe.

"Be careful with her, stupid. The boss doesn't want her hurt," the other voice whispered in a similar accent.

Something cold and metal snapped around her wrists before she was hauled to her feet. Pain ripped through her arms at the awkward jerking motion. "Help!" A scream so loud it burned her throat tore free. "Somebody help—"

The man who'd pulled her to her feet—a dark-haired

man with black eyes that looked like empty pools and a vicious scar running down his face—backhanded her. Pain stung her cheek, but before she could scream again the man shoved something wet over her face. She tried to struggle, but everything in her vision turned fuzzy as her world tilted on its axis.

Chapter 10

Burn phone: prepaid disposable phone.

Ronald jumped in his chair as his cell phone buzzed across his desk. He answered immediately. "Ronald here."

"Who is the man with Sophie Moreno?" Vargas snapped, his voice heated.

"I don't know." Clearly he wasn't with Keane Flight as he'd said or Vargas would have known. Ronald had already betrayed her enough with his silence; he didn't want to add more. Besides, Sophie had told Ronald she'd ditched Jack—or whoever he really was. Had she lied to him?

"My men have been unable to track her and I know she has a partner. Do not lie to me. Are you helping her?"

"No!"

"Has she contacted you?"

Ronald loosened his tie. He assumed Miguel was always watching him, so he decided to go for honesty this time. "Yes."

"What did she say?"

"Just that someone tried to kill her and she doesn't know why. She's scared and on the run. She doesn't know who's after her, which is exactly what I told you. She's not involved in this. You need to leave her alone." His admission wouldn't hurt Sophie. It was the only thing that eased his conscience.

"What about the man she's with?"

"I have no idea who he really is. She told me she ditched him." But now Ronald had a feeling she hadn't. Vargas was far too interested in her, so he must have a reason.

Vargas waited for a beat of silence. It seemed to stretch out for an eternity. "She was at the *hangar* on Sunday night. My men saw a woman running from the building and they were able to get a license plate number when she fled. She could have taken pictures of them or my product. I don't know what she has, but she will be silenced."

Ronald massaged his temple as terror rippled through him. Sophie had been at the hangar? By herself? It was a miracle she hadn't been caught by one of Vargas's men. It was probably what she'd wanted to talk to him about—and he'd blown her off. If she'd truly been at Keane's hangar, then there was nothing he could say that would keep Miguel from tracking her. Ronald's only hope was that he could warn Sophie before she did something stupid. Like come back to Miami.

Miguel continued. "If she contacts you, I want you to set up a meeting with her. I need to find out who this man is. With Keane in a coma, this guy might be trying to take over our operation."

Our? Ronald bit back a snort. He hadn't even thought that the man with Sophie could be trying to take over Vargas's operation. He couldn't deal with another monster. He cleared his throat. "She might not even call me again."

"She will and once you set it up, we will intercept her."

"And if she doesn't?"

Miguel made an angry sound. "Don't try my patience. *When* she contacts you, you *will* let me know. If I find you lied to me, well, I don't need to remind you what a beautiful daughter you have."

It was as if invisible fingers tightened around Ronald's neck as he fought to breathe.

Miguel continued. "Many of my men have expressed a deep interest in . . . getting to know her better. So far she has been unharmed, but if you fail me . . ."

"I won't." The words came out as a strangled whisper. Miguel's not so subtle threat made his stomach heave. His family had been through enough. If he could just get his daughter back, he'd turn himself in, go to jail, whatever it took. He simply wanted his family safe. He'd have called the cops long ago if he had any clue where she was being held. She'd been kidnapped in another country, so the local cops were no good to him anyway. He literally had no one to turn to. Not if he ever wanted to see his daughter again.

"Good. I will call you this evening with further instructions. I'll be in town in a couple days. If you use good sense, you will have your daughter back by this weekend."

Miguel disconnected and Ronald laid his head on his desk. Would this nightmare never end?

As Jack stared at the popcorn ceiling, his watch alarm went off. Sleep had been an elusive fantasy once again. Sophie's words had echoed through his tired brain all night, rattling around with no mercy. *"If you change your mind, I'm right here."*

He sat on the edge of the bed and nearly choked when he saw her. He'd forced himself to avoid looking at her the past few hours, but a small stream of sunlight pierced the room through the opening in the curtain. The beam ran across her chest, illuminating the fact that her sheet was dangerously close to exposing her breasts. Breasts he'd kissed, licked, massaged . . . *Damn it.*

Control yourself.

Careful not to wake her, he grasped her sheet by the edge and pulled it a few inches higher. When his knuckles brushed against her soft skin, he froze for a moment until he found the will to move away. With a silent groan he grabbed a change of clothes and his shaving kit and headed to the bathroom. A cold shower was exactly what he needed.

The icy blast of water was the perfect shock. As the jets massaged his tired shoulders, vicious memories of the last time he'd seen Sophie played in his head, reminding him that if she knew who he really was, she'd run far and fast in the other direction.

He tried to shake the memory, but suddenly he was eighteen again and swimming in guilt over the fact that he hadn't been there to protect the girl he'd cared about more than anyone.

"Damn it," Jack muttered as memories of the last time he'd seen her assailed him. He clenched the bar of soap, his nails leaving half-moon indentations. He'd been doing fine for years, keeping all this shit at bay.

Being around her was just going to bring up stuff that should stay dead and buried. Just like the person he used to be. Sam was dead. He'd supposedly died in Afghanistan many years ago. Something he'd never needed to remind himself of until now. Making the choice to officially "die" had been the easiest thing he'd ever done. He'd had no one and had liked the fast-paced lifestyle. Not being able to admit his true identity to Sophie was the first time he'd ever experienced regret over his decision.

He twisted the shower knob to off, then grabbed a towel and wrapped it around his waist. They needed to get on the road soon, and though he hated waking her, time was their enemy.

After shaving and brushing his teeth, he eased the bathroom door open. Wearing only a towel, Sophie looked up from the small table where she was going through the clothes he'd gotten for her.

A faint smile touched her lips when their eyes locked. "Thanks for getting these. The thought of wearing that dress again . . ." She mock shuddered.

His throat dried up at her state of dress—or undress. She was completely covered, but the thin cotton towel did little more than the sheet had done earlier. Though she was short, her tanned, toned legs seemed to go on forever. He could see the outline of her hard nipples too. The thought of sucking one into his mouth, running his tongue around—

"Uh, Jack?" Sophie's voice jerked his gaze back up to her face.

"Yeah?"

She clutched the towel tighter. "You okay?" She hugged whatever piece of clothing she'd chosen to her chest and watched him with those big brown eyes, obviously waiting for some sort of response.

He cleared his throat and motioned to the bathroom behind him. "I'm done if you want to get in there."

Without a word she brushed past him and shut the door with a quiet click.

Jack rubbed a hand over his face and stared at the closed door. He had to get past this stupid Sophie thing. Nothing could happen between them. Didn't matter how bad he wanted it.

While telling himself not to think about Sophie, he quickly dressed in dark jeans and a dark sweater, then turned on his laptop. Before he contacted Wesley he wanted to see if he could find out more about Levi on his own. His gut told him there was no way Wesley was involved. The man bled red, white, and blue. Still, he'd always thought the same thing about Levi.

After sending out feelers to see if he could pick up any chatter on Levi's whereabouts, he stopped when he heard the bathroom door open. He'd heard the shower shut off, so he'd been expecting her. He tried to brace himself to see her again.

Sophie walked out wearing a snug pair of jeans and a thin green sweater. She rubbed her hands over the jeans pockets and smiled self-consciously. "These are a perfect fit."

"Good." As they'd arrived at the motel last night, he'd seen a drunk couple laughing as they stumbled from their room, heading God knows where. The bars in the Keys were notorious for staying open until dawn, so he'd taken a chance and slipped into their room.

Jack started to close down his computer. "You ready to leave?"

"We're going now?"

"I want to do some reconnaissance of SBMS, you need to call your boss, and I'm going to call Wesley."

"I thought you were going to wait to make any calls."

"I am. I'm waiting until we're out of the Keys. If they do track us down, there's only one road in and out of here and I don't like those odds. Once we hit 95, we'll be able to blend in better."

Her pretty mouth pulled into a thin line, but she didn't argue. He stared at that mouth for a long moment until she nervously moistened her lips. Forcing himself to look away, he packed his stuff while she folded the rest of the clothes he'd acquired for her.

Once they were out of the motel room and on the road, Sophie was quiet, only asking him if it was okay to change the radio station.

When they hit Key Largo he stopped at a cell phone shop and picked up a dozen throwaways and two handheld radios. Sophie stayed in the car. While he hated stopping anywhere that had video surveillance, there weren't many choices and he needed the phones. He managed to avoid looking directly at any cameras.

"Did you get everything we need?" she asked as he got back in.

Jack didn't miss the anxious note in her voice. "For now."

"What made you want to do . . . this?"

He shot her a quick glance as he steered back onto U.S. 1. "What?"

"You know, be a superspy or whatever. Is that the right word?"

A rumble escaped from deep in his gut and he realized he was actually laughing. "I'm not a spy. Not exactly."

"Then what are you?"

"I do a lot of undercover work."

"So you're sort of a spy. Kind of like James Bond?"

"Sort of." A smile tugged at his lips. He wasn't a spy. Not in the sense that she was thinking. So-called spies worked for the CIA or MI6 or a dozen other countries around the world.

"So how'd you get into it?"

Considering that his boss had sent him on this mission when he should have sent him on vacation, Jack actually got perverse pleasure from opening up to her. Sophie already knew who he worked for. When this was all over, she'd be debriefed for hours—or more likely days. And they'd make her sign more than one confidentiality agreement that promised imprisonment and worse if she told anyone what she knew. "I was recruited."

"Were you in the military?"

Her eyebrows were knit in curiosity and he wished he could figure out what was going on in her head. She couldn't possibly know who he was, yet all the hair on the back of his neck stood up as she watched him. "Why?"

"Your tattoos. I saw one on your back. And your . . . bullet. I figured that had some sort of military connection."

Or she hoped it did, was the implication in her unspoken words. Most of his tats had been covered or removed—and the one she was referring to he should have had removed, but he'd kept it out of pride. He'd made it work with all his cover IDs so far, so it hadn't been an issue. The places he'd infiltrated had loved "recruiting" him when they found out he had official training. The bullet he wore around his neck—his hog's tooth—he hadn't worn on his last mission, but he'd snagged it before heading to Miami. He hadn't planned to take his clothes off around Sophie, and the thing was like part of his skin. He hadn't even thought about it this morning, but she'd obviously seen it. Even if she didn't know exactly what it was, she was smart enough to figure it out eventually.

"I was in the Marines." Years of training flew out the window as the admission slipped out. Yeah, he was a real superspy today. Tension hummed through him as he told her way more than he ever should have. He was having a harder time than he'd imagined distancing himself from Sam. Who was supposed to be dead. But being with Sophie made him want to be Sam. He wanted her to look at him the way she'd looked at her high school boyfriend. Not look at him as if he were a fucking stranger who could ever hurt her.

"Oh." She bit her lip, then looked out the window.

"What?"

She looked at him again. "It's just . . . I told you that you reminded me of someone and he was a Marine too. That's all. It just freaks me out a little, I guess."

"Why do I remind you of your friend?" He was playing with fire, but he couldn't stop himself. And fuck all his years of training and even his boss, he didn't *want* to.

Her shoulders lifted noncommittally. "Your eyes. They're . . . unique."

"What happened to your friend?" Oh yeah, he deserved a goddamn medal for his superspy abilities today.

Her jaw twitched once, but she answered, "He died. Roadside bomb in Afghanistan or somewhere in the Middle East. I didn't know, but he'd listed me as his emergency contact, so the military automatically contacted me. I never got the full story and truthfully, I didn't want to know the details. The fact that he'd died was hard enough to deal with."

"I'm sorry."

"Me too," she said quietly.

Jack's fists tightened around the wheel. Just because she was sorry about his death didn't mean shit. Time to change the subject. "As soon as we get to Miami, we're ditching this car and finding a new one. And we're going to get into the building before the nighttime security arrives, so we'll have time to kill before meeting with Weller."

"How do you know the security schedule?" Her voice was cautious.

He lifted an eyebrow at her. Did she even have to ask?

Sophie just shook her head, so he fished out one of the burner phones and handed it to her. "Are you ready to call your boss?"

"I guess." Her words didn't inspire confidence.

"If you don't think you can do this, tell me now. If he senses something's off, we could be walking into a trap. You need to convince him to meet you. I don't care what you say, just make sure he agrees to meet. The sooner the better. And remember, you've got forty seconds." That was how long it would take someone to trace the call if anyone was trying. After being tracked down last night, he wasn't taking any chances.

"I can. I *will*." She nodded as if to convince herself and her loose hair swished seductively around her shoulders.

She had that just-out-of-bed, sexy tousled look. He knew it wasn't intentional either and that just made her hotter. Something he shouldn't be noticing. "Good. As soon as you hit Send, put him on speaker."

With trembling fingers, Sophie took the phone from his hand and dialed. She did as he instructed, then held the phone in her lap as it started ringing.

Her boss picked up in the middle of the second ring. "Yeah?" he growled.

"Ronald?"

His voice softened. "Sophie, are you all right?"

She glanced at Jack as she answered, "I'm fine, but I need to meet you. Soon."

"I thought you were going to get out of town." He sounded panicked.

"I know but I need to see you. It's important."

"Sophie, you can't come back to Miami. Trust me. It's too dangerous," he hissed, his words a whisper.

"I have to. I found some information on Keane Flight that looks sketchy, including pictures I took at the hangar. You *need* to see everything."

There was a short pause. "Why can't you just tell me what you found?"

"I can't talk about any of this on the phone. People with guns tried to kill me. I think this may be part of the reason. If it is, we need to go to the police."

Jack was impressed. Sophie kept biting her bottom lip, but her voice was strong and convincing.

Ronald sighed. "How about we meet at Dorsey Park?"

Sophie looked at Jack. He shook his head and mouthed the word "office." Then he mouthed *ten seconds*.

She nodded. "No. It's too public. I want to meet in your office."

"Sophie, I don't know—"

"I'll be there tonight at eight. Be there or I'm going straight to the cops. I've got to go." With wide eyes, she hung up the phone.

"That was good," Jack said.

"You're sure?"

"Yeah. Not giving him a chance to argue and threatening with the police was perfect."

She sighed and sagged back against the seat. "Thank God."

Jack flipped on his blinker and pulled into a gas station.

"What are you doing?"

"Filling up with gas. Do you mind paying the attendant?" He handed her a couple of bills before getting out of the car.

Keeping an eye on her while avoiding the one video camera outside the station, he started the pump, then used the same phone Sophie had used and called Wesley. He'd be ditching it as soon as this call was over, so he might as well get some use out of it.

"Wesley here." His boss sounded pissed.

"It's me."

"Where the hell are you? You should have checked in by now."

"I think we might have a leak."

"What?"

"Miguel Vargas's men tracked us down last night."

"And where exactly were you?"

Jack ignored the question. "Levi was with them."

Silence.

"You still there?"

"Son of a bitch," he muttered.

"What's going on? You haven't said two words about Levi since I've been back." Truth be told, Jack hadn't asked either. He'd assumed his friend was on a mission and Jack had other things on his mind. Namely Sophie. While Levi was one of the few people Jack trusted, he hadn't spoken to him in over a year. Just the way this business was sometimes. Jack had been so deep undercover for his last operation he'd been unable to reach out to anyone once he'd been completely embedded. Not that he'd been in the right frame of mind to do so anyway.

"He went off the grid six months ago. No one has seen him since."

"Why? What about Meghan?" The gas pump clicked off, so Jack placed it back in the holder.

He slid back into the front seat as Sophie emerged from the gas station carrying two foam cups and a plastic bag. He leaned over and opened the door for her.

"I didn't want to tell you like this, but Meghan is dead." His boss's gravelly voice was strangled.

Bile rose in his throat. *"Dead?"*

Sophie slid into the passenger seat and set his cup in the coffee holder.

"Yeah. Seven months ago she was murdered and Levi disappeared a month later. He's been like a ghost."

Jack started the car but didn't move. "Shit."

"Exactly."

He hated to ask the question because he knew the answer would make him sick. "What happened to her?"

"She was tortured and executed. It was professional. By the methods used, we guess it was the Russians."

Meghan was one of their best agents. No, she *had* been. Even thinking that she was dead felt wrong. After nearly a decade of undercover work, she'd finally taken a desk job because she and Levi had wanted to start a family.

"There's more, Jack. She was five months pregnant when she was killed."

An icy flash of raw anger snaked through him as the words sank in. Torturing a pregnant woman? He was surprised Levi hadn't gone off the deep end completely. "Why did Levi disappear?"

"Revenge is my guess, but I honestly don't know. He sold their home, got rid of all his belongings, and fell off the face of the earth."

"Is there a connection with Vargas and Meghan?" As far as Jack knew, Meghan had never done any work in South America. If there was a link, it was possible Levi was out for revenge. Or maybe he was using Vargas to get to someone else. That would make more sense.

"Not from her time with us," his boss growled.

Jack understood his frustration. There were too many variables. Levi obviously had his own agenda, but it wasn't what Jack originally thought. "Someone on the inside helped them track us. I overheard part of Levi's conversation with Vargas, and that bastard has a contact on the inside."

More silence.

"Wesley?"

"I was afraid of that. Someone sold Meghan out, so after her death I began a discreet investigation. I haven't come up with anything solid."

"So what do you want me to do?"

"Don't call me anymore. Use the same backdoor channel we used when you were in Lebanon."

Most of his missions were off the books, including that one. And that channel hadn't been used in years. If anyone was listening to their current conversation, they'd have no clue what he and Wesley were referring to. "Okay. I'll contact you soon. And, Wesley?"

"Yeah?"

"You should have told me about Meghan before now." It was a shitty thing keeping him in the dark about one of their own. It wasn't as though he could have gone to the funeral, but he should have been told. Because no matter what, he'd have reached out to Levi.

"I know."

Jack disconnected, then rolled down Sophie's window. He popped out the battery and handed it to her. Without him having to ask, she tossed the pieces into the trash can by the pump.

"Is everything okay?" Sophie asked. She'd been completely silent until then, sipping her coffee and carefully watching him.

"Yes." The answer was automatic as he steered out of the lot.

"No, it's obviously not." He nearly jumped out of his skin when she placed a light, reassuring hand on his arm.

The soft way she touched and looked at him tore the truth from him. *How did she do that?* "I just found out a friend of mine died last year." It wasn't like he was telling her details of something classified. It was the only thing that eased his conscience about opening up.

"Oh . . . God, I'm so sorry." And she was. The sincerity in her voice was real. Something else he loved about her. Sophie didn't say anything she didn't mean.

"Thanks," he murmured as he pulled back onto the main road.

Just being close to Sophie grounded him in a way he'd never expected. Or even imagined. He'd learned at a young age to only depend on himself. So why did he feel this sudden need to bare his soul to Sophie? Maybe not exactly bare it, but he wanted to open up to her. For once he wanted to be honest with a woman. Tell her things he'd never told anyone. He just wanted to let someone in. Okay, not someone. Only Sophie. That scared the hell out of him.

Chapter 11

PHOTINT: photographic intelligence, usually involving high-altitude reconnaissance using satellites. Also called IMINT.

Hannah could hear the distant sound of male voices and another, more insistent tapping sound much closer. She kept her eyes shut. She was afraid of what she might see when she opened them. Visions of wrestling with a man, then being knocked out with some sort of drug tickled her memory. It wasn't a dream, that much she was sure of.

"Are you awake?" a soft female voice asked.

Hannah cracked open her eyes at the question. A pretty blond woman wearing jeans and a plain black T-shirt sat huddled against a wall. Her knees were pulled up to her chest, and her arms were wrapped around them. The blonde looked as though she was barely out of college. Glancing around, Hannah realized they were in a matchbox-sized concrete room with one bed and one toilet. And she was stretched out on the uncomfortable mattress.

Pushing up, she tried to ignore the pain splintering through her skull. "Where are we?" Her voice was raspy and unused, making her wonder how long she'd been unconscious.

The blonde shrugged, but the action was a little jerky. "I don't know. Cuba maybe. They just brought me here a couple days ago and one of the guards told me we're moving again very soon. He said I'd be seeing my family, so I think we're going to Miami."

"Moving? They? What's going on?" Hannah gingerly touched the back of her head. A small bump had formed on the bottom side of her skull. She moved her jaw back and forth, not surprised her face was sore.

"The men holding us work for Miguel Vargas. He was here earlier, but you were still unconscious."

"Who's Miguel Vargas?"

The girl frowned at her. "He runs one of the biggest South American drug cartels. You don't know who he is?"

"Oh . . . maybe." She couldn't remember if Sophie had said anything about that on the phone. Her head was still fuzzy. Stretching out her arms in front of her, she looked at herself, then down at her clothes. Dirt stained her white T-shirt and jeans, but she didn't think she'd been hurt anywhere else.

"What's your name?" the girl asked.

She stopped her assessment. "Hannah. What's yours?"

"I'm Holly. Do you know why you're here?" Her voice slightly trembled.

Hannah shook her head. "Not really. The last thing I remember, my best friend called and told me to pack a bag and hide somewhere for a few days. She said someone was after her and . . ." She trailed off as she realized that anyone could be listening to them. The more she came awake, the worse off she knew she was. This was a bad situation. The other girl had said they might be in Cuba? Holy hell. Bad, bad, bad.

"Who's your friend?" Holly asked before Hannah could speak.

She contemplated not answering for a second, but this girl was a captive too. And even if she was faking it for some reason, Hannah had no reason to lie. "Her name is Sophie."

Holly's forehead crinkled. "Sophie . . . Sophie Moreno?"

Hannah couldn't hide her surprise. "Yeah, you know her?"

"She works for my dad. I've known her for years. How is she involved in this?"

Hannah shrugged. "I don't even know what 'this' is. Why is some drug lord holding *you* hostage?"

"It has something to do with my dad's company. I tried to ask one of his men once, but—"

The sound of heated male voices drifted through the steel door of their room. "Who is that?" Hannah whispered.

There was a spark of fear in Holly's eyes as she held a finger to her mouth. "Shh. Roll over and close your eyes. I'll tell them you're still sleeping."

Without pause, Hannah did as she asked. She tried to keep her breathing normal when she heard the door creak open. A man said something in Spanish, but she couldn't understand him. Holly answered, and then another man spoke, but his voice was much softer. Nicer. They continued talking. Hannah could pick out some words, but *bonita* was the only one she understood.

There was some shuffling around behind her. Hannah prepared to be shaken awake—or worse—but nothing happened. The door shut and after a few minutes Holly spoke.

"You can turn over now," she whispered.

She cringed as the mattress creaked. "What happened?"

Holly held out a handful of celebrity Spanish magazines and a faded paperback. "They wanted to know if you'd woken up and they left these."

"Have they . . . hurt you?" Hannah hoped the girl understood what she meant.

For a moment, her blue eyes darkened, but she shook her head. "No, thankfully. One of the men tried to rape me when I was first taken, but the guy who brought these in stopped him." She held up the magazines.

"Have you tried to escape?"

The other girl shook her head and wrapped her arms around herself again. "No way. They all have guns and I don't even know what country we're in now. Before they brought me here, they actually let me out of my room a few times, but I was in the middle of the rain forest. I wouldn't have known where to run anyway. Everyone around here is really scary." Her voice cracked on the last word.

"You said you think we're in Cuba?" Hannah stood on shaky legs and stretched her arms above her head. Her body was sore, but at least she could move.

"Yeah. I heard one of the guards talking."

Hannah had started to ask another question when the door flew open. A man with a scar down the left side of his face looked back and forth between them. He nodded once at her, then said something she didn't understand.

"He wants you to go with him. He said they have questions for you." Holly's voice shook as she translated, and a fresh wave of terror swept over Hannah.

Just because these men hadn't harmed Holly didn't mean they wouldn't hurt Hannah.

His heart pounded wildly in his chest as his fingers flew across the keyboard, entering commands at record speed. *Hurry, hurry,* he ordered himself, even as he tried to will his heart rate to calm down.

But that was impossible. Nothing could soothe his frayed nerves at this point. He'd hacked in through a back door he'd left during a mission that had ended over a month ago. Luckily no one had discovered it. Of course, he'd hidden it extremely well. And it couldn't be traced back to him. Unfortunately if anyone found him in this control room, he'd be in a shitload of trouble. Which would mean questions and detainment and inevitably his arrest if they dug deep enough. And they would.

A dark part of him loved the thrill of going behind everyone's back at work. They would call him a traitor once his sins were discovered—as he knew they eventually would be, but after he'd left the country—but he didn't care. He was smarter than all of them. At first he'd started selling secrets to pay off gambling debts. There had just been so many and he'd been out of control. So he'd had to find a way to pay them or be killed. The answer was simple. He had access to information people would pay good money for. And why shouldn't he cash in?

After he'd paid off his debts, he hadn't stopped. The money, the rush, it was too good. Too intense. He was so addicted to the thrill of making more money. Six figures a year wasn't enough. Some days he wondered if anything would ever be enough. He simply couldn't stop now anyway—even if he'd wanted to. He was in far too deep with very dangerous people. Miguel Vargas would never let him walk away until he was done with this job. But then he was out. Of course he didn't plan to stop working. He had a valuable set of skills, namely hacking, and he planned to use them any way he could.

As the screen he'd been waiting for popped up, an alert dinged that he'd found something. Before leaving work last night, he'd entered Sophie Moreno's picture into his secret program. The NSA hijacked CCTVs all over the country for their own use, so he'd simply piggybacked onto one of their programs and put in his own parameters.

And now it looked as if he might have gotten what he needed. A few clicks later and his breath caught in his throat. A CCTV from a gas station less than an hour from Miami had captured her face clear as day. Thankfully the system was wireless and had an online backup, which was easy enough for him to hack in to. It was set on a forty-eight-hour loop, though, but it looked as if she'd *just* left. Holy shit, he could locate her if he got lucky. He forwarded through the video until he spotted her getting into a car.

From the angle he couldn't see the license plate, so he pulled up a map of the direct area and found a bank a block down. After hacking in to their system, he smiled to himself as the car she was in drove by less than a minute after she'd left the gas station. He couldn't see in the vehicle because the windows were tinted, but he got a clear shot of the license plate from one of the three cameras.

Now that he had what he needed, he quickly shut the program down. All he had to do was enter the license plate number into another database. And this one, he could track from his cell phone. Once he got a hit, it would alert him immediately. Then he could bring something directly to Vargas. Something that would get the man off his back.

It wasn't as if he gave a shit what happened to the Moreno woman, and Vargas was just going to kill her anyway. No torture would be involved. Just a quick, clean kill.

Jack glanced in the rearview mirror and frowned when the white SUV he'd first noticed about ten blocks earlier switched lanes after he did.

Again.

He and Sophie had made it to Miami without any trouble, but he was edgy and ready to ditch this car. They'd had it too long, which increased their odds of being tracked down. And Sophie's friend Hannah still hadn't left a message. Sophie had asked about it a few times and he hated that his answer was always no. The worry and fear on her face tore him up inside. But he shelved those feelings as he smoothly switched lanes. They were leaving the business district and about to enter a sketchy part of town.

The SUV had stayed almost exactly two car lengths back. It kept its distance but didn't stray too far. The driving seemed precise and somewhat trained. Could be nothing. Or it could be a tail.

He was about to find out.

As they neared the upcoming intersection, the light turned yellow, so he gunned it. Normally on an op—and especially since he had Sophie with him—he tried not to break simple traffic laws and draw any unnecessary attention to himself. But he wasn't going to drive around in circles trying to figure out if they were being followed.

Either the SUV would follow and give the occupants away, or Jack was just being paranoid. As he tore through the intersection, the car directly behind him slowed and stopped at the light. But the SUV honked, swerved, and plowed through the line of cars. He cursed under his breath.

Sophie glanced over her shoulder and sucked in a breath. "We're being followed."

"Yep. We're going to have to ditch this car and run on foot. We'll be fine," he said to reassure her even though she seemed calm.

"Okay." She picked up her wallet from the center console and tucked it into the back pocket of her stolen jeans. "Should I have a gun or something?"

He didn't like the thought of her actually needing one, but he still had an extra weapon. And if something happened to him, she needed to be able to protect herself. "Once we're out of the car I'll give you one. And if something happens to me, call Wesley. His number is the only one programmed into the burner phones." Jack wasn't supposed to call him, but if he went down, Sophie had to have someone to turn to and there was no way the local cops could do shit to protect her. Not without knowing all the facts.

Taking a hard right turn, he swerved around the car in front of them, cutting the person off. A loud horn blasted.

"What if we don't lose whoever that is?" Sophie asked quietly.

"We will." He'd taken enough defensive driving courses over the last decade to be secure in his abilities, but the fact was that this was Miami, his original home. He knew the layout better than anywhere else in the world. He might not lose their tail permanently, but he could ditch it long enough to head out on foot with Sophie.

The farther they drove into the heart of Miami, he made a decision. "You're familiar with Bayside Marketplace?"

"Of course." The tension humming through Sophie was almost visible as she remained turned around, watching their pursuer.

They weren't outwardly attacking, but it was the middle of the day and getting into a gun battle on a crowded Miami street was just plain stupid. Whoever was after them would want to get them alone. Which was why Jack planned to make sure that didn't happen. "I don't know for sure who these guys are, but I'm guessing they don't know this city like we do." Unless Vargas had hired locals, but that was something Jack would have to deal with if the man had.

He took another sharp turn, tearing through a yellow light. His adrenaline pumped at rapid speeds, but he kept a controlled grip on the wheel. "I'm going to park right on Port Boulevard. We're going to ditch the car in the middle of traffic, then make a run for it. You on board?"

She nodded, her expression tense.

"You're sure?"

She rolled her eyes. "*Yes.* Would you rather I question your decisions while someone is chasing us? You're the pro here and I don't want to get killed. So yes, I'm sure I'd rather disappear into a crowd than keep driving around in circles."

He bit back a smile at that spark of attitude. She'd been worried all morning about her friend, and he couldn't blame her. But she was still keeping it together. She'd been like that when they were younger too, always compartmentalizing things. Most foster kids who survived the shitty system were like that.

The faster he wove in and out of traffic, the faster the SUV kept pace. And the driver was getting more dangerous. Jack cringed as he glanced in the rearview mirror and saw a homeless man pushing a shopping cart jump back onto the sidewalk to avoid getting hit by the SUV.

"We're almost there." Jack knew she'd be aware of that, but the countdown was on. In less than thirty seconds, they'd be exposing themselves for precious seconds before they disappeared into the crowd. And that was if they could.

As he pulled on to Port Boulevard, his heart rate increased with each second that passed. Swerving to the left around a motorcycle, he jerked the car back into the right lane and sped up. The brake lights in the car in front of him lit up, so Jack pressed down on theirs. Sophie yelped as the vehicle shuddered to a stop. One hand was wrapped around the handle as she unsnapped her seat belt with the other.

He grabbed his backpack as she opened her door and slung it on. Risking a glance behind them, he saw the SUV was about three car lengths behind them. Not far enough away.

The front door and passenger door opened, so there were at least two people. The sight sent a burst of adrenaline raging through him.

"Come on!" He rounded the car, grabbed her hand, and started running.

She wasn't tall, but she was in incredible shape and kept pace as they darted down the west side of the shops. His final destination was the parking garage on the east side of the marketplace, but he couldn't run straight there. First, they had to lose these guys.

Shops flew past them in a blur as they sidestepped people. A cigar specialty store, Gap, Bath & Body Works, a couture shop for women.

A man holding a falafel and a foam cup stepped back from a food kiosk, oblivious of Jack and Sophie barreling through the crowd. Sophie dropped Jack's hand and dodged to the right, avoiding him, but Jack couldn't miss him without slamming into two teenagers.

Scorching coffee sloshed on his shirt as he collided with the Hispanic man. "What the fuck!" the guy shouted as he sprawled on his ass.

"Sorry." Jack jumped over the fallen man and risked another glance behind him. The crowd of people wasn't as thick as it would be on a weekend, and he spotted a man with dark hair wearing sunglasses moving forward at a steady clip.

The guy wasn't running, but his movements were fast and measured as he scanned the area. There were a hell of a lot of places to hide, including the yachts and other boats dotting the bay to their left, but Jack wanted out of this vicinity in the next five minutes. The longer they stuck around, the bigger chance he had of getting caught on a CCTV. And if there was a traitor working for the NSA who was tracking him, pinning his location would be too easy. Grabbing Sophie's hand, he ducked behind the food kiosk as they moved out of the line of sight of the man following them.

"Where are we headed?" she asked as they passed a café, their walk fast, but not sprinting.

They needed to blend in, and running at this point would draw too much attention. They were just lucky their tail hadn't seen Jack slam into that man. He ignored her question as he scanned the various kiosks until he saw what he wanted. "Give me one sec."

Glancing behind them, he slapped a fifty down on the kiosk and grabbed two cheap hats and two pairs of aviator-style sunglasses. Touristy crap, but it would have to do. "Will that cover this?"

The woman with pink and purple extensions nodded. "Yeah, but I need to get your change."

"Keep it."

He handed the hat with the sparkly pink flamingo to Sophie. "Tuck your hair into it."

Not much as far as disguises went, but the bill from the

baseball cap would cover half her features, which would help in avoiding cameras. Which was only part of their problem.

"How many men did you see?" she asked as she scooped her long hair up and shoved it under the cap.

"There are at least two, but I only saw one behind us. He hasn't spotted us yet. The other or others could be anywhere." He slid his own cap on and took her hand in his again. He didn't need to, but he liked holding on to her for reasons he didn't want to admit. As they strode past a kids' shoe store, a loud boom echoed through the air. Then another.

One. Two. Three shots fired.

Jack turned in the direction of the shots, but couldn't see the shooter through the mass of people, who were all frozen.

For a single moment, everything around them quieted. Then another shot rent the air. People screamed and scattered in every direction. Next to him Sophie crouched against the glass window of the store, as if the act could make her smaller.

"There are kids in the shoe store."

"There are kids everywhere." He knew what she meant, though. She didn't want to inadvertently lead the shooter to a bunch of children.

Jack kept scanning, then narrowed his gaze on the same man with the sunglasses he'd seen earlier as he stepped out from behind a kiosk. He had a pistol in his hand, raised above his head as he looked around. At least he'd fired into the air.

Hating the situation and the crowd, Jack raised his weapon. He would only get one shot at this.

The man saw him too late. As he drew his weapon down, Jack fired once. It hit the stranger right between the eyes. The impact from the bullet slammed the guy back a foot, but Jack turned before he'd hit the ground.

One shot, one kill. Best way to deal with a problem like this.

Thanks to the sunglasses, Jack couldn't see Sophie's eyes. If she was disgusted, he didn't want to know.

Following a cluster of screaming women and children, they turned right at the end of the west side shops. "We've got to make it to the parking garage. We can steal another car."

"Sounds good to me," she panted as they started running again.

They raced parallel to the brick wall until they reached the east side of the shops. Peering around the corner, he saw more people running in all directions, most of them screaming.

He'd never understand that reaction. Screaming did nothing but complicate any situation. And it made you a bigger target. Stupid.

But it also made it easier for him to pick out who didn't belong. One man was crouched low, with one hand balanced on the side of a hot dog stand and the other holding a gun at his side. He had dark hair, sunglasses, and he was turned in profile to Jack.

Unfortunately his position was also right on their path to the parking garage and there was no other way to get there. Jack hated opening fire in a crowded place, but there was no time to second-guess himself. Not when he needed to get Sophie to safety.

"We're going to head east." He motioned, pointing toward the garage. "I'm going to run in a straight path and you are going to stay directly behind me. Do you understand? Right behind me."

"Got it."

He nodded, glad she was so calm. Lifting his pant leg, he grabbed his backup weapon and handed it to her. "If I'm hit, keep running. Do not fucking stop for me. You make it to the garage. I don't care if you have to carjack someone, get to safety and call Wesley. Understand?"

"I'm not leaving you behind."

He blinked in surprise. Unwilling to argue, he peered

around the corner again. The guy was still there and the majority of the crowd was gone. They were losing any cover they might have. There was no time to argue. "Stay close," he ordered as they stepped out from their hiding place.

They'd made it ten paces when the man spotted them. He started to push up from his crouch, raising his gun as he moved, but Jack had the element of surprise. Still moving, he fired twice. Once in the head, once in the chest for good measure.

Sophie gasped next to him, but it was the only sound she made. Seconds later, they rushed through a side door to the first floor of the parking garage. Screeching tires peeled through the air as people tried to escape. In the chaos it was a hell of a lot easier to steal a car. After only a minute of searching, he found an older-model truck. It didn't have tinted windows, but it would do and it was easy to hot-wire.

It took another whole minute to get the hell out of the garage. And he lost a decade of his life worrying about getting Sophie out of harm's way. They exited onto Biscayne, and only then did he allow a small sliver of relief to slide through him. He turned left and headed toward Third Street, then took a sharp right.

"Next time I give you an order, you do it." He hadn't meant the words to come out so harsh, but his heart was racing and his palms were sweaty. If he'd been hit and Sophie had actually stuck around—the thought terrified him. He was so used to being in control, and so far she'd been fairly cooperative. He knew it was because she didn't have any other options, but he'd expected total compliance.

"Fuck that," she snapped, the outburst taking him by surprise. "I'm not a soldier and you're sure as hell not my boss. If I agree, hell yeah, I'll follow orders, unless your order is stupid. And telling me to actually leave you behind is *stupid*."

An unexpected laugh escaped. The timing was inappropriate and he shocked himself, but hearing her curse and yell at him after what had just happened soothed a dark part of him.

"Is that funny to you?"

"No. Damn, Soph. That temper of yours . . ." He trailed off when she stilled.

It was subtle, but her hand tightened on the weapon resting in her lap and he was pretty sure she stopped breathing for a moment.

"What?"

"Nothing. What do we do now?" Her voice wavered slightly, but he pushed past it. Hell, he couldn't blame her after everything that had just happened.

"Find a safe house and hole up until you have to meet Ronald tonight." And get the hell out of this area.

Sirens blared in the distance and Jack knew that soon the local cops would be swarming the place and probably putting up roadblocks. They needed to be long gone by the time that happened.

Chapter 12

Infiltration: the secret movement of an operative into a target area with the intent that his or her presence will go undetected.

Sophie jumped as the bang against the wall from their neighboring motel room reverberated through their crappy room. Of course, the bang was followed by a string of obscene curses.

She wasn't sure how it was possible, but Jack had picked the *worst* pay-by-the-hour motel in Little Havana. When they'd first arrived it was still daylight, and in the daytime it wasn't so bad. But it was nearing dusk and she was fairly sure their "neighbors" were either dealing drugs or engaged in some sort of prostitution ring. Probably both. People had been coming in and out of their room all afternoon, and some of the noises had been revolting.

Earlier she'd tried to buy crackers from the vending machines, but had quickly returned to the safety of their room after a couple of men had asked what her "price" was. Apparently something about her jeans and sweater screamed *hooker*. It didn't matter that Jack had given her a gun, she'd still felt incredibly exposed outside.

"When are we leaving?" she asked again, not bothering to keep the annoyance out of her voice this time.

Jack was lounging on one of the double beds and doing God knew what on his laptop, but he looked up when she spoke. For the briefest moment, those pale eyes darkened as he raked an appreciative gaze over her breasts. He got this little smile when he looked at her, as if he was remembering something. She wondered if he was even aware he was doing it. Damn it, the look was so . . . familiar that it jarred her straight to her core. Combined with the way he'd called her Soph in the truck earlier, it put her on edge. More and more he was reminding her of Sam.

Which was insane.

It made her feel unbalanced. She'd done fine not thinking of him for years—or at least locking her thoughts down. Now her life had gone to shit in a matter of days, she didn't know who to trust, her best friend still hadn't checked in—which was eating Sophie alive inside every second that passed—and she had scorching thoughts of Sam almost every time she looked at Jack.

"Give me five minutes," he murmured as he looked away.

"You keep saying that. We need to get out of here. This place is creepy." Gross-looking brown stains were on both bedspreads, so she'd been relegated to sitting at the small table or pacing the room. To entertain herself she'd been figuring out what the stains resembled, almost like watching clouds at the beach. Only a lot grosser.

Jack had been very quiet, constantly working on his computer and not telling her anything unless she asked him a direct question. Which was incredibly annoying. She could almost swear he was purposefully ignoring her. After they'd barely escaped from those two shooters—and her insides were still quaking over that—she guessed that the reason he'd picked such a crappy place to hole up was that cops wouldn't frequent it. Not unless called. And considering that everyone she'd seen looked like they were up to something illegal around here, no one in their right mind would be calling.

He typed some more into his computer, then looked up again. "If it makes you feel better, Homeland Security won't need to talk to you anymore."

Oh yeah, that made everything better. She held off on the rude comment because it wouldn't help and it made her feel petty. "Why not?"

"My boss made some calls. They'll be easing off SBMS until the NSA knows more about what's going on."

"Good." She wouldn't admit it, but she'd actually forgotten about Homeland Security. There were too many other things running through her mind.

He swung his legs—his very sexy, muscular legs—off the side of the bed and snapped the laptop shut. "Bring everything with you because we're not coming back here."

"Thank God."

The hard lines of his lips softened at the corners. "This place isn't *that* bad."

"The fact that you say that scares me. What kinds of places have you stayed in?"

Something dark crossed his face before he schooled his features. All traces of that smile were gone. Immediately she regretted what she'd said even if she'd only said it to lighten the atmosphere. Turning, she grabbed her sad little plastic bag of clothes and the hat with the sequined flamingo on the front and headed for the door.

"You can leave the hat," he said quietly behind her as he gathered his things.

"I know." The hat was impossibly tacky, but she was going to keep it because Jack had given it to her. It didn't matter that it had been part of a disguise. Some weird part of her wanted it. When she looked back at him, he had a guarded look on his face, but he didn't respond. Just palmed the keys to the most recent SUV he'd stolen.

The man was certainly good at that, and while she didn't want to be impressed by his thievery, watching him in action was pretty hot. Once they were out of the stale-smelling room and heading toward SBMS, she thought she'd feel better. Instead she was terrified at the prospect of facing her boss. Which was so ludicrous she almost laughed out of sheer nervousness. She was with one of the most dangerous men she'd ever met, yet she was scared of seeing her boss, a man she considered a dear friend. She still couldn't get the images of Jack shooting those guys out of her head. He'd been so focused, so lethal.

"If we run into any problems with SBMS's security, your only priority is to get out of there. I've watched these guys and they're not going to use lethal force, so no matter what, don't wait for me if you have a chance to get away." Jack glanced in the rearview mirror as they pulled out of the motel parking lot.

She sighed. "I thought we'd been through this. I'm not leaving you behind."

"Sophie—"

"Don't you 'Sophie' me. Having this argument is pointless and one you'll absolutely lose. . . . Would you leave me behind?"

"Never." He shot her a hooded look and for a moment, she thought he'd continue arguing, but he returned his attention to the road. "You're going to call your boss at a quarter till seven and tell him the meeting time has been changed. Then—"

"Jack, I know all this. We've been over it a hundred times." She hadn't just sat around in the motel room. When he hadn't been on his computer, they'd been going over "the plan," and it wasn't hard to remember.

"You can back out of this if you're not ready."

"Isn't it your job to give me a pep talk or something? Not make me second-guess myself?" She wasn't afraid to admit she was terrified right now, and having him question her was freaking her out even more.

His lips pulled into a thin line. "I just want you to know we can figure something else out if you're not comfortable."

Sophie tightly clasped her hands in her lap until her knuckles turned white. "The weapons are bad enough, but if Ronald is really helping terrorists, I can't sit back and do nothing. Actual biological warfare on our soil . . . do you know how far-reaching that could be. Hundreds of thousands of people could die," she said before he could respond, mainly because he would know better than her. "Not to mention someone tried to kill me and I know Ronald knows more than he's letting on. Did you check your voice mail again?" She wasn't sure why she was asking when she knew the answer would shred her up inside.

"Yes."

Sophie dug her fingernails into her palms, hoping the pain would distract her. Hannah obviously hadn't left a message or he would have told her. She was supposed to have called his number to let them know where she was. *Hours ago.* Even though Jack's phone was turned off, her friend would have left a message. She'd promised. There could be any number of reasons that Hannah hadn't called. Some were harmless, but Sophie kept picturing the worst possible outcomes for Hannah not getting in touch with her. Clearly someone wanted Sophie dead. What was to stop them from using Hannah to get to her? It wasn't as if she had many close friends, and it was no secret how tight they were. Unfortunately Hannah didn't know where she was, so even if someone wanted to . . . torture her or something, she had no information. Sophie's stomach lurched and she forced her morbid thoughts to quiet for the moment. She wouldn't do anyone any good if she had a breakdown right now. "Can I use one of your phones?"

"Why?"

"I want to call Hannah's work."

After he handed it to her, Sophie quickly dialed the number to Hannah's sector of the hospital before he could change his mind.

"Miami Children's Hospital," a female voice answered after three rings.

"Hi, is Hannah Young in yet? This is a family emergency."

"I'm sorry but Hannah called in sick tonight."

"When did she call?"

"Who is this?"

Sophie disconnected without answering. They weren't allowed to give out personal information at the hospital. Something she understood, but she didn't feel like getting into a drawn-out conversation with someone who would never give her the answer she wanted.

"Is everything okay?" Jack asked.

"The woman who answered said Hannah called in sick."

"That's a good thing, Sophie. If she simply hadn't shown up, then you'd need to be worried."

"You're right." She tried to give the appearance that she was satisfied, but couldn't shake the feeling that something was wrong. Hannah wasn't a flake. She should have called by now.

The closer they got to SBMS, the more tension built up in the back of her neck. Surprising her, Jack reached out and put a reassuring hand on her arm. He stroked her for a second with his thumb, the move slow, a little sensual, and so much like the way Sam used to comfort her, it was like a slap to her senses, pulsing through her like a wave. She couldn't breathe for a moment as memories of the way her first love had done more than comfort her. She'd never felt so emotionally raw in her entire life as she had these past couple of days. Add to that these strange, conflicting feelings she experienced every time Jack looked at her or touched her in a far too familiar way and she felt herself starting to split at the seams.

At least he looked just as startled as she felt. Maybe he was experiencing the same electric . . . whatever was going on between them. Jack stared at his hand for a second before pulling it back as if she'd scorched him. God, she wasn't going to bite. Unless he asked nicely. Then she'd definitely oblige him. She could feel heat creeping up her neck at the inappropriate thought, but she was helpless to stop those internal needs. She wasn't sure if it was because Jack reminded her of Sam or not, but her draw to him was making her edgy, hungry for his touch. Luckily they were at their destination. Which shouldn't be a relief considering what she was about to do. But it was. Anything to distract herself from the hundred different thoughts running through her head.

"Left here." She pointed.

There were two parking garages, so she directed him to the older one. In order to enter the new one, they would have to get a ticket and wait for a small mechanical arm to lift. Not to mention, there were security cameras in the new garage. Technically they weren't supposed to use the old one, but a lot of the employees did, especially if there was an early meeting and some of them wanted to dip out without being noticed. No one enforced the rules, so it didn't matter anyway.

Instead of parking on one of the top floors, Jack wound down the ramp until they were at the basement-level garage. Not surprising, no one else was parked there.

"What are you doing?" she asked as he put the SUV in park.

"We're going in through the basement entrance."

"So you knew about this garage?"

He nodded and opened his door.

She sighed as she exited the vehicle. Why he hadn't just told her instead of letting her give him directions, she didn't understand.

Jack rounded the SUV and motioned for her to follow. When they came to the door that led to the stairs, Jack tried opening it. It was locked, so he pulled out a small black kit and worked the lock until the door swung open.

"Why am I not surprised?" she said as he held open the door for her. She'd seen him hot-wire cars. This had taken him a lot less time.

He winked at her and her stomach flipped. Just like that. Oh yeah, she was completely lacking all common sense when it came to this man. The man was walking sex appeal. Not in an overt way, but after seeing him without a shirt this morning, she hadn't been able to get the image of his sculpted arms and chest out of her mind. She'd felt how powerful he was when he was carrying her through that icy water, and actually seeing him half-clothed only added to her desire for him. It was so easy to imagine what it would be like to have his body over hers, pumping into her while she—

"Stay behind me." His words echoed in the stairwell, cutting her fantasy short.

Which was probably best. She needed to stay focused even if being distracted by thoughts of Jack was oddly helpful with the rest of the worries she couldn't shake. Once they reached the sixth floor, the panic she'd been expecting settled in full force. Most people would be gone for the day, but it was possible she might run into someone she knew. They had to cross an overpass from the old parking garage to the building. There weren't any cameras, but someone could be exiting the building and they would have nowhere to hide.

"You ready?" he asked before opening the door.

No. "Yeah."

He eased open the door. There were a few cars in the upper level of the garage, but no one was around, so they hurried across the overpass.

The halls were eerily empty as they made their way to her office. Mandy and the other assistants had of course gone home for the day, increasing Sophie's sense of isolation. Anyone could walk in on them and Jack didn't seem the least bit affected.

Without asking, Jack sat at her desk and turned on her computer.

"What are you doing?"

"I'm checking your files." He didn't even look up.

"Why?"

He shot her a quick glance. "I want to see if someone has been tracking your movements on here. Someone knew you'd taken those pictures—which explains the gunmen the day we were out to lunch. But it happened damn fast. I want to find out if someone planted a back door on your computer. I'm pretty sure they did, but I want confirmation."

She blinked. "Back door?"

"It would give them remote access to your files if set up right." His fingers clacked away on the keyboard at rapid speed, as if he was barely aware of her presence.

Okay, then. She scrubbed a hand over her face, but when the doorknob rattled, Sophie completely froze. As the door swung open it was as if everything around her moved in slow motion. Benson, one of her coworkers, walked in. His face turned a dark shade of crimson when he spotted her.

Immediately her gaze riveted back to the desk, but Jack was gone. *What the hell?*

"Sophie, what are you doing here?" Benson asked.

"This is my office." She took a few steps backward and leaned against the edge of the desk, hoping her action seemed casual.

"Ronald said you were out sick."

She ignored the comment. "Did you need something?"

"Oh, no, I didn't mean . . . That is . . ." He cleared his throat and held out some sort of postcard. "I just wanted to invite you to see my band play this weekend."

She stared dumbly at what he was offering. "Your band?"

"Yeah, I thought maybe we could have a couple drinks before my show," he mumbled.

Oh no. No, no, no. She did not have time for this. "I actually have plans this weekend, but I should let you know that I'm dating someone."

"Of course you are," he mumbled, the crimson flush spreading all the way to his neck and ears.

"Listen, Benson, I don't date coworkers anyway, so—"

Looking away, he took a step back toward the door. "Don't worry about it. I'll see ya around."

Before she could respond, he'd shut the door behind him. She quickly locked it, then sagged against the solid door. "Jack?" she whispered.

He popped up from behind the desk. "Did you lock the door?"

"Yeah."

Jack pulled a flash stick out of his pocket and plugged it in. Then he glanced at his watch. "I found a very well-hidden back door. It's closed now, but I'm taking everything from your computer."

"Do you know who planted it?"

"Nope, but I *will* find out." There was a steely edge to his voice that left no doubt in her mind that he would. "And it's time to call Weller."

She pulled the phone from her back pocket and cursed her trembling hand. "What if he won't move the meeting time?"

"Make him do it." He didn't even look up from her computer as he spoke, which made her feel a little better.

Jack acted as if she should have no problem getting Ronald to agree. Which meant her sexy spy trusted her. Except he wasn't hers and she needed to stop thinking like that.

She glanced at the wall clock behind Jack's head. Almost seven. With a shaking hand she dialed Ronald's office number. After three rings, she frowned. Maybe he wasn't even there.

When he finally answered, his voice sounded odd. "Hello?"

"Ronald, it's me."

There was a long pause. "What do you want?"

She frowned at his brusque tone. "We need to meet now."

"Now? Are you in the building?" There was a note of panic in his voice.

"No, but I will be soon. I'll be in your office in five." She disconnected before he could argue.

"Something's not right," Sophie said to Jack.

He stood as he pulled the flash drive from her computer. "What do you mean?"

"He sounded . . . funny. I can't explain it."

Jack pulled a gun from his shoulder holster. "We're going to do things a little differently, then."

As he headed for the door, she placed what she hoped was a firm hand on his chest. "You won't need a gun with Ronald."

"Sophie, we're doing this my way. I need to know you won't question any decisions I make in the next twenty minutes. I can't do my job if I'm worrying about you."

She glared at him. "I can't believe you think you even have to say that."

"Well, you've refused one of my orders. Twice."

She gritted her teeth. "It's because that order is asinine. You need to let that shit go." After everything they'd been through, she trusted Jack with her life. He might be a little intimidating, and okay, scary, when he wanted to be—she still couldn't get over how calm he'd been when he shot those two men—but it was clear he knew what he was doing and wanted to protect her. Hell, he'd kept them alive this long.

He blinked once, as if she'd surprised him, but didn't respond as he unlocked the door. Sophie stayed close to him as they entered the outer office area.

As they crept down the hallway toward Ronald's office, sweat trickled down her spine. The door was closed, so Jack pressed his back against the wall and motioned to her.

"If anything happens, I'm right here." His quiet voice was

so soothing it stilled all the nerves running rampant inside her. She could do this.

Trust didn't come easy for her—never had—but the longer she was around this man, the more she found she actually wanted to trust everything he said to her. She connected with him on a fundamental level that almost defied logic. The only other person she'd felt that way about was Sam. Her protector and lover. And Jack was only one of those at this point.

Nodding once, Sophie knocked and opened the door at the same time, hoping her fear wasn't showing. Jack stood to the right of the door, unseen to anyone inside, but his presence made her feel better. Safer. She stepped in and gasped.

The blinds were drawn, Ronald sat in his chair behind the desk, and her assistant, Mandy, stood two feet away from him. And she was holding a gun.

"Mandy? Why do you have a gun?" Sophie asked loudly.

"Shut the door." Her assistant trained the gun in Sophie's direction.

By the firm way she held it, Sophie guessed she knew how to use it too. She paused but did as she said.

"Now move over next to him."

"What are you doing?" Sophie asked.

Mandy, no longer the sweet assistant Sophie had come to enjoy working with, rolled her eyes. Suddenly she looked older, her gaze remote and icy. "Making a lot of money, that's what."

She glanced at Ronald for confirmation, but he simply shook his head as if he was confused by this.

"Stand up, Ronald," Mandy ordered.

"Are you going to kill both of us? How can you think you'll get away with this?" Sophie asked. It probably wouldn't be that hard, but she just wanted to keep the woman talking.

"I'm only killing you. Rather, Ronald is."

"What?" Her boss finally spoke, horror in his voice.

Mandy rolled her eyes again and spoke to Ronald as if Sophie weren't in the room. "I'm not giving you the gun, you moron. We're going down to the parking garage and I'm killing her. It will look like you did, though. If you try to cross Vargas, he'll send the evidence to the police."

Sophie looked at her boss. Dark circles under his eyes stood out against his pale face. Out of the corner of her eye, Sophie could see the door slowly opening. Mandy had her back facing the door and it took all of Sophie's willpower not to look in that direction.

Unfortunately she wasn't so sure about Ronald. It was stupid. Probably the stupidest thing she'd ever done, but she turned to Ronald and started yelling at him. Somehow she had to distract Mandy and give Jack an opening. If Mandy had wanted Sophie dead, the other woman would have shot her the moment she walked in the door. But it was clear she wanted to do the job downstairs. Probably because dragging a bleeding body through the building would be impossible to explain.

"Did you know about those weapons being shipped by Keane? Is that why someone tried to kill me? Did you set me up, you son of a bitch? Is this all about money?" Sophie's voice rose with each word. She silently prayed Ronald didn't give away Jack's position.

Ronald stared at her. "I can explain—"

Sophie grabbed Ronald's hand, pulling him to the floor at the same time Jack made his move. Everything happened so quickly, Sophie didn't have time to do anything other than stare from her position on the floor.

A loud yelp sounded from Mandy as Jack slammed his gun across her head. The woman crumpled under the force, her body hitting the floor with a loud thud.

Jack kicked her gun away, then immediately trained his own weapon on Ronald. "Move away from her slowly." His voice had a deadly—and damn terrifying—edge to it.

He had that same look in his eyes he'd had after he shot those men. Seeing him in action now sent shivers snaking throughout her body. He'd been bossy as hell with her, but he hadn't been scary. Not even when she'd tried to escape. If anything he'd just been frustrated. She was so glad she wasn't on the receiving end of his wrath.

Wordlessly, her boss pushed up from the floor and stood.

"Now sit. Hands on the desk where I can see them."

"You okay, Soph?" Jack asked, never taking his eyes off Ronald.

"I'm fine." The way he shortened her name warmed her insides, but she brushed it away. Moving quickly, she shut and locked the door.

"Take off your tie," Jack ordered Ronald.

Sophie came up to stand next to Jack. "What are you doing?"

"I want you to tie her up," he said quietly.

Ronald slid the tie across the desk. Without making eye contact, Sophie took it and bound her assistant's wrists tightly behind her back. Mandy didn't move once. When Sophie rolled her over, she was deadweight. Maybe things would register later, but for now it was hard to feel anything for a woman who had just told her with no emotion she was going to kill her.

"You can sit, Sophie," Jack said. She couldn't help noticing that his voice softened when he said her name. And she didn't know what to do with the feelings that evoked inside her. She certainly liked it, though. Way too much.

She sat on the edge of one of the seats across from Ronald's desk. Jack did the same, but his gun never wavered.

"Who are you?" Ronald asked.

"You are going to answer my questions. If I think you're lying, I will kill you." Sophie didn't think he would, but Jack's icy voice was convincing. "How long have you been working for Miguel Vargas?"

Ronald shot a mournful look at Sophie, then returned his gaze to Jack. "Six months."

Hearing him admit it sent a punch of shock slamming into Sophie. She'd known Ronald for years. He'd devoted his life to helping people. It was the reason he'd started SBMS. To get medical supplies to countries that otherwise wouldn't have any. How had he become involved with a man like Vargas?

Jack continued, that same edge in his voice. "Who is he working with in Africa?"

"I don't know."

Jack's gun hand shifted along the desk and Ronald threw his arms up.

"I don't know, I swear. Miguel doesn't tell me anything."

"Why does he want Sophie dead?"

"I . . . I'm not sure. He knows she was at Keane's hangar Sunday night. And now he also *knows* she took pictures."

Jack was silent for a moment as he watched Ronald. "Is that why he tried to have her killed?"

Ronald nodded and once again Sophie felt as if someone had punched her right in the gut. Ronald had *known* Vargas tried to kill her. She struggled to find her voice, wanting to know if it had been before or after she'd almost died the first time.

Jack took a menacing, controlled step closer to the desk. "Did you know he planned to kill her?"

Tears burned Sophie's eyes as she waited for the answer.

"No, I swear it. He called me Monday and said he'd be taking care of her, but then you guys disappeared. When she called me I told her to stay away." He turned to look at her then. "I *told* you to stay out of Miami. Sophie, you have to believe me, I never thought you'd be affected by any of this. It's—"

"Shut the fuck up. You don't talk to her unless I give you permission." Jack tapped the desk with his gun, drawing Ronald's attention back to him.

Ronald paled as he stared at Jack. "How long has Mandy worked here, Sophie?" he asked her, his focus never wavering from Ronald.

She wiped away the few stray tears threatening to spill over, refusing to cry in front of either of them. "About a year, but she interned here her senior year in college."

Jack's mouth pulled into a thin line as he directed his next statement to Ronald. "You said you've been working with Vargas six months."

Ronald shifted nervously in his seat, his eyes on the weapon. "I have. I didn't know Mandy even worked for him until tonight. I swear! She said she's been monitoring Sophie's actions and basically admitted she's the one who told Vargas that Sophie took pictures at the hangar. She found them on her computer."

Sophie gripped the edge of the chair. If Mandy had been monitoring her, then Vargas would definitely have known of Hannah's importance in her life. Hannah was the only friend who called the office. Hell, Sophie had even invited Mandy out to have drinks with the two of them on more than one occasion. That treacherous bitch.

The fear and worry she'd been keeping at bay pushed at her again, making her entire body tense, but she ruthlessly shoved them back down. She had to get through one problem at a time.

Chapter 13

Tradecraft: the methods developed by intelligence operatives to conduct their operations.

Jack tilted his head toward Sophie but still didn't take his eyes off Ronald. "Sophie, I want you to take a picture of Mandy with the cell phone I gave you."

"Uh, okay. Why?"

Always so inquisitive. Jack bit back a smile despite the situation. "I'm going to send her picture to my boss and see if they get a hit." Normally he would handle an interrogation situation *very* differently, but with Sophie in the room, he was keeping himself restrained.

Barely.

Ronald was holding something back. Jack could feel it straight to his bones. Every time the man spoke, Jack could see the lies and worry in his eyes.

Jack waited as Sophie stood and did as he asked. When he heard the faint click of the phone, he spoke again. "Sophie, there's a supply closet at the end of this hall. I want you to find anything you can to further restrain Mandy."

Though he couldn't see her, he could actually feel Sophie pause before leaving. Probably because she could sense the contained violence inside him. It wasn't directed at her. Could *never* be directed at her. But if Ronald had had anything to do with those men going after Sophie, Jack would kill him here and now. Everything else including his fucking job could be damned. The thought of this bastard being in on that hit against her life made the primal man he kept locked down come roaring to the surface with the need to protect a woman who could never be his.

When he heard the door close behind her, he rounded the desk. With a foot, Jack shoved the chair back and placed his weapon over Ronald's knee. "What aren't you telling me?" Getting information out of people could be tricky. And Jack didn't have time to figure out this guy's weaknesses. Information gained from torture was rarely reliable, but the fear of pain was often worse.

"They have my daughter," the other man whispered.

Jack paused, mentally reviewing the dossier he had on Weller's family. It said his daughter was backpacking through Europe with friends. "How long?"

Beads of sweat rolled down his face. "Six months. So far they say they haven't harmed her, but they threatened to kill her if I didn't help with some of their deliveries."

"Who are they working with in Africa?" Jack had already asked, but he still wasn't convinced Ronald was telling the truth.

"I wasn't lying when I said I didn't know. All I'm in charge of is providing a cover to get into places they normally couldn't."

"What about Keane Flight?"

"Paul is—was, I guess—in charge of doctoring flight logs and in some cases he deleted trips entirely. We coordinated our stories and I updated everything here."

Okay, that lined up with what Keane had told Wesley. "When's your next meeting with Vargas?"

"This weekend. Maybe sooner. He's promised I'll have my daughter back."

This was why people should call in professionals when

they were in trouble. "Did you call any law enforcement about this?"

Weller snorted. "No. Who could I have called? The local cops? The feds? She was taken in another country. They have no jurisdiction there, and law enforcement in most South American countries are too scared of Vargas. And . . ." He swallowed hard, fear bleeding into his eyes.

"What?" Jack pressed the gun harder against his knee.

"As soon as Vargas contacted me, he also sent me the bloody ear of someone. Told me it belonged to the son of someone who'd tried to go behind his back and involve cops. He said if I wanted my daughter back in one piece I'd follow his instructions or I'd start receiving boxes of her . . . body parts." His voice cracked on the last word.

"When's the last time you talked to him?" Jack asked, his voice monotone. He needed this guy to keep his cool.

"This morning."

"When's the last time you talked to your daughter?"

His shoulders slumped. "Couple days ago."

Jack sheathed his weapon in his shoulder holster and went back to sit across from Ronald. "You realize that once you give him what he wants, he will kill your daughter?"

Ronald shook his head. "He promised that—"

"He's a drug lord, Ronald. And he's helping a terrorist faction in North Africa bring biological weapons into this country. Do you *really* think he'll keep his word?" *Fucking moron.*

Ronald's mouth dropped open. "I thought he was just running drugs."

Could he really be that naive? Or maybe he'd just wanted to hold on to hope for his daughter's sake. Once a person gave up the last shred of hope, it was over. Jack scrubbed a hand over his face. People never ceased to amaze him. "You have one thing going for you."

"What?"

"You said you're meeting him in days, so if Miguel is coming to Miami, something big is going down. Next time you talk to him, demand to talk to your daughter and don't take no for an answer. You need to make sure he's bringing her with him."

"But what if—"

"You have something he wants. Even if he threatens your daughter, tell him you need proof. If he doesn't comply, hang up on him. You'll push him into a corner and get him off balance."

He shook his head almost violently. "I can't do that. He's been letting me talk to her at regular times. I can't—"

"If you value your daughter's life you will. Trust me when I say I've done this before. If you don't start negotiating with him, he'll push and push until he knows you'll agree to just about anything." It was how predators like Vargas worked.

Jack stood as Sophie entered the room carrying twine.

"What are you going to do now?" Worry and a heavy dose of fear laced Ronald's voice.

Jack pointed to Mandy's unmoving form. "Get rid of one of your problems."

"Are you going to . . . ," Ronald started, but didn't finish.

"No, I'm not going to kill her. She'll be picked up by the people I work for." And they very well might kill her, but that wasn't Jack's problem. Considering that the woman was the reason Sophie had almost been killed, he didn't care if she died.

Ronald stood. "If she's working for him, Vargas will know something's wrong. You can't—"

"Sit down and calm down. He's going to think she skipped town. If Vargas asks about Mandy—which I doubt he will because he'll be admitting she was a mole in your company—you tell him you haven't seen her."

"What do you want me to do now?"

"Nothing. Go home to your wife and act like this conversation never happened. I'll be in contact tomorrow." Jack turned to Sophie. "Did you see anyone in the hall?"

She shook her head, but he didn't miss the hurt look she shot Weller before returning her attention to him.

Jack gritted his teeth. He understood that the man was trying to save his daughter, but he'd been willing to sacrifice Sophie. The pain in her dark eyes as she watched him lift Mandy off the floor tore at his insides like razor wire.

Jack understood how she felt and more than anything, he wanted to wipe that lost look off her face and hurt the person who had put it there. He wanted it so badly he had to contain the sudden, very real urge to clock Weller across the face. It wouldn't do any good other than make him feel better, and Sophie didn't need any more violence in her life.

Hannah couldn't fight the terror forking through her system. The man with the scar hadn't cuffed or tied her hands. Maybe that was a good thing. Or maybe their security was so tight, he wasn't worried about her trying to escape.

Garish yellow lights illuminated their way, creating creepy shadows. There weren't any guards along the hallway, and the three other holding cells were empty. Though she did notice a dark reddish stain on the floor of one. When they came to a steel door with bars covering the small window, the man next to her pulled out keys.

When he opened the door, she was surprised to step out into a garden of sorts. "Where are we?" she asked, even though she knew it would likely be pointless.

No answer.

The ocean was nearby. She couldn't hear waves, but the salty smell was unmistakable. Maybe Holly was right. Maybe they were in Cuba. The air was humid, but it wasn't too hot, which meant maybe they were in one of the Caribbean islands. Or maybe they were still in Florida. She drank in her surroundings as they walked across a grassy incline toward the back of a palatial house. Her breath caught when she saw two armed men standing in the shadows near a giant oak tree.

Okay, then. They were definitely not alone. That was why the scarred man hadn't bothered to bind her wrists. If she ran, she'd be shot. No wonder Holly hadn't tried to escape.

As they neared the house she spotted a familiar-looking man sitting on the brightly lit veranda. *Miguel Vargas.* The name had sounded familiar earlier, but now that she was in front of him she remembered seeing him on the news.

The man next to her roughly grabbed her arm and pushed her onto a cushioned seat across from Vargas. Her skin briefly stung from the treatment.

"Thank you for joining me," Vargas said. His voice was surprisingly smooth and calm and almost charming.

"Did I have a choice?" She inwardly chided herself for the automatic smart-ass answer. Her mother was right, her smart mouth would definitely get her into trouble one day. Probably today.

He ignored her question. "Do you know why you are here?"

She shook her head.

His lips pulled into a thin line and any hint of charm he'd had a second before vanished. "Why were you leaving your house in the middle of the night?"

A battle waged in her head. She couldn't tell him what she didn't know and it wasn't as if she was betraying Sophie. The man in front of her obviously knew something. Something in her gut told her she needed to be smart if she wanted to survive this conversation. "My friend called me and told me to run."

"Friend?"

She shifted in her seat but didn't respond. His dark gaze was penetrating and downright scary.

"Don't make me repeat myself." That razor-sharp edge to his voice sent fear slithering down her spine.

"Her name is Sophie Moreno."

His head tilted slightly to the side. "An honest answer. Good. Who is the man she's with?"

"I don't know."

When his dark eyes flashed in anger, she knew she'd said the wrong thing even if it was true.

"I swear I don't know! She just met him and she didn't expand on who he was. The only thing I know is that she told me my life was in danger and that I needed to hide somewhere that even she wouldn't know about. She was very forceful about that."

"What else? Did she say where she was going?"

"No. I could hear the man in the background and he told her to get off the phone before I could ask any questions."

"How were you going to contact her?" His eyes narrowed a fraction. It was almost imperceptible, but she knew he was testing her.

"What?" Blood rushed in her ears. *Think,* she silently screamed at herself.

"What number were you supposed to call?" He bit the words out.

"She didn't give me one. She was going to call me." She could taste the lie in her mouth, but she prayed he wouldn't sense it. There was no way she was going to give him the number her best friend had given her. For all she knew he could trace it.

He stared at her, his expression unrelenting and hard, but she forced herself not to squirm. Finally he spoke. "Don't get too comfortable. We'll be leaving soon."

"What are you going to do to Sophie?"

He chuckled as he motioned to one of his men. "*I'm* not going to do anything, but your friend is likely dead by now anyway. You are simply insurance in case she's not."

Pain sliced through her. Sophie was her best friend. Hell, one of her only real friends. "You son of a bitch!" Her words were cut off as the scarred man once again grabbed her by the arm and yanked her from her seat.

Tears stung her eyes as he dragged her back across the lawn. She wanted to scream and struggle but knew it wouldn't do any good. Besides, now of all times she needed to keep a level head. If only there was some way she could escape and warn Sophie. She was fairly sure there wasn't an American embassy in Cuba, but there was a naval base. Considering that she didn't know where they were, she sure as hell wouldn't know how to get to the naval base.

If she could escape, though, she'd find a way.

Chapter 14

Sanitize: to delete specific material or revise a report or other document to prevent the identification of intelligence sources and collection methods.

Carrying Mandy down to the garage was a risk, but their window of opportunity was closing fast and Jack needed to get out of this building. He gauged that Mandy was supposed to take care of Sophie, then no doubt check in with her boss.

When they reached the bottom of the stairwell, Sophie finally spoke. "What exactly do you plan to do to her?"

"We're going to tie her up better and lock her in the utility room."

"Won't she be . . . I mean, will she . . . How long are you leaving her here?"

"I need to contact Wesley and have him send someone he trusts to pick her up. Why don't you go sit in the vehicle while I take care of this?" Considering he and Wesley had no clue who the mole was, they had to be careful about who they trusted with this information. Especially since Jack planned to make it look as if Mandy had disappeared.

Sophie took the keys from his hand, not even arguing about staying to help, which told him a hell of a lot about her state of mind. After jimmying the lock, he dragged Mandy into the small room, bound her feet, rebound her hands with twine, and placed the tie around her mouth. Then he tied her arms to a metal cabinet bolted to the wall. Not bad for last-minute business.

When he was finished, Jack found Sophie strapped in on the passenger side.

"You all right?" he asked as he steered out of the garage, keeping his voice low and soothing.

"I guess. What did you guys talk about while I was gone? And don't say nothing." Her voice sounded so small it tore at him.

"Long story short, Vargas has your boss's daughter—"

"Holly?" Sophie gasped. "I thought she was backpacking for a few months."

Jack shook his head. "Not anymore. Vargas has been using Ronald to do his dirty work by using her as leverage. Then when you took those pictures, you became a target. My guess is he wants you out of the way by this weekend. There's probably a big deal going down in a couple days, but we can work this to our advantage."

"How?"

"I think we'll be able to convince Weller to help us bring Vargas down."

"What if Ronald doesn't want to help?"

"Too damn bad." Jack pressed on the accelerator.

Sophie was silent for a few long moments and he wished he knew what she was thinking. Someone she cared about had betrayed her trust, and he knew that cut deep. When she spoke, however, her voice was lighter than he expected. "We're not going back to that motel, are we?"

He shot her a sideways glance. *"No."*

"Where are we going, then?"

"You might not like this place any better. I found a cheap hostel close to the beach. They accept cash and I'm pretty sure they don't have video cameras outside. We'll probably be the oldest people there." They had private rooms, free Wi-Fi, and it was in a safe part of town. That was all that mattered. But first . . . "We have one more stop to make before then."

"Where?"

"Mandy's condo."

"You know where she lives? Of course you do," she said, answering her own question with a shake of her head.

As they pulled into the parking lot of Mandy's condominium complex—which he'd memorized from her small, obviously not thorough enough file—Jack took note of the number of cars and exits. After brief surveillance, Jack was satisfied there wasn't anyone watching the place. She lived on the second floor of a high-rise in an exclusive part of South Beach, but the lock was a low-end Schlage. So damn typical.

They slipped inside the front door without any trouble. He withdrew his weapon and started down the hallway toward the interior. A kitchen to the left was the first entrance. He cleared it, then continued. The hallway opened into a big living room with a sliding glass door that led to a balcony.

Since the living room was clear, he swept the only other hallway to the right. The master bedroom and office were also clear.

"Start with her bedroom. Pack a small bag of her clothes and take all her jewelry and cosmetics. Leave things messy. Make it look like she left in a hurry," Jack said as soon as he finished with the last room.

While Sophie was busy, he started in Mandy's office. After downloading anything that looked as if it might be helpful from her computer, he sent Wesley a message, then riffled through her two-drawer filing cabinet.

"What about shoes and stuff?" Sophie called out from the other room.

"Grab a few pairs. Make it look good . . . Oh, see if she's got any nail polish remover in the bathroom."

Sophie stepped in and handed him a half-empty bottle of pink liquid. "The bag is packed. Why do you need nail polish remover?"

"I'm making this look good." He shoved the drawer shut, then rounded back to the other side of the desk. After tipping the computer tower on its side, he poured the liquid through the round vent, then stomped on it. It might not destroy everything on the hard drive, but it would make Mandy look even guiltier. And it would send Vargas's men in the wrong direction. They'd be wondering where she went and who she talked to before she left. Hopefully this would take some of the pressure off Ronald Weller.

"Her place is very sterile," Sophie commented as he stood.

"I noticed." The place had a few tropical pictures hung up, but all the walls were stark white, and there weren't any personal pictures. The office had an inexpensive fiberboard desk, a metal filing cabinet, and an office chair. Even her bedroom was bleak. No pictures, no television. Just one dresser and a bed. With the exception of her expensive clothes and a few bottles of pricy perfume, the place looked as if she might have been planning to leave anyway.

"Do you think she was planning to leave town?" Sophie asked, reading his mind.

"I think it's more than probable. Vargas probably approached her with a deal she couldn't pass up. He pays well, but she's likely smart enough to realize she's expendable and eventually, she would be a liability to him."

"Expendable," Sophie murmured before turning and walking out.

Damn it. His gut twisted as he watched her disappear from the room. Ronald had treated her as if she was expendable, and he wasn't the first person to do so. She didn't have to say any more for Jack to understand what she was thinking.

At the moment he wanted nothing more than to wrap his

arms around her, but they needed to get out of there. He flipped off the light in the office, then followed her to the master bedroom. Half the hangers were on the floor, and clothes were scattered around the carpet. "Nice job," he said quietly.

He was rewarded by a small smile that did something insane to his insides. Hefting the bag onto his shoulder, he flipped off the light, then drew back the floor-length blinds to reveal another sliding glass door.

Sophie came up next to him. "Think she hid anything on her porch?"

He shook his head. "No, I just wanted to check—"

She stiffened as a rattling sound reverberated through the place. She opened her mouth, but he held one finger to his lips and opened the glass door. He motioned for her to step outside, then shut it quietly behind them.

They stepped into the shadows of the porch, but the darkness wouldn't provide them cover for long. He glanced over the balcony, then tossed the bag onto the grassy area.

"Come on. I'll hoist you over," he whispered.

Sophie's eyes widened as she glanced over the balcony. She shook her head, but loud cursing from inside spurred her into action. He climbed over the ledge and she followed. Staring at him with those big dark eyes, she clutched on to the railing.

He glanced down again. The drop wasn't far, and they had a soft, grassy landing.

"On the count of three," he whispered.

On three he pushed off and landed with a thud. He rolled onto the grass before jumping to his feet. She still hung on.

"Sophie," he whispered, fighting panic. He was too far to help her if someone discovered her.

Staring down at him, she shook her head. It was dark, but with the moon and lighting from other balconies, he could see her expression clearly and she looked terrified.

"I'm right here," he whispered again.

Something must have startled her because she turned back around toward the balcony, then looked at him and pushed off.

She landed with a quiet yelp, but he didn't give her time to react. Jack grabbed the bag and her arm and they started running parallel to the building. Weapon drawn, he rounded the corner of the building and found himself staring down the barrel of a SIG. No matter how many times he'd been in the same position, having a loaded gun pointed at his head didn't get any easier.

Without pause, he lifted his own weapon.

Behind him, Sophie gasped, but he focused on the man in front of him. Thinking about her could get them both killed and he needed to stay calm.

"Put your weapon down," his friend—ex-friend—Levi ordered.

His finger twitched on the trigger. "You first."

A long moment ticked by. "Same time?"

Jack narrowed his eyes but nodded. As Levi lowered his weapon, Jack followed suit so that they both held their weapons at their sides. "What the hell are you doing working for Vargas?"

"You have forty-five seconds to get to your vehicle and get the hell out of here before Vargas's guys spot you."

Jack felt as if he were staring into the eyes of a stranger. "Damn it, Levi, I just heard about Meghan and I'm sorry, but talk to me. What's going on? Why are you working for that piece of shit?"

"My problem isn't with you. Stay out of my way and I'll stay out of yours. You're down to forty seconds now." His voice was icy.

Jack could stand there all day and not squeeze any information out of him. "Fine . . . How deep are you involved with Vargas?"

"Deep enough to know he's got a mole in the NSA. You need to close that leak."

Jack didn't show any outward reaction. He couldn't afford to. Whatever he'd originally thought about Levi, it didn't sound as if he was betraying his country. This *had* to be about revenge. It was the only thing that made sense. Maybe that was wishful thinking, but he'd known this man too long. "Is this about her death?"

Levi's jaw clenched once, but he gave an imperceptible nod.

"Why are you telling me this?"

He snorted. "Because fuck Vargas, that's why. He's a means to an end. You've got thirty seconds now."

Jack blocked Sophie's body with his as they walked around Levi. "You almost got us killed in Marathon. You get in my way again, I'll put a bullet in your head."

"I wouldn't expect any less," Levi said.

Jack stayed close to Sophie as they rushed down the side of the building. But he kept his eye on Levi, who still hadn't moved.

Once they made it to the other corner, he had full visibility of the parking lot. No one was around. Levi must have been their lookout man.

Jack didn't say a word, but Sophie remained close as they maneuvered their way toward the SUV. Tomorrow he'd have to ditch it, but for now they needed it to get to the hostel.

Once they'd pulled out of the parking lot, Sophie breathlessly asked, "Why did he let us go?"

"I have no clue."

"Do you think he'll follow us?"

"No. I don't know what he's doing, but he's not interested in us." This had everything to do with his wife's death. Jack was sure even if he didn't know the details. The truth was, if someone killed Sophie he didn't even want to think about what he'd do to get revenge.

"Do you think . . . we could stop by Hannah's house? She still hasn't called and I'm worried."

Considering he'd already dragged Sophie all over the city and nearly gotten her killed more than once, he couldn't knowingly put her in more danger. "Her house is probably being watched. It's not a good idea."

"Isn't this what you do? Can't you get us in without being seen?" She bit her bottom lip and he could feel himself caving.

"No."

"Unless I'm your hostage, I'm going with or without you. Decide if you want to help me or not, because I'm going."

She would too. He could see it in the stubborn set of her jaw.

And the truth was, he couldn't physically restrain her and keep her captive. Not knowing her history. Hell, he couldn't do it no matter what. Not to Sophie. "We'll drive by, check out the area, and *if* it looks safe, I'll double back and enter from the backyard. Do you know what kind of security system she has?"

"She doesn't have one and she keeps a key hidden in case she locks herself out. Not that breaking in should be a problem for *you*." He didn't miss the wry note in her voice.

"Where's her key?"

"In the fake plant hanging on the front porch. It's in a small magnetic holder."

His hands tightened around the steering wheel. He couldn't comprehend that kind of naivete. "Please tell me you don't have a key anywhere outside your place."

"No."

Thank God. "Do you at least have a security system?"

"No, but I live in a safe neighborhood."

He snorted. "That's going to change."

"Excuse me?" She lifted a dark eyebrow.

"When this is all over, I'm having one installed for you."

She could make whatever she wanted out of that. He knew there was no future for them, but if he could take care of her, even in a small way, he was going to. She looked surprised but didn't respond.

Since he already knew Hannah's address, he took the shortest route there. Sophie was silent on the short drive over. As they cruised by Hannah's bungalow-style home, he didn't see anything out of the ordinary. "Is her garage door normally closed?"

"Yeah, she keeps her car parked in it."

He didn't slow his speed as they cruised past, but there weren't any vans or cars parked across the street. That was a good sign. But it didn't mean her house wasn't being watched.

"So, what are we doing now?"

"*We* aren't doing anything. I'm going to park and do a little recon. *You* are going to wait in the vehicle."

"The hell I am. This is stolen. What if the cops stop me while I'm sitting in it?"

Doubtful, considering he'd switched the plates. "That's not going to happen."

"I'll follow you and you can't stop me." She unsnapped her seat belt as he steered into a spot behind a parked car on the street over.

He bit back a frustrated growl. Her stubborn streak had definitely not faded with time. "This'll be easier if I can get in and get out without worrying about you."

"She's my best friend. I'm going." Her fingers were already wrapped around the door handle.

Sighing, he said, "Come on."

The street was quiet, and after a quick scan of the houses on the neighboring street, he picked the only house with a chain-link fence as opposed to a privacy fence. To give her credit, Sophie didn't chatter and she stuck close to him. After the past couple of days they'd had, he couldn't blame her for wanting to check on her friend. Jumping the fences was easy enough and there weren't any big dogs or men with weapons waiting for them either.

When he was sure they weren't being watched, he jimmied the back lock—which was worse than Mandy's. He could have gotten the key, but didn't want to expose himself more than necessary.

As they entered, all his survival instincts were on high alert, but there was no one in the house. He could feel almost immediately that they were alone. It was indescribable, but that sensation he got when danger was near wasn't knocking away at his brain as it had so many times in the past.

The living room looked lived in, but nothing was broken or tossed. Same with the kitchen. When they reached the only bedroom, he leaned close to Sophie and tried to ignore his body's response when his mouth grazed her ear. Under different circumstances he'd give anything to suck her earlobe between his lips and feather kisses along her soft skin. "Check to see if her suitcase and clothes are missing. I'm going to check the garage."

She nodded and her hair tickled his nose. As she brushed past him, his cock went on full alert. It didn't matter that the timing was inappropriate, his body just reacted around her. He deserved a fucking medal for keeping his distance over the past couple of days. Especially when she'd made it clear she'd welcome him into her bed. But if he crossed that line now, how the hell could he go back to his life without her?

He couldn't.

Pushing back his hunger, he hurried to the garage and opened the door. He swept his flashlight around the empty space and froze when he spotted shards of glass and a red scarf near the garage door. It could mean any number of things, none of which he was informing Sophie about. If Vargas's guys had taken Hannah, they'd have taken her car and disposed of it somewhere. That was why the house wasn't a wreck. If the police were called, nothing in her house would look out of order.

As he pulled the door shut, Sophie's subtle, exotic scent tickled his nose. The mango, citrusy smell would be forever etched in his mind. He schooled his face before turning toward her. "Her car's gone."

"A lot of her clothes and toiletries are gone too," she whispered back. "That's good, right?"

"Yep. Let's get out of here."

Once they were back in the SUV, some of the tension built up in his shoulders loosened a fraction. He felt guilty about keeping what he'd seen from her, but if he told her she'd be eaten alive with worry. And he wouldn't do that to her. Not when she couldn't do a damn thing about it.

She sagged against the leather seat. "I still can't believe all this is happening."

"I know, and I'm sorry you got dragged into any of it. I know I said it earlier, but you really are handling this better than any civilian I've ever worked with." True, he hadn't worked with many, but the few he had normally lost their heads. Hell, he'd worked with trained agents who lost their shit during gunfire.

She chuckled and shook her head.

Something told him that her time in foster care had a lot to do with her coping. She'd grown up learning to hide her emotions and put on a happy face for the world. Except with him. With him, she'd always been herself. Where most people had thought she was a snob growing up, he'd figured out early that she was just quiet. She'd moved around too much to let people in. Something he understood.

"How much longer until we get there?" she asked, drawing his attention to her mouth.

"Soon, I promise." Though he wondered if that was a

good thing. They would soon be sharing a room again, and he only had so much restraint.

"Thank God."

Flashing neon lights and throngs of people wearing skimpy dresses and designer clothes passed them in a blur as they cruised down Ocean Drive. He'd never been to the hostel, but he recognized some of the landmarks from their Web site's photo gallery. After turning down a few side streets, he located it off Washington Avenue.

"*This* is the hostel?" Sophie stared at him as they pulled into the semifull parking lot.

"Yeah, why?"

"It's so . . . nice. I backpacked through Europe one summer and *never* stayed anywhere like this."

Jack shrugged and unloaded their bags. The simple two-story building was located in the Art Deco district, and as long as no one was shooting at them he didn't care where they stayed. He wouldn't mind sleeping on the beach if he had to. Especially if he had Sophie to keep him warm.

As soon as they walked through the front door, they were greeted by two giggling, drunk college-aged girls who placed leis around their necks. There were eight other people in the lounge area. Jack quickly assessed them. They all looked drunk but harmless. And they weren't paying Sophie or him any attention.

The flashing purple lights and modular seating reminded him of a club. Sophie was right. This wasn't like any hostel he'd ever stayed in either.

"Which way do we go?" Sophie asked.

To the right was a bar area, and the room to the left of the lobby had a pool table and a row of computers. "Let's try this way."

As soon as they stepped inside, a man about his age wearing a white polo shirt greeted them. The man stuck out his hand. "Hi, I'm Mark, the owner. Are you folks looking for a place to stay?"

Jack took his hand and smiled. "My name is Robert Smith. I called earlier about the private room."

"Oh, right, dude. Sorry, the one with the two twin beds is gone, but I've still got one private room left. Only one bed, though. That a problem?"

The thought of sharing a bed with her was too damn tempting. He glanced at Sophie—hoping his internal reaction wasn't visible on his face—and she shrugged. "Nope. Show us the way."

They followed the man through the computer room and down a plain white hallway.

The owner opened the last door on the left and turned to face them. "There's a dollar-fifty happy hour every night from six to eight. No curfew, but if you come in after three, try to keep it down."

"That won't be a problem." Jack fished out enough bills to cover three nights and handed them to the man.

The outer areas might be bright and colorful, but their matchbox-sized room was painted a dull white. No cheap art hanging on the walls, just a bed, a nightstand, and a plastic plant.

Sophie sat on the edge of the bed. "Want to hit the shower first?"

"No, you can. I'll take the floor, so don't worry." He unzipped his bag and pulled out the plastic bag she'd shoved her stuff into earlier.

To his surprise, her lips pulled into a thin line. "We're both adults. After everything I've been through in the past forty-eight hours, I *think* I can handle sleeping in the same bed with you." She snatched the bag from his hand and before he could respond, she'd slammed the bathroom door behind her.

*   *   *

Sophie turned the shower on before collapsing onto the closed toilet seat. His offer to take the floor had been sweet, but for some reason it had seriously pissed her off. It was as if he'd just lit the match on her temper. And deep down, she knew why.

Thoughts of Sam had been bombarding her all day. They'd been mixed in with every other crazy thing that had happened. Watching Jack move, the way he'd stood up for her, protected her . . . it was fucking with her head. And all she could picture was one of her last memories with Sam. Not the last, but this one was brutal enough because it had been the beginning of the end for them. She hated that she kept seeing Sam when she looked at Jack but couldn't figure out what was wrong with her.

Squeezing her eyes shut, she tried to banish the memory that wouldn't go away, but it was impossible. The treacherous images played over and over like a bad movie.

Sophie stretched out on Sam's bare chest, resting her chin on her hands as she watched him. They were in his bedroom, where they usually hung out when Ms. Bigsby was gone. His bed was bigger and softer and she liked it better because it smelled like him.

"What are you doing?" he murmured, a half smile playing across his hard features, but he didn't open his eyes.

Pale eyes she swore could see right into her soul. He was the only person she'd ever truly loved. She hadn't told him. She couldn't find the courage yet. If she did, she was afraid he'd be taken from her. Things between them were so good, and in her experience, good things didn't last long.

"Watching you fake sleep," she whispered, wishing he was kissing and touching her. She loved it when he touched her. He made her feel so treasured. As if she mattered.

The humming sound of the air conditioner was steady and loud, filling the otherwise quiet house. Ms. Bigsby was away for her bingo night and there weren't any other kids in the house except them.

Soon Sophie wouldn't be living here and she couldn't wait. Only two months left until she turned eighteen—and in one month she'd graduate from high school. Sam turned eighteen in a month, a week before they graduated. He planned to join the Marines then. He'd told her he was thinking about waiting a month, but she could tell he didn't want to wait, so she'd told him no. Besides, he'd have nowhere to stay except with friends for that month, and that didn't make sense—even if deep down she didn't want to let him go just yet. But she figured she'd rather him be in boot camp while she was still living here. Then when she was free, she could get a place of her own. She had a lot of scholarships for college lined up, but she'd found a small diamond ring hidden in one of Sam's drawers. Well, it wasn't hidden very well since she'd stumbled across it. She might be wrong, but Sophie was pretty sure he was going to propose when she turned eighteen. He was only a month older than her, but he'd probably wait. Even though he hadn't told her he loved her, she knew he did. And the thought of marrying him, of finally belonging to someone, was heaven.

They were so young, but if he asked, she'd say yes. And she'd follow him anywhere. She could put off college for six months and then go to school anywhere with her grades. She'd applied to colleges all over the country simply because she could. And she'd gotten into ninety percent of them. So, wherever Sam was stationed, she could go. She was all about planning and there was no way she was giving up a man like Sam. He was totally it for her.

"What are you thinking of?" *Sam's deep voice had her blinking and she realized that she'd been staring off into space.*

"What we did an hour ago." *She grinned when his face turned red.*

Nothing ever seemed to faze him, but since they'd started dating and having sex, it was so easy to mess with him. She loved that he only got like that with her. With everyone else he was this big, tough guy. Not with her. He was just her Sam.

Before she could blink, he had her pinned flat on her back underneath him. He was wearing boxers, but she was still naked and could feel his reaction to her. It made her entire body tingle. Their first time had hurt a little, and he'd been nervous about making sure it was good for her, but ever since then it had been amazing. Sam liked to take his time and use his mouth on her in places that would have grossed her out only months ago. Now she loved it. Loved doing the same to him in return. As they started kissing and she grew even more turned on, the doorbell rang.

Sophie's eyes flew open and Sam froze above her. Ms. Bigsby wouldn't ring the doorbell and it was way too early for her to be back anyway. The older lady never left bingo night early either. Sam jumped off her and they quickly dressed as someone started knocking.

"Should we answer it?" she whispered, though she wasn't sure why.

He nodded and she stayed behind him as they headed down the hallway and he peered through the peephole. "It's the cops."

Sam looked at her and shrugged as he opened the door. There were two police officers and one woman Sophie recognized from DHS. Dread settled in her stomach. She knew things had been too good to be true right now. Of course something bad would happen to mess it up. The cops and DHS meant one thing: they were moving to another home. And it was unlikely she and Sam would get to stick together.

Chapter 15

OSINT: open-source intelligence; information derived from publicly available sources.

Hannah sagged against the steel door after the guard slammed it shut. The sound of the heavy lock sliding into place made her jump. At least she wasn't in front of that monster Vargas anymore. Just looking into his eyes had made her skin crawl.

"You okay?" Holly was stretched out on the bed, but sat up, her face worried.

"Yeah. That guy Vargas wanted to ask me questions." Hannah just hoped he'd believed her lies.

"About what?"

"He wanted to know more about Sophie. . . . Has he asked you questions too?"

Holly shook her head. "No. He kidnapped me to use as leverage against my dad. I only have one purpose for him."

"Leverage?" Sophie hadn't told Hannah much and she was more than a little curious.

"My dad works with different flight companies to get into some really hard-to-reach places. His company has been around so long that they're basically above reproach, and I think Vargas capitalized on his reputation. . . . Do you think Sophie was working with Vargas or something?"

"Hell no! Whatever's going on, Sophie was trying to keep me safe. There's no way she'd ever do business with some drug runner." That much Hannah knew. Sophie had been her best friend since college. More like a sister actually. If she got too much change at a restaurant, she gave it back to the waitress. No way was Sophie involved in any of this—whatever *this* was. For a moment she felt bad for what she'd just said because it was obvious Holly's dad *was* working with a drug runner or whatever, but that was the least of her worries right now.

Hannah glanced around the room, eyeing the ceiling, which looked like all slab concrete. Just like the walls. The entire room was concrete. No doubt to stop people from escaping through the ceiling. "Have you tried the window?"

Again, Holly shook her head and placed a finger over her mouth, then pointed toward the sink.

Frowning, Hannah crouched down by the sink and peered underneath it. There was a tiny black rectangular device that was blinking red. When Hannah stood, Holly continued.

"Trying to escape is pointless. They'll just catch us." Holly stood near the sink and turned the water on. She nodded toward the window, then motioned with her hands for Hannah to lean closer. "One of the guys must have just put this in while you were gone. They let me out for a walk and when I came back, I found it." Her voice was barely above a whisper.

They were both silent for a moment until Holly turned off the water.

"How were you kidnapped?" Hannah asked since this wasn't the kind of information that could be used against either of them.

"I was in South America on a backpacking trip when two men took me. I'd planned to stay there for a month, then head to Europe for a couple months. They must have been tracking my family's movements and honestly, my trip wasn't a secret. I posted about it on Facebook, so for all I know, that's how they found out about me coming here. Now I wish I'd just gone straight to Europe. I wanted to take some time off . . ."

As they continued making idle conversation, Holly stood by the window, crouched down, and motioned for Hannah to get on her shoulders. Hannah shimmied up her back until she was sitting on her shoulders. Holly tottered for a second, but quickly gained her balance. Hannah barely weighed a hundred pounds, but Holly was probably only twenty more than her. Still, she was taller than Hannah, so that gave them a little more height.

Placing her hands against the glass, she tried to push. There was no give, but it wasn't double paned. Hannah was certain she could break it. Unfortunately it would make noise. Somehow they'd have to cover it—

The door flew open with a bang. Holly swiveled and when she did, Hannah toppled onto the bed. A dark-haired man— not the one who'd taken her to see Vargas—stood in the doorway. *Oh, shit.* There was no denying what they'd been trying to do. Unable to move, she felt like that proverbial deer in headlights.

The man glanced back and forth between them, then spoke quietly to Holly.

Thanks to Sophie, Hannah knew a few Spanish phrases. She picked out a couple of words, and the guy's tone wasn't threatening, so maybe he wasn't going to hurt them after all. After he shut and locked the door, she was almost afraid to ask.

"What did he say?" she whispered.

"He's the one listening to us. He said his shift ends in twenty minutes and the next guy won't be so forgiving. If we want to stay in the same room, and if we want to remain *unharmed*, we need to be quiet. He also said if we had managed to get through the window, there are a dozen men with guns canvassing the area. They'll shoot us on sight." She bit her bottom lip and a few tears spilled over her cheeks. "I just want to go home. I miss my mom and dad," she whispered.

Sighing, Hannah lay on the lumpy mattress and turned on her side. "Me too. I'll sleep with my head at this end. If you want to sleep in the other direction, I think we'll both fit."

"Okay." Holly dimmed the overhead light and lay down next to her.

Moonlight streamed in from the small window, giving them a little light. A lead ball congealed in Hannah's stomach. They were stuck and there was nothing she could do about it. And according to that asshole Vargas, he was going to kill her best friend. She'd never felt so helpless in her life.

After checking the lock on the small window—which was pathetic—Jack stripped down to his boxers, laid his weapon on the dresser, then slid under the covers. He hadn't realized how tired he was until his back hit the cool, cotton sheet. If he was exhausted, he could only imagine how beat Sophie must be.

He closed his eyes, though he wasn't anywhere near ready to sleep. He couldn't until Sophie was in the room with him. Safe and close enough for him to touch. The shower had shut off a few minutes ago, so he knew she'd be coming out soon. He'd decided to put off his shower until the morning because the thought of stripping down completely naked with Sophie only feet away from him . . . yeah, he wasn't even going there right now.

The sound of the door opening forced his eyes open. He ordered himself to keep them shut, but his gaze was drawn to her like a magnet. Sophie walked out wearing skimpy shorts and a tight tank top that molded to every curve. It was one of the outfits he'd grabbed for her. Imagining her wearing it and actually *seeing* her in it were two different beasts. He'd turned off the light, but his eyes had adjusted to the darkness.

With the light from the bathroom streaming in, he got a perfect view of her toned, sleek body and he wanted to slowly peel her clothes off. Or frantically tear them off. It didn't matter. As long as he got to see her naked. To taste every inch of her.

"You awake?" Sophie whispered as she took a few tentative steps toward the bed.

"Yeah," he managed to rasp out. He shifted uncomfortably, cursing his erection.

She set the bag on the floor next to the bed, then slipped under the covers next to him. She smelled fresh. Like vanilla and something exotic. Something that was all her. The familiarity of that scent wrapped around him, threatening to choke him. "I'm sorry I snapped at you. I'm just tired, I guess."

He rolled over to face her, hating that he had no fucking control over his cock. At least the darkness was covering his condition. "You don't have to apologize."

"Yeah, I do. I'm so angry right now and you're the only one I can take it out on."

"Your boss is an asshole." Jack guessed that was probably bothering her more than being almost killed. With both of them lying sideways on the pillows, they were only a foot apart from each other. He could see the bright sheen of unshed tears in her eyes and it killed him.

"That's just it. He's not. He was doing what he thought was best . . . I guess."

Yeah, well, her boss could have found another way to deal with his problem. He could have gone to the feds. Instead his stupidity had upended Sophie's life and gotten her almost killed. That put Ronald Weller at the top of Jack's shit list. "Anyone willing to sacrifice someone like you is an asshole."

A few tears spilled over her cheeks, and something inside him cracked wide open. Crying women had never bothered him before, but tears from Sophie were too much. "Damn it,

Soph, don't cry." He reached out and cupped her cheek, only intending to wipe away her tears, comfort her as he'd done so many times when they were younger. He swiped his thumb across her delicate cheekbone, but couldn't tear his hand away from her soft skin. Touching her was addictive and something he could get used to very easily if he allowed it. Hell, she'd been his addiction years ago. One he'd never wanted to walk away from.

Sophie didn't seem to want him to stop either. The tears abruptly dried and her breathing grew ragged, unsteady. Her pink lips parted as she stared at him with those intoxicating dark eyes. When her gaze dropped to his mouth in a hooded sensual way, he knew he'd lost whatever control he had on himself. Which by this point wasn't much. She moistened her lips and he wondered if she'd done it intentionally to drive him crazy. Either way, he didn't care.

Not kissing her was not an option. Not when he already knew how she tasted. She met him halfway and before he could think about stopping—like that was ever a choice—their lips were dancing with a raw, pent-up need. She tasted sweet, minty, and perfect.

Over the years he'd thought about Sophie a lot, but he'd always tried to tamp down the sexual memories. Buried them deep in his mind because he knew nothing would ever happen between them again. Would be kinda hard considering he'd never planned to see her again. Some days he'd even convinced himself that it was just teenage love that he'd built up in his mind, but he knew better. What he'd felt for her back then just wouldn't die, and the longer he was around her now, the stronger it grew.

She moaned into his mouth and though they were both still lying on their sides, his hips bucked toward her until their entire bodies meshed together. When she hooked one leg around his waist and ground against him, a shudder rolled through him. He slid his hands under her shirt, savoring the feel of her soft skin. Making quick work of it, he peeled her top off.

Blindly, he tossed it onto the floor as he stared. For a moment he couldn't do anything else other than just look at her. He'd tried to tell himself that his memories were faulty, that she wasn't as beautiful as he remembered, but damn. She was better than he remembered. Her nipples were small and brown and perfect for his mouth. Faint triangle-shaped tan lines covered her bare breasts, which brought up a dozen different memories of them together at the beach. They'd made love in the ocean on more than one occasion.

Before she gained her sanity back, he bent down and sucked one of her nipples between his teeth. He lightly bit down and tugged, loving the erotic moaning sounds she made. She'd always been so damn reactive to his touch.

When her back arched, giving him better access, he allowed himself to relax. She wasn't going to change her mind. She wanted this as much as he did. When she let out another whimpering sound of pleasure, he circled the hardened nub with his tongue, flicking and teasing it. He pulled his head back a fraction and blew across the moistened skin.

She jerked underneath him, her hips rolling upward in such a purely sexual way it made him feel a little crazy. "Tell me now if you want to stop," he managed to rasp out.

"Stop and I'll kill you." Her voice came out as ragged as his own.

Exactly what he needed to hear. Though he hated to stop touching her, he paused to grab a few condoms from his bag. This was definitely going to be more than a one-condom night. He threw a couple on the nightstand and ripped one open with shaking hands. Jack had no problem taking down a moving target in rough wind from a thousand yards or stalking someone with patience for weeks, yet this—*this*— had him acting like a randy teenager about to have sex for the first time. Which was kind of what he felt like. Hell, he'd never forget their first time. He'd been nervous as hell, determined that she'd come before him and that he wouldn't hurt her. That hadn't worked out the way he'd thought, but the second time . . . yeah, he'd had her crying out his name as she climaxed.

Sophie sat up and wrapped her arms around her exposed chest. Her damp hair tumbled around her shoulders, and in addition to looking sexy and incredibly seductive, she suddenly looked vulnerable. And maybe a little nervous. Despite the need thrumming through him, he pushed down his disappointment when he realized she'd changed her mind.

After laying the foil packet down, he sat on the edge of the bed. "We can stop right now. You've been through a lot and—"

She blinked once, then dropped her arms, giving him another shot of her very kissable breasts. "No, it's not that. I want . . . this. *A lot*. It's just been a long time for me."

"Me too." Using control he didn't know he possessed, he managed to keep his eyes on her face instead of straying to her exposed breasts when all he wanted to do was kiss them again.

Her dark eyes narrowed slightly, as if she didn't believe him, so he leaned forward and brushed his lips over hers. Gently at first, then more insistently. He teased the seam of her lips open until he'd completely invaded her mouth. Maybe he should do the gentlemanly thing and completely stop, but he wanted to be inside her too much. He hadn't been lying when he said it had been a while for him. His job wasn't conducive to any type of serious relationship, and one-night stands had become depressing a long time ago. And he never slept with anyone connected to his job—until Sophie.

Threading one of his hands through the curtain of her hair, he cupped her scalp as his other hand found its way to her breast. He couldn't get enough of touching her. Wished he had more than two hands so he could stroke her everywhere at once. Slowly he swept the pad of his thumb over her nipple. It hardened even more, the little nub rigid under his touch. When she sighed with complete trust, something inside him shifted.

In his profession, getting too attached to anyone could get him killed. He'd learned long ago not to let any attachments get in the way of the job. Tonight, however, he was breaking all his rules. He was already attached to this woman. *His* woman. Even though he wasn't quite ready to admit it yet, it didn't matter. Tonight was going to change everything for him. Sophie had already changed him in the few days they'd been together.

"Clothes off now," Sophie murmured against his mouth as her fingers dipped under the elastic of his boxers.

When she wrapped her fingers around his cock, he jerked against her. Then she stroked him. Once, twice, three times— he abruptly pulled back. Breathing hard, he shook his head. He couldn't find his voice, but she seemed to understand. If she continued touching him he'd lose it in her hand and there was no way in hell that was happening. Not when he had a chance to be inside her, when his single fantasy for over a decade was about to come true.

He'd wanted to take his time, but everything moved in a flurry. His boxers and her skimpy shorts were off in seconds and then like a fucking miracle he was nestled between her thighs. His heart beat wildly as he stared down at her, his cock resting against her lower abdomen. Stretched out on the sheets with her dark hair pillowed around her and her lips swollen, she looked like a sexy pagan offering. But she didn't belong to anyone but him.

As he shifted down so that his cock was closer to her wet entrance, her legs automatically wrapped around his waist. She dug her heels into his ass, urging him on. Her chest moved rapidly in tune with her shallow breathing. Those dark eyes of hers were staring at him with too many emotions for him to define, but he saw raw lust there and it floored him. Thankfully the erratic beat of her heart matched his own. He wasn't alone in this internal torrent, which made him feel a little saner.

"You're beautiful," he said as he cupped her cheek. Not poetry and the words felt so damn inadequate for how he felt about her, but a soft, almost shy smile touched her lips before he pressed his to hers again.

This kiss was different. Softer, slower, more sensual. His tongue danced against hers while he skimmed her rib cage and hips with his fingers. Her skin was like silk underneath him.

When he moved again and rubbed his hard length against the folds of her sex, her fingers dug into his back. Before things went too far, he grabbed the condom from the night-stand and sheathed himself. Next time he wanted her to do it, but he didn't trust himself to let her touch him at the moment. And as he rolled it on, his hands shook. Actually *shook*.

When he finished, all he could do was stare at her. Her caramel skin was flushed and practically glowing. This was what he'd been remembering and fantasizing about for years and he didn't want to forget any of it.

She sat up on her elbows, the action pushing her breasts up. "Do you need a written invitation?" she asked teasingly.

Hell no. Once again it was skin on skin as she locked her ankles behind his waist in an unrelenting grip. She dug her heels into his ass as he feathered kisses along her jaw and neck. When he sucked on her earlobe, it was as if she reacted with her entire body. They were so connected he could feel when a slight tremor rolled through her. While he kissed her, he continued lavishing attention on her breasts, flicking and rubbing over her already hard nubs with his fingers. With each flick, she writhed underneath him.

He rubbed his erection against her sex but didn't penetrate

yet. He wanted to draw this out just a little longer. It was the best kind of torture. But when she dug her fingers into his backside and let out a frustrated growl, he knew she was ready. He slipped one finger inside her to test her slickness. She was drenched. Her inner walls clenched around him and her hips rocked against his hand, urging him on.

A low buzz hummed in his ears as a new reality wrapped around him in a hard embrace. She wanted him as bad as he wanted her and was holding nothing back. The realization was frightening to his sense of survival. He was getting too attached. She was making him want things he'd never imagined for himself. Never imagined he deserved.

Stability. A little happiness and just maybe . . . a shot at a normal life.

Banishing those thoughts, he focused all his attention on the here and now. On the beautiful woman underneath him. After withdrawing his finger, he hovered at her entrance for a fraction of a moment. He wanted to remember everything about this moment.

As he rocked into her, Sophie arched her back. Her inner walls were so tight he couldn't hold back the growl of possession he felt for her. Each time he stroked into her, her fingers tightened against him. In seconds they found their rhythm.

Part of him wondered if the reason she'd wanted to sleep with him was that she needed to remind herself she was alive after the past few days, but he truly didn't care. He hadn't felt connected to anyone like this in—ever. And this wasn't just anyone. Sophie was his. Being with her now brought back so many damn memories. A flood of them hit him all at once.

When she raked her fingers down his back and ordered him to go faster, he nipped at her bottom lip. As he increased his movements, he palmed her breasts, and before he realized she was even close she surged into orgasm. Her inner walls clenched around him with a fierce intensity as the rush of her climax hit.

Just as suddenly, he found his release too. The thought that he'd given her this pleasure was a bigger turn-on than anything she could have physically done to him. He'd always been able to last as long as he needed. He controlled his body. His body didn't control him. Not tonight. Not with Sophie. She totally owned him.

They both rode out the waves of their release together until he was spent and her legs loosely relaxed their hold on him. Catching himself on his forearms, he slowly withdrew from her and rolled onto his side. Still facing her, he kept a protective hand across her stomach. She looked at him almost in a daze as a satisfied smile played across her lips.

His heartbeat jumped at her sultry expression. Unable to stop himself, he leaned over and kissed her, still wanting to taste every inch of her. He gently feathered kisses over her face before pulling away and discarding the condom.

Words eluded him, but she didn't seem to want to talk either. Stretching out on his back, he wrapped his arm around her shoulder and tugged her until she was nestled into the crook of his arm, her head on his chest. Sleeping this close to someone was a foreign experience, but tonight he needed to feel her. Wanted to wake up to Sophie's face. Hell, he'd sleep inside her if he could.

Chapter 16

Eyes only: data that shouldn't be discussed without explicit permission.

Ronald sat across the dining room table from his wife as they ate in silence. Again. He didn't know why they even bothered having their meals together anymore. They didn't talk and when they did, they fought. Rather, she yelled at him.

He cleared his throat. "The casserole is delicious."

"It was Holly's favorite," Margaret snapped before taking a healthy gulp of her martini.

His fork fell onto the plate with a clatter. "Damn it, Margaret, we can't keep living like this."

It was as if he'd flipped a switch. She threw her fork down onto the table. "You never should have let her go!"

"How many times are we going to have this same argument?" Pushing away from the table, he stood. He was unwilling to fight back this time. It wouldn't matter what he said. He couldn't win. Hell, there was no winner. He just wanted his daughter back.

He took his plate with him into the kitchen and dumped the majority of his food in the trash. As he contemplated whether he'd be making it a scotch or vodka night, the designated cell phone Vargas had instructed him to always have on him buzzed in his pocket.

What little food he had in his stomach roiled. "Hello, Miguel."

"Where are you?"

He wasn't sure why the man asked, when Ronald had no doubt he knew. He was sure someone was watching the house. "I'm at home." He leaned against the kitchen counter and bit back a sigh. They'd been virtual prisoners the past few months, too afraid to go anywhere for fear Miguel would think they were talking to the police or involving outsiders. After receiving that bloody ear in the mail, he was too terrified to even think about it.

"Have you heard from your friend tonight?"

This was going to be tricky, but he'd rehearsed what he'd say. "She called and wanted to set up a meeting, but she never showed."

"And you haven't heard from her since?"

"No."

"What about her assistant? Is she asking questions?"

Ronald silently prayed he could get through this and be convincing. "No, she thinks Sophie is out sick. Just like everyone else in the office."

"So she hasn't come to see you about anything lately?"

"What are you talking about? Why do you want to know about everyone in my office all of a sudden?"

Instead of answering, Miguel veered in another direction. "The meeting has been moved to Thursday."

"I thought you said this weekend."

Miguel ignored him. "You will be at the hangar at exactly noon—"

"I'm not doing anything else until I speak to my daughter." Ronald fisted the phone tightly against his ear, trying to calm his shaking hand.

Again, Miguel continued as if he hadn't spoken. "After you sign the necessary documents—"

Months of repressed anger and worry trumped the rising

bile in his throat. "Either I speak to my daughter now or this ends right here. In fact, she better be with you on Thursday or I'm not only *not* giving you what you want, but I'm calling the cops. I'll turn myself in, Miguel." He meant it too. He'd rather go to jail than continue living in constant terror with a wife who couldn't even look at him.

"You might want to think before you speak any further, Mr. Weller. I hold your daughter's life in my hands."

"And I have something you want. I have nothing left to lose." After having a gun shoved in his face and nearly losing someone he cared about, he'd hit his breaking point today. His marriage was all but over if he didn't get his daughter back. It was sad that it took a stranger to convince him of what he needed to do. He needed to start pushing back.

"Stay close to your phone," Miguel said, before disconnecting.

"Margaret, get in here," he called out.

His wife appeared in the entrance but didn't make any further movements toward him. "What do you want?"

"Hold on."

She crossed her arms over her chest and leaned against the door frame, her face a mask of fury.

When the phone buzzed in his hand, he prayed he was doing the right thing. He answered and immediately put it on speaker.

"Hello?"

"You have thirty seconds," Miguel said.

"Daddy?" Holly's voice came over the line, and sharp tears stung his eyes.

He grasped the phone in his hand as if it were a lifeline. "I'm here, baby. This is almost over, I promise. You're going to be home soon."

His wife flew across the room to stand next to him. "Holly? Sweetie, are you all right?"

"I'm fine, Mom. It sucks here, but they haven't hurt me."

"We'll be seeing you soon, I promise. One more day and we'll be together again."

"I love you guys—"

Holly was cut off by Miguel. "That's enough. We will see you on Thursday at noon. You know where the hangar is. Don't be late."

The line went dead, but he stared at the phone. After months of living in fear, he would finally be reunited with his daughter. Maybe this nightmare would finally be over.

In a surprising move, his wife stumbled toward him and wrapped her arms around his waist while she bawled against his chest. He held her tightly, comforting her the only way he knew how. He knew the next thing out of his mouth could be cause for another argument, but for now he was going to take what he could get.

Sophie opened her eyes to find Jack sitting on the floor with his computer in his lap, frowning at the screen. He sat against the wall near the open bathroom door, using the other room as his source of light. Did the man ever rest? The fact that he'd let her sleep instead of turning on the overhead light touched her. It was a small thing, but it was still thoughtful. In fact, everything he'd done since they met had been pretty thoughtful. He was sometimes brusque and blunt, but they were in life-and-death situations and he'd always taken care of her. No matter what. She wasn't an afterthought to him, but someone who mattered. Maybe the way he was treating her was part of his job, but she didn't think so. Not after last night.

When she shifted, the mattress creaked, drawing his attention to her.

"Morning." Last night was still vivid in her mind and she was pretty sure she wouldn't be forgetting it any time soon. If ever. After their first frantic coupling, they'd made love again not long after. He'd touched and kissed practically every inch of her body with a sensual intensity, so she couldn't understand why this inexplicable wave of shyness rolled over her.

His unreadable expression didn't help either. "Morning. You want me to grab some coffee?"

"You don't mind?" She tugged the sheet a little higher against her chest. Not that it mattered. The sexy man had seen all of her in great detail.

He shook his head. "We've got a long day ahead of us, so I'll grab a couple breakfast bars too. Unless you want to eat breakfast here?"

"Whatever you get is fine. Just make sure you get coffee."

He grinned and slid the computer off his lap and onto the floor. "I'll get anything you want."

Still holding the sheet around her, she twisted so that she was sitting halfway off the bed, her feet touching the carpet. "Have you checked your voice mail this morning?"

"Yeah." By his muted tone, she already knew the answer to the next question.

"Hannah still hasn't called?"

"No, but it could mean nothing. I haven't heard any chatter that Vargas has a new bargaining chip."

"Chatter?" What did that mean?

"Since I'm trying to avoid phones, I've been communicating with my boss through . . . We've been staying in touch through a secure method online and he hasn't heard anything about your friend."

She wondered what he'd been about to say, but brushed it off. Chances were, she wouldn't understand his spy lingo anyway. "That doesn't mean anything, though."

"If they had her, chances are we'd know about it."

It was impossible to tell if he was saying this for her benefit or if he meant it, and that drove her just a little bit crazy. "You didn't know they had Ronald's daughter and you didn't know Mandy worked for Vargas."

His eyebrows lifted, but he didn't disagree. "We're doing everything we can to find your friend. If Vargas did take Hannah, she won't be harmed. They'll need her alive."

The small thought gave her a little hope, but the fact that a drug lord might have kidnapped her best friend erased most of her optimism. "Okay."

Before she could blink, he'd crossed the small room until he was kneeling in front of her. He crouched down so they were at eye level. "I promise I'll find your friend."

She nodded, but when he started to rise, she grabbed his hand. "Jack?"

This time he sat on the bed next to her and he didn't let go of her hand, which gave her some comfort. "Yeah?"

"Are things going to change with us now that it's morning?" She hated the almost desperate note she heard in her voice, but couldn't stop herself. Over the years she'd learned to compartmentalize her life. It was the only way she knew how to survive. For once she didn't *want* to separate things. When all this was over—if she survived—she was making some serious changes, but she couldn't bear it if what they'd shared last night was a one-time thing. While there was no way she'd take it back, she wanted more from this man. Admitting it to herself scared her, but she was ready to put her feelings out there.

He gave a slight nod. "Last night changed everything."

"What does that mean?"

He shook his head and for the first time since she'd met him, he looked lost. "I have no idea."

Okay. Not making her feel any better.

"I do know that I want more than last night. I want to spend more time with you." He sounded almost hesitant, as if he was unsure of her response.

Relief punched through her, warming her insides. "Me too."

They stared at each other for a moment until he leaned

over and kissed her forehead. The chaste act shouldn't do anything, but her entire body tingled and ached for more at the brief contact. Yep, she was so a goner.

"I already showered, so if you want to shower while I grab coffee, we're probably going to be leaving soon."

Her stomach flipped. "We are?"

"Yes, you'll get to meet my boss soon."

"Why?"

"It looks like Weller was telling the truth. Vargas is definitely planning a trip to the States. If we can get your boss to help, we're going to bring Vargas down for good."

"Okay." She was sure there were a million other details he was leaving out, but for now it didn't matter. If they could bring down that monster and get Ronald's daughter back, maybe she could get her life back.

"I have more to tell you, but we'll talk on the way there."

Where was *there*?

He pushed up from the bed and grabbed a Polo T-shirt from his bag. Before he slipped it over his head, she saw something that made her freeze. He had a small birthmark on his left shoulder in the shape of a heart. It was unique and she'd only seen it once before.

Just like Sam.

She fought to draw in a breath. The mark was unmistakable. She used to tease Sam about his all the time. She'd been so focused on Jack's tattoos—and the rest of his body—earlier that she hadn't seen it.

He started to turn back toward her, so she wrapped the sheet around herself and bent down to grab the shorts she'd discarded the night before. She managed to avoid looking at him as she busied herself gathering her clothes.

When she heard the door click shut, she dropped the sheet and tossed it back onto the bed. With shaking hands, she dug into Jack's bag and pulled out a pair of jeans and a long-sleeved pink T-shirt. The air-conditioning wasn't running, but there was a chill in the room. Florida weather was erratic during the winter months, but she guessed today she'd need an extra layer of clothing. After grabbing what little toiletries she had, she locked herself in the bathroom and flipped the shower on.

Jack had the same eyes and same birthmark as Sam. Logically, it was impossible. There was no way Jack and Sam could be the same person. Could they? God, could she really be seeing what she wanted? She rubbed a hand over her face, questioning her sanity. The past few days had been highly stressful, but there was no way she was making these things up about Jack. When the room filled with steam, she drew the curtain back and stepped inside. The cascading jets beat against her shoulders in a steady stream. What the hell was going on? She had to be imagining a connection that wasn't there, unless . . . Unless what? Sam was really alive. No way he would hide that from her. Not the boy she'd been in love with.

No fucking way. He couldn't be that cruel.

Sam had died. *Died.* She knew that. So why had she felt this unexplainable sense of familiarity from the *moment* she'd met Jack? A strange numbness started at her toes and worked its way up to her fingers. Her fingers were so jittery it took a few tries before she could pop open the shampoo bottle.

Jack worked for the government. She supposed they could have changed his face. She shook her head and increased the water pressure, letting the jets massage away her soreness. This was insane. Maybe she was seeing things because she still had unresolved issues over Sam's death. Maybe . . .

"Sophie? I'm back." Jack's deep voice from outside made her jump.

"I'll be out in a sec," she called, thankful her voice didn't shake.

Instead of focusing on her crazy *Is Jack really Sam?*

thoughts, she hurriedly got ready. She didn't have time for any of those thoughts anyway because there was no way in hell it was possible. After washing her hair, shaving, and drying off, she towel-dried her thick hair as best she could. She hadn't seen a hair dryer anywhere and didn't feel like hunting one down. She smoothed on lotion she'd found at Mandy's place before tugging on her clothes. Perhaps she should feel guilty at using the woman's stuff, but Mandy had tried to kill her. She was way past guilt.

She glanced at her reflection in the mirror and cringed. She still didn't have a bra or panties. The long-sleeved shirt she wore was snug enough to support her, and even though it was warm in the bathroom, she could see the faint outline of her nipples.

Sophie tugged at the shirt one more time before gathering up the toiletries against her chest and exiting the safety of the bathroom.

When she walked out she found Jack sitting on the bed, staring at that damn computer screen again.

"Any news?"

He blindly glanced at her before returning to the screen. "Yeah. We're meeting my boss soon."

She folded up her worn clothes and tucked them back into his bag. "Is one of those mine?" Sophie gestured to the two foam cups on the nightstand.

"Yeah, sorry." He handed her one of the cups. As he did, he raked an appreciative glance over her, letting his heated gaze linger on her chest. A small, knowing smile played at his mouth before his eyes met hers.

"Okay, we need to make a stop before meeting your boss," she said as she took the extended drink.

Picking up his cup, he frowned at her. "Why?"

"I don't feel like going commando anymore and I really don't want to meet your boss with my nipples showing."

He choked on his coffee before setting the cup down. "Good point," he rasped out.

She watched in amazement as a shade of red crept up his neck. She hadn't thought it was possible to make him uncomfortable. Biting back a grin, she took another sip of her coffee, which was surprisingly good.

Once they'd packed up what little they had, they were in the stolen SUV cruising down the road. Oranges and yellows streaked the sky so that even the clouds draping across the city had a bright and cheerful tint. It seemed almost wrong with everything going on in her life.

She took a sip of her warm coffee, letting the heat flow through her. "Where are we headed?"

"A warehouse . . . Can you text your boss while I drive?"

"Uh . . . yeah."

"Instruct him to walk outside his home and call this number." He handed her one of the throwaways and repeated the number as she punched in the digits.

When the phone buzzed in her hand, Sophie hit the green SPEAKER button.

"Who is this?" the familiar voice of her boss asked.

Jack took over the conversation. "It's me. Are you still at home?"

"Yes, I'm in the backyard," Ronald said.

Jack continued. "Did you talk to Vargas?"

There was a moment of silence before Ronald answered, "Yeah . . . I did what you said. He let me talk to my daughter."

Sophie listened to the conversation, wishing she could feel something other than hurt. The man had been willing to sacrifice her without even attempting to contact the police or another government agency. Expendable. That's all she was. She'd considered Ronald family, but he considered her . . . nothing.

Jack glanced at her as Ronald continued, and gave her a reassuring smile. Jack's smiles were so rare that he gave her a boost of confidence. She wasn't *nothing* to Jack. Unless sleeping with her was part of his job. Even thinking that made the coffee in her stomach roil.

"What else did he say?" Jack asked as he turned back to the road.

"How do I know you'll be able to protect my family?"

"No matter what happens, you have a better chance with my team as backup than if you meet with him *alone*."

There was a long beat of silence. "He wants to meet in hangar eight at the Opa-Lopka Airport tomorrow."

"What time?" Jack glanced over his shoulder and switched lanes.

"At noon. He says . . . He says he's bringing my daughter with him."

"You and I are going to need to meet today, then."

"What if they're watching me?" His voice rose with panic.

"They probably are, so head to work like you always do. I'll be in contact within the hour." Jack disconnected and left the phone on the center console.

"Is Walmart okay?" he asked as he pulled off the main road and into a parking lot.

"What?"

"You said you needed to pick up a few things."

"Oh, it's fine. What are you going to do about Ronald?"

"Bring him in to meet with the team, explain that we'll be watching the whole time, and explain how everything needs to go down."

"How do you know someone isn't following him?"

"He's definitely got a tail, but I doubt he's being tracked by satellite. It costs too much money and would draw too much attention to constantly track your boss like that. I guarantee they've got his house bugged, though. So far he hasn't been a problem to Vargas, so security's probably gotten lax.

That's good for us." He put the vehicle in park and shut off the engine.

"You're coming with me?" she asked as he opened his door.

His brow furrowed. "I'm not letting you out of my sight."

The thought of shopping for any sort of undergarments with Jack was . . . interesting. "If you say so."

Chapter 17

C-4: a common variety of the plastic explosive known as Composition C.

He looked up from his computer screen as Wesley walked up. "What's going on, boss?"

"Conference room. Two minutes." Wesley headed toward another desk, making any questions pointless.

He wiped sweaty palms on his pants, then logged off his computer. Over the past twenty-four hours, he hadn't been able to get anything useful from Wesley, especially regarding Sophie Moreno and everything surrounding SBMS. His boss had switched phones, and hadn't been communicating on many open channels. At least not that he could find. Wesley was paranoid by nature, but lately his boss had been taking extra precautions—as if he knew he was being watched.

And now the Abarca woman had disappeared according to Vargas. He hadn't heard that she'd been picked up by the NSA, but for all he knew, he was being kept out of the loop. At least Vargas didn't seem to think she'd been arrested. He was pissed about her disappearance but seemed to think she'd decided to run with what money she had. Even if she had been picked up by a government agency, the woman didn't know much. She'd been recruited to watch the inner workings of SBMS, but she wasn't privy to any real knowledge.

Grabbing a notepad, he headed toward the conference room, wondering if it was possible anyone was on to him. No, he'd been too diligent. He'd cleared all his tracks after running the facial recognition scans, but before that he'd even pointed those tracks toward someone else in case someone got really suspicious and managed to extract his online trail. And he hadn't gotten any dings on his offshore accounts, so no one should know about his growing stash. *Just breathe,* he ordered himself.

As he walked down the hallway, he was surprised to see two other analysts and five field men heading toward the room also.

Once they were all seated, Wesley closed the door. "We're all leaving in thirty minutes, so shut down whatever you're working on. If it's necessary, delegate your work to someone else. We'll be gone for a few days."

"Where are we headed?" one of the new field guys asked.

"That's classified." Wesley glanced around the room expectantly, but no one else said a word.

They all had bags packed for emergencies or special operations. That was just the way things worked. This wasn't the first time he'd gone on a mission when he had no clue what was going on and no previous notice.

Wesley glanced at his watch. "If that's all, everyone better be on time."

As they all started to rise, Wesley spoke again. "One more thing. Leave work cell phones and computers at your desks. All materials will be provided on-site. There will be a security check when we get to the hangar, so don't let me catch you with anything."

Hangar. That meant they were flying. But to where? He picked up his notepad and exited the room with everyone else. Sweat rolled down his back as he headed back to his desk. No one was paying attention to him, so he slipped into the nearest restroom. There was one person in there, so he waited in a stall until the man left. Then he called Vargas.

"Yes?"

"Something's going down in the next few days, but I don't know what it is." He kept his voice low.

"What do you mean, you don't know?"

"It's all hush-hush. There's nothing on file either. I'm getting on a plane in half an hour to God knows where."

"Call me when you know more."

"That's going to be a problem. They're taking away all our communications."

"Do they know about my arrival?" Vargas asked.

"It's possible, but I don't know where we're going." He hadn't heard anything, but that didn't mean shit anymore. The past couple of days he might as well have been invisible. Wesley hadn't confided anything to him. Not that he hadn't tried to subtly get his attention. He'd been making pointless trips to his office with excuses to talk to him. Nothing was working.

"Contact me if you can."

"Are you still coming to the States?"

"Of course. If they try to interfere, I have another—how do you say?—ace in the hole."

He frowned but didn't comment. He didn't like being kept in the dark, especially when he might need to use Vargas. "When are you going to wire the rest of my money?"

"When this job is over." His answer was expected, but it still annoyed him. He'd put his neck on the line and now he might lose everything he'd worked so hard for. Now that he didn't have to worry about paying off his debts, he could enjoy the benefits of his work. He deserved it. He was underappreciated here, and for how smart he was, the pay was a joke. Besides, it wasn't as if he was actually harming anyone.

He might pass on valuable information for the right price, but his hands were clean.

"Fine, I'll be in contact when I can."

Vargas disconnected without responding, so he slid his personal cell back into his pocket. He'd have to get rid of this before he left.

All his survival instincts told him to disappear now, but there was no way he could get out of the building undetected, and more important, Vargas still hadn't paid him the majority of what he was owed. Even if he managed to get to his car, they'd send someone after him, track his accounts, and freeze his money. Without all of his funds, his early retirement wouldn't be as lush as he'd like and everything he'd done would be for nothing.

"Why did you buy all those cap guns?" Sophie asked as she slid into the passenger seat.

He didn't miss the amused note in her voice. Jack loaded their bags into the backseat, then got into the driver's seat. Trying to banish the image of watching Sophie pick out undergarments—simple cotton panties had never been so sexy—he said, "For the sulfur."

"Care to elaborate?"

"I need it."

"Again, care to elaborate?" She crossed her legs toward him as she shifted against the leather seat.

"Wesley is bringing a team in with plenty of firepower, but I always like to be prepared."

"Like a Boy Scout?" Her lips curled up slightly, the vision seriously tempting him to lean over and take her mouth the way his body was urging him to. Last night definitely wasn't enough. It had only enflamed his lust and need for her.

"Exactly." He knew she didn't understand what he was saying, but the less she knew the better.

Jack's boss would be bringing in a good team, but he didn't know some of the men and Jack always liked to have a backup plan in case things went wrong.

He pulled out another one of the throwaway phones as he steered out of the parking lot. Jack had contacts all over the country—hell, the world—and while he *hated* using this particular one now, he didn't have a choice.

After five rings, he was about to give up when someone answered. There wasn't an audible response, but Jack could hear muted movement on the other end. "Alexander?"

"Who is this?" his contact barked.

"It's Dante."

"Holy shit, man. It's been what, four years?"

"That sounds about right. I hate to call and ask for a favor like this, but I'm in town for an unexpected job and need some packaging material." Code for C-4.

Alexander Lopez wasn't the brightest weapons dealer Jack had ever dealt with, but he was careful. Which was why he was still in business.

"How much?"

"Enough to wrap up a small warehouse." More code. Not exactly genius code, but if someone was listening they couldn't bring Alexander down on anything without solid proof.

"I don't know, man. That'll take some time."

"Payment up-front."

"Why didn't you say so?"

"So we have a deal?"

"Remember that abandoned warehouse we used to party at?" Code for a storage container they'd made exchanges at twice.

"Yes. When can you meet?" Jack asked.

"Tomorrow?"

"Sooner. How about twenty minutes?"

"Man, how do you even know I'm in town?"

Jack snorted. The man rarely left Miami and they both knew it. "Can you do it or not?"

The other man sighed. "I'll be there."

Jack disconnected, then took the battery out of the phone. This was one phone he wouldn't be using again. The others he was using he was fairly sure weren't being tracked, but he was ninety percent sure Alexander was being watched by someone. The DEA, FBI, who knew? Hell, he was probably being watched by the local cops too.

"What was that about, *Dante*?" Sophie asked as he headed toward I-95.

He suppressed a smile at her sarcastic tone. "I hate bringing you with me, but I've got to pick up some stuff and I've got to do it now."

"Packaging material, huh?" She raised a dark eyebrow at him.

"That's right."

"Mm-hmm," she murmured. "So, what do you do when you're not busy being a spy?"

"What do you mean?"

"You know, for fun. Spies are allowed to have fun, aren't they?"

The past few years he hadn't had much downtime, but there was one thing that never got old. "I like to fish."

"Really?"

"Why is that surprising?"

She lifted her shoulders slightly. "I don't know. That just seems so . . . normal. And pretty boring. For someone like you, I mean."

"Nah, I love it. Maybe it's my Irish blood, but being on the water is the only time I feel grounded." Maybe he should have left that part out. Jack Stone was Irish, but so was his former self. She didn't seem to notice. "What about you?"

"I love to paint and draw."

"I know." *Damn it!* The words were out before he could

stop himself. This was why he needed to keep his mouth shut around her. The more he let his guard down, the more likely he was to slip up. When she was a teenager she'd always been drawing and sketching. The girl had filled up notebooks.

"You know?"

"Your file. It said you minored in art. Why didn't you pursue anything after school?"

"I wanted stability." Her answer was immediate and real and he loved that she was being honest with him.

He'd already guessed why, but couldn't tell her that. "Are you going to go back to work at SBMS when this is over—if there's a company to go back to?" Which Jack wasn't sure there would be. It might end up being dismantled.

She snorted in a very un-Sophie-like manner, completely taking him off guard. "No way. Even if he doesn't go to jail, I don't know if I can ever look Ronald in the face again after all this."

Jack was pretty sure Weller wouldn't go to jail, not if he helped them enough to bring Vargas down. If the threats against him ended up being bad enough, he'd likely be put into WITSEC. There were too many variables and Jack didn't give a shit what happened to Weller anyway. "What are you going to do?"

"I . . . have no idea. After the past couple days, I've started to realize that no matter what I do, I can't be truly safe from everything. I want to do something that makes me happy." She paused and bit her bottom lip. "Is that totally cheesy?"

"No." He pulled off the next exit and circled back under the overpass.

"Okay, where exactly are we going? Because this area looks a little like that gross motel."

"We're almost there." They were in one of the worst parts of town. As they drove past an abandoned apartment complex covered with graffiti, he pointed toward an eight-foot chain-link fence across the street. The fence surrounded what used to be a parking lot but now housed storage boxes and garbage. "See those green storage boxes? That's where we're going."

She lifted an eyebrow. "Your friends hang out in some interesting places."

"This guy isn't my friend, so you're staying in the car. And remember, my name is Dante, not Jack."

"How many names do you have?"

"Too many," he said as he steered into the deserted area. Gravel and dust flew up as he turned into the only cutout opening along the fence.

Avoiding potholes and bags of trash, he parked in front of one of the containers. He glanced in his rearview mirror as an old pickup truck pulled up. Withdrawing his backup pistol from his ankle holster, he laid it on the center console. "This should be over soon, but if something happens to me, drive away and don't look back."

Her lips pulled into a thin line. "Really, again with this? You expect me to leave you behind?"

"Sophie—"

"Fine. I'll do it." There was no conviction in her words and he knew she was lying, but there was nothing he could do about it. Even though he hated the thought of her not following his orders, he felt another crack around his chest at the thought of her sticking by him. It was one of many things he'd always adored about her. Once she decided she was on your side, she was loyal to a fault.

Alexander was the only person that he could see in the truck, so after another visual scan of the area, he reached behind his seat and grabbed a small duffel bag, then got out first. He'd called this meeting, so he needed to make the first move.

When he stepped out, the other man did the same.

"It's been too long, my friend," Alexander said. Wearing

a bright green and blue Hawaiian button-down shirt and faded cargo pants, he didn't look like the typical weapons dealer Jack usually dealt with. As long as Jack had known him, he'd never seen him wearing a suit or anything other than the tacky getup he was in now. Maybe that was another reason he'd stayed alive so long. He knew how to blend in with his surroundings.

"I've been out of the country. Had to lie low after that last job."

Dante nodded knowingly, then quickly switched gears. "Have you brought the money?"

"I assumed you'd want it electronically. Just like old times." For all Alexander's old-school ways, he rarely dealt with cash.

The other man motioned with his hand. "This way."

Jack glanced back at Sophie before following the other man toward one of the locked storage boxes. Alexander unlocked it, disabled what looked like a booby trap—which would probably cause an explosion if anyone tried to break into the unit—then opened it for Jack. With the flip of a switch, an overhead fluorescent light came on. The low buzz reverberated around them. Rows of packaged explosives and stacks of M-4s, M-16s and other military-grade weapons lined the small facility.

Alexander pulled a laptop from the briefcase he'd brought and opened it. "First things first."

Jack leaned against one of the metal walls as he waited. He hated not having a visual of Sophie, but she had a gun. It was the only thing that eased his growing tension.

"Who is the woman with you?" Alexander asked as he typed in his password.

"A close friend."

"She must be, you bringing her here. Normally I wouldn't allow a guest, but it's you, so I'll make an exception."

Jack didn't respond. He was fishing for information. In

this business, anytime someone could get a leg up on anyone, they did. Law of the jungle.

"Okay, here's the account number." Alexander handed him a white strip of paper with a string of numbers hand written on it.

With a few keystrokes, Jack wired the fee, then handed the piece of paper back. "Ready to do business?"

"One moment." He pulled out his phone. After a brief conversation with his bank, Alexander was off the phone and smiling. "Take what you need."

Jack kept his eyes on the other man as he loaded up his duffel bag. Once the bag was stocked, he hoisted it over his shoulder. "Thanks again."

He didn't wait for Alexander to lock up. As soon as he was outside, he scanned the area for any threats, then headed for the SUV. Jack knew that within an hour that storage container would be cleaned out and the rest of the product moved. Alexander might have let him see this place, but the weapons dealer had a habit of moving his products constantly.

"Did you get everything you needed?" Sophie asked as he strapped in.

"Yep." He slung the bag into the backseat. The good thing about C-4, it was incredibly stable. He could hit it with a hammer and it wouldn't do a thing. Hell, he could light it on fire and nothing would happen. Of course if he hit it with a hammer while it was burning, now, that was a different story.

Revving the engine, he hit the accelerator and tore out of the parking lot.

"Everything okay?"

"Yeah, I just don't want to hang around here longer than necessary." For all he knew, Alexander had been tailed and Jack really didn't want to deal with local law enforcement. Considering the shooting at Bayside Marketplace yesterday, he definitely didn't need to be noticed right now. According to Wesley he hadn't been caught on any cameras and there weren't any witnesses that had come forward, but tangling with the locals until this op was completed wasn't something he needed.

"Are we going to meet your boss now?"

Jack glanced at the clock on the radio. "Not yet. He should be landing soon and we've got one more stop to make."

"What's in the duffel bag?"

He debated telling her when she swiveled around and unzipped the bag. "Holy shit, is this what I think it is?"

His lips quirked up. "What do you think it is?"

"Don't be a smart-ass. Is this some kind of explosive?" She zipped up the bag and straightened back against her seat, her eyes a little wide.

"I told you it pays to always have a backup plan."

She muttered something in Spanish and turned to stare out the window.

The silence in the SUV was almost deafening until they pulled into the Opa-Lopka facilities. There was tight security at the front gate, but there was a back entrance on the far side of the airport. Something Jack had never understood. A simple fenced gate with a cheap lock was the only preventative measure. Once he'd picked it, they drove through. He slowed his pace as they circled the pavement. Then another thought hit him. "How did you break in here?" For some reason he couldn't see Sophie picking the lock.

She shrugged. "We've been doing business with them forever and I knew that the fence behind Keane's hangar has a small opening. It's hard enough to see during the day, so if you don't know about it, at night it's impossible to locate without a guide. There are places like that all over this airport. Their security is complete shit half the time. And I didn't actually break in—I have a key."

"With you?"

She shook her head.

He could pick the lock easily enough. What killed him was that she'd come here alone. She was damn lucky she'd been able to escape the other night. Jack shuddered to think what could have happened if any of Vargas's men had gotten ahold of her. He kept his driving slow until he was parked behind hangar seven.

There weren't any people around and most of the private planes were grounded, but he didn't want to draw undue suspicion by parking near hangar eight.

Sophie frowned at him. "Are you planting bombs or something?"

"I'm setting up an insurance policy for us. Stay here."

In response, she opened the passenger door and jumped out. "I'm going with you."

"Sophie, I don't—"

She slammed the door and walked around to his side. "I don't care what you want. I'm helping. Last time I was there they had *two* security guys and no cameras."

He almost laughed at the way she said two. As if that would ever stop him. He already knew they didn't have cameras. If they had, the NSA would have hacked them if possible. But after her recent break-in and the fact that Vargas was expected in the country, they would have increased security. Hell, he hoped it was only two. They wouldn't even know he was in there. And he wasn't bringing Sophie in with him.

Covering the distance between them in a few steps, he had her pinned up against the vehicle door in seconds. Her eyes widened and she swallowed hard, eyeing him with surprise.

The thought of intimidating her with his body sickened him, but he did what he had to. "I'm not going to stand here and argue with you. Even with their security, I can move around without being seen. I can't do that if I have you slowing me down."

She flinched at his words, but finally nodded. "Fine," she said tightly, her jaw set.

Against his better judgment, he threaded his hands through her hair and cupped the back of her head in a completely dominating grip. Her lips parted in surprise as his mouth descended on hers. Hell, he surprised himself. It wasn't the time or the place, but damn if he could leave her looking so vulnerable.

For a moment she resisted, but as his tongue swept past the seam of her soft lips, she moaned into his mouth. Her body melded against his, her breasts rubbing against his chest as she clutched on to his shoulders with a wrenching hold. He'd parked close enough to the hangar that they had cover from outside, prying eyes, but they were still in the open. That knowledge was the only thing that pulled him back to reality.

Somehow he tore his mouth away. She blinked once, her gaze lust-filled even as she watched him warily and let her hands fall away. "You can't use sex to get what you want from me."

He snorted. "That isn't what this is about. I can do this quicker if I'm alone. And that kiss was because *I* needed it." Let her make what she wanted of that. "Stay in the vehicle."

After grabbing his duffel bag he waited until she got in the passenger seat and shut the door. Then he checked to make sure there weren't any spotters outside before sprinting across the asphalt to the next building. He hated how much open space he had to cross without any cover. But there was no way around it. At least there were no cameras.

The hangar next door was exactly like the one he'd parked behind. It was a square metal building with a ceiling high enough to house planes. There was a hatch that rolled up in the front with an opening big enough to let a plane through and a single door in the back. Just like the rest of the hangars. Not a lot of design went into these buildings, and that was a good thing for him. He had a general idea of the layout without actually having been inside this particular one.

Once he was hidden behind the cover of the other building, he crept along the wall to the entrance. There was a small window on the back door, so he was able to see inside. He could see one man lounging against a wall with his back turned to him, but he knew there would be more inside. The lock was easy enough to pick. Getting inside undetected would be the real trick.

Luckily he was really good at being invisible.

Twenty minutes later he slipped back out the way he'd entered. There had been one plane inside and about ninety crates stacked around the back and side walls. He'd been able to use the wooden boxes as cover as he set up his homemade bombs. Adding foil-protected detonators had been tricky, but he'd gotten everything into place. If it became necessary, he'd have the ability to set off the bombs using a high-powered laser pulse. Something that would piss Wesley off if it ever came down to it, but Jack didn't care.

The government had trained him to think outside the box. Hurrying back across the pavement, he only stopped once he'd reached the steel wall. He'd been away from Sophie too long, and even though she had a weapon, he didn't like being separated from her. He glanced around the wall to eye the vehicle and almost froze when he saw a man dressed in all black peering into the passenger window of the SUV. Jack might have been able to dismiss him, but the man had a pistol in one hand. Jack doubted the guy was security. With the man's black pants, long-sleeved black shirt, and enough bulk under it that he was likely wearing a Kevlar vest, Jack guessed he worked for Vargas.

The hangar they were parked behind was empty and he didn't see a golf cart or other transportation for the dark-haired man. He also didn't see Sophie in the passenger seat, which sent his heart rate into overdrive.

Dropping his now empty duffel, he crouched low and hurried to the driver's side of the SUV when the man started walking to the back of the vehicle.

"Hey, I see you in there!" the man shouted in a heavily accented voice. A harsh tapping followed. The sound of a gun hitting the window. "Come out now or I shoot."

Over my dead body. Using the element of surprise, Jack stayed low and rounded the front of the SUV. Not drawing his weapon because he wouldn't need it in close combat, he hurtled himself at the man before the guy had even fully turned to face his attacker.

The weapon fell from the man's hand as Jack slammed his body onto the ground. Not wanting to draw this out longer than necessary, he hauled back and head-butted the guy. Bone crunched and blood spurted everywhere and the man's hands automatically went to cover his nose.

Flipping him onto his stomach, Jack wrapped one arm around his neck and pulled tight, cutting off his air supply. The man started struggling, instinct kicking in as he clawed at the asphalt and tried to buck Jack.

But he had at least fifty pounds on the guy and clearly a lot more experience. Less than thirty seconds later, the man passed out. After retrieving the fallen weapon and his own duffel bag, he'd started securing the man's wrists behind his back when the back door opened.

Jack glanced up to find Sophie watching him, her mouth pulled into a thin line. Immediately she frowned. "Are you hurt?"

He didn't have to look to realize what she meant. "Not my blood. You okay?" When she nodded, he hefted the guy up and carried him to the back, where he dumped him.

His chest ached painfully as he watched Sophie wordlessly get into the passenger seat. This was the last thing he should be doing with her. For once in his life Jack wanted to do something normal. Like take Sophie on a fucking date instead of have her wait for him while he set up high-powered explosives and then knocked a man unconscious.

Scrubbing a hand over his face, he got in the driver's side. "Where did that guy come from?"

She wrapped her arms around herself, traces of fear evident in her dark eyes. "I'm not sure, but he came from the direction of the hangar you were in. I thought maybe . . . you'd gotten hurt or something. I was worried."

That's when he realized the fear wasn't for herself, but for him. He wasn't used to anyone worrying about him. Despite what they'd shared last night, he told himself he couldn't get used to it. "I'm fine," he said, the words harsher than he'd intended.

He didn't trust himself to say more, so he started the vehicle and slowly backed up. They didn't have far to go, so he continued driving behind the next couple of hangars until he parked in front of number five.

"Why are you stopping?"

"We're here."

"*This* is where we're meeting your boss?" She sounded incredulous.

Jack nodded. "We need to be close to whatever's going down with Vargas." He jumped out of the vehicle and punched in the code for the hangar door. It immediately started rolling up.

"What's going to happen to me now?" Sophie asked as he slid back into the driver's seat.

"What do you mean?" Glancing in the rearview mirror, he slowly pulled through the entrance. Wesley's team should be here soon.

"Will I still, uh . . . never mind." It was as if the temperature in the vehicle dropped a few degrees. He could practically see her shutting him out, shutting down. She'd done it numerous times when they were teenagers.

If something was bothering her, her automatic reaction

was to pull away emotionally. Jack had never done the comforting thing well, but he hated Sophie pulling away from him. Especially now. "Sophie, I'm not letting you out of my sight if that's what you're worried about. You are mine to protect. No matter what happens, I'll keep you safe."

Her expression softened a fraction, but she didn't respond. As if she wasn't quite sure she believed him. Before he could say more, three black SUVs with tinted windows drove through the opening, parking in a perfect row.

"Looks like everyone's here. . . . Remember, don't mention what I just did to anyone."

She nodded, her expression guarded. "I promise."

Levi was silent as he walked down the tiled hallway in Vargas's house. As he passed one of the open doors, he overheard two of the guards arguing. He stayed in the doorway, but neither of them took notice of him.

As their voices escalated, he frowned when he realized what they were discussing. "What the fuck is going on?" he asked. Stupid fucker, always looking at the two women Vargas held captive. There weren't many things Levi would ruin his cover for, but protecting a woman was about it. He hadn't been with the team to pick up Hannah Young—because he would have made sure the girl got away—but she was here now and there wasn't anything he could do about it. Unfortunately he had a feeling he'd be leaving soon.

"Why don't you mind your own business, *pendejo*?" Manuel took a step back from Rico and squared off at Levi.

Rico waved a hand in the air as if to dismiss him. "Don't worry about it, man."

Levi ignored Rico and focused on Manuel instead. He leaned casually against the door frame. "You touch either of those girls and Vargas will cut your nuts off. He'll probably make you eat them before he kills you."

Manuel let out a string of curses before storming past him.

Levi waited until he saw the scarred man disappear down the hall before turning back to Rico. "Keep him away from those girls."

"I'm trying to get it through his thick skull that Vargas will kill him. . . . Man, whatever, it's his fucking hide." Rico shook his head and brushed past Levi.

The world would be a better place if Manuel was dead, but the only way Vargas would kill him was if he actually hurt one of the girls. On that front, Vargas was a strange man. Levi had overheard him threaten to hurt the blond girl to her parents, but he'd never actually do it and he'd never let his men hurt them. Levi wasn't sure why, but there was a rumor that someone had raped and killed Vargas's wife a decade ago.

But that's all it was. A rumor. If it was true, it was the only thing Levi had in common with the drug-running bastard. Whatever, everyone had a fucking sob story. Right now the only thing he cared about was vengeance. He couldn't worry about anyone else's shit.

When his phone buzzed, he frowned at the number on the caller ID. "Yeah?"

"You still looking to get in bed with the Russians?" a familiar voice asked.

Fuck yeah. "I'm in?"

"Your time with Vargas was worth it. Your credentials are solid."

"When do they want me?"

"I can get you a ride off the island in three hours. You know the place."

"I'll be there." Levi's hand shook as he disconnected. This was it. He hated that he couldn't free the women, but they weren't his problem. A year ago he'd have died trying to get them out of here. But if he was dead, no one would avenge his wife's death. Right now that was the only reason his heart was still beating. Once he'd ended the bastards who'd cut down his life, his soul, he didn't care what happened to himself.

He glanced down the hall. Empty. Most of Vargas's men guarded the perimeter. Getting off his estate without being seen would be tricky. His friend was doing him a huge favor flying him out of Cuba, and he couldn't risk Vargas following him to the airstrip.

It wasn't as if he owed Vargas anything. Not to mention that something big was going down if Jack was involved. Vargas had been very vague about what he was doing with SBMS other than running weapons. Deep down Levi knew it was bad and that if he dug deep enough he'd find out what it was, but the driving need for revenge inside him kept pulling him back. Levi couldn't get caught up in that mess if he wanted to stay alive. It was definitely time for him to disappear and get his revenge.

Chapter 18

Op center: location where an operation is being run.

Sophie watched an older man get out of one of the SUVs. He was followed by two men wearing what looked like battle gear. They were dressed in all black, wore Kevlar vests, and carried some big freaking guns. Everything about the situation had her on edge. When she'd seen the man they now had tied up coming toward her, she'd tried to hide, but it had done no good. Then to see Jack disarm and knock him unconscious so easily . . . it was jarring. Though she wasn't sure why. She'd seen him take down two men with a bullet between the eyes—while he'd been running. He moved with such fluidity, his actions natural and graceful—in a terrifyingly deadly sort of way. And the longer she was with him, the more she couldn't shake the feeling that she knew him. Had known him for a long damn time.

It didn't matter what reality told her, something bone deep recognized Jack and it was starting to drive her a little crazy. Now she couldn't get rid of the fear that their time together was coming to an end. She wasn't sure how she felt about it. Okay, that was total bullshit. She didn't like the thought at all. Wrapping her arms around herself, she asked, "Who are those guys?"

"They're part of the tactical team. There are probably six

or seven of them and they won't know anything about us or the mission until they get set up in the hangar." Jack answered her, but she could tell he was only half listening. His eyes narrowed as he scanned everyone, probably looking for a possible threat.

All in all, there were seven men dressed like commandos, four men wearing suits and ties, and one woman in a pantsuit. She guessed the older man was the boss. He turned to everyone, shouted something, and people fanned out like ants, pulling boxes and bags from the backs of the vehicles in a quick but orderly manner. One of the men shut the hangar door, which gave her a surprising sense of claustrophobia. She didn't know any of these people.

When the older man looked through their windshield and nodded at Jack, Jack turned to her. "You ready?"

No. "Yeah." For the past two days she'd been running for her life, but she'd been with Jack. Which, in her mind, translated to safe. Now all of a sudden, she was nervous. Before she'd even shut her door, Jack had rounded the vehicle and was standing protectively close to her. His nearness was wildly soothing.

"Just relax," he said, low enough for only her as the older man walked up to them.

"Ms. Moreno, I'm Wesley Burkhart. We spoke on the phone. I'm sorry you've had to be a party to all this." He held out his hand.

"Thank you, and please call me Sophie." She shook his hand before sticking her hands in her pockets.

When Jack placed a comforting hand on the small of her back and pulled her a fraction closer, the older man's green eyes narrowed. Not in a dangerous sort of way, but he looked almost surprised.

"I've got an unconscious guy tied up in the back of the SUV. Probably one of Vargas's. He spotted our vehicle and he's definitely not airport security. I left his weapons under

the driver's seat." Jack's statement tore his gaze away from
the way he was holding Sophie.

"Where you'd run into him?"

"Outside hangar seven after I'd finished recon of Keane's.
So either he got nosy or they've got guys doing larger-scale
sweeps." Or the guy could have been smoking a cigarette and
noticed the vehicle. Who knew?

His boss frowned. "The satellite hasn't caught anything
like that," he murmured, almost to himself. Then he turned
and shouted an order to someone. Two of the men wearing
all-black gear stopped what they were doing and headed for
the vehicle.

"This way." Without waiting, he turned and headed toward
a far corner of the hangar.

Jack nodded, so she fell in step with him. The other people barely glanced their way as they unloaded the vehicles.
Unlike in the other hangar, there weren't any crates. Just tables with computers and a couple of the men were in the
process of setting up cots and dry-erase boards.

"Are they going to sleep here?" she whispered.

"Probably."

Once they'd reached the far corner of the building, Wesley
stopped. "The two guys from Bayside were likely hired
thugs. We couldn't find a concrete connection to Vargas, but
they've done work for hire in the past. The locals are wrapping the case up as we speak," he informed them.

Sophie had wondered about those men—though she
hadn't cared much about their deaths considering they'd been
hunting her and Jack.

Jack simply nodded, his expression blank, as if he felt the
same way.

"Did you get a chance to scope out Vargas's hangar?" he
asked Jack.

"Yeah. Five men guarding the place now. Well, six if you
include the guy I took out. After Sophie's break-in, I'm

guessing they increased the security, because she said there were only two men there Sunday night."

His boss glanced at her, so she just nodded in confirmation. Then he looked back at Jack. "Have you contacted Weller yet?"

"No, I was waiting for you."

Wesley's eyes narrowed, but he didn't comment. Sophie didn't understand what was going on, but she was under the impression the other man wasn't happy. As if they were having a conversation without actually talking.

"Contact him and pick him up," Wesley ordered.

"Send someone else." There was an unexpected edge to Jack's voice. She'd heard the same tone before, but this was his boss he was talking to.

Wesley's jaw clenched. "She'll be protected."

"I'm not letting her out of my sight. You're the one who *insisted* I take this mission, and I'm doing things my way."

Jack's boss gritted his teeth, but he conceded after a few tense moments. "Fine. I'll go with one of the guys. *You* need to call him, though. You've been his only contact and he trusts you."

Without responding, Jack pulled out one of his phones and texted her boss.

As they stood there waiting for Ronald to return the call, she decided to take a chance. It was constantly weighing on her mind to the point she wanted to scream in frustration. Jack had promised he'd tell her if he heard anything, but maybe his boss knew something he didn't. Asking was worth a shot. "Has there been any news on my friend Hannah?"

Wesley shot a glance at Jack. It was almost too quick, but she saw the warning glance in Jack's eyes as he looked at his boss.

"What aren't you telling me?" she demanded. Raw panic slithered down her spine, leaving her cold and numb.

Jack rubbed a hand over his face and sighed. "When we were at her house I saw some broken glass and some of her clothing scattered in her garage."

His admission was like a stinging slap to the face. He'd kept this from her the entire time they'd been together. "Why didn't you tell me?"

"It could be nothing and I didn't want you to worry."

"You should have told me." Her hands automatically balled into fists at her sides.

"Why? So you could needlessly worry? There's nothing you can do and now this knowledge only hurts you. I . . . just wanted to protect you." The way his voice softened smothered the majority of her previously spiking anger. But it didn't soothe her growing panic.

She hated that he was right. There wasn't a damn thing she could do. Still, Hannah was her best friend. Sophie pressed a shaky hand against her abdomen. Hannah was okay. She had to be. But this was the real world and she knew all the bad things that could happen. Staring into those pale eyes, she felt absolutely betrayed. "I thought we were in this together."

"I didn't want . . . You're right. I should have told you. I'm sorry." He said the last part quietly.

Wesley raised his eyebrows as he glanced between the two of them. But she didn't care about him right now.

"Is there anything *else* you're not telling me?"

"No."

"Should we call the police, then? Her parents?"

Wesley shifted his feet, looking slightly uncomfortable. "I've spoken with a local contact about her, and we have her house under surveillance, but we're not involving her family. The timing is too coincidental, so we're assuming Vargas has her. If he'd wanted her dead, he'd have just had her killed at her house and left her there."

Sophie nodded because she'd heard what that man in

Marathon had said about taking Hannah. But she didn't understand why they weren't calling the police.

Before she could ask, Jack cut in as if he'd read her mind. "If we contact the locals, it might alert Vargas that we know a lot more than he's aware of. Right now he knows that people are asking questions about SBMS, but he doesn't know more than that. He thinks *you* are a threat because of the pictures you took, but he doesn't know who's helping you or why. For all he knows, you're working with competition looking to move in on his territory.

"He clearly had her call in to work, so he wants the world to think she's just sick, not missing. He might think he has a bargaining chip with her and we need to let him think that. Either way, it changes nothing."

A bargaining chip. Sophie felt sick to her stomach.

Jack started to say more when his phone buzzed. "Yeah?"

The conversation was one-sided, but after some smooth talking, Jack convinced her boss to meet some people with the NSA. Worry for her friend ate at her, but she knew it wouldn't do Hannah or her any good to freak out right now.

"Set up a table for when I get back. I don't want anyone else touching the recording devices," Wesley said before turning on his heel and heading back across the open floor.

"You could have gone, Jack." Sophie wrapped her arms around herself.

"I'm not leaving you." He reached out a hand and cupped her cheek, his thumb gently stroking her skin. She almost pulled away, but there was something vulnerable in his gaze that stopped her. She was so damn angry he'd lied to her, that feeling battling with the worry inside her, and she wasn't sure what to do. Finally he cleared his throat and dropped his hand. "Come on, I want to get the audio equipment ready by the time they get back."

Sophie fell into step with Jack, thankful he'd kept his word. He'd said he wouldn't leave her, but she hadn't been sure if she'd truly believed him until this moment. She wasn't sure what it meant, though. He'd lied to her about Hannah and while she understood, it pissed her off beyond belief. She'd been handling everything pretty well and she hated that he'd kept that knowledge from her. She didn't need him to think for her or make her decisions.

He watched the interaction between Jack Stone and the Moreno woman. That had certainly been interesting.

Jack was more or less a legend in the agency, a man who killed with no compunction. No one but Wesley really knew him. For all he'd heard about Jack—and it wasn't much—he'd never imagined the man had a soft spot. But seeing the way he'd just comforted the Moreno woman—there was definitely something going on between them. The sexual tension was practically tangible. And he couldn't believe *he* was the man who'd been working with the Moreno woman. Now that he actually had intel for Vargas, he couldn't tell him that the mystery man wasn't someone trying to take over Keane's operation, but one of the NSA's own. Wesley had certainly kept this operation close to the vest.

So far he hadn't been able to contact Miguel. Wesley was taking security to a new level and ruining all his plans. Everything they did was being monitored by their Georgia office. And there was no way in hell he could get his hands on a cell phone now. He wouldn't even try.

He was more than a decent hacker, but there was only so much he could do under these circumstances. If only he'd left town a few days ago. He wouldn't have had as much money, but he'd still be free. He wanted to kick his own ass for not following his instinct and leaving when there wasn't a chance he'd be tracked right away. If he tried to leave now, Wesley would know something was off and it would be damn near impossible to get out of the country. His boss would spare no expense hunting him down if he knew he was dirty.

The NSA would plug his picture into all the facial recognition programs around the country. And even if he somehow managed to make it through an airport undetected, he didn't have any of his fake passports or near enough funds to live the way he wanted. The way he deserved.

As Stone and the Moreno woman walked in his general direction, he turned his back to them and started setting up one of the laptops. He couldn't afford to be caught staring. Getting Sophie Moreno alone would be tricky, but when the time was right, he wouldn't waste an opportunity.

Hell, maybe he wouldn't have to use her at all. He really hoped he wouldn't need her, but if by some chance Miguel was captured alive, he knew the drug lord would turn him over with little incentive. If Wesley had to make a deal with Vargas or him, he knew his boss would choose to deal with Vargas. The man was a criminal and he didn't hide what he was.

He'd worked with Wesley long enough to know that no matter how much information he offered up, they'd never offer him immunity if Vargas was offering the same intel. He was considered a traitor, and for that, Wesley would turn his back on him. The best he could hope for would be life in maximum-security prison. And that was if they were feeling generous. If not, he'd get the death penalty for treason. Which was more likely.

That was why it always paid to have a backup plan.

Jack carefully laid out a listening device one of the analysts had given him on the six-foot fold-out table. Sophie sat next to him, her hands clasped tightly in her lap.

As he inspected the device, his phone buzzed in his pocket. He frowned when he saw the number. "Yeah?"

"I think I'm being followed," Ronald whispered.

Jack massaged his temple. He'd given the man simple instructions. "Where are you?"

"A couple blocks from the restaurant you told me to go to. On Ocean Drive."

"Walking?"

"Yes."

"Okay. At the next intersection, cross the street and pay attention to anyone who follows you."

A horn blared in the background. "I'm across but I don't know if anyone followed me."

"Turn back in the opposite direction from the restaurant."

"Why?"

Jack contained his frustration. "Just do it."

"Okay."

"Is there anyone across the street mirroring you?"

"Not that I can tell, but a green sedan just made a U-turn."

"Good, that means your tail is driving. What kinds of stores are you near?"

"There's a deli, a photo shop, a touristy—"

"Go into the deli. It'll buy you more time."

"I'm inside. Now what?"

"Look for a back exit." Restaurants had to take out the trash multiple times during the day, making it less likely that an alarm was on the back door. Jack could hear people talking in the background, and so far it sounded as though Ronald was handling things relatively well. When everything went silent, Jack guessed the other man had made it.

"I'm outside now."

"Head back in the direction of the restaurant, but stay on the street you're on now. Do not go back to Ocean Drive. I'm going to put in a call to our guys. They'll meet you out back."

"Okay."

"Problems?" Sophie asked, her tone distant as he disconnected.

Normally he loved the thrill of a new job, but he simply wanted this one to be over. Then maybe he and Sophie could hole up somewhere for a couple of weeks and do nothing but have sex. That was of course if she forgave him for lying about her friend. But if her friend actually died—fuck, he couldn't even think like that. He had to take care of one problem at a time. "I don't think so."

"Jack? This may not be the best time, but where do you live exactly?"

"What?" He wasn't sure what to make of the random question, and her expression gave away nothing.

"When you're not working."

"I don't have a home." It had never felt weird before, but not having any roots was beyond depressing. Nothing and no one had ever grounded him before—except Sophie. He was constantly working, constantly on the move, but right now he desperately wished he had a place to call home. Someplace to take Sophie to. And not on a temporary basis. The more he thought about that, the less it scared him. Hell, the thought of her walking *out* of his life was more terrifying than anything.

"Oh." She frowned, then glanced around the expansive room, avoiding his gaze.

Jack struggled for a response but knew he'd have to wait until tonight when they'd be able to talk more in-depth about everything without prying ears. "Want to see how we're going to be able to monitor Ronald?"

She turned back toward him and nodded, her expression tight. "Sure."

Chapter 19

Bona fide: proof of a person's true identity.

By the time Wesley walked into the building with Ronald, Jack had already set up four chairs. The two field agents who flanked Ronald wordlessly left him at the table.

Jack had felt a few curious stares at his back, but he ignored them. The only thing that bothered him was a few of the obviously appreciative glances in Sophie's direction. He'd never thought of himself as possessive, but he'd also never been with a woman long enough to develop anything other than a physical relationship. The only woman he'd ever felt that way about had been Sophie—and that definitely hadn't changed. They'd been operating in such a vacuum the past few days that seeing other men look at her made him edgy.

The agents and analysts had set up a sleeping area, a work area, and even a private area to shower. Jack knew Wesley was going to have an issue when he told him that he and Sophie weren't staying, but his boss could deal with it.

Wesley ordered the rest of the agents away before he and Ronald sat across from Jack and Sophie.

Weller cleared his throat and looked at Sophie. "Sophie, I'm so sorry—"

"Save it," she ground out. She stood and pushed her chair

back as she looked at Jack. "Is it okay if I walk around until you're done?"

"Sure." He nodded before focusing on Ronald. "This is how it's going to work. When you meet with Vargas, his men will probably scan you for any sort of listening or tracking device." Jack held out what looked like an ordinary ballpoint pen. "This is something the NSA has been working on. There's a minuscule listening device in here that uses an unusual frequency. We're the only ones plugged into it. It should hold up under any scrutiny."

Ronald held out a tentative hand. "It *should*?"

"It's passed all our tests," Wesley said.

"Is that it?" Ronald asked.

"No, you're also going to be wearing this on your tie." Jack held out a small silver, basically unnoticeable tie pin with a camera in it. "We'll be able to see everything going on, and if anything happens, we'll storm the place."

"What about my daughter?"

"He's going to call you before the meeting. Insist on talking to your daughter right then. If he doesn't let you, it's doubtful she's with him."

"What if he doesn't let me?"

"Then you refuse to meet him," Wesley said.

"What if he does something else? Tries to make me?"

Jack scooted his chair closer to the table. "We're going to have someone stationed at your house watching your wife and a couple guards at your office. If he makes a move, we'll know."

Ronald wiped a hand across his sweaty brow. "What exactly do you want from him?"

"Getting him on United States soil is the most important thing, and you've already done that. What we really need is more information on who he's dealing with in North Africa," Wesley said.

"What if I can't get that? What about my daughter?"

"No matter what happens, we're going to get your daughter back. Vargas will be prosecuted for his crimes, but you need to look at the big picture. If he gets any kind of biological weapons into this country, your entire family could be wiped out along with hundreds of thousands of others. Your friends, everyone you know." Wesley's voice had a reassuring quality to it.

"Is there anything else I should do?" Weller asked.

"Stay calm and don't do anything that could tip Vargas off. Remember, we'll be watching you at all times," Jack said.

"Okay. . . . Do you think it would be possible to talk to Sophie before you guys take me back?" Ronald's voice cracked.

Wesley started to respond, but Jack interrupted. "No."

"I just want to tell her how sorry I am."

"Maybe you should have thought about that before throwing her to the wolves." Jack knew the last thing he should do was rile this man up, but the bastard had almost gotten Sophie killed.

Ronald's face paled as he took the silver pin and slipped it into his jacket pocket. "I guess I deserve that."

Wesley shot Jack a warning glare before standing. "I think we've covered everything. We'll be in contact tomorrow before the meet to test out the audio." He motioned to a couple of the agents cleaning their weapons. "If you'll go with these men, they'll make sure you get back into your office undetected."

Ronald nodded as he stood and shot a pitiful glance in Sophie's direction as he left.

"What the hell was that?" Wesley asked the second Ronald was out of earshot.

Jack shrugged, even though he understood what he was referring to. "What?"

"We need him calm for tomorrow. It wouldn't have hurt to let him talk to Sophie."

"I'm not letting anyone upset her. She's been through enough thanks to that asshole."

"You're letting yourself get too involved with this mission."

Damn straight he was. Jack lifted his shoulders again because he knew it would piss Wesley off. Jack didn't care how involved he was. At this point he wouldn't change a damn thing about the decisions he'd made. "You're the one who insisted I take this job."

"I thought you'd be able to get close to her because of your history—but I expected you to remain professional."

"I guess you were wrong." And Jack wouldn't apologize for anything he'd done. He stood abruptly, his chair scraping loudly against the concrete floor. "I'm getting Sophie out of here."

Wesley started to argue, but Jack cut him off. "We're not staying here. I'm taking her to a nice hotel tonight, and the agency is paying for it. She's been through a lot."

"She seems like she's doing okay."

"She is, but she just found out I lied to her and that her friend is likely being held captive by Vargas. I'm not forcing her to stay here with a bunch of armed men for the next twelve hours."

After a pause, Wesley gave him a tight-lipped nod. "Let me know where you're staying."

"I will. What about the guy I brought in?" When Wesley had been gone he'd seen two of the field agents escorting him out, but he wasn't sure where they'd taken him.

"Took him to a place off-site where he's being questioned. My guy has checked in once, but the man doesn't seem to much. Could be lying, but we'll find out."

"What about Abarca?"

Wesley's face darkened at the mention of her. "Still in federal holding. Won't be put into the system until we bring Vargas down."

Jack nodded, figuring that was the case. They couldn't risk Vargas getting tipped off by someone that Mandy Abarca had been arrested. They weren't sure how far his reach was or what kind of contacts he had. Jack glanced around to make sure no one was within earshot. "What about the other problem?"

"I've got a short list of suspects and an official investigation, but no one on my list is here. No one even knew what was going on until after we'd unpacked everything."

Which meant there was still a mole somewhere within the NSA. A problem that needed to be dealt with, but it wasn't something he could do anything about now. "I'll call you when we get there." At least now he wouldn't be driving a stolen vehicle and he had a clean new ID courtesy of Wesley.

Jack spotted Sophie talking to one of the analysts, Steven something, and pushed down the foreign twinge of jealousy in his chest. The man wasn't acting inappropriately or leering, just politely talking.

She must have felt the weight of his stare on her, because she looked up. For the briefest moment she appeared vulnerable, like the girl he'd lived with. The expression was gone so fast he could almost pretend he'd imagined it. But he hadn't. He'd hurt her by lying about Hannah and he needed to make it right. She turned to the other man, said something, then strode toward him, closing the small distance between them.

"You ready to get out of here?" he asked.

Her eyes widened. "We don't have to stay?"

When he shook his head she let out an appreciative sigh and it made him feel like the king of the fucking world. All the woman had to do was smile and he was lost.

After sweeping the hotel room for bugs, Jack shrugged out of his jacket and laid his weapon on the nightstand. Sophie was sitting in an armchair by the expansive window, staring outside, but he didn't think she was really seeing anything. She'd been quiet the entire drive here, and he hated that she was pushing him out.

His cell phone buzzed with a text from Wesley. He shot off a quick reply and told him he'd be going offline for a while. At least until he could iron out everything with Sophie. He crouched next to her on one knee. She stiffened, completely aware of him, but didn't glance his way. Yeah, he was going to have to work for this.

He wanted to reach out and touch her but held off. "I'm sorry I lied, Soph. I just didn't want you worrying. I knew it would eat you up inside."

She turned to look at him, her dark eyes guarded, almost accusing. "What else have you lied about?" There was a *knowing* about the way she asked that question.

He swallowed hard. "What do you mean?"

"Are you answering with a question because you don't want to tell me the truth? I want to know your *real* name," she snapped, pushing up from the chair, anger radiating off her in waves. Her hands were balled into fists at her sides.

He stood to face her, not sure how he could keep lying to her anymore. His soul couldn't take it. "I already told you."

She advanced on him, covering the distance between them until inches separated them. Her sweet scent wrapped around him as she looked up at him. "The truth. Now. What's the name you were given when you were born?"

Time seemed to slow as everything but Sophie's face funneled out around him. She *knew* and was just waiting for his confirmation. The vein on her neck pumped wildly. She might be nervous about his answer, but she wasn't pushing him away. Part of his brain screamed at him to lie to her. Just give her the easy answer. But the part that cared far too much for this woman knew it was time for the truth. Still, he steeled himself for her rejection. "I think you know the answer."

Triumph flared in her eyes. "I want to hear you say it."

Her strangled whisper sounded overpronounced in the silent room.

"Sam Kelly." The two words dropped with the intensity of a grenade.

Without warning, she shoved at his chest. Hard. Then she slammed her fists against him again and again. "I knew it, you fucking *mentiroso*!" Her loud shout echoed through the room. "I thought I was going crazy!"

Jack cringed as she shouted a few other choice words he understood clearly. His Spanish might suck, but he knew enough that she'd just called him a liar. And she was right.

He grabbed her upper arms and tried to pull her close, but she struggled against him. He was desperate to keep her from pulling away. "Let me explain!"

She struggled to free herself, but he refused to let go. He couldn't let her run out on him. Not now. Not until he'd explained things. And he could tell by the look in her eyes that she was two seconds away from sprinting out the door and never looking back. He tightened his grip. "Damn it, Sophie, I don't want to hurt you."

"Then let me go," she said through gritted teeth as she tugged against his hold again. Her breathing was erratic and the angry fire in her eyes scorching.

His heart was pounding like a jackhammer. "Will you listen to me if I do?"

Her jaw clenched and her body tensed, so he held firm. He didn't squeeze because he was afraid of bruising her, but he kept her in place. "I didn't want to lie to you."

"Was sleeping with me part of the job?" she asked, the words a razor-sharp edge. Her eyes flashed with barely concealed rage.

His answer was immediate. "No. I never should have started something with you. That was a mistake—"

"So now you think it was a *mistake*!" It was as if he'd lit the main fuse on her rage. She hauled back and tried to knee him in the groin. He turned, taking the brunt of her strike against his hip.

"That's not what I meant! I just meant that had nothing to do with the job. That was my choice." Damn it, his thoughts got so muddled around her.

As he tried to shift away and deflect another knee shot without hurting her, she yanked one of her hands free. She slammed her fist square in his chest again and it was clear she wasn't going to stop pounding him.

"Damn it, Soph!" Jack twisted their bodies until they were flat on the bed with her underneath him. Her blow didn't hurt as much as being the target of her rage and mistrust. Hell, he almost welcomed the physical pain. "I couldn't tell you the truth."

"Fucking liar! Did you know I mourned for you? I cried for months and months when I learned you'd died. I lost so much weight I had to see a doctor. You bastard. . . ." Her voice cracked as she trailed off. She closed her eyes and looked away from him as if she couldn't stand to look at him. Tears started rolling down her cheeks and he felt like the biggest bastard in the world.

Rolling off her, he lay flat on the bed and cursed. She instantly jumped up, hovering near the foot of the bed, watching him warily. "I could strangle you right now."

He sat up, ready to move on her if she tried to run. "Are you going to run away or are you going to stay and talk?" Jack tried to keep his voice calm when he felt anything but. Raw panic scraped over him. If she tried to leave, he'd have to stop her, and the thought of restraining her that way shredded him.

"Why did you lie to me?" Her glare sliced into him.

"I didn't have a choice. Besides, what would you have done if I'd waltzed into your office and announced I was your childhood friend, back from the grave?" He hated the hurt look in her eyes as she angrily swiped away the remaining errant tears, but he forced himself to hold her gaze. He needed her to know that he'd only been trying to protect her. That he'd do *anything* for her.

"How long have you been Jack Stone?" Her voice was cold, unforgiving.

"Since Sam died in Afghanistan."

"You talk about yourself in the third person?" That temper flared in her gaze again, white hot and ready to burn him.

The vise around his vocal cords loosened a little. "It keeps me sane. . . ." He hadn't struggled to bury Sam, but he *had* struggled to bury his past with Sophie. It had been the only damn thing that had been hard about leaving his old life behind. "How'd you know who I was?" he asked once he found his voice again.

She wrapped her arms tightly around herself. "Little things. Your birthmark, your eyes, the way you look at me, and the way you called me Soph like it was natural was a big tip-off. Then when we made lo—had sex—it was . . . intense. The way you made me come so easily, the way you touched me, it was like we'd done it before. Damn it, you even smell the same! I kept thinking I was crazy for even thinking you might be Sam. I can't believe you let me mourn you!"

"I swear I didn't want to lie to you," he rasped out.

"But you *did*. Just like you lied about Hannah. How do I know anything you say is the truth and not part of the job? Why did they send you on this mission? There's no way it was a coincidence we used to know each other."

His paused for a moment as he tried to choose the right words. "Because of our history."

Her face tightened. "So what do you want from me?"

That was easy. "Everything."

She pressed a shaky hand to her abdomen and exhaled. When her dark gaze met his, he saw confusion and something a lot like resolution there. She took a step back. "Jack—Sam, whatever, I can't even look at you. I need to leave. . . ."

Her voice broke and the fresh, unshed tears he saw glistening in her eyes cut right through his chest.

He tried to reach out for her, but she shook her head and stepped back before retreating to the bathroom. She slammed the door behind her with incredible force, and though she turned on the shower he could hear her crying. Sobbing, actually.

Fuck.

Though he wanted to go in there, demand that she listen and forgive him, he knew he couldn't. It would just make things worse. She needed time to adjust, to digest everything he'd told her. He couldn't leave her completely alone, so he headed for the attached room with the extra television and couch. Walking away from her tonight was killing him, but if it was what she wanted, he'd do it. But only for the night. He'd give her time to digest everything he'd told her. That was it. Then he was making his claim and his intentions clear. She was his, had been since she was seventeen.

He wasn't walking away from her again.

His job, everything else could be damned. Sophie was the one thing he couldn't walk away from. Ever again.

Sam checked the address for the tenth time and knocked on the door. A woman with graying hair he didn't know answered. He assumed it was Sophie's new foster mother. At least this woman looked nice. Soph hadn't been answering any of his attempts to contact her, and once he'd found out what happened . . . fuck, he wanted to kill that bastard. Technically Soph was too old to still be in foster care, but the state was letting her stay a couple of extra months until she got on her feet. Probably because they were afraid she'd sue them.

He cleared his throat. "Is Sophie here?"

The woman eyed him skeptically, no doubt taking in his desert cammies. He'd be shipping off soon, but his staff sergeant had given him a few days' leave.

"Who are you?"

"My name is Sam. We used to live together, with Ms. Bigsby." In eighteen years, Ms. Bigsby was one of the only decent foster parents he'd ever lived with. Unfortunately she'd been in a bad car accident on the way back from her bingo night and wouldn't be able to keep any kids for a while.

The woman frowned but opened the door wider to let him in. *"Why don't you wait here and I'll go get her?"*

"Yes, ma'am." He clasped his hands in front of him and waited in the foyer. The two-story house looked nice enough. From what he'd learned, Sophie was the only kid living here.

He stared at his watch until he heard Sophie descending the stairs. Her long, dark hair was pulled into a ponytail and she wore a baggy sweater and loose faded jeans. When she reached the bottom she crossed her arms over her chest and stared at him with a blank expression. *"What are you doing here?"* Her voice was flat, lifeless, so unlike the girl he loved.

"I'm leaving in a few days and you haven't been returning my calls. I'm so sorry about . . ." At his words she averted her eyes to the floor, and his throat seized. He'd never been good at expressing himself. His words always got jumbled. Especially around her. He didn't know what to say to make this right. Deep down, he knew nothing ever would. But he still wanted to be there for her.

"There's nothing you can do, Sam. I don't know why you're even here," she mumbled.

He took a step forward and she immediately took a step back toward the stairs, so he kept his distance. *"I still want you to come with me. I'm being sent to Afghanistan, but when I get back we can get a place together. Even if you don't want that anymore, I thought . . . maybe you could write me."*

In an instant her head whipped up and her gaze sharpened on his face. *"I'm not going to write you. I hate you, Sam. You promised you'd always be there for me. You promised."* Her voice broke on the last syllable.

"I didn't know the home would be like that." If he had, he'd have run away with her. *"I didn't even want to go to boot camp right away, but you told me to and—"*

"So it's my fault?" she snapped, anger flaring in her eyes.

"No! I just . . . fuck, I'm sorry. I shouldn't have left. I—"

"Do you know what that monster did to me? He held a knife to my throat and raped me for hours. His wife was in the next room, but she didn't do anything! You should have been there. You promised you'd always be there for me! I can't stand to even look at you, Sam! I hate you and I never want to see you again. Don't call and don't write."

At that, she turned on her heel and raced up the stairs. He knew she was saying the words out of anger, but that didn't stop the jagged edge from piercing his gut. If he'd just waited thirteen weeks, he might have been able to stop what happened. It wasn't as if he would have been living under the same roof as Sophie, but maybe . . . hell, maybe he could have protected her, made sure no one hurt her.

But he hadn't, and someone had.

Jack's eyes opened with a start. It was just a dream. One he hadn't had in years. His heart beat erratically in his chest as he tried to catch his breath. He felt as if he'd run a marathon.

Looking at his watch, he realized it was three in the morning. Sophie hadn't come out of her room once since he'd left her. She'd eventually come out of the bathroom, but she'd shut the door to the bedroom and had been quiet. When he'd asked her if she'd wanted room service, she ignored him.

He scrubbed a hand over his face, hating the helpless sensation that had overtaken him. Against his better judgment, he quietly moved to the bedroom door and peered inside. Curled on her side with her eyes closed, Sophie was breathing and completely fine. Maybe not fine, but alive and safe.

It would have to be good enough for now. He'd fucked up so bad he wasn't sure anything would ever be right again. Now that he'd gotten a taste of her after keeping all his feelings locked up for years, he wasn't sure how he was going to go back to life without Sophie in it.

Chapter 20

Detonator: a device or a small, sensitive charge used to detonate an explosive.

Ronald shut down his computer with shaking hands. This was it. After six months, he was finally going to see his daughter again. He hadn't wanted to come to work today, but both the NSA and Vargas didn't want him to draw any undue attention to himself. Ronald shook his head at the irony.

His cell phone buzzing across his desk made him jump. The number wasn't one he recognized. "Hello?"

"Are you ready?" Wesley Burkhart didn't have to introduce himself. His gravelly voice was distinctive enough.

"I think so." He wiped a clammy palm on his slacks.

"The equipment is working. Remember, we're listening and watching the whole time. As soon as you get what we need, we're taking him down."

"I know." Even to his own ears, he didn't sound convinced. If he was going in by himself, he didn't think he'd be as scared. His daughter was going to be there, though. That made the chance for a screwup unimaginable. Part of him wished he'd gone to law enforcement sooner, but he still didn't know who he would have turned to if the NSA hadn't approached him. If he'd turned to the wrong people and gotten his daughter killed, he'd have never forgiven himself. Hell, he still wasn't sure that wouldn't happen today.

"We're trained for this sort of thing, Mr. Weller."

Easy for him to say. It wasn't his daughter's life on the line. "I need to get out of here."

"Take it easy driving. We all know how stressful this is, but you need to show up in one piece."

"I will. . . . I guess I'll be seeing you soon."

After they disconnected, he checked his shirt pocket one more time to make sure the pen was still there. As he gathered his things to leave, he started to finger his tie, then forced himself to stop. He couldn't afford to draw anyone's attention to it, and Vargas would be watching his every move.

There was a quiet buzz of anticipation humming through the hangar. Jack had cleared off a table so he could prep and give him and Sophie some privacy. Not that she was speaking to him. She'd been quiet, withdrawn, her eyes puffy and red from crying last night—which made him feel like shit—and he didn't want to push her too much until this operation was over. Until the threat of death wasn't hanging over her head anymore. Maybe then she'd listen to him. Or at least think about forgiving him. Then . . . no, he didn't even want to hope for more. Right now he just wanted to bring Vargas down and save her friend.

Ronald Weller would be meeting with Vargas soon, so all the team members were in position. Analysts were ready at their laptops and the agents were waiting for Wesley to give them the go-ahead. A few men were staked out in a nondescript van near Vargas's hangar watching the place, just waiting for him to arrive. As soon as the agents checked in with Jack and Wesley, the team would make their move.

Sophie wrapped her arms around herself in a defensive gesture. "I don't understand why you have to go in there too."

He automatically checked his Kevlar vest and weapon one more time. Maybe he was stupid to feel any sort of hope that she might forgive him, but he liked that he heard concern in her voice. It meant she still cared. "I started this and I'm seeing it through." Not to mention he couldn't let any of these men head into a situation where he wasn't willing to go himself.

He didn't personally know any of the men he was working with today. Wesley had handpicked the agents from various special ops outfits for that very reason. No risk of a leak. He recognized two of the men from a classified Delta Force file, so he had no doubt the rest of the men were just as qualified. They'd have to be. Discovering how deep Vargas's connection was to the Middle East directly impacted national security and the safety of hundreds of thousands of civilians.

Sophie didn't respond. She leaned back against the table and watched him with those big brown eyes as he adjusted his gear.

"You'll have video and audio of me at all times," he added softly.

"I know. It's just I'm afraid I'll lose you . . . again." Her voice cracked and he forced himself to look away from her.

He didn't know how to respond. They hadn't resolved shit after last night, but hearing her say those words stripped him completely raw. It gave him the tiniest sliver of hope that just maybe she could forgive him. "Sophie, I . . . I'll see you soon," he managed to rasp out.

Avoiding her gaze, he turned and strode across the concrete floor. Now was not the time for him to be thinking of anything other than the mission. Fate had a way of taking things away from a person when he least wanted it. He'd seen it too many times before. He'd seen guys get killed in action weeks after their wedding, and he'd witnessed veterans get blown up by a roadside bomb two days before their retirement. It was the way of the world. No matter how much he wanted to be with Sophie, he had to let this play out.

Wesley stood in a semicircle with five other men around one of the tables. They were going over the layout of the other building again. Despite the fact that everyone had gone over the plan more than a dozen times, no one was worried about being overprepared.

As he neared the table, Wesley's phone rang. His boss pressed the SPEAKER button. "We're all here."

"Weller has arrived alone," the other man said.

"Good. How many men around the perimeter?"

"Same as before. Three total. Two static, one roving at four-minute intervals."

Three wasn't bad—though he knew there'd be a lot more men inside. The only problem Jack could foresee was taking down the roving man by surprise. Each hangar sat alone with a little less than a hundred yards in between any two. They had to get to him before he could contact anyone on the inside and they had to take down the other two men without that guy realizing it. Everything came down to precise timing.

"We've got visual contact," one of the analysts shouted from a few yards away.

"Everyone, you know what to do." Wesley's words were all they needed to hear.

Everyone moved into position and Jack resisted the urge to look back at Sophie before falling in line with the other men. He couldn't afford that kind of distraction.

Sweat rolled down Ronald's back and face as he arrived at the hangar. Despite the air-conditioning blasting in his car, he couldn't cool down. Before he could decide if he should park outside, one of the men standing guard banged on the side of the metal building.

Instantly the oversized hangar door rolled back, giving him just enough room to drive through. The man waved him by. He glanced in the rearview mirror and watched the door slam shut. The sound echoed loudly even in the enclosed vehicle.

Dread was a live thing inside him, bringing his body temperature up a few more degrees. He wiped his face with a napkin before getting out of the car and ordered himself to keep his shit together. This wasn't about him right now.

Immediately one of Vargas's men frisked him from ankles to shoulders. Then he ran a wand over his entire body. When nothing beeped, the tense knot in his belly loosened a fraction. Not much, but suddenly his chest wasn't as tight either. Looked as though the NSA's technology worked. He could do this.

He *had* to do this.

In addition to half a dozen armed men lounging around on crates, a small Cessna and two black SUVs were in the hangar. So far there was no sign of Vargas.

Ronald turned to the man who had just frisked him. "Where's your boss?"

The man grunted and nodded toward the plane. As if on cue, the stairs extended and out walked Vargas and two heavily armed men. "You're late."

Ronald didn't have to glance at his watch to know the other man was wrong. "Where's my daughter?" The question came out shakier than he'd intended. He'd spoken to her on the phone but still couldn't believe he would be seeing her soon.

Vargas paused halfway down the stairs, lifted a hand dismissively, and one of his men turned back inside.

A few seconds later, Holly and a familiar-looking Asian woman came through the hatch. They were both dressed almost identically, in jeans and plain white T-shirts. Holly's eyes widened when she saw him, but she didn't say anything. He couldn't see any bruises, so he silently prayed both of them were unharmed.

"You ready to do business?" Vargas's voice jerked his gaze away from his daughter's.

Ronald focused on Vargas as he walked toward him. His

expensive-looking loafers made snapping sounds as he walked across the concrete floor, echoing and bouncing off the vaulted ceiling.

"Who's the other woman?" Ronald asked when Vargas stood a foot away from him.

Vargas ignored him and looked to the man on the left of Ronald.

"He's clean, boss."

Vargas looked back at him. "No more questions. We're finishing this now. Then you can go back to your life."

"Let my daughter go first. Then I'll sign whatever you want." It wasn't part of the plan, but his only concern was getting his daughter to safety. Now that he'd seen with his own eyes that she was alive, he didn't care about anything else. Including his own life.

Vargas's dark eyes narrowed as he took him in from head to foot. "Or I could break every bone in her body and let you watch. I have been very patient up until now. Do not test me."

Mouth dry, Ronald could only nod. There were men watching his every move, he reminded himself. He wasn't alone.

"Good." Vargas turned and motioned toward one of the armed men leaning against two stacked crates. "Rico, get off your lazy ass."

Immediately the man grabbed a suitcase sitting on top of one of the wooden boxes and strode toward them. As if from thin air, another of his men appeared with a folding card table and two folding chairs. Moments later Ronald was sitting across from the only man he'd ever wanted to kill.

Vargas riffled through a few of the papers, then slid them across the table. "Sign these."

Ronald quickly scanned the documents. Vargas wanted him to authorize a lot of flights. A lot of *unusual* flight paths. The kind Ronald would have to personally sign off on. SBMS didn't travel to the Sudan often, and Djibouti held an American military base. "Why do you need to go to these places? I thought you ran cocaine."

Instead of responding, Vargas turned toward one of the men and said something in Spanish that Ronald didn't understand. Without question, the man turned and strode in the direction of his daughter and the other woman.

"Wait." Instinctively Ronald's hand flew out and grasped Vargas's arm.

Vargas shouted something else and the man froze. His eyes traveled to Ronald's grip.

Ronald immediately let his hand drop. "You're going to kill me anyway." His words were spoken so low there was no way Holly could hear.

The drug lord's jaw clenched, but then he shrugged. "I'm picking up a delivery for an associate of mine in the Sudan."

"What about Djibouti?" Ronald knew he was pushing, but he had nothing to lose.

"Why all the questions?"

"I want to know before I die. I deserve that much."

Again, Vargas didn't negate that he would eventually kill him. His mouth curved into a cruel smile. "Djibouti will be a testing ground before we introduce a new *strain* of war against your weak country." He said the words proudly, as if bragging.

Other than a few poor shantytowns, there was an American military base in Djibouti. "War?"

"Your country grows weaker every day. They can't keep out my drugs and they won't be able to keep out, what does your government call it . . . biological warfare. A stupid term for the plague."

"Plague?" Ronald asked dumbly.

Vargas pounded a fist on the table, causing some of the papers to shift. "Enough. Sign now and your daughter will not suffer."

With a shaking hand, Ronald picked up the pen and began

authorizing what could kill thousands. Hundreds of thousands.

It didn't matter, though. Wesley and Jack promised it wouldn't matter in the end. They wanted to find out who Vargas was working with, but they said if things got too dicey they'd storm the place.

So why weren't they here yet? As he authorized the last change, sweat dripped from his forehead onto the paper, smearing some of the ink.

Vargas snatched it from him just as he lifted the pen. Then he glanced to his right at one of his men. With a tilt of Vargas's head, the other man headed toward the women.

Panic settled deep in Ronald's gut, twisting like a rusty blade. Where the hell were those guys? This situation qualified as bad to him. "What are you going to do with us?" he asked.

"Kill you. You will not suffer, though." He stood as he spoke.

One of the men grabbed the chair Ronald was in, forcing him to stand.

Ronald waited with barely concealed impatience as the guard walked toward him, gripping both women by their upper arms. "What do you want me to do with this one?" The man shoved the Asian woman toward Vargas but didn't release his tight grasp.

Even Ronald could see how much pain the woman must be in. The man squeezed her small arm so fiercely, red stained down her skin.

Vargas stared at her for a long moment. "Keep this one alive for now. We might need her later if the Moreno woman decides to show her face."

"You son of a bitch! You're not going to get away with any of this!" The shouting of the petite woman surprised everyone. A stunned silence descended on the hangar.

The pause was short-lived. A loud crack echoed as Vargas

backhanded her across the cheek. "Do not speak unless you are spoken to."

At that, he nodded at the man holding both women. The man shoved Holly in Ronald's direction, then dragged the other woman back toward the plane.

"Daddy," she sobbed as she stumbled forward and wrapped her arms around him.

Ronald held her tight because that was all he could do.

"Take them to the swamp," Vargas ordered.

Ronald wasn't sure what he meant, but he guessed the Everglades. They could dump their bodies and his wife would never know what happened.

Before the thought had a chance to settle in, gunfire and shouting erupted. Holly screamed in his arms and all he could think about was keeping her safe. Using his body as a shield, he threw himself over her. They landed on the floor with a thump. She'd probably have some bruises, but as long as she was alive, it didn't matter.

Sharp pain sliced into his side. He yelled in agony but didn't move from his position. Keeping Holly's head protected with his arms, he risked a glance around. Wesley's men swarmed the place like bees.

Pops sounded everywhere. Everything was so loud and bright. Like the movies, but a hundred times worse. He put his head back down. Holly was trembling underneath him and he was afraid he was dying. He didn't know if he'd been shot, but the needles of pain slicing down his left side told something had hit him.

Suddenly the viciously loud staccato pops stopped. Or maybe he'd gone deaf.

Jack trained his SIG on Vargas, who had a gun placed directly on Hannah Young's head. Sophie was back in the other hangar and he knew she had to be seeing all this through the live video feed.

"Drop the weapon, Vargas," Jack shouted.

"You're not taking me in," the other man shouted back. He pulled Sophie's friend tighter against his body.

From his limited vision, it looked as though their team had neutralized everyone but one man. Through the video feed, they'd been able to get a decent head count, and one man was definitely missing. He spoke low into his radio. "Johnson, you copy?"

Johnson stood off to the left of him with another agent behind some crates and out of Vargas's line of sight. They had one of Vargas's thugs restrained facedown on the floor. Jack didn't look at him, but he saw him tilt his head and speak into his radio. "I'm here."

"There's still one guy missing. Do a full sweep of the crates. Then try to get a shot at Vargas."

"Copy that." Jack still hadn't taken his eyes off Vargas, who was slowly backing toward the plane. As if he thought they'd actually let him leave.

"You're surrounded. Give it up."

"Why should I?"

The fact that he asked told Jack he might be interested in cutting a deal. "You're not who we want. You know that. Let the girl go and we'll talk. So far no one's been hurt." It had been a long time since he'd negotiated with anyone. Normally Jack was undercover as one of the bad guys or the places he infiltrated had no clue he was even there.

Before Jack could respond, one of the thugs he recognized from earlier walked out from behind one of the crates with a gun to Johnson's head. "Boss?" The guy looked around nervously at all his fallen associates.

Shit. Jack hadn't wanted to do this. With measured, slow movements, he reached into his pocket and pulled out the cylindrical detonator he'd been holding on to. "Vargas? See this? It's a pulse laser. I press this button and you die in a fiery explosion."

Vargas took another step back. "You lie!"

"One of my guys is going to open up the crate labeled X6. Tell your boy not to do anything stupid."

"Fine." Vargas nodded at his man.

One of the Delta Force guys kept his weapon trained on Vargas, but walked across the floor. He eyed everyone, then set his weapon down and opened the top of the crate. After digging through stuffing and bubble wrap, the agent gingerly pulled out the rigged pack of C-4 and held it up for everyone to see.

"There's more placed all over this warehouse. And you're within strike range, Vargas. You are not getting out of here alive if you don't cooperate."

When Vargas didn't respond, he continued. "Let the girl go. You don't have a way out of here. Even if you take her, you know we'll be forced to shoot your plane down—but you and I both know you'll never even get that far. We only want to know about your Middle Eastern contact."

"I want immunity."

Of course he did. Jack gritted his teeth. "It depends on your information."

"I know names, times, dates, and meetings. You get it all as long as I get immunity."

At that moment, the hangar door was pulled back. Jack didn't bother turning around. He knew who it was. After disarming the outside security team, his guys had come in the back and through a ventilation shaft.

This would be Wesley coming in to wrap things up. His boss had heard everything and no doubt would deal with this scum.

"Who are you?" Vargas shouted.

Jack felt before he saw Wesley walk up next to him.

"My name is Wesley Burkhart. I'm deputy director of the NSA. You give us what we want, you'll be granted complete immunity but you won't be allowed to step foot in this country again. If you do, the agreement will be void. This is a onetime offer and if I don't like what you have to say, I'll hand you over to the DEA."

"How do I know you're telling the truth?"

"You have my word and you have it in writing." Wesley held up a piece of paper signed by the president.

Jack had known they'd have to deal with Vargas. He hadn't realized Wesley had been *this* prepared. Though he should have expected it. The one thing he hated about this job was the politics. Intellectually he understood that sometimes it really was all about the bigger picture, but he hated making deals with someone like Vargas. Of course, Jack also knew that once they cut Vargas loose, his days would be numbered. Someone would kill him. A sniper, no doubt. The CIA, the NSA, it didn't much matter who. The guy was a walking dead man.

Vargas shoved the girl away from him and laid his gun on the floor. He looked at the man still holding a gun on Johnson and bit out something in Spanish.

Jack figured out enough that Vargas threatened the guy's family if he didn't let the agent go.

Almost immediately the thug dropped the gun and put his hands behind his head.

"Sorry it had to work out like this," Wesley said low enough for Jack's ears only.

"It was inevitable." Jack holstered his weapon and watched as the other men rounded up Vargas's guys.

Wesley squeezed his shoulder. "Go check on Sophie. We can handle things from here."

"Thanks." Jack had turned to leave when Wesley stopped him.

"Check on her, but I want you to help interrogate Vargas."

"No problem." He hurried out of the building and borrowed one of the SUVs to drive down to their building.

The sensation humming through him right now was foreign. Different—better—than any rush he'd gotten before. Better than when he'd graduated from boot camp. He had no clue what the future held for them—hell, if they even had one—but he did know he was taking an extended vacation. If Sophie forgave him, they deserved a chance to see where this thing between them could lead. And some part of him he hadn't known still existed was burning with hope that they might actually have a second chance.

There would be a ton of paperwork and days, maybe weeks, of questioning Vargas, but afterward, he was making some changes in his life. Starting with Sophie. Yeah, he'd lied, but they'd make it over that hurdle. He'd spend the rest of his damn life making it up to her if he had to. And he could think of *plenty* of ways to make it up to her.

As he pulled up to the building, one of his burner phones buzzed. Only the members of the team here had this number. Frowning at the unfamiliar number, he answered, "Yeah?"

"If you ever want to see your girlfriend alive again, you will do exactly as I say."

"Who is this?"

"Thomas Chadwick. Now listen carefully. Sophie's life depends on it."

Chapter 21

Immunity: protection or exemption from something like prosecution.

Ten minutes earlier

Sophie stared at the live video feed and tried to digest the sight in front of her. Vargas had a gun to her best friend's head.

She clutched the edge of the crappy fold-out table as she watched the horrifying events unfold on the computer screen. Pieces of wood were splintering off as she dug into the table. Hannah looked so scared it brought tears to her eyes. This whole thing was too surreal.

"Do you need a drink of water?" the man sitting next to her asked. He was one of the analysts.

Her eyes were glued to the screen. "No, thank you."

Two more analysts sat behind them at another table. They'd been kind enough to set her up with her own computer so she could watch what was going on. Now she wished they hadn't.

It was as if an invisible weight pressed down on her chest, making it impossible to breathe. In addition to Ronald's video feed, which was now obstructed, a few of the field agents had worn cameras, giving her multiple views of the situation in the other warehouse.

As a wave of nausea swamped her, she abruptly stood. The chair scraped against the floor, echoing loudly in the large room. She turned to the man sitting next to her. "Bathroom?" Saying any more was impossible. If she attempted she was likely to puke on his shoes.

His eyes widened, but he pointed toward the back. "Small one near the back door."

Her shoes made rapid clacks as she sprinted across the floor. Focusing on the sound was the only thing that prevented her from hurling. *Breathe in and out.* She repeated it over and over, trying to push down the bile.

Her best friend and the man she'd never stopped loving were in that warehouse. If something happened to either of them, it would kill her.

The bathroom door made a soft snicking sound as it closed. She barely made it before emptying the contents of her stomach into the toilet. Her entire body was chilled, but drops of sweat rolled down her neck and back.

When Sophie was finished, she closed the lid and flushed it. She forced herself to stand on wobbly knees. The stark white bathroom was cold and sterile, but at least the facilities worked. She turned on the cold water and rinsed out her mouth before splashing her face.

The icy sensation jolted through her. With shaking hands she grabbed a paper towel and patted her face dry. Clutching the side of the white sink, she managed to steady herself.

Over the past few days she'd surprised herself by keeping a level head. Maybe it was because Jack had been by her side the entire time. So contained and sure of himself. Now she felt anything but calm. His revelation last night had left her raw and shaken. Jack was Sam. Her first love. The *only* man she'd ever loved. She still couldn't find the right words to say to him, but she wanted the chance to try. God help her, she prayed he was okay.

The door handle was cold as she grasped it. Clutching it, she pulled the door open and found herself staring down the barrel of a gun. She let out a terrified, instinctive yelp. Though she was ready to scream, she froze at the man's words.

"Scream and die." The analyst—Thomas something—roughly grabbed her arm and jerked her toward the lone back door. He kept glancing behind him, but his grip on the gun and her never wavered. "You're coming with me."

She seriously contemplated screaming but knew it would be a stupid move. He might shoot not only her, but the other two analysts too. She wouldn't have that blood on her hands.

He shoved open the back door with startling force, then dropped her arm and pulled out a key fob. She jumped when an alarm beep sounded. He trained his gun on her once again and handed her the keys. "You're driving."

"Where are you taking me?"

"We're just taking a little drive." He took a step forward and pushed the gun to her chest.

She froze at the feel of cold steel pressing through her shirt. Uncontrollable shivers rippled through her. She'd only ever felt like this once before. When her foster father had pressed a knife to her neck—*No! Keep it together,* she ordered herself. After all she'd been through the past few days, now wasn't the time to lose it.

She clutched the keys in her hand. The jagged metal piercing her skin forced her to think. Wordlessly she moved away from him and toward the SUV. He followed suit and got into the passenger side, never taking that gun off her.

"There's a back way out of here, so follow my directions. If you listen, you just might make it out of this alive."

She started the engine, then kicked it into drive. "Why are you doing this?"

"You're my ticket out of the country." He pulled a cell phone out of his pocket and laid it in his lap. "Follow this way." He pointed toward the right. The private airport was large, but the layout was simple.

She knew exactly where he was taking her. The back exit was where she and Jack had entered the first time. She kept driving parallel to the surrounding fence until they came to the opening. She started slowing the vehicle even before he ordered her to stop.

"Get out and roll the fence back. Don't do anything stupid." As if to prove his point, he shifted his gun to his other hand, straightening it in her direction.

Without looking at him, she slid from the vehicle and did as he instructed. If there had been neighboring woods or any place she could run, she'd have taken the chance. As it was, there was nothing but a semi-demolished building across the street. The building might provide some cover, but it wasn't likely she'd make it across the four-lane road, over the other fence, and into the building without being shot in the back.

And she really didn't want to die that way. Okay, she didn't want to die period. The only thing that gave her hope was the fact that he hadn't shot her yet. He needed her for something, which meant he would keep her alive until then.

"Turn left and follow this road until you see signs for 95 South, then get on," he ordered as she slid back into the driver's seat.

Then he pulled out a phone and dialed a number before pressing SPEAKER and placing it on the dash.

When Jack's familiar voice came on the line, her hands jerked against the wheel.

"Yeah?" Jack said.

"If you ever want to see your girlfriend alive again, you will do exactly as I say."

"Who is this?"

"Thomas Chadwick. Now listen carefully. Sophie's life depends on it."

Sophie clutched the wheel so tightly her knuckles turned white. She thought about speeding up and trying to crash, but he was strapped in too and still firmly held the gun on her. If she tried, she'd probably end up shot.

"I'm listening," Jack growled.

"You're going to trade Vargas's life for Sophie's."

"No." Jack's answer was automatic.

With that one word, Sophie's heart cracked wide open.

"I don't think you understand the situation."

Out of the corner of her eye, Sophie watched her captor reach into his pocket. Before she realized what he was doing, he flashed a knife in her direction. With the click of a button, the blade whipped open and he sliced into her arm.

"Aah." Instinctively she swerved as he cut her. She cried out as the pain registered. Blood dripped all over the seat and her jeans. Her arm throbbed, but the laceration was shallow at best.

"Sophie?" Jack's deep voice raked over her.

Thomas answered. "She's fine. Just a little cut. If you don't do what I say, she'll have bigger cuts all over her body. Bitch won't be recognizable by the time you get to her."

Ice chilled her veins. She'd die before she let that bastard torture her.

"Why do you want Vargas?" Jack asked.

"He owes me a lot of money and I can't get out of the country without it or him. I *need* that money. It was only a matter of time before he gave you my name."

For a moment Sophie's world went fuzzy. That meant Vargas had definitely been captured. Before she ran to the bathroom, he'd still been free. "Is Hannah alive?" she asked before she could think about censoring herself.

"She's fine," Jack answered.

"One more word out of you, and I'll cut through your

muscle." Thomas didn't yell, but his voice had a deadly edge to it that told her he'd have no problem following through with his threat.

Biting her lip, she focused on the road in front of her and tried to block out the pain in her arm.

"As I was saying, you'll bring Vargas to a location of my choice and I'll give you the girl. It's a simple trade and no one has to get hurt."

Jack was silent on the other end for painfully long. "You know I can't give you Vargas. He's too valuable."

Thomas looked in her direction, but she stared straight ahead. Tears stung her eyes, but she fought them back.

"You don't care what happens to the girl?"

"Vargas is too valuable, so if that's all you've got, you're barking up the wrong tree." Jack's voice was monotone, uncaring.

Then he disconnected.

All the air sucked from Sophie's lungs. Tears blinded her vision, but she managed to keep the vehicle straight. There was a sign for 95 South, so she turned right as the man next to her cursed.

"How long have you known Stone?" Thomas demanded.

"A few days." Her words came out scratchy and unsteady. She tried to ignore the jagged talons of the raw pain raking through her, but it was impossible. Jack didn't care what happened to her. She was expendable. A sob built in her throat, but somehow she managed to shove it down. Just barely.

"Damn it! I thought . . ." He tapped the gun against his leg, then made another call. Thomas didn't put him on speaker this time, but in the quiet vehicle, she could hear every word.

Jack answered immediately. "I told you I'm not making a deal."

His words were just one more nail in her coffin and one more punch to the gut.

"I can give you information on Vargas, but, more important, on his contact, Abu al-Ramaan. No matter what he says, Vargas doesn't know shit about the man. I've got a list of probable targets and a list of Abu's contacts along the East Coast and some in California. He wants to unleash biological terror within the next couple months. I'm the only man who can help you."

"How could you possibly have this information?"

"You think I keep all my eggs in one basket? Vargas would kill or betray me with no problem. Unfortunately I need my fucking money. I've worked too hard to get shortchanged now. I know you guys will hunt me down, but with enough cash, you'll never find me. It always pays to have a backup plan." He sounded so proud of himself. So smug and sure.

"Where do you want to meet?"

"Uh-uh. You get Vargas, then head south. Once you're on the road, call me and I'll give you further instructions. If I even think you've brought a team, I'll put a bullet in her head before you can get within a mile."

"Your information better be good."

"Trust me, it is. Oh, and, Jack?"

"Yeah?"

"Don't waste your time trying to track me. I disabled the GPSs on all the vehicles earlier today."

Jack hung up.

Thomas snapped the phone shut and glared at her. "Maybe you don't mean as much to him as I thought."

On one level Sophie understood national security was a priority, but this wasn't just Jack rejecting her. She'd never say his name aloud, but this was Sam. *Her Sam.* And she wasn't enough for *him.* A vise tightened and twisted around her heart, the screws puncturing so painfully it was all she could do to keep the vehicle straight. He might as well have reached into her chest and ripped her heart out with his bare hands. She meant nothing to Jack.

Jack slid his phone into his pocket with shaking hands. More than rage, raw fear snaked through his veins like liquid fire. Hanging up on Thomas Chadwick had been the hardest thing he'd ever done. It had been a huge risk and if Sophie hadn't been part of the equation, he wouldn't have second-guessed himself.

Chadwick needed Jack's help, so Jack knew he wouldn't kill Sophie. The only way to convince him of that had been to bargain. If Jack had given in too quickly, Chadwick would have realized just *how* important she was to him. Then he'd have had all the bargaining power and Sophie would be dead.

Jack exited the vehicle and pulled up the hangar door a few feet. The two other analysts still clacked away at their computer. Good. They didn't know Chadwick was missing. Both glanced at him but just as quickly returned to what they were doing.

"Hey, I need Chadwick's help. He's over at Vargas's hangar helping set up the interrogation room." He casually dropped the information as he walked toward their table, trying to gauge their reactions.

The only female of the group frowned at him. "But Wesley said—"

"Change of plans. I've worked with Chadwick before and I requested him."

"Fine." The woman shrugged, then returned to her computer.

While they were busy, he made his way to one of the farthest stations set up in the corner of the building. He glanced over his shoulder as he grabbed a tracking device. Not that it technically mattered. He doubted they'd question him, but he needed to be above suspicion for the next ten minutes. Just enough time to get the hell out of there. To get to Sophie.

What he was planning was illegal and if he failed he'd

probably get thrown in jail. Okay, there was no probably. Letting Sophie die wasn't an option, though. He'd sell his soul for her without question.

Without wasting time worrying about the consequences, he headed back to the other hangar. Instead of parking in the front, he parked in the back where there weren't any other vehicles. Inside the building, everyone still had their guard up, but things had broken down into routine. Round up the bad guys, question them, and get ready to head home. That was the way things always worked, and the routine was the only advantage he could count on.

Plastic sheets were draped over the fallen bodies, and Vargas's other men had been restrained and were being guarded by a few agents.

As Jack crossed the open floor, he kept his eyes open for any sign of Vargas, but didn't see him. Wesley nodded in his direction and motioned Jack over to him and an agent.

"I was just telling Johnson I want you to take point on the interrogation. He'll be standing by, but you make the calls," Wesley said.

Jack glanced between the two men. "Where is Vargas now?"

Wesley pointed toward the back. "We put him in an office in the back. Once we get everything squared away here, we'll transfer him."

"Where are we taking him?"

"One of our satellite offices," Wesley answered.

Jack nodded. He was aware of at least one office in Miami, but for all he knew, there could be more. The NSA had nondescript offices all over the country. Half the people who worked for them couldn't tell their families what they did every day. Even Jack wasn't privy to all their locations. That was the kind of information people would kill for.

As they headed to the back, Johnson cleared his throat. "Listen, man, thanks for earlier."

"No problem." Jack guessed the guy was embarrassed that one of Vargas's guys had managed to disarm him and put a gun to his head in front of everyone, but there wasn't much he could do about it now. Shit happened.

Johnson was silent for a moment before continuing. "I can't believe that guy got the drop on me."

"Don't let it get to you. It happens to the best of us." Jack pushed down the foreign twinge of guilt. He could ruin this guy's career by what he was about to do. "Stay here for a second, will ya?"

Johnson frowned but nodded. Jack made his way back toward his boss. Wesley was talking to one of the Delta Force agents. Perfect.

"Is there a problem?" Wesley asked.

"No problem, I just want someone more experienced with interrogation, especially after what happened earlier." He nodded at the other agent. "You're with Delta Force, right?"

The man nodded. "Max Schaeffer."

Jack looked at his boss. "I want him."

Wesley's lips pursed into a thin line as he studied Jack, but he nodded. "Fine."

As they headed back to where Johnson waited, Wesley stopped him. "How's Sophie?"

Jack didn't bother turning around. "Fine," he threw over his shoulder. Wesley had an uncanny ability for weeding out bullshit. As they neared Johnson, Jack slapped him on the shoulder. "Wesley wants to see you, man."

Johnson would be pissed at first, but later when he realized what Jack had done, he'd probably thank him. Of course Jack would likely be in jail by then, so it wouldn't matter. In order to get Vargas out of the building, he was going to have to take out the Delta Force guy. If he'd done it to Johnson, the man would be demoted and probably fired for screwing up twice within the same day. And Jack couldn't have that hanging on his conscience.

"How do you want to work this?" Schaeffer asked as they turned down the small hallway.

"You can take the lead." Jack held open the door for the other man.

Jack quickly assessed the situation. Vargas sat at a small desk with his hands cuffed in front of him. One agent leaned against the wall standing guard. He straightened as they entered.

Jack didn't have any time to waste. In one swift move, he landed a sharp blow to the agent's right temporal lobe. Near the eye, but not hard enough to inflict any lasting damage. It was a move he'd used too many times to count. Never on one of his own guys, though. Before the agent's body hit the floor, Jack struck out at Schaeffer.

The guy started to turn as Jack slammed his fist, then elbow across Schaeffer's back and neck. If he'd reacted a second sooner, things might have turned out differently. Thank God for small miracles. Tension thrummed through Jack, but he kept his focus on the goal.

Get Vargas out of the holding room alive. Get him out of the direct hold of the NSA. Free Sophie.

After that, he would worry about consequences.

Jack stepped over the unconscious body and roughly yanked Vargas up by the collar. When he did, he slipped a tracking device under his shirt.

"What the hell are you doing?" Vargas's voice held a trace of fear.

"Getting you out of here." Jack snagged the handcuff keys from the first man he'd knocked out, but didn't release Vargas.

Easing open the door, he glanced down the short hallway. No one was there, but the men he'd knocked out wouldn't stay down for long.

"What are you—"

Jack shoved Vargas against the wall, wrapping his hand

around his neck. "Keep your mouth shut and you might get out of this alive."

The other man's dark eyes narrowed, but he nodded.

There hadn't been a guard at the back door before, but Jack wasn't taking the risk. They rushed down the rest of the hallway. When they reached the metal door, Jack opened it two inches.

Relief slammed into him. It was clear. Grasping Vargas's upper arm, he jerked him outside. Once they were in the relative safety of the SUV, Jack secured the man's cuffs to the side handle, then gunned the engine. Their window of opportunity to escape undetected was rapidly shrinking.

Getting Vargas out of holding was only half of his problem. Actually getting off the property undetected was going to be the hard part. Instead of driving parallel to the fence outlining the property, he drove behind two hangars, then made a sharp left and sped across the tarmac. The NSA had given orders that all flights be grounded. By driving this way he was putting them out in the open, but the path to the back gate was a lot shorter.

"Where are you taking me?" Vargas snapped.

"Your friend Chadwick wants to make a trade." Fear for Sophie's safety a living thing inside him, Jack glanced in the rearview mirror as he maneuvered around parked planes. No one was behind them.

"You know about him?" Vargas's voice was cautious.

"I do now."

"I take it from our escape that you are working alone." It wasn't a question.

"Your friend has something I want." Jack's fingers flexed around the steering wheel. The back gate was still open. No doubt from when Sophie and Chadwick left. Jack was counting down the seconds until he wrapped his hands around that bastard's neck. When he'd heard Sophie cry out in pain, he nearly lost it. The knowledge that if he'd reacted he would have put her in more danger was the only thing that stopped him.

"Something or someone?"

Yeah, as if he was going to have that conversation with Vargas. "How long have you worked with Chadwick?"

He shrugged. "Long enough."

Nice, evasive answer. "Who approached whom?"

Vargas shifted uncomfortably in his seat. "We approached him, of course."

Somehow Jack doubted that. Jack was silent as he followed the signs toward I-95.

"Ninety-five South? Where are you taking me?"

"Your guess is as good as mine." Intentionally, Jack jerked the vehicle sharply as he took the ramp onto the highway. When he did, he retrieved his phone from his pocket and held it down next to his left leg. His phone was usually set to silent, but he'd also set the tone to mute.

Wesley was going to be pissed, but texting him was the only way to communicate. *Chadwick has Sophie. Wants 2 trade Vargas. Activate small tracking on V. C has info on Ramaan. Follow. No choppers.*

The message was choppy at best, but Wesley would figure it out. Or at least Jack hoped he would.

After pressing SEND, Jack made a show of pulling his phone out of his pocket and dialed Chadwick. Even though Vargas looked uninterested, Jack knew the man was watching his every move. He redialed Chadwick's number and waited.

He answered midring. "Do you have him?"

"Yes."

"Good, put me on speaker."

Jack did as the man ordered.

"Miguel?" Chadwick spoke.

"I'm here," Vargas said.

"Is anyone following you?"

Vargas turned around as he answered, "Not that I am aware of."

"Is anyone with you?"

"No, he's working alone. Took out two of his men to free me."

"Can you get us out of the country?"

By now Wesley would have grounded every flight in Florida. Something he had the power to do and something Chadwick no doubt knew. Chadwick's order to free Vargas was a tricky bet, but Jack understood why he'd done it. He clearly didn't have all the funds he wanted to live his life on the run, and a man like that, who'd betrayed his country, would never be satisfied without all the money he'd been counting on. However much it was, Jack could only guess.

Vargas looked at Jack, a smirk playing across his hard features. "Do not worry about the transportation. I have men on standby."

"Good. As soon as we get off the phone, Jack, you're going to throw your phone out. If you don't, Miguel will tell me at the meet and your girlfriend will pay."

"Where's the meet?"

"Do you know where the Channel Five Bridge is in Long Key?"

He'd grown up in south Florida. Of course he knew. "Yes."

"Turn off onto that abandoned strip right before the original Overseas Highway."

"We'll be there."

"If you're not, your girlfriend dies."

"If you don't have the information you promised, you won't make it to jail."

Chadwick hung up.

Though he was loath to do it, Jack tossed his cell out the window. He'd give the slimy bastard credit. He'd covered a lot of his bases. Just not all of them.

"What information has he promised you?" Vargas asked.

Jack shrugged and increased his speed.

"How do you know he won't betray you?" Vargas spoke again.

Jack internally smiled. Vargas was getting nervous. "I don't, but he's got better information than you. I'm willing to take the risk."

Vargas was silent, so Jack reopened the conversation. "There's a man that works for you I'm interested in. You sent him after me a few days ago."

"I don't know who you are talking about."

Jack gave a brief description of Levi but didn't say his name because he assumed Levi had used an alias. Vargas didn't respond, so Jack guessed he knew exactly who he referred to. "Why wasn't he with you today?"

"Why do you want to know?"

"Like I said, it's personal." Jack couldn't give the guy a reason, so either he told him or he didn't.

Vargas shifted against the leather seat, causing his handcuffs to jangle against the side bar. He didn't speak for so long Jack gave up on him answering. Finally Vargas sighed. "What does it matter? The man you speak of doesn't work for me anymore."

"Why not?"

"He did a few contract jobs, then left to hook up with some Russians—which he thinks I don't know about. He did not follow orders well. Who is he?"

"I've been after him for a few years. Thanks for the tip." Jack made a mental note about the Russians. He'd put Levi out of his mind for the past day, but he wanted to find his friend when all this was over. He just hoped Levi hadn't gotten in over his head.

Chapter 22

FUBAR: Fucked-up Beyond All Recognition.

In the deafeningly silent vehicle, Sophie fought to keep it together. Tears burned her eyes, but she blinked them back. It was hard, though, when she knew she was going to die.

Had no doubt about it. Jack didn't give a shit about her. Only information and his damn job were important to him. Her heart might still be beating in her chest, but it wasn't working. As a young woman she'd loved Sam, but she loved Jack, the man he'd become, just as much. More, even. Something she could finally admit and it didn't matter. He not only didn't feel the same but was just like everyone else.

She was disposable. A means to an end.

Her throat and muscles were so tight from holding back the avalanche of tears pressing at her, she was practically shaking.

As Chadwick tapped his gun against the center console, Sophie forced herself to stay calm. She was terrified that any overt movement would set this maniac off. She had one foot inside death's door, and time was not on her side.

Every time Chadwick glanced at his watch, the more antsy he got. At least he wasn't chatty. Since his last call to Jack he'd said a few words to her, but only to give her directions. If he wanted to talk she'd start crying and she'd never stop. God only knew how he'd react to that. Probably knock her out or cut her again.

Her yellow sweater sleeve had turned a crimson red, but the bleeding had stopped. Now the dried material was stiff against her arm. Every time she moved she was afraid she'd open the wound again.

They were parked just off the road, right before a long bridge in a gravelly spot that couldn't be called an actual parking area. From where they sat she had a good view of the new bridge and the older, crumbling one that ran parallel to it.

The turquoise water glistened under the bright sun and there literally wasn't a cloud in the sky. It seemed impossible that she was being held at gunpoint on such a beautiful day. Cars zoomed past in sporadic intervals, but traffic was fairly light. Every time she saw a dark vehicle in the rearview mirror, she nearly jumped.

Then she cursed herself for the reaction. She had to stay immobile and not give Chadwick a reason to lash out at her.

When the SUV she was watching started to slow and turned off the road she automatically swiveled around in her seat. Chadwick did the same.

"You're going to do everything I say or you're getting a bullet in your back."

Ice slithered through her veins. Swallowing hard, she nodded. The SUV pulled up next to them on her side, but she didn't make a move to get out.

Chadwick glanced around nervously, then motioned with his gun. "I'm getting out on this side. Climb over the center console."

She did as he said and the moment her feet touched the ground, he grabbed her by her injured arm, then shoved his gun into her spine.

Little needles of pain splintered up her arm, but raw fear overtook any agony.

Sophie watched as the passenger-side window of Jack's SUV rolled down. Miguel Vargas was handcuffed to the side handle and Jack was in the driver's seat.

"Miguel, did he toss his phone?" Chadwick asked.

"Yes."

"Were you followed?"

"No."

"Jack, get out where I can see you." Chadwick's voice rose.

Blood rushed in Sophie's ears, but she kept her focus on Jack. It killed her to even look at his face knowing he cared so little for her, but she knew he'd save her if he could. Even if she wasn't a priority in this trade-off. The small consolation did little to ease the clawing ache in her chest.

Jack got out but stayed behind the front of the vehicle. "I want what you promised me," he shouted.

"First come out from behind the SUV. I want to see you." Chadwick's voice rang in her ears.

"I'm not putting my weapon down."

"Fine. I still want to see you."

Without moving her head, her eyes strayed to Vargas. He sat immobile, looking so calm, as if this were something he did every day.

She was barely keeping it together.

Jack still had his gun drawn as he walked around the vehicle toward them. "Let the girl go, Chadwick. I've held up my part of the bargain."

The girl. God, he didn't even say her name. She truly meant so little to him.

"First you unlock Miguel."

Jack's pale eyes narrowed. "Not until you give me what I came for."

"Take the minicomputer in the middle seat."

Gun still pointed in their direction, Jack sidestepped until he opened the door, retrieved it, then transferred it to his vehicle. He then unlocked Vargas with one hand, jerked him from the vehicle, and clasped the man's hands behind his back and secured the cuffs again. "We exchange at the same time, Chadwick."

"After the exchange, we leave first," her captor snapped.

Jack nodded in agreement. "If the information you gave me doesn't pan out, I'll hunt you to the ends of the earth. You know that."

"I haven't stayed alive this long by being stupid. All I want is to get out of here alive and get my fucking *money*," Chadwick snarled. "And if you try anything, I'll take her down with me."

Shit, shit, *shit*. She had no doubt he meant it. Could only imagine what it would feel like to have a bullet ripping into her.

Jack, however, didn't seem to break a sweat, which further embedded that dagger in her chest. "On the count of two. One, two."

When Chadwick released her, Sophie jerked her arm close to her chest. Without the gun pressing into her back, she no longer felt as if the Grim Reaper was about to claim her. Keeping her steps measured, she resisted the urge to sprint. Everything around her funneled out as she walked toward Jack. This entire time he'd barely made eye contact with her, but even now she knew he was aware of her gaze on him.

Jack was aware of everything—even if he didn't give a shit about her.

When she and Vargas passed each other, he tossed her a disdainful glance. She picked up her pace.

As soon as she was a foot from Jack he spoke low enough for her to hear. "Get behind the truck."

She nodded and continued past him, rushing the last few feet to gain cover. A second later Jack joined her. "Stay low. I'm letting them go and I don't want anything to happen to you."

The sound of the other engine revving, tires squealing, then the loud pop of gunfire sent her diving for cover. Sophie shielded her ears and hit the ground. This sound was becoming all too familiar.

"Damn it!"

She looked up to find Jack pounding on the hood.

"What happened?" Standing, she brushed off her hands on her jeans.

"They shot the engine." He holstered his weapon in the back of his pants, then rubbed a hand over his face.

She couldn't find it in her to care. All she felt was betrayal and she just wanted to see that Hannah was truly safe, then go home.

Recovering quickly from his outburst, Jack assessed her from head to toe in such a clinical fashion she felt like a specimen under a microscope. "Is this your only wound?" He gently held her arm and moved the material of her shirt to the side.

Even though what she really wanted to do was strike out at him and hurt him the way he'd hurt her, she just nodded.

"Did that bastard hurt you in any other way?" There was a sharp bite to his question.

Still not trusting herself to speak, she shook her head.

"We'll take care of your wound later. I hate bringing you with me, but we've got to go after them now, Sophie."

She nodded again. If she started talking, she feared she'd open the floodgates and would never stop crying. And God help her, she refused to let Jack see how much he'd affected her. How he'd basically flayed her insides.

Sophie was safe and with him. The reality went a long way in letting Jack focus and do his damn job.

His woman was safe.

That was the only thing that mattered. She was quiet and possibly in shock, but she was alive. He kept saying the words over and over, but they did nothing to still the beast raging inside him. That bastard Chadwick would eventually pay.

But first Jack had to catch him. He ran through their options in his head. He needed to upload the information he had to Wesley and he really needed to track Vargas and Chadwick. As a car whizzed past them, he grabbed the small computer case and handed it to Sophie. "Just stay behind me."

With her injured arm he didn't like giving her anything to hold, but he needed both hands free. He made his way across the gravelly area until they stood on the edge of the highway. Despite the cooler weather and the ocean breeze, the heat from the black asphalt reflected off the road, warming his entire body.

Glancing in both directions, he said a silent prayer that someone would come along. As if on cue, a green Jeep came barreling across from the other side. No doubt coming from Key West. Jack put one foot out and waved frantically, hoping the driver would slow. As soon as the driver crossed the bridge to their side, he went past them, but slowed and did a U-turn before pulling off a few yards away.

A college-aged guy wearing board shorts and flip-flops got out and walked toward them. "Are you guys okay?"

"Yeah, my wife hurt her arm and our SUV broke down. We're just trying to get to Marathon." Jack hated lying to a Good Samaritan, but there was no other choice.

"I'm heading back to the mainland, but I can get you to an auto shop or something."

Jack withdrew his weapon and pointed it at him. "Step away from the vehicle."

The man eyed him warily but took a few steps in the opposite direction. "Are you serious, man? You robbing me?"

"You'll be compensated. Do you have a phone?"

With his eyes on the gun, the guy nodded and reached into his pocket. "Here, man, take whatever you want." He tossed it to Jack.

Without turning, Jack called out to Sophie. "Soph, get in the vehicle." He could hear her moving around behind him and when she slid into the passenger seat, he walked the few feet to the driver's side and got in.

The road was clear in both directions, so he flipped a quick turn and headed in the direction Chadwick had gone. It was odd they were heading *toward* the Keys instead of the mainland, but he guessed Chadwick and Vargas had already worked something out. Which meant they were leaving either by private plane or boat very soon. Though it was more likely by boat since Jack knew without even asking that Wesley had grounded all flights in the area—if not the entire state. It was protocol.

He risked a glance at Sophie, who'd been quiet. She was safe. It was pathetic but he kept looking at her, needing to reassure himself of it. "Sophie, honey, check the back and see if there's a first aid kit."

"I'm fine," she croaked out.

Frowning, he looked at her again, but she turned her face away from him to stare out the window. "Sophie, you can tell me if he hurt you in some other way. . . ." His gut twisted as scenarios ran through his head. He'd gut Chadwick if he'd touched Sophie. The guy would never see the inside of a prison cell.

A light sheen of tears glistened in her eyes when she looked back, but she shook her head. "He just cut my arm. I'm fine." Her voice was tight.

He wanted to pull over and comfort her. Pull her into his arms and make sure she understood she'd never be in danger again as long he was alive. "This nightmare is almost over, Soph. Soon you'll be able to go back to your life." When she didn't respond, he frowned but decided to let it go. She'd been handed a lot of shit the past couple of days. If she needed to decompress in silence, he'd let her. "Can you turn on the computer?"

When she nodded he reached into his pocket and handed her a wireless USB connector. "Once it's on, connect to the Internet."

As she started pulling out the computer, he punched Wesley's number into the stolen phone.

"Yeah?" Wesley barked into the phone.

"It's me."

"Where the hell are you and what the hell is going on? All of our GPS trackers have been disabled."

"Did you get my text?"

"Yeah, Chadwick's the mole and you've put a tracking device on Vargas. Does that about cover it?"

"More or less. Did you figure out which tracker I used?"

His boss snorted. "Yeah, we're following him now."

"Where's he headed?"

"Straight down U.S. 1. Looks like he's moving through Islamorada now."

"Have you got him on satellite?"

"No, there's a problem with the signal. For all we know, Chadwick did something to our system."

It was highly possible. "I'm going after them. Have you sent another team?"

"They're preparing to fly out as we speak. . . . How's Sophie?"

"Shaken up, but she'll be okay." She had to be. If she decided that everything that had happened was too much to handle and she wanted nothing to do with him—*hell no*. Jack wouldn't think like that.

"Was breaking Vargas out worth your career?"

He glanced at Sophie, who was staring intently at the computer screen. "Yes."

"You might get jail time."

"I know."

Wesley swore loudly. "I can't believe you did this, Jack. What the hell were you *thinking*?"

He was thinking Sophie was the only damn thing that mattered to him. That if he lost her he might as well put a fucking bullet in his head. He'd seen and waded through so much shit the past few years, and while some of it was hard to deal with, losing Sophie—he simply couldn't do it again. It would be like ripping his own heart out of his chest. As they crossed one of the minibridges, Jack slowed down and pulled into a local gas station. "Hold on, Wesley." He turned his attention to Sophie. "Can you drive?"

Again she nodded. He wanted to ask her what else was going on, but couldn't afford to waste the time. If Vargas got away, it was more than likely Jack would go to jail. He knew Wesley would try to pull some strings, but Jack had understood the risk when he made the choice. Even so, he wanted a shot at a life with her.

They quickly switched seats. While Sophie drove, Jack pulled up the files from Chadwick and started e-mailing them to his boss. "Wesley, I'm sending you everything on the computer he gave me. From the looks of it, if these dates and names are real, we've got a jump on a few big hits."

"You better pray this information is good."

"Believe me, I am—"

"Wait, looks like they're turning onto Coco Plum Drive. . . . Okay, we've got the satellite up. Hold on."

Jack moved the phone away from his mouth. "Once we cross into Marathon, look for Coco Plum Drive. It'll be on your left."

"I know where it is. It leads to the city beach," Sophie said without looking at him.

Her flat, almost monotone voice sent off alarm bells.

"You there, Jack?" Wesley's voice came over the line.

"I'm here."

"We've got a team headed your way. One chopper and we've notified the Coast Guard."

"Can you link the satellite image to this computer?"

"I've already got someone working on that. . . . One more sec. . . . Okay, should be streaming in."

"Got it. I'll stay behind them. See if you can cross-reference any of those names with—"

"Jack, focus on catching Vargas. I'll delegate this information later."

"I'll call you if we have any problems, but I had to steal a Jeep. Left the guy standing near the Channel Five Bridge. Can you contact the locals?" The last thing he needed was to get pulled over by a local cop.

"Done."

Jack kept his eye on the screen. Coco Plum Drive was a few miles long. It shot south toward the Atlantic, then sharply curved back up northeast. Along the first stretch there were a few homes on the right and a thick cluster of trees on the left. After the turn, the city beach and one or two multimillion-dollar homes were the only things along the water.

A makeshift shack proclaiming to sell lobsters and shrimp was up on the left near their turn.

"This is it, right?" Sophie asked.

"Yes. . . . Shit," he muttered as he watched the satellite image on-screen. What looked like a cigarette racing boat was moving fast toward the city beach. Exactly where Vargas and Chadwick were headed. He couldn't allow them to get on that boat, especially since that particular type was known for being able to outrun the Coast Guard. "Speed up, Soph."

"Don't call me Soph anymore!" she snapped, her voice sharp as she pressed harder on the gas.

"What's going on? And don't say you're fine because you're obviously not. You can't shut me out like this."

She snorted.

"I'm not a mind reader. . . . Wait, follow where the road curves." He looked back at the screen and ran through scenarios. "When we near the entrance to the city beach parking area, speed up until we pass it, then pull off about thirty yards down." As he watched, the vehicle Vargas was in slowed and turned into the city beach parking lot. Well, parking lot was a bit of a stretch. There were about ten spaces drawn out in a badly paved area. He couldn't see that much from the satellite view, but he'd been there before. After most of his undercover operations, he usually spent his downtime fishing and vacationing in the Keys.

With the exception of a house half a mile down the road and another house a mile down from that on the point, mangrove and palm trees surrounded the area. He'd have plenty of cover.

Though he wanted nothing more than to grill Sophie until she told him what the hell was going on in her head, he called Wesley. If he didn't stop Vargas, he'd never get to talk to Sophie again. Or it would be from behind bars.

"Are you seeing this?" Jack asked the second his boss answered.

"Yeah. That boat is tearing through the water. Do not let them get on."

"Am I authorized to use deadly force if necessary?"

"If you can't bring them in alive, you have to take them out. We can't risk either of them escaping."

"Understood. . . . Park here." Jack pointed to a stretch of grassy area but kept his eyes trained on the computer.

The vehicle had parked, but only one person got out. The images weren't crystal clear, but he could see one of the men walk around to the passenger seat and pull a body from the vehicle. One man dragged the other toward a cluster of trees— with difficulty—then only one individual emerged. Jack couldn't be sure, but his money was on Vargas being the one still alive. Chadwick had nothing to gain by killing Vargas.

Jack moved the computer to the backseat, then turned to face Sophie. "I've gotta go. Stay here and wait for me. If anyone comes up to the vehicle, drive away and don't look back."

She opened her mouth as if to argue, then snapped it shut and nodded.

Jack pulled out his SIG and after a brief scan of the area got out of the Jeep.

"Be careful." Sophie's soft words cut through the air as he shut the door. He paused for a brief second but didn't turn back before rushing into the underbrush.

That speedboat was either very close or already on the shoreline. He dashed through the mangrove trees at full speed, ignoring the snapping branches and leaves hitting him in the face. When he neared a clearing on the beach, he stayed hidden in the shadows and bushes. The boat he'd seen on the satellite was cruising full speed toward the shore, ready to beach on the white sand.

Jack guessed Vargas was hiding under some sort of cover until the last moment possible. At least that's what he'd do if he was in the man's position. Jack glanced down the stretch of beach, thankful it was deserted. The few times he'd visited, there had usually been one or two kite surfers, but there was no wind today so the place was dead. Using the trees as cover, he inched his way closer to where the parking area joined with the beach.

As soon as the boat hit the sand, Vargas appeared from a cluster of mangroves. Jack hated revealing his position, but there was no other choice. He couldn't wait for backup to arrive.

Weapon drawn, he rushed from the trees. "Stop where you are!" Moving across the sand was difficult in shoes, but Vargas was having the same problem.

He stopped midstride to look at Jack, then looked back toward his escape. He had twenty feet to go.

The two men with the dark sunglasses in the boat shifted slightly, so he continued shouting. "A chopper and the Coast Guard are on their way. Leave now and we have no problem."

The men hadn't made any sudden movements, so he'd bet

his life savings they had guns in their hands. Only their heads and shoulders were visible above the dash. As they glanced at each other, the faint sound of a helicopter rent the air. They spoke for a few seconds, then reversed as if they were in a Super Boat race. The twin-engine speedboat was gone in milliseconds, leaving a raging wake in its path. Water and foam lapped against the shore.

Jack guessed it was the mention of the Coast Guard that changed their mind.

Vargas still hadn't moved, though Jack was sure he had a gun tucked in his pants. The movement wasn't overt, but Jack saw his hand twitch. He was almost a hundred percent sure Chadwick was dead, but he paid close attention to the parking area using his peripheral vision. "Don't even think about it, Vargas. You're coming back with me."

A large vehicle out of the corner of his eye momentarily distracted him. For a split second Jack thought it was the Jeep he'd stolen. Before he could react, Vargas reached for his weapon.

Vargas swung his arm up, gun in hand, and Jack fired twice. The loud pops thundered, echoing loudly along the coast. The weapon dropped from Vargas's hand as crimson liquid spread out like a river across his chest, lapping and twisting as it covered his entire shirt. The man hit the ground knees first, then fell onto his face.

The sound of squealing tires pulled him out of the funnel. He turned to see a Jeep—thankfully not the one Sophie was in—tearing out of the lot. No doubt whoever that was had already called the police. Even though he was sure Vargas was dead, he checked his pulse and retrieved the man's weapon.

He'd left Sophie alone far too long. Once he was sure Vargas wasn't breathing, Jack sprinted across the pavement, only pausing at the entrance to scan the road in both directions. His heart rate tripled when he saw the dark green Jeep still parked about thirty yards north.

When he was a foot from the driver's-side door, she opened it and jumped out. "You're okay?" The words came out hoarse and scratchy and her eyes were red and glassy.

"I'm fine. It's all over." He wanted to take her in his arms and bury his face in her neck, but he kept a little distance.

She wrapped her arms around herself and leaned back against the seat. "Will I be able to see Hannah soon?"

"Of course. She's probably still being debriefed."

"Good." She stared at him for a long moment, then looked down at her feet.

He could hear a chopper in the distance and knew he should call Wesley, but before she was debriefed—and he was possibly arrested—they needed to talk. "Will you please tell me what's going on?"

Her shoulders lifted noncommittally, but at least she looked at him. "Thank you for saving my life, Jack."

"I don't want your fucking thanks! I want you, *forever*. Fuck, Sophie. I'm sorry for lying to you, but—"

"It's not about that." Her pretty lips pursed into a thin line as she watched him. "I just realized we feel differently about each other."

"What?" He fucking loved her and while she might not feel the same, he knew she cared for him. She could grow to love him. Even if she didn't, he still wanted a life with her. Wanted to see her face every morning when he woke up.

The chopper was getting louder now. Since they couldn't land on the beach, they'd probably land in one of the empty lots across the street.

She took a step closer and placed a gentle hand on his chest. "I understand you had a difficult choice to make, and in my head, I get that you had to choose catching Vargas over saving me."

"What the *hell* are you talking about?"

All pretense of gentleness gone, she shoved his chest, but he refused to budge. "Chadwick had you on speaker. I *know* you weren't going to trade me for Vargas until he sweetened the deal." The pain that flashed in her eyes clawed at him, but it also pissed him off that she didn't realize what he'd gone through.

"Are you out of your mind? I always planned to make the trade."

She let out a harsh, bitter laugh. "*Right*. I owe you my life, Jack, but don't patronize me. I *heard* you. I heard every word."

He started to respond, but the familiar *whop-whop* of the helicopter blades was increasing in decibel and drowning everything else out. The chopper zoomed over them, then hovered across the road before landing in an empty lot.

When the engines shut off the silence was almost deafening. "Sophie, I swear, I *never* would have let Chadwick take you. I would cut off my own fucking nuts before I let that happen."

She shoved her hands in her pockets but didn't respond. Her expression made it clear she didn't believe him.

He looked at the men emptying out of the chopper. Wesley was one of them. Though his boss was about half a football field away, Jack could tell by the set of his boss's jaw that he was going to be taken in. Jack might not be arrested in the end, but Wesley would have to take him in, at least in front of the other men.

"Wait here a sec, okay?"

When she nodded he jogged toward his boss.

"I've got to take you in," were the first words out of Wesley's mouth.

"I know. Can you keep this from Sophie?"

Wesley's gaze strayed past him. "Yeah, I'll have one of the men bring her in for debriefing. You've got to come with me now, though." He took Jack's arm and led him toward the helicopter.

Jack resisted the urge to turn around. Things weren't over between them. Not by a long shot. But if he was going to jail, he wasn't going to bother explaining anything further to her. Until he knew the outcome of his situation, he couldn't drag her through any more of this bullshit.

Chapter 23

To go private: to retire.

Jack tapped his finger against Wesley's desk. He'd been away from Sophie too long, and his boss still hadn't let him contact her. They'd flown to one of the NSA's branches in Georgia, and he'd been on lockdown for the past twenty-four hours. Wesley hadn't even let him take a shower, which in the big scheme of things wasn't important. At least he wasn't going to be arrested. He deserved it, but considering how many times he'd put his ass on the line, he simply couldn't apologize for saving the woman he loved.

The woman who was *very* angry with him. He scrubbed a hand over his day-old stubble. How could she have thought he'd just let her die? After everything they'd shared?

He swiveled at the sound of the office door opening. Wesley gave him a curt nod. "Come on."

"Is Sophie okay? Where is she?" he asked as they strode down the hall.

"She's fine. She and Miss Young are done debriefing and I had someone escort them to Sophie's place."

"What about—"

"They don't know it, but I've placed two armed guards in a car across the street." Wesley jerked the conference room door open and motioned for Jack to enter.

Giving Sophie an armed guard was probably unnecessary, but it eased the growing tension in Jack's shoulders. He hated being away from her. Especially now. He needed to clear the air so that she understood exactly what she meant to him and what his intentions were. Maybe he should have told her how he felt in the hotel. Just admitted he loved her. But yeah, he'd been scared of her rejection after he admitted who he really was. Okay, he'd been terrified.

He took a seat next to Wesley as a female analyst pulled up images on three of the various flat screens against the wall. One was a satellite view of what he guessed was Africa if the terrain was anything to go by. The other was a satellite view of a rain forest. Maybe South America. The third was a list of flight records. "What's all this?"

"Images from the files Chadwick gave you. We've also torn apart his computer at work and I've got a team at his apartment now. There isn't much. He covered his tracks better than we expected."

"That Africa?" He nodded to one of the images.

"Yep. That's one of Abu al-Ramaan's training camps even we didn't know about. With the information from Chadwick, we're now aware of his movements over the past six months."

"Have you briefed the CIA?"

"Yes, but this isn't why I called you in here." He tilted his head at the woman in the room. Without pause she exited, leaving them alone.

"What's up? Decide you want to arrest me after all?"

"Push it and I just might. I wanted to let you know we've got a lead on Levi. He's using an old alias—Marcus Tirado. Just got wind that he's surfaced in Odessa."

"What's he doing there?"

"Don't know. The CIA is putting a team together and they've asked for you to piggyback."

Part of Jack wanted to hunt Levi down for nearly getting Sophie killed—and oddly enough, to help him out of whatever he'd gotten into—but neither reason was worth it. At one time it would have been. Not now. Getting back to Sophie was all that mattered.

"You're not going to take the job, are you?"

"No."

Wesley cleared his throat and gave him that father look he was accustomed to. "You're not going to be taking any more jobs." It wasn't a question.

"Sorry, boss. I'm done. For now anyway." He couldn't rule out coming back in the future, but right now the only thing he wanted in his future was Sophie.

"She's really worth it?"

Jack didn't bother with a response. Sophie was worth everything.

Sighing, Wesley dug into his pants pocket and handed his car keys to Jack. "I have no one but myself to blame, I guess. Go back to my place and get a shower. You smell like a donkey. I might see you tonight. If not, be here at seven sharp. Your woman will be here."

Jack paused, unsure he'd heard right. "What are you talking about?"

"She's left a handful of nasty messages threatening to cut off my balls if I don't tell her where you are."

"Sophie actually said that?"

Wesley grinned. "Not exactly, but it was definitely implied."

The painful vise around Jack's chest slackened an inch. If she was worried about his well-being, they could work things out. Either that or he was going to make love to her until she forgot all about why she was so angry with him. Until she couldn't breathe without scenting him on her.

Chapter 24

Uncle: headquarters of any espionage service.

Sophie held out her arms for the third time as another man wearing a gray, nondescript security uniform patted her down. "Do you really think I'm carrying a weapon?"

The man shrugged as he straightened. "Sorry, ma'am. Simply following procedure."

Gritting her teeth, she yanked her purse off the security scanner and hooked it over her shoulder. She was beyond her patience limit. She wanted to see Jack and she wanted answers yesterday. "I'm here to see Wesley Burkhart."

"I know why you're here, ma'am." The guard sounded as if he was humoring her—which was just insulting. "Please follow me."

At this point she wasn't exactly sure where *here* was. After Jack had disappeared onto that helicopter, she'd been ready to rip him a new one. Until she'd heard one of the men talking about Jack being arrested. Then anger had dissolved into panic when she realized the gravity of exactly what he'd done for her.

Ever since then she'd been trying to get ahold of Wesley. Like a maniac, she'd threatened the director of the NSA with bodily harm—very descriptively—if he didn't help her. Wesley had finally called her back and offered to fly her to his office. So now she was somewhere in Pine Mountain, Georgia, wandering around the most boring building she'd ever seen. On the outside, the building was a drab gray. After a security check just to get past the building doors, she'd had to go through another scan in the lobby, and after the incredibly long elevator ride she'd just endured, another pat-down. Where did they think she was hiding these supposed weapons?

She stayed close to the guard as they walked down a hallway that actually had decent Renoir and Monet prints. After they took a left, the guard stopped in front of the first door on the right. He knocked once, then turned back the way he'd come.

"Come in," Wesley's familiar voice barked.

She stepped inside and closed the door firmly behind her. Wesley stood and motioned for her to take a seat.

With shaking hands she pulled out one of the maroon chairs and perched on the edge. "Thank you for agreeing to see me."

In response, he nodded. "What can I do for you?"

Really? He actually had to ask? She bit back a growl of frustration. "I want to see Jack. *Now.*"

"That's impossible right now."

"Nothing's impossible. . . . Is it true he's been arrested?"

Wesley shrugged noncommittally. "Why do you want to see him?"

"It's important."

"That's not an answer."

She shifted against the seat, unwilling to tell this man what she'd come to see Jack about. She wasn't going to tell a virtual stranger that she was in love with Jack and needed to apologize for the awful way she'd behaved toward him. "I just really need to talk to him. He saved my life." Before she could continue, the sound of the door opening interrupted them. Her stomach did crazy flip-flops when she saw Jack standing in the doorway. It had only been two days, but he looked leaner. His sharp face seemed even more angular. That hungry look in his pale eyes was still there, but he was somehow different.

Wesley said something, but she wasn't paying attention. She was vaguely aware when he walked past Jack and shut the door, but she had eyes only for Jack. Abruptly she stood, knocking her purse to the floor and spilling the contents, but she didn't care. "Are you okay?"

"I think that should be my line." He didn't take any steps toward her.

Okay, she deserved that. She'd accused him of betraying her when he put her first. Even before himself. The frustrating man had been willing to go to jail for her. He'd been protecting her, just like always. His familiar scent was intoxicating, but she forced herself to focus. "I guess you're not arrested?"

He shook his head. "No. After what I pulled, Wesley had to bring me in, but with the information we recovered from Chadwick, they'll probably give me a medal."

Relief punched through her. "So you caught that Abu whatever guy?"

"Not yet, but they're closing in on him. With Vargas dead and your former assistant in jail, there aren't any more loose ends."

She shifted on her feet as they stared at each other. The last two days without him had been calm and uneventful. Well, with the exception of filling out a novel's worth of paperwork for the NSA, things had been quiet. She'd also been living in a suspended state of pure hell without Jack. She hadn't even realized anything was missing from her life until he'd barreled into it. "I'm so sorry for not believing you. I didn't know what you'd put on the line for me."

He shoved his hands in his pockets but still didn't make a move in her direction. That's when she noticed a light sheen of sweat had formed across his forehead. Under the most intense gunfire, the man barely flinched. *Now* he was sweating?

"Why did you come here?" he rasped out.

"Because I love you." Saying the words released the pressure around her chest. She'd never said those words to a man before. Not even Sam. She'd loved him but had never found the courage. Saying them now should terrify her, but after everything she'd been through, it was a relief. She'd spent a decade running from anything resembling commitment, and it was time to stop. If any man was worth risking her heart, it was the brave one standing in front of her.

His lips curled up at the corners in an almost smile, but he didn't say anything. Maybe she'd made a mistake in coming here. Maybe he was nervous because he didn't know how to let her down easily. He might have told her that he wanted her forever in the heat of an intense moment, but now that everything had settled down, he could have realized she wasn't what he wanted. Even if that was true, she wouldn't let herself regret telling him.

She averted her gaze and bent to retrieve her fallen purse. Stupid tears stung her eyes, so she kept her head down as she reached for a tube of lip gloss. She stilled when Jack's strong, callous hand clasped over hers. She hadn't even heard him move toward her.

"I love you too, Sophie." The words were so low she wasn't sure she'd heard right. "I know we still have stuff to work out. We need to talk about . . . Sam."

It was a little weird the way Jack talked about himself in the third person, but she thought she understood it. He'd shed that life and started a new one when he became Jack. Sam had been the old him. The truth was, she didn't care what name he went by as long as he stayed in her life and let her be a part of his. But before they went any further, she needed to get some more stuff off her chest.

"When you . . . when I thought you died—in Afghanistan—there was so much I wanted to say to you. I had *so* many regrets. You were the one real friend I had and . . . I'm so sorry for the hateful things I said. I know what I said, but I never actually hated you. I loved you back then, but I felt dirty, ashamed of what had happened to me. I thought you'd eventually realize I wasn't good enough and push me away, so I pushed you first. I was just trying to survive."

"You don't have anything to apologize for," Jack said, his voice rough with emotion.

"Yes, I do. You were going to war and I know you had that ring for me and . . . I was *horrible*. Everything I said to you—" Her voice broke off as a tear escaped.

"*Stop.* You were seventeen, hurting, and dealing with being raped. I never held what you said against you. I might have hated myself, but never you."

Her throat was tight with so many years of regret, but now it seemed they were getting a second chance. Or she prayed they were. "So what do we do now?"

A slow, seductive smile spread across Jack's face. "Whatever we want. I quit my job."

Her eyes widened at his admission. "You love what you do."

"No. I love *you*. This is all I've ever known, Sophie. I want . . . Hell, I don't know what I want. I never thought much about it until you were back in my life. The only thing I do know is that I want to come home to you every night and wake up to your face every morning. Everything else, we'll figure out together."

She opened her mouth to protest, but he held a finger to her lips.

"I'll give it a year. If I'm miserable, I'll find a job in some sort of law enforcement, but I'm not going back to this kind of lifestyle."

"This is a big decision to make so suddenly." Despite her

protest, joy pulsed through her at the thought of starting a life with him.

"This is the easiest decision I've ever made."

The sincerity in his voice slammed through her. Smiling to herself that they'd been lucky enough to get a second chance against all odds, she leaned forward and touched her lips to his.

The kiss was tentative at first, and then his animalistic side took over. Their lips and tongues collided in a hungry frenzy. She wrapped her arms around his neck, threading her fingers through his hair, until a loud slam pulled them apart. They both turned at the sound.

Wesley shook his head and stepped past them. "I didn't leave the two of you alone so you could go at it on the floor of my office."

Sophie fought the heat she felt creeping up her cheeks. Jack, however, was completely unfazed.

In one swoop he gathered the rest of her things, shoved them in her purse, and took her hand before standing. "Don't worry, we're getting out of here."

With her hand clasped in Jack's, Sophie's heart swelled to ridiculous proportions. They were both jobless and she had no clue what the future held, but this was the happiest she'd been in her entire life.

Epilogue

One year later

Sophie glanced up as the bell to her and Jack's shop jingled. A dark-haired man with a full beard and mustache walked in. He wore a Rusty T-shirt, board shorts, and flip-flops.

He looked harmless enough, but she was thankful she had the counter as a barrier between them. "Are you interested in renting a Jet Ski or chartering one of our boats?"

Glancing around, the man cleared his throat and shoved his hands in his pockets. "Actually I was wondering if you guys were hiring."

Instinctively she glanced out the open window. Jack was busy tying up two of the Jet Skis a couple of college students had just returned. "We're not hiring right now, but in the next three months we're looking to. Do you want to fill out an application?"

He nodded enthusiastically, so she pulled out the standard form and slid it across the counter. In any other place it would be inappropriate to wear board shorts while looking for a job, but life was a lot more laid-back in the Keys.

As the man left the store, the phone rang. She grabbed it on the second ring. "Island Rentals, how can I help you?"

"Sophie?"

"Uh, yes?" She pressed a hand to her stomach at Wesley's voice. They hadn't heard from him in almost six months. The last time he called, he'd tried to convince Jack to come back to work. She was still pretty pissed about that. "What do you want?"

He chuckled lightly. "Don't worry, I'm not calling to bug Jack. I'm calling to ask you a favor. My niece is going to the Keys for spring break with a couple friends and I wanted to know if you could cut her a deal for some Jet Skis one afternoon."

"That won't be a problem. Does she need a place to stay?" They had a small guesthouse above their garage, as most houses in Key West did. It gave guests, and them, complete privacy. Not that they'd had any guests except Hannah. And she'd stayed in their house.

"No, she's staying with friends, but if you could keep an eye out for her, I'd appreciate it."

"Just e-mail Jack all the information on her and we'll watch out for her."

"Thanks."

As soon as they disconnected, Jack walked in. His face broke into a relaxed smile when they made eye contact. Something he seemed to be doing more and more every day. "You about ready to take lunch, babe?"

"Yes—I'm starving." She grabbed her purse and rounded the counter.

Before she'd taken two steps, Jack grasped her hips and pulled her close, holding on to her as if his life depended on it. Tingles shot down to her toes as he ran his tongue over hers in erotic strokes.

When he pulled away she immediately missed his touch. "What was that for?"

"I think we should take lunch at the house." His words were a seductive growl and let her know exactly what he had in mind for "lunch."

"Sounds good to me." Somehow she managed to rasp out the words, though it was hard to even find her voice. A year later and he still made her knees weak with just one look.

For the first time in her life she knew exactly where she belonged. In Jack's arms was the only place she wanted to be.

ACKNOWLEDGMENTS

Even though writing is a solitary profession, getting a book published takes an amazing team and I'm grateful to have so many wonderful people to support me. First, thanks to my editor, Danielle Perez, for pushing me to make this the best book possible. I'd also like to thank Christina Brower, Courtney Landi, Katie Anderson, and the rest of the team at NAL for all their behind-the-scenes work. Publishing a book truly is a team effort. I'm also very thankful to my agent extraordinaire, Jill Marsal, for always being in my corner.

Kari Walker, Laura Wright, Cynthia Eden, and Carolyn Crane, I'd be lost without you ladies! I'm lucky to call you friends. Another great big thank-you for my husband, sister, and parents, who have always supported my decision to become a writer—long before I actually finished that first book. For my readers, you guys are amazing and I hope you love this new series as much as I do! Your e-mail and kind words mean more than you'll ever know. Last, but never least, I'm grateful to God for so many wonderful opportunities and never-ending support.

Don't miss the next thrilling novel in the

Deadly Ops series from Katie Reus,

coming in summer 2014 from Signet Eclipse.

Maria Cervantes grasped the interior door handle of the SUV limo as her family's regular driver took what would hopefully be the last sharp turn of the night. Either he'd forgotten how to drive or she was sicker than she'd realized. Every little bump in the road made her afraid she'd puke. After being laid up in bed with flulike symptoms for five days and missing work for a week straight—something she'd never done before—she'd been positive she had kicked the nasty stomach bug this morning. Now she wasn't so sure.

Nausea roiled in her stomach and she swallowed hard, forcing the sickness back down. *Just a few hours,* she reminded herself. That was all she had to get through; then she could go back home and pass out.

As the vehicle straightened, then slowed, she peered through the divider. She'd asked the driver to keep the partition down. If she got so sick she needed him to pull over, she didn't want to waste precious seconds buzzing him. Still, she was clutching one of the empty silver ice buckets she'd snagged from the minibar in case she didn't have time to warn him.

"We're almost there, Ms. Cervantes." His voice was ridiculously polite despite the fact that she and Nash had known each other for two years.

She knew why, though. He was annoyed with her for going to this party when she was sick. "I swear to God, if you call me Ms. Cervantes again, I'm going to crawl up there and puke on you. We're the same age, Nash."

"Damn it, Maria—"

She let out a raspy laugh, loving that she'd gotten Nash Larson to curse, since it was a rarity. He'd been working for her parents for two years. Before he started working for them he'd done private security work for a year, and for eight years before that he'd been in the Army. Maria's father, Riel, had needed an outside security company to oversee one of his projects in Mexico two years ago and Nash had been assigned. After witnessing the man at work, her father had snatched Nash away with a hefty pay raise and better benefits. Now he was more or less a personal bodyguard/driver/fix-all man for her parents. While her dad often used Nash as extra security when traveling on business, he hadn't for his current trip since it was so short.

Nash let out a growl of frustration as the vehicle slowed to stop. Maria barely paid attention as she heard him talking to one of the security personnel outside the gated mansion, where a very exclusive party was going on. She didn't need to listen because she knew he was showing them her elegant gold and cream embossed invitation. If it were any other event, she would have bailed, but Bayside Community Center, where she worked, needed the donations that would come in from tonight. And there was one potential donor in particular Maria desperately wanted to talk to.

Maria had grown up with incredibly wealthy parents and they'd taught her to give back. They weren't exactly happy with her chosen profession, but they supported her career as a counselor. After getting a bachelor's degree in behavioral psychology and a master's in counseling, she couldn't imagine doing anything else. She was also the acting director of the community center, since her predecessor had suddenly retired a couple of months ago. Until they found a replacement, she was in charge. She'd thought the added responsibility would be overwhelming, but Maria found she liked the challenge.

Since there was no way her parents would have let her arrive at the Westwood gala driving her Prius, she had a chauffeur. Any other night it would have been annoying, but there was no way she could operate heavy machinery right now. She'd stopped taking her over-the-counter antinausea medicine so she wouldn't be drowsy but the side effect was that she was now nauseated. She was just impressed she'd managed to get dressed on her own.

The Westwood family wasn't originally from Miami, but California. They liked to do things over the top and a bit garish, but Maria didn't care. They were friendly, donated to local charities, and in addition to three food banks and another community center in Miami, Bayside was one of the recipients of the donations from tonight. Which meant Maria had to be here. She was the public face for Bayside and she took her position very seriously. Though it wasn't the only reason she was here. She also had to meet Joann Hood, an insanely wealthy woman who wanted to "talk numbers" in regard to donating money to Bayside. And this was the only time the well-known, eccentric woman could meet Maria. So here she was.

"You look like shit, Maria. As soon as we stop I'm texting your mother to let her know I'm taking you home." Nash's expression in the rearview mirror was almost scolding.

Despite their both being twenty-nine, he sometimes seemed light-years older. She put a hand to her unsettled stomach before saying, "One hour. That's all I need." Or she hoped it was. "And I'll be fine. Just don't take me through the main entrance." There would be a silly red carpet and photographers hoping to snap shots of some of the politicians and celebrities who might come. She definitely wasn't newsworthy, but there would be an extra crush of people there and she knew there was another entrance.

"I wasn't planning to," he growled. "And I'm not letting the valet take the SUV. I'll be waiting in the parking area.

Call or text when you're ready and I'll pick you up." The driveway leading to the main house was long and winding. Instead of following the drive to the left, where it curved, Nash continued straight until they reached one of the service entrances. There was more security there, but after a quick conversation with someone Nash clearly knew, they were allowed past.

"You know him?" she asked, glad her voice sounded stronger. If she could get some decent face time tonight, it meant she'd get an invite to next year's party and Bayside would be on the list to continue receiving donations. Since it was the first year she'd received an invitation, she wasn't taking any chances of insulting the Westwoods by not showing up. With the economy the way it was, Maria had to look out for her kids. That community center was the only form of family some of them had and she refused to let them down.

"Yeah, when I heard you were sick I called the security team and found out who was on duty. I still don't think you should be here."

Maria sighed, not bothering to respond to Nash's comment as he pulled up next to a catering van and parked. "Didn't you used to work for the same security company as that guy?" Even though the man at the front gate wore a suit, the one who'd just stopped them had been wearing a black polo shirt with a familiar security logo and cargo pants. He'd also had a gun strapped to his belt, much like the police wore. Definitely not trying to hide what his job was for the evening.

"You know I did. Don't try to change the subject."

"Argue all you want. It's a battle you'll lose."

He muttered something under his breath as he got out of the vehicle. She straightened her long, violet gown and glanced down at herself. While she hadn't been able to do much with her hair other than curl it and leave it loose around her shoulders, her dress was so gorgeous it wouldn't matter.

Before she could open the door, it swung open and Nash held out a hand for her.

Even though his smile had an almost boyish quality, there was nothing boyish about the man in front of her. His normally relaxed face was drawn into a tight expression and his blue eyes flashed with annoyance. Well, he wasn't her freaking boss and certainly not her boyfriend—though she had a feeling he had a small crush on her, so she tried not to get too angry. Despite his obvious annoyance he held out an arm and helped her from the vehicle.

Normally she wouldn't need help, but tonight she was taking it. She'd already gotten the okay from her doctor that she wasn't contagious—otherwise she wouldn't have come.

"You—"

"Nash, enough," she snapped, at the end of her rope. She was barely keeping it together and didn't have the strength to argue.

"I was just going to say you look beautiful," he muttered, his ears turning pink.

"Oh, thank you." Not wanting things to get awkward, and because she wanted to get inside as soon as possible, she stepped away and held up her simple clutch purse. "I've got my phone. As soon as I'm ready to leave I'll call you and meet you right out here." She glanced toward the part of the mansion they were parked outside. There was a security man standing by a side door, clearly waiting for her. In the distance she heard music and voices, but it was fairly quiet where they were. "Mansion" probably wasn't the right term for this home. It was more like a castle. Sure, her parents were wealthy, but the Westwoods were in a totally different stratosphere. They were like royalty. "You're sure I can go in through there?"

"Yes. I worked it out ahead of time." Nash tilted his head in the direction of the man patiently waiting. "Cormac will lead you into the party and"—he glanced down at his cell phone when it pinged—"your mother is waiting by the ice sculpture of a dragon. It's near the . . . room of weapons?"

"Room of . . . Oh right. Tell her I'm on my way." She was so grateful that her mother had taken to texting Nash instead of her. The thought of trying to focus on tiny letters now . . . no thank you.

She was also glad she knew where the weapons room was. Well, sort of. Once she got in the house she was certain she could find it. The Westwoods were huge history buffs and had an actual room designated solely to displaying various weaponry from the past two centuries. It was actually pretty cool, if a little weird.

Her heels clicked along the pathway as she walked toward an intimidating man wearing all black. His expression was cool and assessing as he took her in. "Normally I'd check you for weapons, but Nash says you're all right." He opened the door for her and gave a sharp gesture for her to enter.

Okay, then. They stepped into a kitchen that was humming quietly with activity. Various people were setting up dessert trays and plates, but this definitely wasn't the main kitchen. Maria had been in that one a couple of years ago.

"This way," the security man urged, clearly not liking that he was her temporary escort.

All the food aromas were overwhelming so she hurried after him, but not before snagging a minicupcake. She hadn't eaten in hours and sugar probably wasn't the best idea, but she needed something in her stomach. Shoving it in her mouth, she stumbled trying to keep up with the long-legged man. He took her down a lot of hallways and too many turns to count. Dizziness swarmed her as they reached the end of a hallway that opened into a room where well-dressed people were all drinking either champagne or martinis. Female servers were walking around wearing . . . *Holy shit, they were wearing only body paint made to look like tuxedos.* Maria blinked and tried to listen as Cormac gave her directions to the weapons room. Nodding politely, she fought more nausea as he hurried away while talking into an ear mic. Before she'd taken two steps a woman named Greta Dobbins latched onto her arm.

Maria guessed the white-haired woman was pushing eighty. She was slim, a few inches taller than Maria, and had a wicked grip. "Hi, sweetheart. I just saw your mother. She told me you were coming and I'm just so glad. It's amazing how much time you dedicate to that center. Of course, I know your dear mother wishes you'd settle down and get married. . . ."

Oh, sweet Lord. Maria's eyes and ears glazed over for a moment as she took in the room. Two sparkly chandeliers hung above them and classical music was being piped in from somewhere. About forty people in long, glittery gowns or tuxedos talked among themselves. She recognized some of them, but not everyone. Pasting on a smile for Mrs. Dobbins, she tried to focus on the woman's face, but bile rose in her throat as clamminess descended over her skin.

"Maria, you don't look so good." Without waiting for a response, Mrs. Dobbins practically dragged her across the marble floor to the other side, ignoring the calls of her husband.

"Where are we going?" Maria had no strength to fight the other woman and just prayed there was an empty bathroom nearby.

Taking Maria by surprise, the older woman opened a door Maria hadn't even seen. It was built into the dark wood paneling, seamless in its architecture. "We're going to find you a place to rest and I'm going to get your mother. You shouldn't be here. She told me you weren't feeling well, but you look like death warmed over. I know how dedicated you are to that center, but this is unacceptable."

Even though she wanted to argue, Maria knew the woman was right. Her face and hands were clammy, but sweat had started to blossom across her forehead, between her breasts, and down her back. A chill snaked through her body, making her shiver. "How did you even know about that door?"

Mrs. Dobbins chuckled. "Oh, I know a lot about this place. Flora has me over for tea at least once a month. And that's code for martinis, but don't tell Kingsley. It'll just raise his blood pressure and . . ."

Everything went hazy again as the woman chatted away. Maria had forgotten how close Mrs. Dobbins was with Flora Westwood. Even though the woman was a total chatterbox, Maria was incredibly grateful for her kindness now. While she wasn't sure where they were going, she couldn't hear the crowd of people anymore and her heels were silent against the carpet runner covering rich wood floors. Finally the woman stopped in front of a door and peered inside. She let out a breath. "Okay, no one's in here. There's a bathroom right through there." Mrs. Dobbins pointed even though Maria couldn't see past the heavy door. "I'll be back in ten minutes; I promise. Just as soon as I find your mother."

"She's near a dragon ice sculpture." Or she had been. Maria wasn't even sure how much time had passed since she'd arrived. Or where she now was in the giant house, for that matter.

"Make that twenty minutes, then." The woman ushered her into what turned out to be a lavish guest room. It was dimly lit by a Tiffany table lamp, but Maria didn't care about the décor.

Racing toward the door Mrs. Dobbins had pointed out, she hurried inside and barely made it to the toilet before she threw up the cupcake. After a while she was just dry heaving.

The bathroom lights were too harsh so she crawled to the entry and shut them off. Relief rolled over her at the sudden dimness. There was still a little stream of light from the bedroom, but her eyes didn't hurt anymore. Wanting to call Nash and her mother, she opened her clutch, but frowned when she didn't see her phone. The purse wasn't big, so it wasn't as if it was hiding in a compartment. Which meant it had likely fallen out in the SUV. Lord, she couldn't even remember whether she'd brought it. Everything about tonight and the past few days was too fuzzy. Cursing, she snapped the clutch shut and struggled to her feet. She shouldn't have come tonight and didn't want to be lying on the floor when Mrs. Dobbins and her mother found her.

As Maria entered the bedroom she heard loud male shouting coming from the next room. At least three men. Two had accents she couldn't place, but one man she recognized. She wanted to say hello, but was too ill to face anyone and the shouting was escalating.

A low hum of panic threaded through her veins as the yelling suddenly increased in volume. She couldn't make out the words, but then everything got quieter. Curious and worried, she hurried to the shared wall and pressed her ear against it.

"You cannot bomb the Freedom Tower last," the familiar voice said, anger punching through each word.

"We can and we will. It is symbolic," an accented voice growled.

"No—the Tower is a landmark. If you try to wait, it won't work. The police, FBI, and everyone hunting you will—"

Maria wavered on her feet. Bomb the Freedom Tower? Panic gripped her with sharp talons, digging into her chest until it was hard to breathe. Blood rushed in her ears and she shook her head, trying to clear her fear so she could hear better. Straining, she held her breath as a man talked about bombing other Miami landmarks. Then there was a vile curse about hating the United States.

When everything suddenly went quiet, she pushed away from the wall. What the hell had she just heard? Terror was like a living thing inside her, pushing back most of her nausea. She had to tell someone what she'd just heard. While she didn't recognize two of the voices, she knew one of them. And that scared the holy hell out of her that he was involved with . . . whatever was going on.

Her gaze landed on the door, but she backed away from it. There was no way she could exit through it. What if she ran into one of those men in the hallway? Looking around the unfamiliar room, she hurried to a double panel of floor-length curtains. Peering behind one of the thick silk panels, she realized the curtains covered two French doors.

When she disengaged the lock, the sound seemed overpronounced in the stillness even though she knew no one could have heard it. Slipping outside onto the small balcony, the cool air rushed over her skin and a chill ran through her that had nothing to do with the weather or her sickness.

Glancing around the expansive moonlit acreage, she looked for a guard or any sign of life. *Are you freaking kidding me?* The place had to be crawling with extra security.

Maria slipped off her heels and hurried across the small stone patio outside the room she'd been in. Immediately her feet hit grass. It was cool under her toes, but nothing could calm her right now. Pure panic raged through her as she hurried across the yard. On all sides she could see only a wall of hedges engulfing this place. Heading east across the yard in what she thought was the direction where Nash had originally parked, she picked up her pace. She still felt shaky and nauseated, but nothing could stop her now. The hair on the back of her neck raised as another fear set in. What if someone had seen her leave that room? Or was watching her right now?

Those men had been serious about the destruction they meant to cause. She had to get help.

When she reached one of the giant hedges, a small sliver of relief slid through her. It wasn't an actual wall, just thick bushes that she could slip through. At this point she didn't care what was on the other side. She just had to escape from this place and get to the limo. Her phone should be there and, more important, Nash would be able to help.

As she tried to find an opening she could shove through, she heard a rumble, and then a horrific blast filled the air. She spun around, her heart in her throat. Not truly comprehending what she was seeing, her stomach pitched when a giant ball of orange flames tore through the sky, engulfing the mansion.

Another rumble ripped through the air as the place started collapsing in on itself. Her mouth opened but no sound came out as the knowledge that her mother was in there pierced through her numbed mind. Darkness edged her vision, but she started to run toward the fire, needing to get to her mom, when another ball of flames tore through the night sky. Her entire body trembled under the impact, heat warming her despite the distance from the building. She blindly reached for something to hold her up but collapsed to her knees as her legs gave way. Unable to help, unable to breathe, she felt tears stream down her face as she watched the place implode.

Though she tried to fight it off, the darkness that had threatened to overtake her earlier suddenly claimed her as she passed out.

ALSO AVAILABLE FROM

USA TODAY BESTSELLING AUTHOR

Katie Reus

First book in the Moon Shifter series

Alpha Instinct

Ana Cordona has been a strong leader for the few remaining lupine shifters in her pack. But with no Alpha male, the pack is vulnerable to the devious shifter Taggart, who wants to claim both their ranch and Ana as his own. When Connor Armstrong comes back into her life, promising protection, it's *almost* enough to make Ana forget how he walked out on her before—and she reluctantly accepts his offer to mate.

But Taggart and his rival pack are not their only enemies. A human element in town is targeting shifters. Their plan not only threatens Ana and Connor's future—but the existence of the entire pack.

"A wild, hot ride."
—*USA Today* bestselling author Cynthia Eden

Available wherever books are sold or at
penguin.com

facebook.com/ProjectParanormalBooks